STAR TREK®: THE NEXT GENERATION™
TECHNICAL MANUAL

WRITTEN AND DESIGNED BY
RICK STERNBACH AND
MICHAEL OKUDA

with a special Introduction by
GENE RODDENBERRY

POCKET BOOKS

New York   London   Toronto   Sydney   Tokyo   Singapore

"Some men see things the way they are and say, 'Why?'
I dream things that never were and say, 'Why not?'"

—Robert F. Kennedy

An *Original* publication of Pocket Books

POCKET BOOKS, a division of Simon & Schuster Inc.
1230 Avenue of the Americas, New York, NY 10020

This book is published by Pocket Books,
a division of Simon & Schuster Inc.,
under exclusive license from Paramount Pictures.

ISBN: 0-671-70427-3
Library of Congress Catalog Card Number: 91-61228

First Pocket Books trade paperback printing November 1991

10 9 8 7 6 5 4 3 2

POCKET and colophon are registered trademarks
of Simon & Schuster Inc.

Printed in the U.S.A.

CONTENTS

INTRODUCTION BY GENE RODDENBERRY

The Starship *Enterprise* is not a collection of motion picture sets or a model used in visual effects. It is a very real vehicle; one designed for storytelling.

You, the audience, furnish its propulsion. With a wondrous leap of imagination, you make it into a real spaceship that can take us into the far reaches of the galaxy and sometimes even the depths of the human soul.

The purpose of all this? To show humans as we really are. We are capable of extraordinary things. I am stunned and thrilled by events such as the falling of the Berlin Wall, the spectacular spread of democracy in Europe, incidents of humanitarian gestures for AIDS victims, the magnificent achievements of the *Voyager* spacecraft team, efforts toward hunger relief, and the rapprochement with those we saw as forever bitter enemies.

For example, our character Worf is something of a symbol of the reduction of global tensions in the world today. Just a few years ago when we first conceived of a Klingon officer on the *Enterprise*, the Soviet Union seemed to some a dangerously intractable enemy. Now through a fictional *Star Trek* character, we are living out the same high drama. This is not to suggest that the path to world harmony will ever be an easy one – witness the agony of the Persian Gulf crisis – but Americans are increasingly beginning to see the Soviet people not as enemies, but as fellow citizens of Planet Earth. At its best, our starship can help us explore many possible human futures.

The *Enterprise* is also a symbol of the vast promise of technology in the service of humankind. On *Star Trek*, we've tried to show technology not as important in itself, but as a tool with which we humans can better reach for our dreams. It is one of my fondest hopes that *Star Trek* may help people see the importance of our present-day exploration of space. Not just the possibility of contact with alien intelligences – although I am confident that this will indeed eventually happen – but in a myriad of benefits closer to home. We look forward to space spinoffs providing new communications technologies, extraordinary new energy sources, lifesaving advances in medicine, and revolutionary new industrial processes. Space exploration helps us to better understand both our home planet and its neighbors in our solar system. And on a more philosophical level, it will help us find a sense of cosmic perspective by letting us better see our place in the universe. What we've seen thus far has been an important and very humbling experience.

Documents such as this *Technical Manual* help give some background to the vision we work so hard to create on *Star Trek*. Rick and Mike have obviously had a lot of fun filling in the gaps and trying to find technical "explanations" for some of our mistakes. (Actually, considering the sometimes crushing pressures under which episodic television is produced, I'm quite amazed at how well it usually hangs together.) This is not only great fun, but it also suggests how much work will have to be done to achieve the dreams of tomorrow.

We must remember that the promise of tomorrow will not be fulfilled easily. The collective commitment of our nations, as well as the vision, wisdom, and hard work of many, many individuals will be required to bring our dreams to fruition. In a way, the *Enterprise* and the optimistic future in which it exists might be thought of as a reminder of what we can achieve when we really try.

We certainly don't pretend that our television starship is a blueprint from which NASA or Intercosmos or ESA can immediately begin construction. Let's face it: A faster-than-light warp drive is still far beyond our current understanding. And there are thousands of other areas still waiting to be tackled and built upon. The hard work – and the rewards – remain for the next generation.

I think our future will be worth it.

–Gene Roddenberry
Creator and Executive Producer
Star Trek: The Next Generation

AUTHORS' INTRODUCTION

How "official" is this stuff? Well, this is the first technical manual done by folks who actually work on *Star Trek*. It's closely based on source material we've developed in conjunction with our writers and producers in our role as technical consultants for the series. In that sense it can be considered pretty "official." On the other hand, we believe quite firmly that the "real" *Enterprise* exists in the imaginations of our audience, so it is each individual viewer's imagination that will determine the "true" form of the starship. Nevertheless, it is one of our hopes that this volume will serve as a reference for writers of future *Star Trek* scripts, novels, and other stories. *Star Trek* has always prided itself on its technical and scientific consistency, and we hope that this work will help further that tradition. In writing this book, we wanted to give an idea of the enormous complexity of the systems that would be required in a starship like the *Enterprise*. We wanted to fill in a few of the blanks, and to show some of the background that can only be hinted at in our episodes. On the other hand, we'd like to make it very clear that it is not our intention for this document to serve as a straitjacket, limiting the options of future writers. We have deliberately left significant gaps to permit future writers to "discover" parts of the ship that we haven't seen yet.

To would-be *Star Trek* writers, we'd like to emphasize that this is NOT required reading. If you're writing a *Star Trek* story, you will probably be doing yourself and your audience a disservice if you use more than a very tiny amount of this material. Remember, *Star Trek* is about people; the technology is merely part of their environment. As Gene points out in his Introduction, the real mission of the starship *Enterprise* is to serve as a vehicle for drama.

An important word of caution: All Starfleet personnel are hereby advised that any previous technical documentation in your possession may be suspect because of an ongoing Starfleet program of disinformation intended to confound and confuse the intelligence assets of potential Threat forces. Such documents should therefore be verified with Federation archives and this *Manual* for authenticity.

Acknowledgments

A lot of people have contributed to this project. We want to acknowledge the work of Martin "Bucky" Cameron, Doug Herring, George Peirson, Debra Peirson, Patrick Minyard, James Takahashi, and Daniel Gauthier, who are responsible for ink work on many of the illustrations in this volume. We are indebted to *Star Trek* research consultant Richard Arnold, who was an invaluable resource on the *Star Trek* scenario in general, as well as to Leslie Blitman, Richard Barnett, Susan Sackett, Jon Singer, Peter Cavanagh, Ralph Winter, Terry Erdman, Marcia Evans, Michael Lim, Guy Vardaman, the staff of U.S. Space Camp in Huntsville, and the folks at Star Base Osaka. We also want to recognize the efforts of Dave Stern and Kevin Ryan at Pocket Books, as well as the indefatigable support of our agent, Sherry Robb. Rick wants to thank his dad, Paul Sternbach, for explaining machines to him at a very early age. Mike wants to specifically thank his wife, Denise, for her support, understanding, and love during this project. It's bad enough when your husband is occupied full-time on a demanding television show, but even worse when he spends his free time on a book.

A special word of "thanks" is due to the folks who served as technical resources for this project: Stan Starr (Boeing Corp.), David Krieger (RAND Corp.), G. Harry Stine (Enterprise Institute), Dr. Gregory Benford (UC Irvine), Sue Cometa (Rockwell International), Gordon Garb and Larry Yaeger (Apple Computer), Naren Shankar, Steven Agid and Brian J. Young (McDonnell Douglas), and John O'Connor (YPS). We listened to them all, but didn't always do what they suggested, so any quibbles you may have aren't their fault.

We want to express our gratitude to *Star Trek* producers Rick Berman, Michael Piller, and David Livingston, who gave us the chance to contribute to the show as technical consultants. We are honored that they let us help with the care of what we think is an important part of the *Star Trek* universe.

We would very much like to thank the writers of *Star Trek: The Next Generation* with whom we have collaborated on technical matters. Their strong desire to keep our show as technically consistent as possible has not only improved the series but has led to much of the material in this volume: Hilary Bader, Dennis Bailey, Ira Steven Behr, Hans Beimler, David Bishoff, David Carren, Larry Carroll, Richard Danus, Dorothy Fontana, Sandy Fries, David Gerrold, Shari Goodhartz, Mike Gray, Maurice Hurley, Robert Lewin, Richard Manning, John Mason, Robert McCullough, Joe Menosky, Ronald D. Moore, Hannah Louise Shearer, Lee Sheldon, Melinda M. Snodgrass, Jeri Taylor, Tracy Tormé, Michael Wagner, Lisa White, and Herb Wright.

Our colleagues (past and present) in the *Star Trek* art department are responsible for handling the enormous design challenges we face on a weekly basis in producing this show: Production designers Herman Zimmerman and Richard James, as well as Art Department staffers Jim Bayliss, Charlie Daboub, John Dwyer, Les Gobrugge, Joseph Hodges, Dan Jennings, Paul McKenzie, Richard "Spuds" McKenzie, Jim Magdaleno, Jim Mees, Andy Neskoromny, Greg Papalia, Elaine Sokoloff, Cari Thomas, and Sandy ("Where's lunch?") Veneziano. We would be remiss if we did not acknowledge the very significant contributions of designer Andrew Probert to the overall look of *Star Trek: The Next Generation* and to the *Galaxy* class USS *Enterprise* in particular. We are all in debt to the pioneering work of Matt Jefferies, art director on the original *Star Trek* television series, in whose very large footsteps we follow.

We want to recognize our enormously talented and hardworking co-workers on the staff and crew of *Star Trek*, at Paramount Pictures, and our contractors, all of whom have helped shape the *Enterprise* and the universe she explores. It is on their work that this *Technical Manual* is built: Camille Argus, Burt Armus, Kim Bailey, Tom Barron, Brett Bartlett, Daryl Baskin, Jim Becker, Melinda Bell, Tom Benko, Greg Benson, Alan ("Quiet!") Bernard, David Bernard, Ramsey Bieber (and her amazing singing frog), Bob Blackman, Cha Blevins, Paula Block, Cliff Bole, Adriene Bowles, Buddy Bowles, Rob Bowman, Brooke Breton, Ed Brown, Jr., Dick Brownfield, LeVar Burton, Ruth Carpenter, Chip Chalmers, Mandy Chamberlin, Ed Charnock, Jesse Chavez, Joe Chess, Richard Chronister, Ray Clarke, James Crawford, Denise Crosby, Rhonda Crowfoot, Dan Curry, Dick D'Angelo, Andy Davis, Larry Davis, Helen Davis, Doug Dean, Michael Dorn, Monty deGraff, Charlie Drayman, Joel Dreskin, Susan Duchow, Anet Dunne, Syd Dutton, Wilson Dyer, Carol Eisner, Manuel Epstein, J.P. Farrell, Lolita Fatjo, Kelly Ferguson, Sharyl Fickas, Marian Fife, Wilbur Finks, Fred Fish, Kim Fitzgerald, Don Foster, Jr., Jonathan Frakes, Steve Frank, Sam Freedle, Debbie Gangwer, Cosmo Genovese, Ken Gilden, Dave Glick, Bill Gocke, Whoopi Goldberg, Mike Green, Walter Hart, June Haymore, Dennis Hoerter, Ed Hoffmeister, Steve Horch, Merri Howard, Bill Hoy, Tom Hudson, Gary Hutzel, Tim Iacofano, Fred Iannone, and Phil Jacobson.

Also: Greg Jein, Ralph Johnson, Heidi Julian, Bob Justman, Eric Kuehnapfel, Jon Koslowsky, Andy Krieger, Carol Kunz, Les Landau, Peter Lauritson, Bob Lederman, Don Lee, Rob Legato, Nora Leonhardt, Bob Lewin, Joe Longo, Junie Lowry, Tim "Spike" McCormack, Gates McFadden, Scott McKnight, Scott Marcus, Terri Martinez, Elaine Maser, Mace Matiosian, Joe Matza, Colm Meany, Tony Meininger, Lorine Mendell, Bob Metoyer, Ed Miarecki, Eddie Milkis, Brian Mills, Ronald B. Moore, Peter Moyer, Eric Nash, Emi Negron, John Nesterowicz, Wendy Neuss, Ernie Over, Diane Overdiek, Frank Palinski, John Palka, Bill Peets, Price Pethal, Vince Pope, Steve Price, Tom "The Happy Camper" Purser, J.R. Quinonez, Jerry Quist, Maricella Ramirez, Ed Reilly, Tomaz Remec, Mel Renning, Maury Rosenfeld *(Endeavour* pilot), Wendy Rosenfeld, "Mad" Marvin Rush, Charles Russo, Richard Sabre, Richard Sarstedt, Stew Satterfield, Michael Schoenbrun, Fernando Sepulveda, Dick Sheets, Adele Simmons, Alan Sims, Marina Sirtis, Al Smutko, Bob Sordal, Brent Spiner, David Sterner, Patrick Stewart, Eric Stillwell, Mark Stimson, Janet Strand, Babu Subramaniam, Bart Sussman, David Takemura, Bill Taylor, Bill Theiss, Kim Thompson, Bill Thoms, Tomi Tomita, Tim Tommasino, Dennis Tracy, Steve Tucker, Elaina Vescio, Jana Wallace, Lazard Ward, Charlie Washburn, James Washington, Michael Westmore, Wil Wheaton, Dana White, Cecil Wilson, Murphy Wiltz, Bill Wistrom, James Wolvington, Durinda Wood, Edmond Wright, and Brad Yacobian. (It takes a lot of people to make a television show, especially one as complex as *Star Trek*. And believe it or not, this is *not* a complete list.)

Finally, a very special "thank you" to Gene Roddenberry, creator and executive producer of *Star Trek*. Thanks for letting us play on your starship, Gene!

–Rick Sternbach

–Michael Okuda

This book was written on Apple Macintosh computers using Microsoft Word software. Page layouts were designed using the Aldus Pagemaker program. Illustrations were mostly done with conventional pen-and-ink drawing techniques with a little help from Adobe Illustrator and Swivel 3D.

1.0 USS *ENTERPRISE* INTRODUCTION

1.1 MISSION OBJECTIVES FOR GALAXY CLASS PROJECT

Starfleet has long been charged with a broad spectrum of responsibilities to the citizens of the Federation and to the lifeforms of the galaxy at large. As the volume of explored space continues to grow, and with it the Federation itself, so do Starfleet's duties.

These duties range from relatively mundane domestic and civil missions, to cultural contact and diplomacy, to defense, to our primary mission of exploration and research. Many of these responsibilities are best carried out with relatively small, specialized ships. Yet there continues to be an ongoing need for a small number of larger, multimission vehicles that are capable of implementing the complete range of Starfleet's objectives. This need has in fact grown as the volume of relatively unexplored space within Federation influence continues to expand.

The *Galaxy* class starship represents Starfleet's most sophisticated achievement in multimission ship systems design.

Pursuant to Starfleet Exploration Directive 902.3, the following objectives have been established for the *Galaxy* Class Starship Development Project:

• Provide a mobile platform for a wide range of ongoing scientific and cultural research projects.

• Replace aging *Ambassador* and *Oberth* class starships as primary instruments of Starfleet's exploration programs.

• Provide autonomous capability for full execution of Federation policy options in outlying areas.

1.1.1 Galaxy *Class Starship Development Project logo*

• Incorporate recent advancements in warp powerplant technology and improved science instrumentation.

To provide for these objectives, the Starfleet Spacecraft Design Advisory Commission recommended to the Advanced Starship Design Bureau that the *Galaxy* class starship meet or exceed the design goals in the following specification categories:

PROPULSION

• Sustainable cruise velocity of Warp Factor 9.2. Ability to maintain speeds of up to Warp 9.6 for periods of up to twelve hours.

• Fifth-phase dilithium controlled matter/antimatter reactor primary power. Sustainable field output to exceed 1,650 cochranes, peak transitional surge reserve to exceed 4,225% of nominal output (170 ns phase).

• Warp driver coils efficiency to meet or exceed 88% at speeds up to Warp 7.0. Minimum efficiency of 52% to be maintained through Warp 9.1. Life cycle of all primary coil elements to meet or exceed 1,200,000 cochrane-hours between neutron purge refurbishment. Secondary coil elements

Authors' note: *We will occasionally step out of the* Star Trek *scenario for a moment to relate a bit of trivia or background information. Footnotes such as this will be separate from the main body of the* Technical Manual. *A key to many of the acronyms, abbreviations, and units of measure used in this book can be found in the Index, beginning on page 182.*

1.1.2 Galaxy *class Starship USS* Enterprise, *NCC–1701-D*

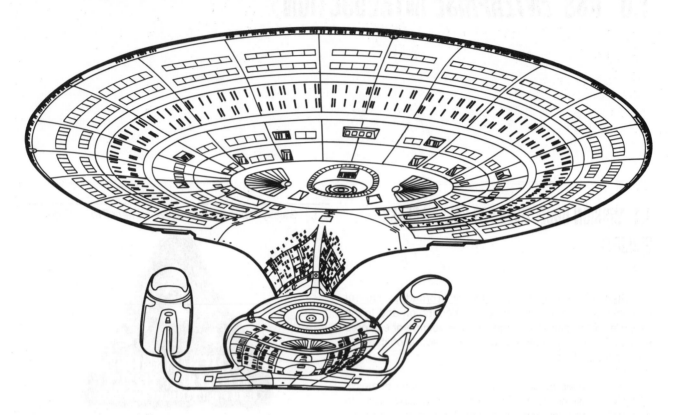

to meet or exceed 2,000,000 cochrane-hours between neutron purge refurbishment.

• Warp field geometry to incorporate modified 55° Z-axis compression characteristics on forward warp lobe for increased peak transitional efficiency. Warp nacelle centerlines to conform to 2.56:1 ratio of separation to maximum field strength.

• Secondary (impulse) propulsion system to provide sublight velocities up to and including 0.92 lightspeed *(c)*. Engine systems of choice to include but are not limited to at least two YPS 8063 fusion drive motors. All units to be equipped with subspace driver accelerators, field output not less than 180 millicochranes at 1.02×10^7K. Reactor modules to be field-replaceable. Independent impulse propulsion system of choice for primary hull to include but not be limited to YPS 8055 fusion drive motors.

MISSION

• Ability to operate independent of starbase refurbishment for extended periods. Independent exploration mode capability of seven Standard years at nominal Warp 6 velocity for docked configuration. Ability to execute deep-space exploration missions including charting and mapping, first

cultural contact scenarios, and full biologic and ecologic studies.

• Space allocation for mission-specific facilities: Habitable area to include 800,000 m² for mission-adaptable facilities including living quarters for mission-specific attached personnel.

• Ability to support a wide range of mission-related ongoing research and other projects (including sufficient habitable volume and power generation for facilities and operations) without impact on primary mission operations.

• Full spectrum EM, optical, subspace flux, gravimetric, particle, and quark population analysis sensor capability. Multimode neutrino interferometry instrumentation. Wideband life sciences analysis capability pursuant to Starfleet life contact policy directive. Two-meter diameter gamma ray telescope. Upgradable experiment and sensor array design. Ability to support both on-board and probe-mounted science instrumentation.

• Support facilities for auxiliary spacecraft and instrumented probes needed for short-range operations to include at least two independent launch, resupply, and repair bays.

Gene Roddenberry tells us that there are presently five Galaxy *class starships in existence, presumably including the USS* Galaxy, *after which the class is named. A sixth, the USS* Yamato, *was destroyed in the episode "Contagion." Other ship names are being left to writers of future episodes.*

ENVIRONMENT/CREW

• Environmental systems to conform to Starfleet Regulatory Agency (SFRA)-standard 102.19 for Class M compatible oxygen-breathing personnel. All life-critical systems to be triply redundant. Life support modules to be replaceable at major starbase layover to permit vehiclewide adaptation to Class H, K, or L environmental conditions.

• Ability to support up to 5,000 non-crew personnel for mission-related operations.

• Facilities to support Class M environmental range in all individual living quarters, provisions for 10% of quarters to support Class H, K, and L environmental conditions. Additional 2% of living quarters volume to be equipped for Class N and N(2) environmental adaptation.

• All habitable volumes to be protected to SFRA-standard 347.3(a) levels for EM and nuclear radiation. Subspace flux differential to be maintained within 0.02 millicochranes.

TACTICAL

• Defensive shielding systems to exceed 7.3×10^5 kW primary energy dissipation rate. All tactical shielding to have full redundancy, with auxiliary system able to provide 65% of primary rating.

• Tactical systems to include full array of Type X phaser bank elements on both primary and stardrive (battle) sections capable of 5.1MW maximum single emitter output. Two photon torpedo launchers required for battle section, one auxiliary launcher in primary hull.

• Ability to separate into two autonomous spacecraft comprising a battle section, capable of warp flight and optimized for combat, and a primary section capable of impulse flight and defensive operations.

• Full independent sublight operational capability for command section in Separated Flight Mode.

DESIGN LIFE

• Spaceframe design life of approximately one hundred years, assuming approximately five major shipwide system swapouts and upgrades at average intervals of twenty years. Such upgrades help insure the continuing usefulness of the ship even though significant advances in technology are anticipated during that time. Minor refurbishment and upgrade to occur at approximately one- to five-year intervals, depending on specific mission requirements and hardware availability.

1.2 DESIGN LINEAGE

The *Galaxy* class *Enterprise* maintains Starfleet's tradition of honoring the original starship *Enterprise*. Like her predecessors, this ship bears the original Starfleet registry number of that illustrious first *Enterprise*, NCC–1701. In this case, the suffix "-D" indicates this is the fourth successor to the name and number. Few other ships in the Starfleet have been so recognized. So significant were the exploits of this original ship and its crew, that in 2277 the practice of having a separate insignia for each starship was abolished, and the *Enterprise* emblem was adopted as the official symbol for the entire Starfleet.

1.2.1 The original Enterprise *emblem (ca. 2245) and the current version of the Starfleet emblem*

The first starship *Enterprise* was a *Constitution* class vehicle commissioned in 2245 at Starfleet's San Francisco Yards, orbiting Earth. This ship, first commanded by Captain Robert April, then by Captain Christopher Pike and Captain James Kirk, became a historic figure in Starfleet's early exploration of deep space.

This ship was refitted several times, remaining in active service until 2284 when it was assigned to training duty at Starfleet Academy. It was destroyed in 2285 while defending the Mutara sector against a Klingon incursion.

The second *Enterprise*, NCC–1701-A, also a *Constitution* class ship, was commissioned in 2286. Originally named *Yorktown*, this ship was redesignated *Enterprise* and assigned to the command of Captain Kirk following an incident in which Kirk and his crew were responsible for saving the planet Earth from the effects of an alien spacecraft. This ship later played a vital role in the success of the Khitomer conference, which had such a profound impact on the political climate of this part of the galaxy.

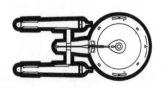

1.2.2 USS Enterprise, *NCC–1701*

The third *Enterprise*, NCC–1701-B, was an *Excelsior* class ship built at Starfleet's Antares Ship Yards. Although the decision to model this ship on the failed original experimental *Excelsior* was at the time controversial, the economics of using the existing (and otherwise successful) engineering of the basic spaceframe were compelling. The wisdom of this decision has been borne out by the large number of *Excelsior* class starships that still serve Starfleet in a variety of capacities. (Indeed, the *Excelsior* herself ultimately proved to be a distinguished part of the Starfleet.) The third *Enterprise* was a key figure in the exploration of space beyond the Gourami Sector. This ship and her crew were responsible for mapping over 142 star systems, including first contact with seventeen civilizations.

The fourth *Enterprise*, NCC–1701-C, was an *Ambassador* class ship built at the Earth Station McKinley facility. Commanded by Captain Rachel Garrett, this ship was lost in 2344 near the Narendra system while attempting to defend a Klingon outpost from Romulan attackers. The heroism of Captain Garrett's crew was a crucial step leading to the current alliance between the Federation and our former enemies, the Klingon Empire.

The fifth *Enterprise*, NCC–1701-D, is a *Galaxy* class starship built at the Utopia Planitia Fleet Yards above Mars. It was commissioned in 2363, and is currently under the command of Captain Jean-Luc Picard. This latest starship to bear the name *Enterprise* is Starfleet's flagship and has already distinguished itself in an impressive number of significant missions of exploration, as well as in several crucial incidents defending the security of the Federation.

1.2.3 USS Enterprise, NCC–1701-A

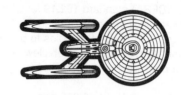

1.2.4 USS Enterprise, NCC–1701-B

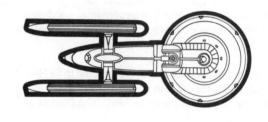

1.2.5 USS Enterprise, NCC–1701-C

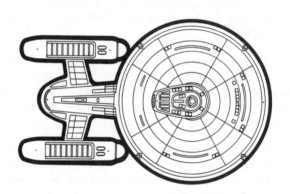

1.2.6 USS Enterprise, NCC–1701-D

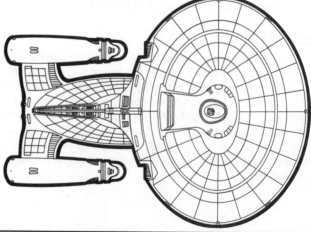

We assume that other Federation starships have had histories as illustrious as that of the Enterprise, *even though Kirk's ship seems to have become the most famous. It's a big galaxy, and there are presumably a lot of adventures out there, enough for many, many starships.*

1.3 GENERAL OVERVIEW

Any discussion of the *Galaxy* class starship that attempted to detail all of the possible attributes and applications of the vessel would fill many volumes of this size. As with living organisms, a mobile environment as large as the USS *Enterprise* is undergoing constant evolution. Were one to make a close examination of the starship at ten-year intervals over the next one hundred years, one would see a slightly different vessel each time.

At present, the starship is still in the early operational phase of its lifetime, a few years out of the Utopia Planitia Fleet Yards, its components and crew settling in, slowly becoming a totally integrated working unit.

The USS *Enterprise* is categorized as an Explorer, the largest starship in a classification system that includes cruiser, cargo carrier, tanker, surveyor, and scout. While most starships may be adapted for a variety of mission types, the vessel type designations describe their primary purpose. Smaller vehicles with impulse or limited warp capability, such as shuttles, are referred to as craft, to distinguish them from the larger starships.

Seen from a comfortable distance of two or three kilometers, the starship takes on the graceful lines of a nonrepresentational organic sculpture. Nature has determined the flow of the design, adhering closely to mathematical formulae at work in the universe surrounding the builders. Even in the desire to expand beyond the apparent limits of the natural world, familiar forces create familiar shapes. As the rapid aquatic and avian creatures of dozens of habitable worlds independently developed the unmistakable attributes of streamlining, so too did their interstellar cousin.

The combination of forces produced within the warp engine core and the flow of space and subspace around the vessel created the particular engineering solution to the problem of faster-than-light travel. The initial Starfleet requirement that a single spacecraft be able to perform as three distinct vehicles presented some rather complex — though some engineers not normally afraid of numbers preferred the word "daunting" — computational challenges.

The docked configuration presented the most efficient use of warp flight forces, but the Battle Section was also required to perform to specifications at warp velocities on its own, and the Saucer Module would have to have the capability of high sublight speed and possibly survive a separation at high warp. Scientists and engineers throughout the Federation, with all the deportment of composers and conductors, arranged sweeping curves, described vast volumes, and summoned up fantastic energies to bring their creation into existence.

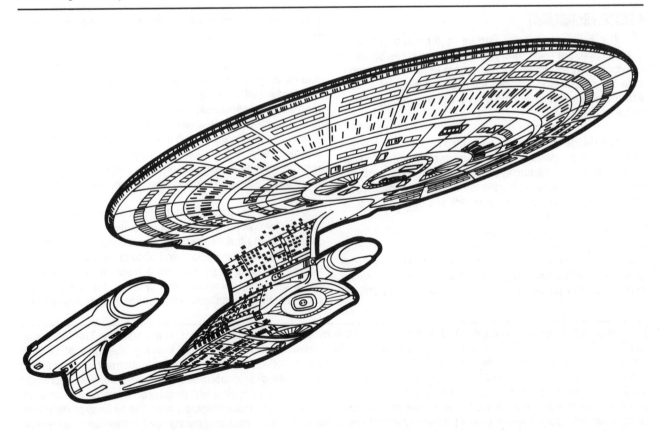

1.3.1 Galaxy class starship *Enterprise*

1.3.2 USS Enterprise *front elevation*

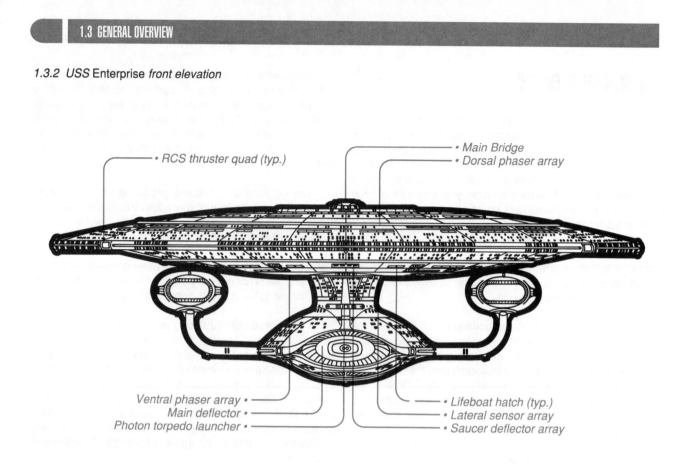

• RCS thruster quad (typ.)

• Main Bridge
• Dorsal phaser array

Ventral phaser array •
Main deflector •
Photon torpedo launcher •

• Lifeboat hatch (typ.)
• Lateral sensor array
• Saucer deflector array

PHYSICAL ARRANGEMENT

The hulls, remarkably birdlike in their strong, hollow construction, are reinforced against flight stresses by active energy fields that tighten and flex where required to compensate for natural and artificial internal and external forces. Structures integrated into the hulls allow for a variety of necessary functions.

The Bridge consolidates command positions for the rest of the starship, windows give crewmembers needed vistas while in space, phaser arrays and photon torpedo launchers provide defense against hostile forces, and subspace radio arrays communicate with other worlds and other ships.

Lifeboats allow for escape in dire emergencies, transporter emitters afford reliable movement of crew and gear nearly instantaneously, navigational sensors and deflectors give the starship distant vision and a method for clearing obstacles, and powerful warp engines propel the ship at

speeds only dreamt of when most spacefaring races begin their climb to the stars.

The forty-two decks are internally divided around major load-bearing structures. A great many systems, especially the pressurized habitation sections, are suspended within the open spaces, essentially "floating" on flexible ligaments to minimize mechanical, thermal, and conductive radiation shocks. As the *Enterprise* left the Utopia Planitia Fleet Yards, approximately 35% of the internal volume was not yet filled with room modules and remained as empty spaceframe for future expansion and mission-specific applications.

The interior spaces validate the concept of the interstellar organism, with the level of complexity rising dramatically once inside the hull. The starship possesses structures akin to a central nervous system and circulatory apparatus, food storage areas, a heart, locomotor mechanisms, waste removal paths, and numerous other systems. Many of these are self-maintaining, with crew intervention required only occa-

The starship Enterprise *was originally designed back in 1964 by Matt Jefferies, art director on the first* Star Trek *television series. The current incarnation of the ship was designed by Andrew Probert. The actual working blueprints of the ship miniature were drafted by set designer Greg Papalia, and a six-foot model was built at Lucasfilm's Industrial Light and Magic under the supervision of Ease Owyeung. A slightly smaller (but more detailed) four-foot model was built under the supervision of Greg Jein during our third season. These models are constructed from cast resin and Fiberglas on a precision-machined aluminum framework. Interior lighting is created by a maze of neon and incandescent lights, controlled by an external power supply console. (Greg Jein is also responsible for the* Nebula *class starship introduced during our fourth season, as well as the USS* Stargazer *from "The Battle" and the* Enterprise-C *from "Yesterday's Enterprise.")*

sionally to monitor their operation. Other hardware requires high levels of crew service and control.

In a sense, the crew act as caretaker cells watching over the health of the total vessel to achieve a homeostatic balance. During crisis situations, the total system responds as would an organism, working to produce higher levels of energy and to deal with adverse conditions at a faster pace.

The living areas of the starship have been designed for maximum comfort and safety while the crew is conducting a mission. Long-term studies of humanoid cultures have confirmed that as each race embarked upon permanent occupation of space, large personal living spaces had to be established, especially on early sublight expeditions. The *Enterprise* allows for some 110 square meters of living space per person, in addition to community space and the areas allocated to purely working functions. While some engineers on the *Galaxy* Class Project questioned the relatively large size of the vessel, opting for a smaller, more efficient design, it was conceded that the large size provided a greater number of mission options, given the changing social, political, and economic conditions in the Milky Way.

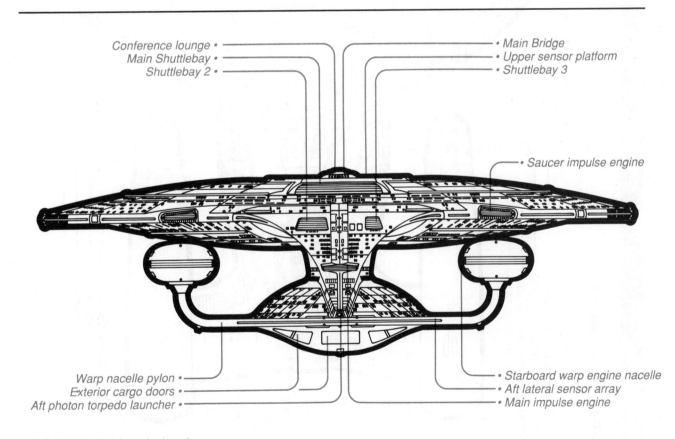

Conference lounge •
Main Shuttlebay •
Shuttlebay 2 •

• Main Bridge
• Upper sensor platform
• Shuttlebay 3

• Saucer impulse engine

Warp nacelle pylon •
Exterior cargo doors •
Aft photon torpedo launcher •

• Starboard warp engine nacelle
• Aft lateral sensor array
• Main impulse engine

1.3.3 USS Enterprise *aft elevation*

1.3.4 *USS* Enterprise *dorsal plan view*

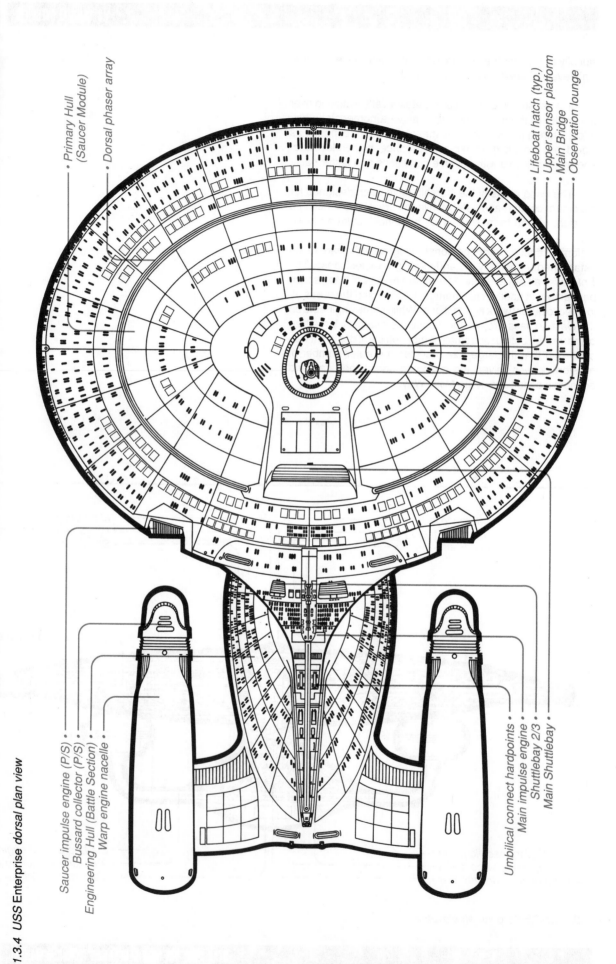

- Primary Hull (Saucer Module)
- Dorsal phaser array
- Lifeboat hatch (typ.)
- Upper sensor platform
- Main Bridge
- Observation lounge

- Saucer impulse engine (P/S)
- Bussard collector (P/S)
- Engineering Hull (Battle Section)
- Warp engine nacelle
- Umbilical connect hardpoints
- Main impulse engine
- Shuttlebay 2/3
- Main Shuttlebay

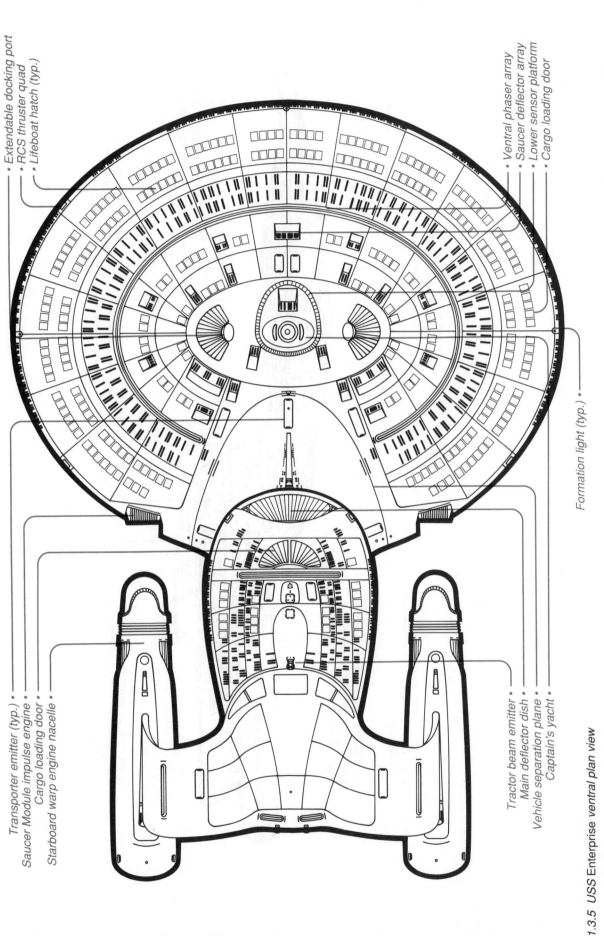

- Extendable docking port
- RCS thruster quad
- Lifeboat hatch (typ.)

- Ventral phaser array
- Saucer deflector array
- Lower sensor platform
- Cargo loading door

Formation light (typ.) •

Transporter emitter (typ.) •
Saucer Module impulse engine •
Cargo loading door •
Starboard warp engine nacelle •

Tractor beam emitter •
Main deflector dish •
Vehicle separation plane •
Captain's yacht •

1.3.5 USS Enterprise ventral plan view

1.3.6 *USS Enterprise starboard elevation, exterior*

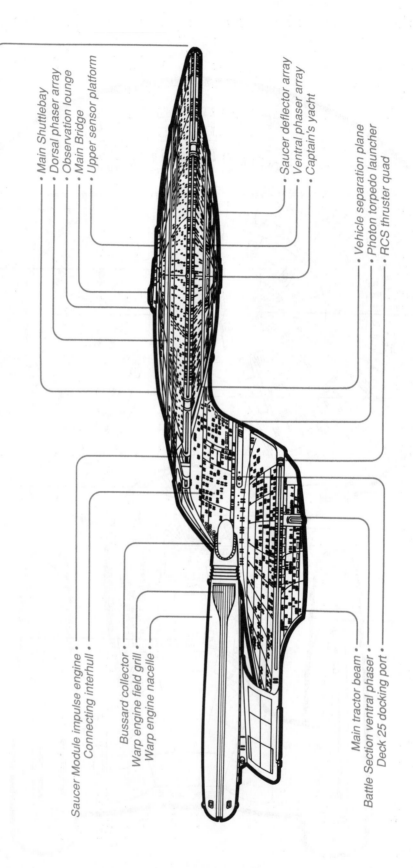

Ten-Forward lounge ·

· Main Shuttlebay
· Dorsal phaser array
· Observation lounge
· Main Bridge
· Upper sensor platform

· Saucer deflector array
· Ventral phaser array
· Captain's yacht

· Vehicle separation plane
· Photon torpedo launcher
· RCS thruster quad

Saucer Module impulse engine ·
Connecting interhull ·

Bussard collector ·
Warp engine field grill ·
Warp engine nacelle ·

Main tractor beam ·
Battle Section ventral phaser ·
Deck 25 docking port ·

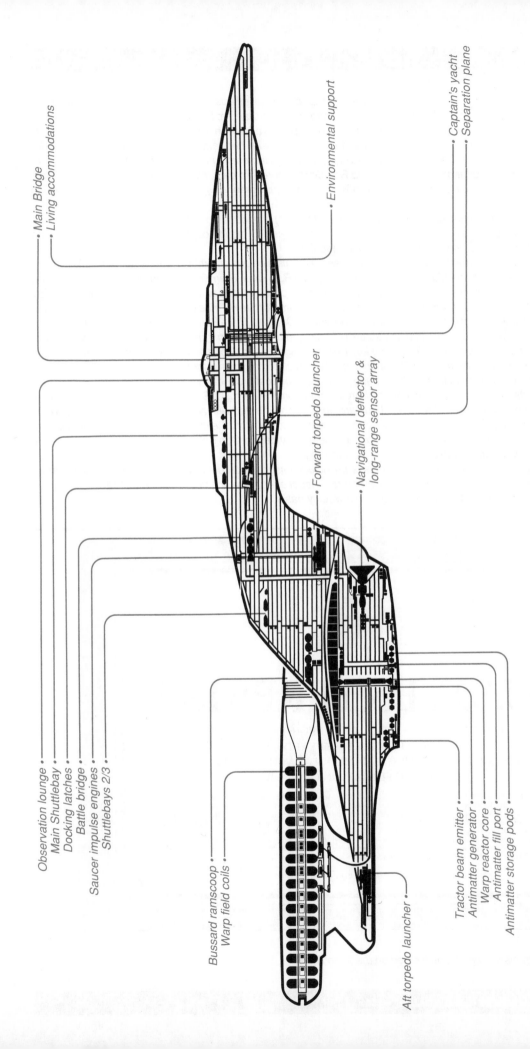

Main Bridge ·
Living accommodations ·

Environmental support ·

Captain's yacht ·
Separation plane ·

Observation lounge ·
Main Shuttlebay ·
Docking latches ·
Battle bridge ·
Saucer impulse engines ·
Shuttlebays 2/3 ·

Forward torpedo launcher ·

Navigational deflector &
long-range sensor array ·

Bussard ramscoop ·
Warp field coils ·

Aft torpedo launcher ·

Tractor beam emitter ·
Antimatter generator ·
Warp reactor core ·
Antimatter fill port ·
Antimatter storage pods ·

1.3.7 USS Enterprise starboard elevation, section at centerline

Star Trek: The Next Generation *uses an enormous number of special visual effects, far more than even most movies. A typical episode will have fifty effects shots, while some episodes have had more than two hundred! Even more amazing is that effects for a typical episode are produced in just a few weeks on a budget that is a fraction of a movie's.* Star Trek *visual effects supervisors Rob Legato and Dan Curry are in overall charge of these weekly visual, budgetary, and scheduling miracles, under the aegis of producer Peter Lauritson. These guys are constantly juggling an incredible number of projects at the same time, ably assisted by visual effects coordinators Gary Hutzel and Ronald B. Moore. To date, over five hundred spaceship shots have been created for the series, which may make the* Enterprise *the most photographed spaceship in the history of television and motion pictures.*

Model photography for our first episode (which became stock footage) was done up at Lucasfilm's Industrial Light and Magic. New model shots for episodes are done at Image "G" in Los Angeles by motion control programmer Eric Nash and stage technician Dennis Hoerter under the direction of Legato and Curry.

The complex job of compositing the model elements into a seamless illusion of a starship in flight is accomplished at The Post Group by visual effects editors Peter Moyer and Pat Clancey. (Fred Raimondi, Stan Kellam, and Don Greenberg served in these positions during our first three seasons.) They also do our transporter effects with the help of assistant editor Ray Clarke. Phasers, photon torpedoes, and similar effects are created by animator Steve Price on the Quantel "Harry" electronic paintbox system. Another key element of our visual effects is the work of Don Lee, Price Pehthal, and Kevin Cox at Composite Image Systems, responsible for the sophisticated bluescreen effects and the precision transfer of film images to videotape.

The use of this computerized video technology is the key to producing such an enormous amount of work on such a tight schedule. In contrast, the traditional methods of film optical effects can cost many times more. More important, it would be impossible to complete the work in the extremely limited time available for post production.

Matte paintings such as the cityscape on the Klingon home planet from the episode "Sins of the Father" are produced by Syd Dutton and Bill Taylor of Illusion Arts. These paintings are often supplemented with such touches as moving clouds or tiny people seen in windows. (Bill Taylor also wrote the song "Benson, Arizona" from the cult s-f film Dark Star.*) Special film animation effects such as the "energy entity" in "The Child" have been provided by Dan Kohne. Maury Rosenfeld (currently of Planet Blue) has contributed Mirage video animation programming.*

Other important players on the Star Trek *visual effects team include associate producer Wendy Neuss and post production department staffers Wendy Rosenfeld and David Takemura. Visual effects are an important part of* Star Trek, *and we are fortunate to have such a strong team creating magic on a weekly basis.*

1.3.9 USS Enterprise *commissioning plaque located on the Main Bridge*

1.3.10 USS Enterprise *forward dorsal perspective*

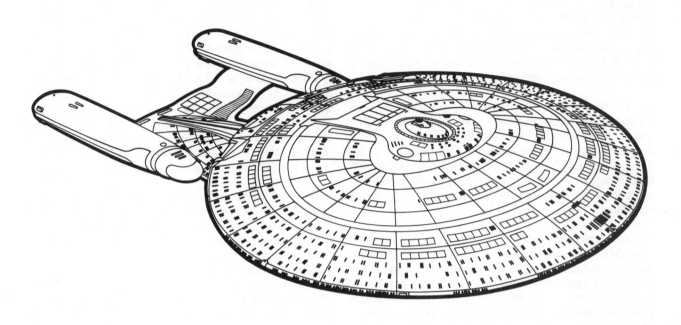

The very nature of Star Trek *frequently requires new types of visuals, so our people are constantly pressed to invent ingenious new effects. The catch is, of course, that they have to be ingenious, new, and achievable in the time and within the budget allocated for a particular episode.*

Such innovation often takes unexpected forms. Dan Curry once created a phaser hit effect using a Mylar pom-pom. That infamous pom-pom also saw use as a nebula and as the mysterious forcefield that imprisoned Riker in "Arsenal of Freedom." (Dan, like most Trek *staff members, often tries to help out in areas beyond his normal job responsibilities. One of his more unusual projects was the Klingon "bat'telh" bladed weapon from the episode "Reunion." A martial arts enthusiast, Dan consulted with our prop makers on the design of the weapon, then assisted actor Michael Dorn to develop the ritual dancelike movements associated with its use.) Rob Legato, faced with the daunting task of creating the end of the universe ("Where No One Has Gone Before"), made use of the shimmering reflection patterns from a pan of water. Visual effects associate David Takemura often helps supply similarly mundane items with equally exotic results. Some of these have included pumicelike rocks from the Balboa Brick Company, used for asteroids in such episodes as "Galaxy's Child," and an ordinary garden hose, used to create a water spray that became another forcefield effect.*

One dramatic example of Star Trek technical innovation is a new ultraviolet light matting process used for model photography. This technique was proposed by Don Lee of CIS and developed by Gary Hutzel and the staff of Image "G." It involves the use of a fluorescent orange backdrop instead of the traditional bluescreen used for model photography. This technique makes it much easier to generate "holdout mattes," which allow the image of the model to be combined with a background of stars and planets. It is such a big improvement over "normal" methods that it allows Star Trek's *effects team to produce literally four times as many ship shots in the same amount of time. (And since time is money, it means that we get to see a lot more new spaceship scenes than we would otherwise.)*

Less obvious but equally important is the logistic and organizational wizardry of visual effects coordinator Ron B. Moore. Ron developed systems to help organize the massive numbers of projects, jobs, contractors, and other elements needed to produce each week's visual effects. Such coordination is essential to enable our people to get the most "bang" for their visual effects bucks on the most ambitious weekly science-fiction television series ever produced. (One of the greatest illusions that our people create every week is the impression that they have a whole lot more money to spend than they really do!)

1.4 CONSTRUCTION CHRONOLOGY

The construction of any new starship is said to begin, as in the days of sailing ships, with the laying of the keel in the shipbuilding yard. While the wooden hull of old has been replaced by metal alloys and ultrastrong synthetic compounds, the significance of laying the keel has survived undiminished. The inception and completion of a conveyance, whether tailored for crossing distances on the scale of an ocean or the galaxy, has for millennia filled its creators with a sense of accomplishment and purpose.

The history of the *Galaxy* Class Project, and of the USS *Enterprise* in particular, is a story of technological innovation and teamwork spanning more than twenty years. Research and fabrication centers throughout the Federation, under the direct authority of Starfleet Command's Advanced Starship Design Bureau (ASDB), combined their efforts to plan and execute the newest and most complex vessel to join Starfleet's inventory.

When the official start for the project was announced in July 2343, much original theoretical work had already been accomplished, particularly in the propulsion field. While the attempt to surpass the primary warp field efficiency barrier with the Transwarp Development Project in the early 2280s proved unsuccessful, the pioneering achievements in warp power generation and field coil design eventually led to the

uprated *Excelsior* and *Ambassador* class starships. Both vessels served Starfleet in exemplary fashion. They continue to do so, even beyond their original design lifetimes. The *Galaxy* class is expected to remain true to its predecessors.

The construction of the USS *Enterprise* followed a path similar to that taken by the pathfinder vehicle, the prototype USS *Galaxy*, and the first production starship, the USS *Yamato*. As with any large space vessel project, improved materials and construction techniques were incorporated into the USS *Enterprise* assembly process, allowing the minimum flyable starship to be delivered to Starfleet in two years less time than the previous class. On June 3, 2350, the first two spaceframe components, the Deck 10 computer core elliptical compression member and the starboard main longitudinal compression bulkhead, were gamma-welded during a brief ceremony at the Utopia Planitia assembly site 16,625 kilometers above the surface of Mars, in synchronous orbit.

The initial procurement order issued by Starfleet Command was for six *Galaxy* class ships. A projected total of twelve vessels is held as an option to be activated by Starfleet and the Federation, should conditions warrant. Once the initial spaceframe design was finalized, it was decided to proceed with the completion of six vessels and to take the other six to the end of the framework stage only. These six spaceframes have been broken down into manageable segments and dispersed by cargo carriers to remote sites within the Federation as a security measure.

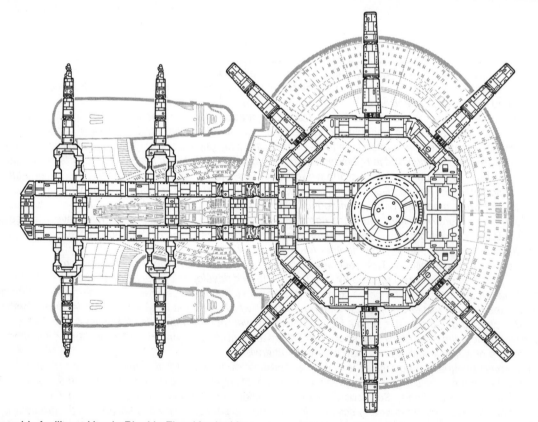

1.4.1 Assembly facility at Utopia Planitia Fleet Yards, Mars

1.4.2 Structural frame assembly at Utopia Planitia

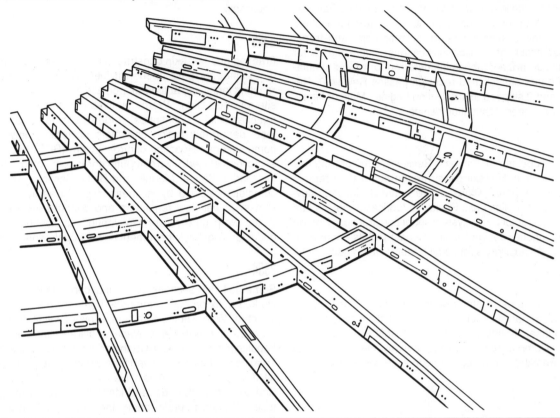

The following events describe the construction of the USS *Enterprise*. There exists little difference in the general construction logs of the *Enterprise* and those of its dockmates, the pathfinder vessel USS *Galaxy*, and the second starship off the line, the USS *Yamato*. Major installation and testing milestones for the first two ships precede those of the *Enterprise* by six months to one year. Certain design and fabrication lessons learned were applied to the *Enterprise* in rapid order, once the soundness of the yard changes was verified. Certain problems, such as the warp engine development, were common to all ships, and do not necessarily indicate a unique situation. Where the *Enterprise* experienced a ship-specific success or failure, it is so noted.

2343

Galaxy Class Project officially approved. Design centers begin drawing upon previous starships once general specifications are transmitted. Vehicle frame, engine systems, computer cores, and hull receive high priority.

2344

ASDB begins early definition work on *Galaxy* class mission simulators programmed with basic vessel characteristics. Detail design work continues.

2345

Mass and volume studies proceed for all internal systems,

based on first cut of frame designs. Field narrows from forty to fifteen. Computer core and software architecture passes Design Review 0.

2346

Testing of hull materials proceeds; final design must include conduits for structural integrity field (SIF), inertial damping field (IDF), and deflector shield grid. Warp and impulse systems pass Design Review 0; materials difficulties foreseen in warp coils. Impulse system design frozen. Computer design passes Reviews 1 and 2. Sensor systems evolving. Habitation and workspace module design frozen; fabrication begins. Redesign of transporter biofilter is requested. Phaser emitter undergoes redesign; photon torpedo upgrade proceeds with standard launcher and casings. Main deflector design frozen.

2347

Warp engine systems design tentatively frozen; anticipating nacelle design frozen later in the year. Impulse design undergoes tweaking. Computer cores pass Reviews 3 and 4. Transporter biofilter design frozen; system fabrication begins. Phaser emitter redesign passes Review 0. Main deflector power supply redesigned to accommodate science instruments.

2348

Vehicle frame design and docking latch system pass Review

0. Final selection of frame alloys; materials ordered. Warp engine and nacelle designs frozen; nacelle passes Reviews 0 and 1. Warp engine components begin test fabrication. Impulse engine components, main computers, and transporter begin fabrication. Communications system and tractor beam design frozen; fabrication deferred for power simulations. Phaser emitter third redesign passes Review 0; Reviews 1 and 2 skipped as fabrication begins. Main deflector power redesigned; fabrication begins.

2349

Frame and docking system pass Review 1; structural latches begin fabrication. Hull skin design frozen; some areas remain under development. Warp engine materials failures slow fabrication. Nacelles pass Review 2; fabrication begins late in the year. Tractor beam system under construction. Photon torpedo launcher design frozen. Sensor pallets under construction. All auxiliary spacecraft under development.

2350

First frame members gamma-welded in Utopia Planitia ceremony. Warp nacelle shells under construction; coils remain in test phase. Impulse components test-fit within frame at midyear. Computer core framing underway. Habitat modules test-fit. Phasers and photon torpedo assemblies under construction.

2351

Frame construction and major hardware installations continue simultaneously. Hull layers begin attachment. Warp engine core 65% complete; nacelles pass Review 3 with assumptions of successful fixes to coil materials problems. Major impulse engine installation complete. Computer cores 50% complete off-site. First layers of habitat modules installed. Transporter installation deferred in labor rescheduling. Tractor beam emitters modified to accommodate hull skin changes. Phaser bank installation proceeds. All other power and consumables conduits continue installation.

2352

Warp engine core completed; materials difficulties eliminated. Warp field coil manufacture delayed by furnace facility complications; other system assemblies completed. Preparations made for impulse run-up tests. Main computer cores 80% complete; nonflight mock-ups complete fit checks. Habitat and connecting passages 55% installed. Transporter systems minus hull emitters begin installation. Phaser bank installation complete; electro plasma power supply to phasers deferred until warp engine power levels verified. Photon torpedo magnetic launcher power supplies reworked. Tem-porary gravity generators installed; network active only where necessary.

2353

Framing and hull skin construction continues. Docking system latches and pass-through fit checks continue. Deuterium reactant tanks and antimatter pod assemblies arrive from off-site for integration. Warp coil fixes effected; production of matched coil sets continues. Impulse engine system run-up tests performed; fusion chambers powered singly and in combinations. Reaction control system (RCS) thruster assemblies installed. Two computer cores completed; one each installed in Saucer Module and Battle Section. Third core completion slowed by isolinear chip availability problems. Phaser power flow regulators and conduits installed; predicted warp core power tap verified as adequate. Main deflector piggyback instrument power supply work complete.

2354

Some hull skin sections show unacceptable welds; 2% reworked to fix problem. Imbedded defensive shield grid not affected. Warp engine core begins low-power tests; reaches Warp 2 equivalent energy. Nacelles still awaiting coil delivery. Impulse tests continue; RCS thruster software problem fixed. Third computer core delayed for additional two years; affects all downstream starships. Habitat layers 70% complete. Shuttlecraft, work pods, and lifeboats arrive for integration tests. Photon torpedo loader thermal expansion anomaly fixed.

2355

Final outer framing members completed; minor design change in forward dorsal requires added longitudinal members. Warp engine core tests continue. Impulse engine system complete. Permanent gravity generator network complete. Habitat modules and storage volumes complete. Transporter and subspace comm system antennae modified; made compatible with deflector shield grid emissions. Structural integrity field (SIF) runs at low power; works out starship's framing "kinks." Main deflector field focus test successful after start-up failure repaired. Starboard pylon phaser bank swapped with one from USS *Yamato*; better operational fit for each. Photon torpedo loader thermal problem returns; new fix is final. Sensor pallets 50% installed; minimum for flight.

2356

Starship skin 95% complete. Warp engine power up tests to Warp 8 equivalent. Warp coils delivered and installed. Impulse fusion generators perform full power nonpropulsive tests. Third computer core delivered and installed; additional

---

When a script calls for a new spaceship to be seen, the initial task of design usually falls to Rick Sternbach. Rick will often create the initial design on his trusty Macintosh computer, using 3-D software to visualize the general shapes on his computer screen. This allows him to try many different variations very quickly before settling on a final design in consultation with our visual effects supervisors. Rick then draws up the final plans (using conventional drawing tools), which are then turned over to modelmakers like Greg Jein and Tony Meininger.

programming and tests continue. First habitat module swapout by transporter successful. Transporter tests complete. Final SIF and inertial damping field hookups complete. Comm system 90% complete. Impulse power to phasers certified. 30% of lifeboats delivered and docked. USS *Galaxy* is launched from orbital dock on maneuvering thrusters.

2357

Hull integrity complete; all SIF and IDF systems operational. Warp nacelles buttoned up and certified for flight. Final impulse system adjustments underway. Computer core subspace field shielding problem arises on *Enterprise* only; threatened one-third of power systems on starship, traced to conflicting power-up procedures, then fixed. Comm system complete after minor rerouting to avoid computer problem. Photon torpedo system remote firing successful. Defensive shields final hookup complete. Sensor pallets certified. USS *Galaxy* is commissioned; declared deep-spaceworthy and warp-capable; moves to outer solar system.

2358

Tests continue on total warp and impulse propulsion systems. All other internal spacecraft systems powered up; cross-system tests continue. New flight software installed in all three computer cores. Ejectable bridge module docked. Minimum flight test program crew completes preliminary training aboard ship. Captain's yacht test article docked, nonflight version. USS *Enterprise* is launched; leaves dock on maneuvering thrusters.

2359

Flight test crew continues developmental shakedown trials in Mars space. USS *Enterprise* computers receive continuous performance updates from USS *Galaxy* orbiting Pluto. Tasks include extensive sensor operations, simulated emergency conditions, simulated combat exercises, and power system stress analysis. Warp field coils receive first power, nonpropulsive, Warp 1 equivalent. Power conditioning of warp coils continues up through Warp 8 equivalent. Performance analysis continues on all vehicle components. Main computers developing "systems awareness," learning and recording how ship behaves as a total entity. USS *Enterprise* declared deep-spaceworthy and warp-capable. Yellow warp-stress visibility hull coatings applied.

2360–2363

USS *Enterprise* achieves warp flight in outer solar system. Initial vibration difficulties transitioning to higher warp factors

smoothed out by computer adjustments to warp geometry control software. Skin reinforcements and frame stiffening performed during dock layovers. Final hull coatings and markings applied. Live-fire phaser and photon torpedo exercises test crew and systems. Low-level defensive shield power deficiencies appear; enhanced shield generators designs put into work. All lifeboats and auxiliary spacecraft docked, including flight-qualified captain's yacht. Operational bridge module docked.

4 OCTOBER 2363

The USS *Enterprise* is officially commissioned in a ceremony at the Utopia Planitia Fleet Yards. The USS *Galaxy* and USS *Yamato* send congratulatory messages via subspace radio.

Given the existence of matter replication devices (like the show's "food replicator" terminals), a very logical question is: "Why can't they just replicate entire starships?" The real reason is that such an ability would allow us to create entire fleets of starships at the touch of a button. This might be great for Federation defense and science programs, but makes for poor drama. For this reason, starship construction facilities (seen at Utopia Planitia in "Booby Trap" and Earth Station McKinley in "Family") have been depicted as construction platforms rather than large replicators. We assume that replication is practical for relatively small items, but that energy costs would be prohibitive for routine replication of larger objects. (Jon Singer points out that if you could make a starship at the push of a button, you wouldn't need to....)

2.0 SPACECRAFT STRUCTURE

2.1 MAIN SKELETAL STRUCTURE

The primary spaceframe of the *Galaxy* class starship is fabricated from an interlocking series of tritanium/duranium macrofilament truss frames. These members average 1.27 m^2 in cross section, and are located an average of every 25 meters across the ship's exterior.

Larger numbers of these trusses are located integral to the main and saucer impulse engine sections, the warp nacelle pylons, both saucer and battle sides of the docking latch interfaces, and along the centerlines of both hull struc-

tures. Smaller trusses, averaging 0.53 m^2 in cross section, are located every five meters on average, and also provide internal supports within the deck and core structure of the spacecraft interior.

This basic mechanical framework provides physical integrity to the vehicle while at rest. A parallel series of aluminum crystalfoam stringers are phase-transition bonded to the primary trusses, providing low-frequency vibration attenuation across the main truss structure, as well as support for certain utility conduits.

Also attached to these stringers are various conformal

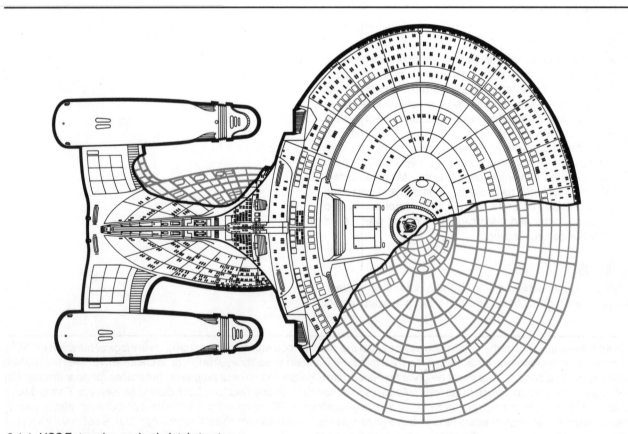

2.1.1 *USS* Enterprise *main skeletal structure*

2.1.2 Structural integrity field dynamic stress points

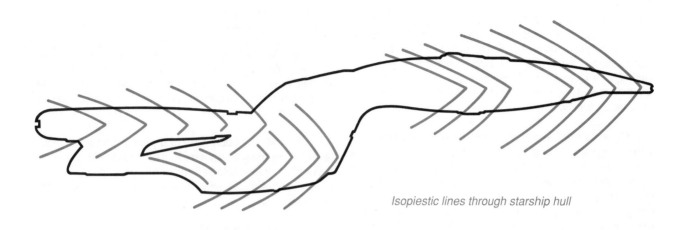

Isopiestic lines through starship hull

devices built into the hull structure, including elements of the deflector shield grid, as well as subspace radio antennas, which are incorporated into the exterior skin of the spacecraft.

SECONDARY FRAMEWORK

Mounted to the primary spaceframe is a secondary framework of microextruded terminium trusses to which the inner hull structure is directly attached. The secondary framework is mounted by means of 3.2 cm diameter x 5.1 cm long semirigid polyduranide support rods, permitting a limited amount of mechanical isolation from the primary spaceframe for purposes of strain relief, plus sound and vibration isolation. Secondary spaceframe segments are also separated from each other (although mechanically attached) to permit replacement of inner hull segments and associated utilities infrastructure during major starbase layover.

Structural integrity during powered flight is provided by a series of forcefields that reinforce the physical framework. This structural integrity field energy (SIF) is distributed through a network of molybdenum-jacketed waveguides, which in turn distribute SIF energy into ceramic-polymer conductive elements throughout the spaceframe. Without the structural integrity field, the vehicle would be unable to withstand accelerations greater than 7.4 m/sec^2 without significant deformation, or greater than 19.5 m/sec^2 without unrecoverable structural damage (in other words, the spacecraft would

sag under its own weight in Earth's gravity without the reinforcement of the SIF [See: 2.4]).

The exterior hull substrate is joined to the primary load-bearing trusses by means of 4.8 cm diameter electron-bonded duranium pins at 1.25 meter intervals. These pins are slip-fitted into an insulating AGP ceramic fabric jacket that provides thermal insulation between the spaceframe and the exterior hull. The pins, jacketing, and hull segments are gamma-welded together.

2.2 USS *ENTERPRISE* COORDINATE SYSTEM

EXTERNAL COORDINATE SYSTEM

An integrated system governing control of all manufacturing, repair, and operational structural reference points exists for the USS *Enterprise* and all other Starfleet vessels. The system utilizes a standard three-dimensional vertex and vector measuring scheme, with centimeters as its operative value. The three axes are labeled X, Y, and Z. The X axis runs port-starboard, with +X to starboard. The Y axis runs dorsal-ventral, with +Y to dorsal. The Z axis runs fore-to-aft, with +Z to aft. Note that this is opposite in sign to translational maneuvers, which consider +Z to be in the direction of flight.

All single points, vectors, and planes can be determined with this scheme, creating a common ground for structural topics. The *Enterprise* is considered to have three vessel configurations: Docked, Saucer Module, and Battle Section. Each configuration maintains a specific measurement origin, designated by the XYZ value of the forwardmost structure. For example, the center forward edge of the Saucer Module is labeled XYZ_S 0, 0, 0. Coincidentally, it is also the origin for the docked vessel and can be labeled XYZ_D 0, 0, 0. The origin for the Battle Section, designated XYZ_B 0, 0, 0, also corresponds to a point on the docked vessel as XYZ_D 0, -1676, 25146, meaning that the Battle Section origin is at 25146 cm aft of the ship's forward edge and 1676 cm below.

Specific components, such as the warp engine nacelles, are given their own origins and coordinate values, and these will also have corresponding values relative to their parent assemblies. For example, the origin of the port warp nacelle is labeled XYZ_{NP} 0, 0, 0. This point, relative to the Battle Section origin, is XYZ_B −12954, −1524, 13716.

Planes passing through the different vessel configurations are labeled according to their axes. XY planes of the docked starship run vertically and laterally, XZ planes intersect the ship parallel with the saucer equator, and YZ planes run vertically and fore-to-aft. Planes may be called out as existing at specific XYZ station points, and coordinates may be given within that plane, especially in locating key starship components or processes.

Normally, all coordinate and planar data are manipulated by the main computers in their monitoring and repair tasks and are available to Engineering crew members as an option in considering exact three-dimensional relationships within the ship.

INTERNAL COORDINATE SYSTEM

Structures and objects within the USS *Enterprise* spaceframe are located with the following coordinate system. Intraship locator addresses are based on a fifteen-digit code which follows the form: "12-1234-000/000/000."

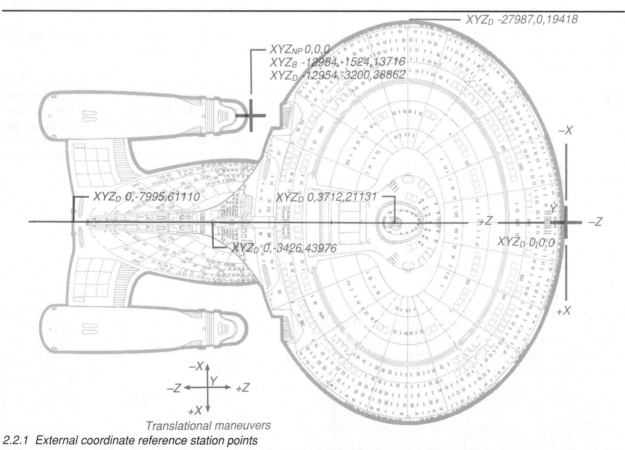

Translational maneuvers

2.2.1 External coordinate reference station points

The first group of two digits refers to the deck number. Possible values within the Primary Hull range from 01 (Deck 1, the Main Bridge) to 16 (the captain's yacht docking port on the underside of the saucer). Within the Engineering Hull, deck numbers range from 08 (the Battle Bridge at the top of the dorsal) to 42 (Deck 42, the bottom of the Engineering Hull).

The second group of four digits specifies the sector and compartment number. For locations within the Primary Hull, the first two digits of this group refer to one of 36 ten-degree sectors (See: 2.2.2).

For locations within the Engineering Hull, the first digit of this group is always a 5, with the second digit designating one of ten sectors (See: 2.2.3). A first digit of 6 indicates a location within the port warp nacelle or pylon, and a first digit of 7 indicates a location within the starboard warp nacelle or pylon.

The third and fourth digits in this second group indicate the compartment or station number within the sector.

Note that the first and second group of the locator address (totaling six digits) are generally used as room designator numbers within the habitable volume of the spacecraft. By keeping in mind this general scheme of room and compartment numbering, it is possible for crew members to locate virtually any room on board the ship by use of the internal coordinate system.

The final group of three three-digit numbers refers to the XYZ coordinate address within a compartment. In cases where greater precision is required, decimal values are appended to each of the XYZ coordinates.

2.2.2 Saucer Module sector coordinate (third digit in internal coordinate address)

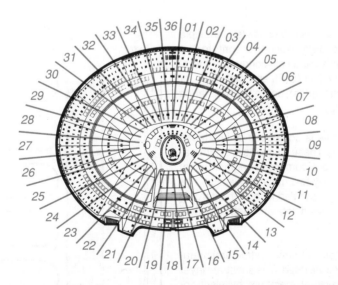

Mike was responsible for the signage in the Enterprise *interiors and by default became responsible for keeping track of all the room numbers of all the rooms seen in the show. This fairly simple task is sometimes made difficult because many doors are reused and redressed to represent different parts of the ship. The actual room numbers are fairly difficult to read on television, but he has gotten letters from viewers who let him know when he's made a mistake (for example, by putting the wrong deck number on a particular door sign). By the way, for any aerospace types out there, our external coordinate system is loosely based on the numeric references used by Rockwell for building the space shuttle. The axis labels are based on motion-control notation (used when programming the computerized special effects cameras used in filming the ship miniature) rather than those used by the present aerospace industry.*

2.2.3 Sector coordinate address in Engineering Hull

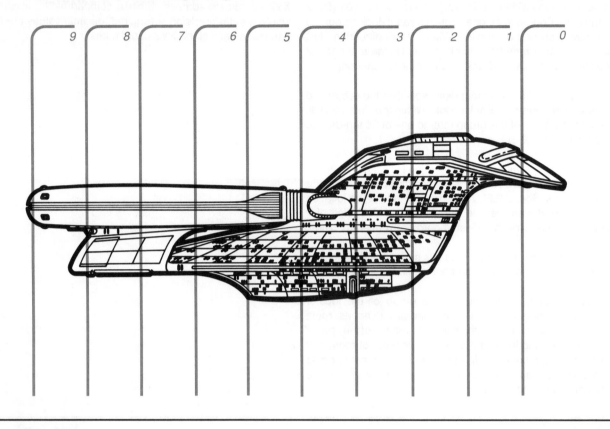

2.3 HULL LAYERS

The exterior shell of the spacecraft consists of multiple layers which afford structural and atmospheric integrity for the spaceframe, integral waveguides and field conductive members for the structural integrity field (SIF), and pathways for other utilities (including deflector grids), as well as resistance to radiation and thermal energy.

The exterior shell substrate is composed of interlaced microfoam duranium filaments. These filaments are gamma-welded into a series of contiguous composite segments that are 4.7 cm thick and are typically two meters in width. The substrate segments are electron bonded to three reinforcing layers of 1.2 cm biaxially stressed tritanium fabric, which provide additional torsion strength.

In areas immediately adjacent to major structural members, four layers of 2.3 cm fabric are used. The substrate layer is attached to the major structural members by electron-bonded duranium fasteners at 2.5 cm intervals. The substrate segments are not intended to be replaceable, except by phase-transition bonding using a transporter assembly jig during major starbase layovers.

Thermal insulation and secondary SIF conductivity are provided by two 3.76 cm layers of low-density expanded ceramic-polymer composites. These layers are separated by

• Exterior   *Interior •*

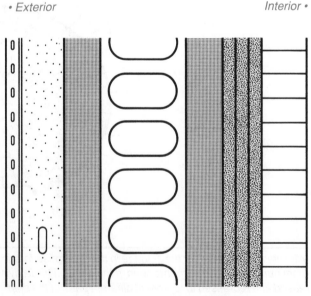

2.3.1 Hull layers

an 8.7 cm multiaxis tritanium truss framework, which provides additional thermal insulation and a pass-through for fixed utility conduits.

Radiation attenuation is provided by a 4.2 cm layer of monocrystal beryllium silicate infused with semiferrous polycarbonate whiskers. This layer is networked with a series of 2.3 cm x 0.85 cm molybdenum-jacketed conduits. These conduits, which occur at 130 cm intervals, serve as triphase waveguides for the secondary structural integrity field. Conductive tritanium rods penetrate the waveguides at 10 cm intervals and transfer SIF energy into the ceramic-polymer conductive layer.

The outermost hull layer is composed of a 1.6 cm sheet of AGP ablative ceramic fabric chemically bonded onto a substrate of 0.15 cm tritanium foil. This material is formed into segments of approximately 3.7 m² and is attached to the radiation attenuation layer by a series of duranium fasteners, which allows individual segments to be replaced as necessary. (Micrometeoroid erosion is kept to a minimum by the deflector shield system, but is sufficient to warrant replacement of 30% of leading-edge segments on the average of every 7.2 Standard years.) Individual outer hull segments are machined to a tolerance of ±0.5 mm to allow for minimum drag through the interstellar medium. Joints between segments are manufactured to a tolerance of ±0.25 mm.

Also incorporated into the outermost hull layer is a series of superconducting molybdenum-jacketed waveguide conduits which serves to distribute and disperse the energy of the tactical deflector system. Selected segments of this network also serve as radiators for starship thermal management.

2.4 STRUCTURAL INTEGRITY FIELD SYSTEM

The mechanical integrity of the physical spaceframe is augmented by the structural integrity field (SIF) system. This system provides a network of forcefield segments that compensate for propulsive and other structural load factors that otherwise exceed the design limits of the spaceframe. The SIF applies forcefield energy directly to field conductive elements within the spaceframe and increases the load-bearing capacity of the structure.

Field generation for the SIF is provided by three field generators located on Deck 11 in the Primary Hull and by two generators located on Deck 32 in the Secondary Hull. Each generator consists of a cluster of twenty 12 MW graviton polarity sources feeding a pair of 250 millicochrane subspace field distortion amplifiers. Heat dissipation on each unit is provided by a pair of 300,000 megajoules per hour (MJ/hr) continuous-duty liquid helium coolant loops. Two backup generators are located in each hull, providing up to twelve hours of service at 55% of maximum rated power. Normal duty cycle on generators is thirty-six hours online, with nominal twenty-four hours degauss and scheduled maintenance time. Graviton polarity sources are rated for 1,500 operating hours between routine servicing of superconductive elements.

The output of each SIF generator is directed by means of a network of molybdenum-jacketed triphase waveguides which distributes the field energy throughout the spaceframe. SIF conductivity elements are incorporated into all major structural members. When energized by the SIF, the load-bearing capacity of these conductive structural elements is increased by up to 125,000%. Secondary feeds also provide for reinforcement of the vehicle's external shell.

Cruise Mode operating rules require at least one field generator to be active at all times in each hull, although the Flight Control Officer may call for activation of a second generator when extreme maneuvers are anticipated. During Alert modes, all operational units are brought to hot standby for immediate activation. Reduced Power Mode rules permit a single field generator to feed the entire spaceframe using the field conduit umbilical connect between the primary and engineering sections.

Fairly early on, Rick did a drawing for our writers showing the Enterprise *superimposed over a map of the Paramount Studios lot. This was fun because it gave us for the first time a concrete idea of how big the ship "really" is. A bit later, though, we started to think of some of the implications of this enormous size. We began to realize that it would be pretty difficult for a structure that size to maintain its rigidity and form, especially under the tremendous accelerations that impulse and warp drive would likely entail. (We envisioned the main impulse engines firing, squashing the ship like a partially deflated blimp. This might actually be a valid way for a space vehicle to operate, but it would probably look pretty silly on film.) Because of this, we came up with the "structural integrity field," which we envision as a powerful forcefield that helps to hold the ship together.*

2.5.1 Inertial potential cancellation using IDF

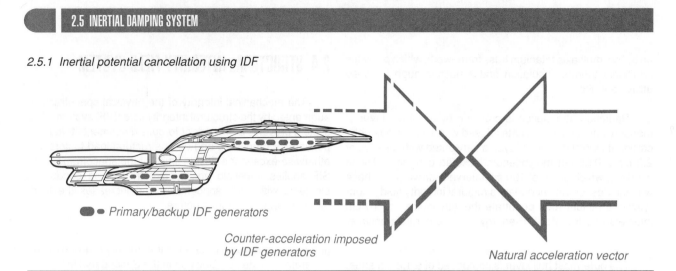

• Primary/backup IDF generators

Counter-acceleration imposed
by IDF generators

Natural acceleration vector

2.5 INERTIAL DAMPING SYSTEM

Operating in parallel with the structural integrity field (SIF) system is the inertial damping field system (IDF). This system generates a controlled series of variable-symmetry forcefields that serve to absorb the inertial forces of spaceflight which would otherwise cause fatal injury to the crew. The IDF is generated separately from the SIF, but is fed by a parallel series of waveguides that are then conducted through synthetic gravity plates.

The IDF operates by maintaining a low-level forcefield throughout the habitable volume of the spacecraft. This field averages 75 millicochranes with field differential limited to 5.26 nanocochranes/meter, per SFRA-standard 352.12 for crew exposure to subspace fields.

As acceleration effects are anticipated, this field is distorted along a vector diametrically opposed to the velocity change. The IDF thereby absorbs the inertial potential, which would otherwise have acted upon the crew.

There is a characteristic lag time for the shifting of IDF direction and intensity. This lag varies with the net acceleration involved, but averages 295 milliseconds for normal impulse maneuvers. Because IDF control is generally derived from Flight Controller data, normal course corrections can be anticipated so there is rarely any noticeable acceleration to the crew. Exceptions to this sometimes occur when power for IDF operations is restricted or when sudden maneuvers or other externally caused accelerations occur more rapidly than the system can respond.

Flux generation for the IDF is provided by four field generators located on Deck 11 in the Primary Hull and by two generators located on Deck 33 in the Engineering Hull. Each generator consists of a cluster of twelve 500 kW graviton polarity sources feeding a pair of 150 millicochrane subspace field distortion amplifiers. Heat dissipation on each unit is provided by a pair of 100,000 MJ/hr continuous-duty liquid helium coolant loops. Three backup generators are located in each hull, providing up to twelve hours of service at 65% of maximum rated power. Normal duty cycle on generators is forty-eight hours online, with nominal twelve hours degauss and scheduled maintenance time. Graviton polarity sources are rated for 2,500 operating hours between routine servicing of superconductive elements.

Cruise Mode operating rules require at least two field generators to be active at all times in each hull, although the Flight Control Officer may call for activation of additional units when extreme maneuvers are anticipated. During Alert modes, all operational units are brought to hot standby for immediate activation. Reduced Power Mode rules permit a single field generator to feed the entire spaceframe, using the field conduit umbilical connect between the primary and engineering sections.

The tremendous accelerations involved in the kind of spaceflight seen on Star Trek *would instantly turn the crew to chunky salsa unless there was some kind of heavy-duty protection. Hence, the inertial damping field. The reason for the "characteristic lag" referred to above is to "explain" why our crew is occasionally knocked out of their chairs during battle or other drastic maneuvers despite the IDF. The science of all this is admittedly a bit hazy, but it seems a good compromise between dramatic necessity and maintaining some kind of technical consistency.*

2.6 EMERGENCY PROCEDURES IN SIF/IDF FAILURE

Failure of the structural integrity field (SIF) or the inertial damping field (IDF) can have potentially catastrophic consequences to the starship and to its crew. For this reason, multiple redundancy has been built into these systems, and emergency protocols have been devised to anticipate the possibility of failure of one or more of these units.

The *Enterprise* is dependent upon its structural integrity field to maintain the spaceframe during the tremendous accelerations encountered during impulse flight as well as the differential subspace field stresses experienced during warp flight. The inertial damping field also provides vital cushioning to the fragile crew during such maneuvers. Without such protection, the spacecraft and crew are unable to survive accelerations in excess of 30 m/sec^2 (approximately 3g) without serious structural damage to the spaceframe and severe — probably fatal — injury to the crew. By way of contrast, accelerations considerably in excess of 1,000g are not uncommon when under full impulse power. Warp flight operations do not produce direct acceleration stresses, but SIF/IDF protection is needed because of the potential for warp field differential stresses and local variations in inertial potential.

Under Cruise Mode operating protocols, two field generators are active at all times, although one unit is sufficient to provide adequate protection for both spacecraft and crew except during extreme maneuvers. In case of failure of one field generator, a backup unit will automatically engage, keeping the number of active units at two. If a third unit is available to be placed in service, Cruise Mode rules allow operations in progress to continue without interruption.

In the event of failure of two field generators, or in the case where an additional backup cannot be brought on line, operating rules require a Yellow Alert status to be initiated, and the Commanding Officer is required to make a determination whether to allow primary or secondary mission operations in progress to continue.

In the event of failure of three or four field generators, regardless of the availability of backup units, Yellow Alert status must be initiated and the vehicle must attempt to decelerate to an inertially safe condition, subject to sufficient generator capacity. If the spacecraft is presently at sublight speed, that speed must be reduced to the point where further deceleration can be absorbed by minimal inertial damping and structural integrity capacity. If the spacecraft is traveling at warp, an immediate reduction to sublight must be initiated, subject to maximum allowable subspace field differentials. Such downwarping must be a simple field collapse maneuver; differential field maneuvers are not permitted. Operating rules provide for exceptions during combat situations or when the failure of the remaining field generators is believed to be immediately imminent.

The failure of all five field generators requires an immediate Red Alert status. The Commanding Officer is first required to stabilize the situation, take steps to minimize potential risk, and then to begin deceleration maneuvers. Severe operational limits are imposed on vehicle maneuvers. Immediate downwarping to sublight must be performed, except during active combat situations. Such downwarping must be a simple field collapse maneuver; differential field maneuvers are not permitted.

Once the Commanding Officer or supervising Operations Manager has determined that further system failures are no longer an immediate threat, power conservation procedures are initiated because of the possibility that the ship may be unable to make a significant change in course or speed for a period of several months. Starfleet Command is notified for possible assistance or rescue efforts.

Until the arrival of assistance, the ship should maintain power conservation procedures and perform the maximum deceleration consistent with vehicle and crew safety. Rescue and salvage options include replacement of field generation components, evacuation of crew to permit unprotected deceleration using the ship's own engines or a tractor beam. Under certain conditions, it is possible for a rescue vessel to project an SIF/IDF onto the ship, although this is a difficult and extremely power-intensive procedure. A final option is the evacuation of the crew and abandonment of the spacecraft, although even this option should not preclude the possibility of salvage at a later date.

We assume that these operating protocols are somewhat conservative. In "Tin Man," the ever resourceful Geordi La Forge was able to divert some power from the structural integrity field to keep the shields up. The computer warned that doing so would compromise safety limits, but Geordi was obviously able to keep the ship together and the shields up.

2.7 SAUCER MODULE SEPARATION SYSTEMS

The USS *Enterprise* consists of two spacecraft systems integrated to form a single functional vessel. Under specific emergency conditions, the two vehicle elements may perform a separation maneuver and continue independent operation. The two elements, the Saucer Module and the Battle Section, are normally joined together by a series of structural docking latches, numerous umbilicals, and turbolift pass-throughs.

Eighteen docking latches provide the necessary physical connections between the major load-bearing members of both vehicles. The active side of the latches is located on the dorsal surface of the Battle Section around the periphery of the Battle Bridge and upper sensor arrays. The passive apertures for the latches are set into the aft ventral surface of the Saucer Module. Each active latch segment consists of two spreading grab plates driven by four redundant sets of electrofluidic pistons. The grab plates measure 6.9 x 7.2 m and are constructed of diffusion-bonded tritanium carbide, similar to the main load-bearing spaceframe members. These are designed to accept and transfer energy from the structural integrity field generators, locking the two vehicles together. The dorsal surfaces of the grab plates are layered with standard ablative hull coatings for exposure to the general space environment and warp flight stresses. The latching system has been designed to accept a failure rate of 1.5 latch

pairs per ten separations; in the event a single pair fails to seat properly within its passive aperture, the structural loads can be shared adequately among the other latches.

Each electrofluidic piston consists of a main fluid reservoir, magnetic valve controller block, piston computer controller, attach brackets, pressure manifolds, and redundant sensor assemblies. Piston operation is maintained under computer control to assure smooth activation of all latches simultaneously, though under emergency conditions a manual latching option is available.

Quick-disconnect umbilicals set into the vehicle interface, which normally allow for the unbroken flow of gases, liquids, waveguide energy, computer information, and other data channels, are isolated once the separation sequence is commanded.

The vehicle interface also accommodates a set of standard turbolift pass-throughs, including the dedicated emergency turbo to the Battle Bridge. These shafts are equipped with automatic path termination seals, which have been designed to double as airlock modules. If either separated vehicle docks at another Starfleet facility at the vehicle interface, the termination seals retreat to their default positions just off the turbolift shafts.

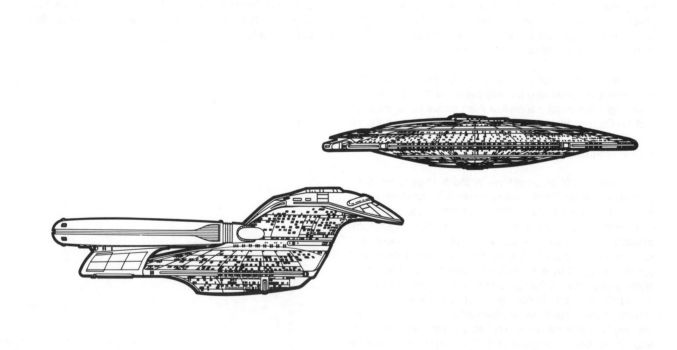

2.7.1 Saucer Module separation

2.7.2 Latching system

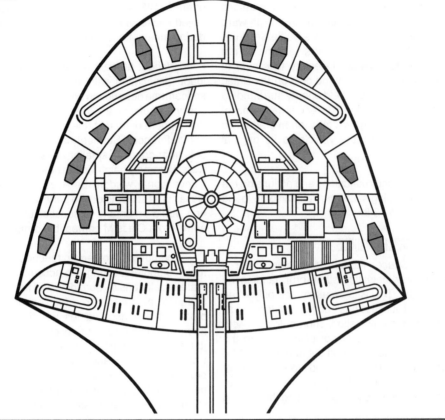

SEPARATION SYSTEM OPERATION

In the docked configuration, the passive apertures retain the grab plates in their fully deployed positions, and a structural locking wedge is driven into the gap between the plates. Energy from the structural integrity field (SIF) is conducted through the grab plates to rigidize the combined vehicle. All umbilicals would operate normally to transfer consumables and information. The turbolifts move normally between the Saucer Module to the Battle Section. At the confirmed signal for Saucer Module separation, once an assigned crew has occupied the Battle Bridge, computer event timers deadface all interconnects by commanding all umbilical blocks to shut down and retract to safe housings, and turbolift termination

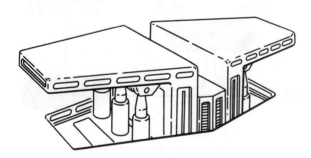

2.7.3 Docking latch (Battle Section side)

seals to drop into their deploy positions. Should any key umbilicals or turbo paths show a failure condition at the vehicle interface, the computer will close off the affected elements at the best possible points upstream of the failure. Hardware and software failures will then be dealt with later, once the emergency situation is resolved. Crews on both sides of the vehicle interface monitor the progress of the separation sequence, and are then on standby awaiting reconnection duties.

Once all systems are safed, preparatory to the −Y translational maneuver, the latch wedge blocks are retracted and the grab plates are moved together. If the maneuver is conducted at sublight, there exists an option to postpone the latch retract into the Battle Section, in case a rapid reconnection is required. Once into warp flight, however, this option is canceled, as the latches must retract quickly to minimize vehicle stresses and any chance of collision with the Saucer Module.

The separation maneuver will cause the two vehicle components to behave differently from a flight dynamics standpoint, and vehicle velocity at the time of separation will further increase the differences in handling characteristics. The main computers aboard each vehicle, interacting with their respective engines, SIF, and the inertial damping field (IDF), will perform realtime adjustments to compensate for vehicle-induced oscillations or externally forced motions. As the Saucer Module is equipped only with impulse propulsion, computational modeling has verified that special cautions must be observed when attempting separation at high warp factors. Prior to leaving the protection of the Battle Section's warp field, the Saucer Module SIF, IDF, and shield grid are run at high output, and its four forward deflectors take over to sweep away debris in the absence of the dish on the Battle Section (See: 7.4). Decaying warp field energy surrounding the Saucer Module is managed by the driver coil segments of the impulse engines. This energy will take, on average, two minutes to dissipate and bring the vehicle to its original sublight velocity.

Discussions of emergency conditions and actions on the parts of both vehicles following separation can also be found in Sections 11.5, 11.6, and 15.8.

EMERGENCY LANDING OF SAUCER MODULE

In the event the Saucer Module is disabled near a planetary body and cannot maintain a stable orbit, landing the saucer is the final option. This is to be attempted only when an acceptable chance of success has been computed and all other available procedures have failed, short of total evacuation by lifeboat modules. If the senior officer aboard the Saucer Module makes the decision that the attempt must be made, special sets of crew procedures and stored computer commands will be implemented. While extensive computer modeling has been taken into account in creating the landing

programs, no guarantee as to their effectiveness can yet be offered. SIF reinforcement of the saucer framework is believed necessary to avoid exceeding saucer structural limits during atmospheric entry of a Class M planet.

Without at least minimal reinforcement, aerodynamic loads associated with most entry profiles may result in spaceframe destruction prior to landing. As it was deemed too costly to subject a *Galaxy* class spaceframe to a full-up atmosphere entry test, the computer model is the best available reference. Starfleet has recorded a total of three data sets from previous smaller starship hull landings, and these were extremely helpful in the design of the computer routines. Conventional wisdom believes, however, that the *Galaxy* class hull is still outside the survivable performance envelope and would be unable to successfully perform a deorbit and entry into a Class M compatible atmosphere.

A complex set of terrain touchdown options reside in the main computers, taking into account such factors as contact material, air density, humidity, and temperature. If there is an adequate amount of time for sensor scans during the approach, the sensor values will be compared to those in memory, and the appropriate control adjustments can be sent to the impulse engines and field devices. Beach sand, deep water, smooth ice, and grassy plains on Class M bodies are preferable sites; in contrast, certain terrain types have not been modeled, such as mountainous surfaces. Other nonterrestrial bodies may possess survivable surfaces, and their

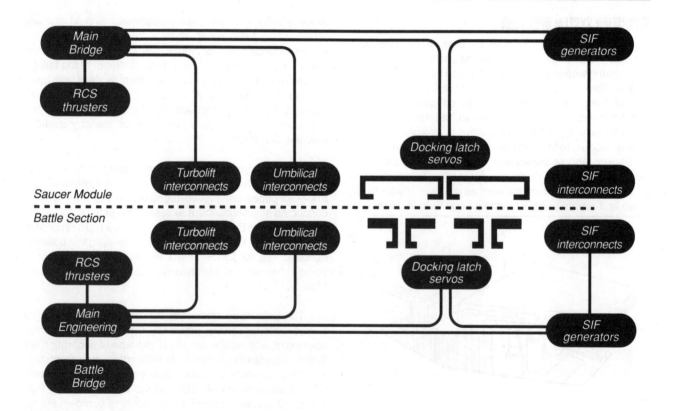

2.7.4 *Saucer separation latching and umbilical systems*

2.7.5 Best-case atmospheric entry profile for Saucer Module

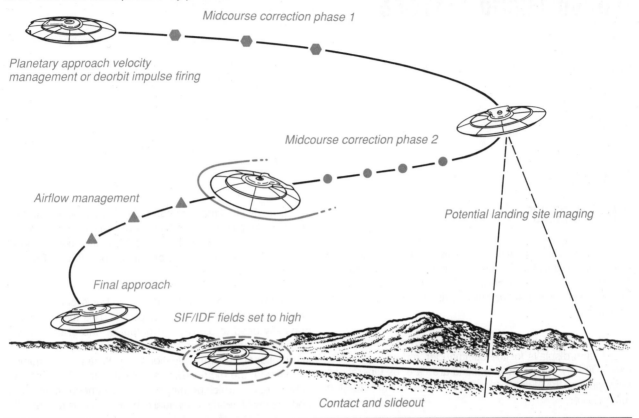

Midcourse correction phase 1

Planetary approach velocity
management or deorbit impulse firing

Midcourse correction phase 2

Airflow management

Potential landing site imaging

Final approach

SIF/IDF fields set to high

Contact and slideout

suitability as landing sites will depend on the specific situation, computer recommendations, and command decisions.

Naturally, many planetary types will possess environments so hostile to crew survival that remaining in orbit will be a preferable option, unless emergency landing is mandated by tactical considerations.

Prior to landing on a Class M planet (as only one example), the structural integrity field and inertial damping field would be set to high output, with the SIF also set to flex the vehicle in small, controlled amounts for shock attenuation. The deflector grid will be set to a high output as well, with its field decay radius configured to optimize the Saucer Module's final slideout distance while applying a controlled friction effect. During approach the computer would take atmospheric readings and make adjustments along the descent, and command the deflector field to perform airflow and steering changes. In the event computer control is limited, the Flight Control Officer (Conn) should be able to make manual attitude control inputs from his/her panel. The IDF would be configured to "jolt mode" during major impacts, if they exceed certain preset translational limits. The deflector field is designed to protect the vehicle hull, though only up to the specified load limits when the hull must make contact with the ground. If the SIF, IDF, and deflector grid are all functioning during slideout, they can add a great deal to minimizing impact forces.

It is assumed that the vehicle would be a total loss insofar as ever being returned to operational service, due to the extreme loads placed upon it, which would result in deep, unrecoverable alloy damage. Postlanding mission rules call for full security measures to protect the crew and vehicle while awaiting Starfleet assistance. Numerous options have been documented, from simple waiting within Federation or allied territory, to total evacuation and vehicle destruct in areas controlled by Threat forces.

3.0 COMMAND SYSTEMS

3.1 MAIN BRIDGE

Primary operational control of the *Galaxy* class starship is provided by the Main Bridge, located at the top of the Saucer Module on Deck 1. The Main Bridge directly supervises all primary mission operations and coordinates all departmental activities.

The central area of the Main Bridge provides seating and information displays for the commander and two other officers. Directly fore of the command area are the Operations Manager and the Flight Control Officer, both of whom face the main viewer.

Directly aft of the command area is an elevated platform on which is located the tactical control station. Also located on the platform are five workstations, nominally configured as Science I, Science II, Mission Operations (Ops), Environment, and Engineering.

At the very front of the bridge chamber is located a large (4.8 x 2.5 meter) visual display panel. This main viewer is generally used to display the output of one of the forward optical scanners, but can easily be reset for any other visual, informational, or communications use. When in communications mode, the main viewer shares the use of a dedicated subprocessor, which permits near-instantaneous conversion and display of nearly any visual communications format. The

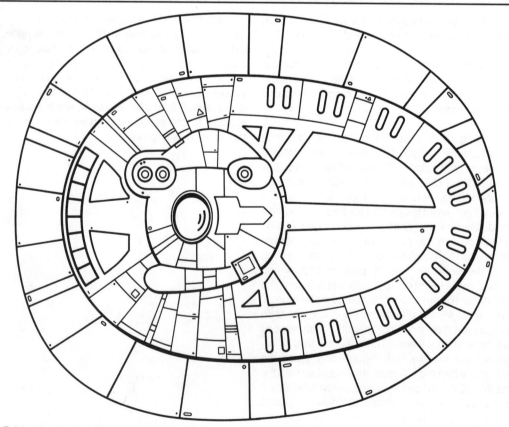

3.1.1 Main Bridge location on Saucer Module

main viewer display matrix includes omni-holographic display elements and is thus capable of displaying three-dimensional information.

Behind the aft workstations is a 3.2 meter equipment bay, normally sealed to crew personnel. This equipment bay houses three of the seven dedicated bridge computer optical subprocessors, and six of the twelve shared subprocessors. Also located in this equipment bay are several power, environmental, and optical data trunk connects. The remaining computer subprocessors are located in smaller equipment bays integral to the aft stations, in the side bays port and starboard of the command area, and in the deck structure between Conn and Ops and the main viewer.

Other facilities located on Deck 1 include the captain's ready room and head, the aft observation lounge, and the crew head adjoining the bridge itself. Both the bridge and the captain's ready room are equipped with food replication terminals.

Major connects to the bridge include two standard turbolift shafts, one emergency turboshaft, and four electro plasma power distribution waveguide conduits. Additional connects include four environmental support plenum groups, nine primary and two backup optical data network trunks, two replicator waveguide conduits, and three service crawlways.

Because of the criticality of bridge systems, especially in

emergency situations, the Main Bridge is designated as an emergency environmental support shelter, receiving priority life support from two special protected utilities trunks. These feeds permit Class M conditions to be maintained for up to seventy-two hours even in the event of failure of both primary and reserve environmental systems. Also provided within the bridge shell are two emergency atmospheric and power supply modules, each capable of providing up to twenty-four hours of atmosphere and lighting in the event of total environmental systems failure.

The Main Bridge module is connected to the spaceframe structure with a series of 320 7.2 cm duranium fastening rods. These fasteners can be disengaged at major starbase layover, permitting disconnect and replacement of the entire bridge module. Torsion relief and vibration damping are provided by a series of 17 mm microfoamed AGP semiflexible ceramic gaskets which form the mechanical interface between the structures. The Main Bridge shell is constructed

The Enterprise *bridge was one of the first things developed for* Star Trek: The Next Generation. *It was initially designed by Andrew Probert, then finalized and built under the direction of production designer Herman Zimmerman. Working blueprints were drafted by set designer Les Gobrugge. Since our second season, set design (including* Enterprise *interiors) has been supervised by production designer Richard James, who was honored with an Emmy award for his art direction in "Sins of the Father."*

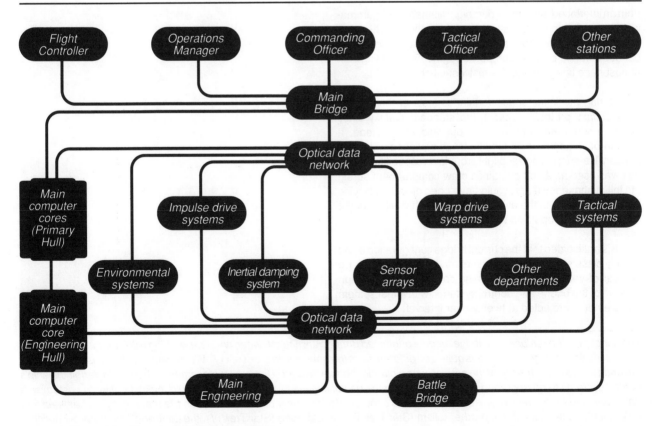

3.1.2 Command intelligence links to major systems

3.1.3 Main Bridge

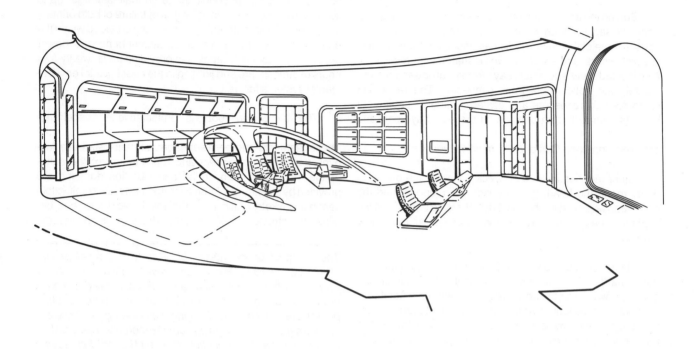

from an interlaced microfoam duranium filament shell gamma-welded to a tritanium truss structural framework. The inner environmental envelope is fabricated from low-density expanded ceramic-polymer composite segments, providing both atmospheric integrity and thermal insulation.

During the initial spaceworthiness tests of the original USS *Galaxy* prototype vessel, the standard *Galaxy* class bridge module was not yet fully operational. Instead, a custom-built module was used that was equipped with independent life-support and sublight propulsion capabilities. This unit was used as a self-contained crew compartment during the initial shakedown and could have been ejected, carrying the crew to safety in the event of a catastrophic failure of the spaceframe or propulsion system.

It is anticipated that the current bridge configuration of the *Galaxy* class starship will remain relatively unchanged for a number of years. Current planning calls for annual design reviews of the bridge and control systems, with major system replacements projected at twenty-year intervals.

The concept of the replaceable bridge module originated during Star Trek V, *when we were working with Herman Zimmerman on a new* Enterprise *bridge that was quite a bit different from the one seen in* Star Trek IV. *We rationalized that this was because the bridge, located at the top of the saucer, was a plug-in module designed for easy replacement. This would permit the ship's control systems to be upgraded, thereby extending the useful lifetime of a starship, and would make it easier to customize a particular ship for a specific type of mission. This concept also fits the fact that we've seen the main bridges of at least four different* Miranda *class starships, the* Reliant (Star Trek II), *the* Saratoga (Star Trek IV), *the* Lantree *("Unnatural Selection"), and the* Brattain *("Night Terrors"), each of which had a different bridge module.*

3.2 BRIDGE OPERATIONS

Operational authority for the starship rests with the Commanding Officer (usually the captain or duty officer). The Commanding Officer is responsible for execution of Starfleet orders and policy, as well as for interpretation and compliance with Federation law and diplomatic directives. As such, the Commanding Officer is directly answerable to Starfleet Command for the performance of the ship.

The Main Bridge is directly responsible for the supervision of all primary mission functions. Through the Operations Manager, the bridge also monitors all secondary mission functions to provide an optimal operating state. The multimission operational profile of the *Enterprise* requires extensive coordination between different departments.

The Main Bridge also serves as a command center during alert and crisis situations. During Separated Flight Mode, combat operations are managed from the Battle Bridge, while control of the Saucer Section remains with the Main Bridge. In such scenarios, the ship's captain and senior officers will generally command the Battle Section, while a designated junior officer will assume responsibility for the Saucer Section.

BRIDGE OPERATIONS DURING ALERT CONDITIONS

• **Cruise Mode.** This is the normal operating status of the spacecraft. Cruise Mode operating rules require a minimum bridge staff of Commanding Officer (typically the captain), Flight Control Officer, Operations Manager, and at least one other officer available to serve at tactical or other stations as required. Other stations may be attended as specific mission requirements dictate (See: 15.4).

• **Yellow Alert.** During Yellow Alert condition, all active bridge stations are automatically brought to Full Enable Mode. Auto diagnostics (Level 4) are initiated for all primary and tactical systems. Ops is responsible for evaluating all current operations and shipboard activities and suspending any that may interfere with ship's readiness to respond to potential crisis situations (See: 15.5).

• **Red Alert.** During Red Alert condition, all bridge stations are automatically brought to Full Enable Mode. Tactical systems are placed on full alert and, if unoccupied, the duty security chief will occupy the bridge Tactical station (See: 15.6).

3.3 BASIC CONTROL PANEL/TERMINAL USE

Control/display panels aboard the USS *Enterprise* are software-defined surfaces that are continually updated and reconfigured for maximum operator efficiency and ease of use. Each panel is tied into a local subprocessor that continually monitors panel activity and compares it to predefined scenarios and operational profiles. This permits the computer to continually update the panel configuration to provide the operator with a current menu of the most likely current actions. This also provides the operator with sufficient information and flexibility to determine and execute nonprogrammed instructions, if desired.

Layout of the display surface is designed for maximum intuitive grouping of related functions and for logical organizational flow of operation. The library computer access and retrieval system (LCARS) software continually monitors operator activity and continually reconfigures the display surface to present the operator with a selection of the most frequently chosen courses of action in that particular situation. The LCARS software also provides the operator with full information (to the level selected by the operator or by operating rules) to choose any other legal action.

Most panels are also configured to accept vocal input, although keyboard input is preferred in most situations for greater operating speed and reduced chance of input error by voice discriminator algorithms.

Cruise Mode operating rules allow each crew member to define a customized operating configuration for his/her work station. This means that crew members are free to configure panel layout and procedural menus to suit personal working styles and levels of training. In the case where a system upgrade has recently been installed, but the duty officer has not yet been trained on the new configuration, panel software can usually be instructed to emulate the previous version until the individual has been properly certified. Standard configuration can be activated at any time, and Full Enable configuration is automatically activated during Alert status.

CONTROL/DISPLAY PANELS

Control/display surfaces are composed of three basic layers. The outermost layer is fabricated from a 2.5 mm tripolymer-coated transparent aluminum wafer into which is imbedded a sensor matrix. This matrix detects tactile input by the operator's fingertips. Also incorporated into this layer is a transducer matrix that provides tactile and auditory feedback to the operator, indicating that a particular control surface address has been activated.

Mike actually spent a fair amount of time trying to come up with a graphic "user interface" that would be the design basis of the various control panels on the ship. His design goal was to create a visual style that suggests an extremely simple means of organizing and controlling very complex processes and hardware. However, a closer examination of the actual panels used on our soundstages would reveal that many of the buttons and indicators are labeled with the initials of members of the Star Trek *production crew. (You'll have to take our word on this — they're too small to be legible on television.)*

The aluminum surface wafer is chemically bonded onto a triaxial optical display crystal membrane, which serves as a high resolution graphic display medium. Monocrystal microwaveguides at 1.8 mm intervals provide electro plasma system power transmission to the upper sensor matrix and transducer layers.

The substrate of the control surface is composed of microfoamed polyduranide sheeting, which provides structural integrity to the assembly. Incorporated into this layer is a matrix of optical nanoprocessors that permit the display surface sheeting to be self-configuring, once addressed and initialized by the local processor node. For redundancy's sake, the panel nanoprocessors include sufficient nonvolatile memory to permit system operation, even in the absence of main computer support.

3.3.1 Display panel layers

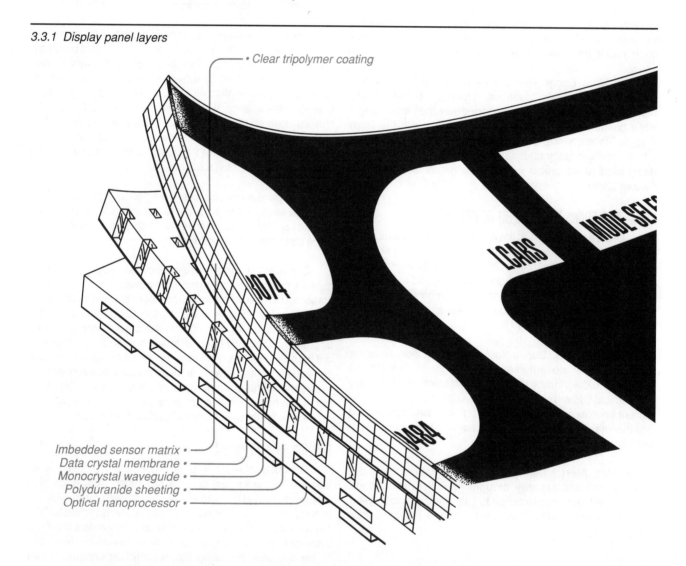

• Clear tripolymer coating

Imbedded sensor matrix •
Data crystal membrane •
Monocrystal waveguide •
Polyduranide sheeting •
Optical nanoprocessor •

We incorporated the concept of software-definable, task-specific panel layout into our controls because Mike thought it a logical way of simplifying designs that would otherwise have been nightmarishly complex. The basic idea is that the panels automatically reconfigure themselves to suit the specific task at hand. A side benefit we discovered is this gave our actors much more freedom in hitting controls to accomplish various tasks. (Even though our cast tries to get things right, there are numerous occasions when a particular shot will require an actor to hit a button on a specific area of a panel, which may not reflect our original design for that panel.) Variable-layout control panels mean that the button that fires phasers this week is not necessarily the same button that fires them next week.

3.4 FLIGHT CONTROL (CONN)

The Flight Control console, often referred to as Conn, is responsible for the actual piloting and navigation of the spacecraft. Although these are heavily automated functions, their criticality demands a human officer to oversee these operations at all times. The Flight Control Officer (also referred to as Conn) receives instructions directly from the Commanding Officer.

There are five major areas of responsibility for the Flight Control Officer:

- Navigational references/course plotting
- Supervision of automatic flight operations
- Manual flight operations
- Position verification
- Bridge liaison to Engineering department

During impulse powered spaceflight, Conn is responsible for monitoring relativistic effects as well as inertial damping system status. In the event that a requested maneuver exceeds the capacity of the inertial damping system, the computer will request Conn to modify the flight plan to bring it within the permitted performance envelope. During Alert status, flight rules permit Conn to specify maneuvers that are potentially dangerous to the crew or the spacecraft.

Warp flight operating rules require Conn to monitor subspace field geometry in parallel with the Engineering department. During warp flight, the Flight Control console continually updates long-range sensor data and makes automatic course corrections to adjust for minor variations in the density of the interstellar medium.

Because of the criticality of Flight Control in spacecraft operations, particularly during crisis situations, Conn is connected to a dedicated backup flight operations subprocessor to provide for manual flight control. This equipment package includes emergency navigation sensors.

SPECIFIC DUTIES

- **Navigational references/course plotting.** The Flight Control console displays readings from navigational and tactical sensors, overlaying them on current positional and course projections. Conn has the option of accessing data feeds from secondary navigation and science sensors for verification of primary sensor data. Such cross-checks are automatically performed at each change-of-shift and upon activation of Alert status.

- **Manual flight operations.** The actual execution of flight instructions is generally left to computer control, but Conn has the option of exercising manual control over helm and navigational functions. In full manual mode, Conn can actually steer the ship under keypad control.

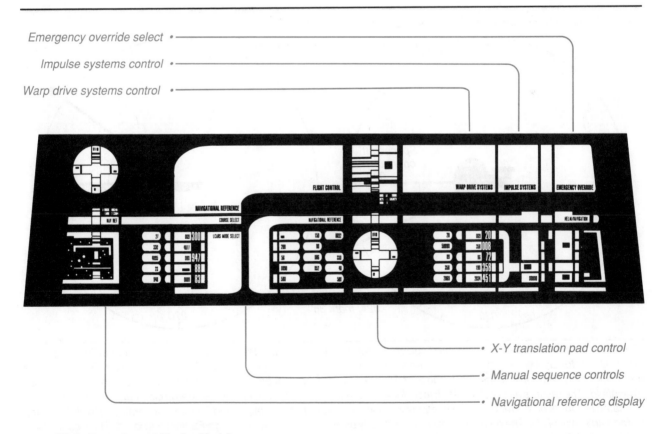

Emergency override select •
Impulse systems control •
Warp drive systems control •

• X-Y translation pad control
• Manual sequence controls
• Navigational reference display

3.4.1 Flight Control panel (Cruise Mode)

• **Reaction control system (RCS).** Although the actual vector and sequence control of the system is normally automated, Conn has the option of manually commanding the RCS system or individual thrusters.

Conn also serves as a liaison to the Engineering department in that he/she is responsible for monitoring propulsion system status and providing system status reports to the commanding officer in the absence of an engineering officer's presence on the bridge.

FLIGHT INFORMATION INPUT

There are five standard input modes available for specification of spacecraft flight paths. Any of these options may be entered either by keyboard or by vocal command. In each case, Flight Control software will automatically determine an optimal flight path conforming to Starfleet flight and safety rules. Conn then has the option of executing this flight plan or modifying any parameters to meet specific mission needs. Normal input modes include:

• **Destination planet or star system.** Any celestial object within the navigational database is acceptable as a destination, although the system will inform Conn in the event that a destination exceeds the operating range of the spacecraft. Specific facilities (such as orbital space stations) within the database are also acceptable destinations.

• **Destination sector.** A sector identification number or sector common name is a valid destination. In the absence of a specific destination within a sector, the flight path will default to the geometric center of the specified sector.

• **Spacecraft intercept.** This requires Conn to specify a target spacecraft on which a tactical sensor lock has been established. This also requires Conn to specify either a relative closing speed or an intercept time so that a speed can be determined. An absolute warp velocity can also be specified. Navigational software will determine an optimal flight path based on specified speed and tactical projection of target vehicle's flight path. Several variations of this mode are available for use during combat situations.

• **Relative bearing.** A flight vector can be specified as an azimuth/elevation relative to the current orientation of the spacecraft. In such cases, 000-mark-0 represents a flight vector straight ahead.

• **Absolute heading.** A flight vector can also be specified as an azimuth/elevation relative to the center of the galaxy. In such cases, 000-mark-0 represents a flight vector from the ship to the center of the galaxy.

• **Galactic coordinates.** Standard galactic XYZ coordinates are also acceptable as a valid input, although most ship's personnel find this cumbersome.

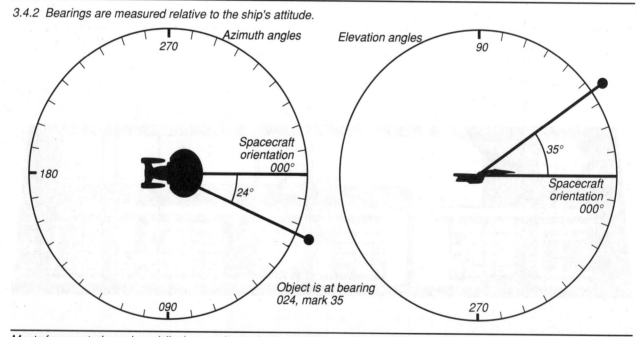

3.4.2 Bearings are measured relative to the ship's attitude.

Azimuth angles — 270 — 180 — 090 — Spacecraft orientation 000° — 24° — Object is at bearing 024, mark 35

Elevation angles — 90 — 35° — Spacecraft orientation 000° — 270

Most of our control panels and displays are large photographic transparencies designed by Mike Okuda and Cari Thomas using Adobe Illustrator, as well as conventional pen-and-ink techniques. These large sheets of film are mounted on Plexiglas sheets and backlit with electronic "blinkies" by the Star Trek special mechanical effects department under the supervision of Dick Brownfield. The result is a very clean "high tech" look to our panels. When a panel must be seen in close-up, Mike often creates animated readouts on his Macintosh II computers using such programs as Macromind Director, Supermac's Pixel Paint, and Paracomp's Swivel 3D. The resulting graphics are directly outputted to videotape using a Raster Ops board. The visual effects department is then responsible for digitally superimposing these displays onto the control panels in postproduction.

3.4.3 Headings can be measured relative to the center of the galaxy. This is analogous to a directional system used on Earth that is based on angular differences to a reference point located at the northern rotational axis. In both cases, a heading of 000 from any point in the galaxy (or the planet's surface) represents a vector directly toward the reference point: the center of the galaxy or the planet's North Pole. Both these ships have azimuth heading of 030.

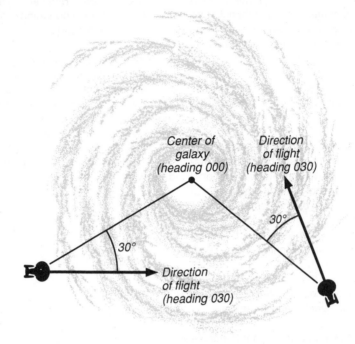

3.5 OPERATIONS MANAGEMENT (OPS)

Many shipboard operations involve scheduling resources or hardware (such as power or the use of sensors) that affect a number of departments. In many such cases, it is common for various operations to present conflicting requirements. It is the responsibility of the Operations Management Officer (normally referred to as the Operations Manager or Ops) to coordinate such activities so that mission goals are not jeopardized. Having a crew member in this decision-making loop is of crucial importance because of the wide range of unpredictable situations with which a starship must deal.

The Ops panel presents the Operations Manager with a continually updated list of current major shipboard activities. This list permits Ops to set priorities and allocate resources among current operations. This is especially critical in cases where two or more requests require the use of the same equipment, entail mutually exclusive mission profiles, or involve some unusual safety or tactical considerations.

An example might be a situation where the Stellar Physics department is conducting an experiment using the lateral sensor array to study a nearby binary star. Simultaneously, part of the same array is being time-shared with a long-range cometary population survey. A request from the bridge for a priority scan of a planetary system might jeopardize both studies unless Ops authorizes a minor change in ship's attitude, permitting the Stellar Physics observations to use the upper sensor array. Alternatively, Ops may weigh the option of placing one of the ongoing studies on a lower priority to provide the bridge with immediate use of the lateral array.

PRIORITY AND RESOURCE ALLOCATION

Most routine scheduling and resource allocation is done automatically by the Ops program. This frees the Operations Manager from routine activity, leaving him/her able to concentrate on decisions beyond the scope of the artificial intelligence software. The level of these decision filter programs can be set by the Operations Manager, and also varies with the current Alert status of the ship.

In cases where priorities are ambiguous or where specific Ops approval is required, the panel will display a menu of the most probable options for action. In virtually all cases, the Operations Manager also has the ability to input choices beyond those presented by the action menus. This is important because it is impossible for mission planners to anticipate every possible situation. Action menus may be displayed for any current activity (even those which would normally be handled automatically) upon keyboard request from Ops.

During crisis situations and Reduced Power Mode operations, Ops is responsible for supervision of power allocation in coordination with the Engineering department (See: 15.9). Load shedding of nonessential power usage in such situations is based on spacecraft survival factors and mission priorities.

The Operations Manager is also responsible for providing general status information to the main computer, which is then made available to all departments and personnel. Ops routes specific information to specific departments to inform them of anticipated changes and requirements that may affect their operations.

An example is a scenario where an Away Team is to be sent on a mission to a planetary surface. Typical Ops responsibilities might include:

• Notification of Away Team personnel of the assignment and providing said personnel with mission objective information. When Away Team personnel are drawn from operational departments, Ops will sometimes coordinate to provide cross-trained replacement personnel from other departments.

• Coordination with Mission Ops for assignment of comm relay frequencies and preparations to monitor Away Team tricorder telemetry.

• Notification for issuance of tricorders, phasers, environmental gear, and other mission-specific equipment.

• Assignment of personnel transporter room to handle

transport operations, as well as the assignment of a transporter chief to the mission. If available, Ops will also provide transport coordinates to the transporter chief.

• Notification of Engineering to prepare for power allocation for transporter operations, as well as deflector shield shutdown, if necessary.

Such notifications are generally accomplished automatically without the need for active intervention by Ops. However, because preprogrammed functions cannot be expected to anticipate all possible situations, Ops is responsible for monitoring all such coordination activity and for taking additional action as necessary. Such flexibility is particularly important during alert and crisis scenarios, during which unpredictable and unplanned conditions must frequently be dealt with.

3.5.1 Operations Management control panel (Cruise Mode)

3.6 TACTICAL

The Main Bridge station dedicated to defensive systems control and starship internal security is Tactical. As currently configured on the USS *Enterprise*, Tactical occupies a unique place in the overall command environment, situated directly between the center command area and the aft work stations.

The physical layout of the raised Tactical station console describes a sweeping curve affording an unobstructed view of the main viewer, and an equally clear view of the command stations below. This allows for an uninterrupted exchange between the Security Officer (doubling as senior Tactical Officer) and other bridge officers during critical operations, as well as exchanges with crew members occupying the aft stations. The console lacks a seat and is therefore a standup position, deemed ergonomically necessary for efficient security functions. While the length of the control/display panel can accommodate two officers, most scenarios will see the Security Officer conducting operations alone. Even during crisis situations, when action levels are highest, a single tactical officer will respond in the least ambiguous manner, with a minimum number of significant order confirmations and command interrogatives. A second Tactical Officer will be available as necessary, in the event the senior officer is called to Away Team duty or is otherwise indisposed.

SHIPBOARD SECURITY FUNCTIONS

Part of the default control layout, depicted in 3.6.1, presents the Security Officer with information readouts dealing with the internal protection of the *Enterprise* and its crew. The first tier of coverage involves a benign, low-level approach, watching over basic crew safety. The second tier activates during diplomatic and cultural missions, providing security for ambassadorial personnel or other important visitors. As an adjunct to these measures, high-level counterintelligence measures may be brought into play to negate possible sabotage or terrorist penetrations on board the *Enterprise*.

Security teams can be directed from Tactical via voice command or keyed instructions by the Security Officer or authorized deputy. Armory inventories, Security team personnel assignments, and detailed directives are but a few of the items handled with panel inputs.

STARSHIP DEFENSE FUNCTIONS

The very survival of the ship will often rest in the hands of Security Officer in the performance of operations in hazardous situations including close-in missions to energetic celestial objects, dealing with dangers posed by certain artificial constructs, and potential hostilities with Threat vessels. A wide variety of systems are available to the Security Officer from the Tactical station, including the ship's defensive shields, phaser banks, and photon torpedoes, all first-line devices (See: 11.0).

Tactical coordinates with the Flight Control Officer and Flight Operations positions in all situations involving external hazards. Guidance and navigation information, targeting data, and external communications are networked through all three stations, providing expanded options for dealing with unknowns as they present themselves.

Other systems that may be commanded by Tactical include long- and short-range sensor arrays, sensor probes, message buoys, and tractor beam devices.

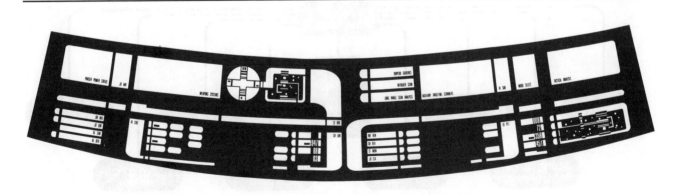

3.6.1 Tactical systems control panel (Cruise Mode)

3.7 COMMAND STATIONS

The Main Bridge command stations provide seating and information displays for the Commanding Officer (normally the captain) and two other officers, typically the First Officer and the counselor. The command stations are centrally located, designed to maximize interaction with all key bridge personnel, while permitting an unobstructed view of the main screen.

The captain's chair features armrests that incorporate miniaturized status displays, and simplified Conn and Ops controls. Upon keyboard or vocal command, the captain can use these controls to override the basic operation of the spacecraft. Such overrides are generally reserved for emergency situations. The other two seating positions in the command area include somewhat larger information display terminal screens, which permit these officers to access and manipulate data as part of their duties.

Cruise Mode operating rules require a shift Commanding Officer to be on duty at all times, although the presence of other command personnel is optional, depending on specific mission requirements. Yellow and Red Alert operating rules generally require the presence of at least two command personnel, in addition to Conn and Ops.

3.8 SCIENCE STATIONS

Science stations I and II are the first two aft stations located directly behind the Tactical station on the upper level of the Main Bridge. They are used by bridge personnel to provide realtime scientific data to command personnel. These stations are not assigned full-time technicians, but are available for use as needed.

In some cases, the science stations are used by personnel attached to secondary missions including researchers, science officers, mission specialists, and others who need to coordinate operations closely with the bridge. A typical example might be an ongoing study of stellar composition, normally handled down in the stellar spectroscopy lab, but which has occasional periods of large-volume observations better managed from the bridge. Another example would be the control of an automated probe, gathering interstellar dust samples from a hazardous area, later requiring specific ship maneuvers in order to successfully recover the probe and its samples.

Science I and II are generally configured for independent operation, but can be linked together when two researchers wish to work cooperatively. The aft Science stations have priority links to Conn, Ops, and Tactical. During Alert status, science stations can have priority access to sensor arrays, if

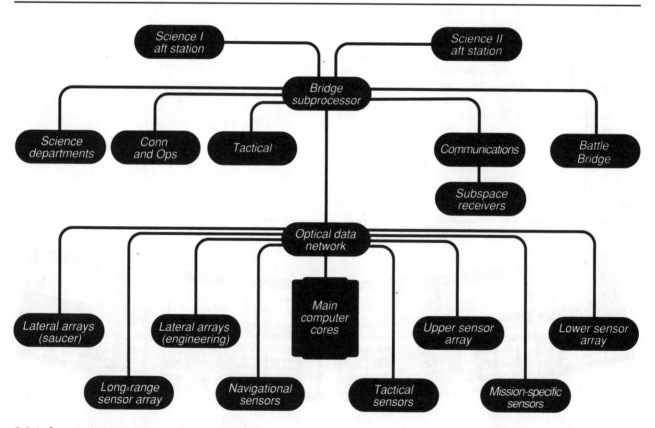

3.8.1 Sensor tie-ins to bridge science stations

necessary overriding ongoing science department observations and other secondary missions upon approval by the Operations Manager.

The Science I station incorporates an isolinear chip matrix panel that permits specialized mission profile programs to be loaded as needed, and also permits investigators to accumulate data for later study.

SCIENCE STATION FUNCTIONS

Primary functions of Science stations include:

• The ability to provide access to sensors and interpretive software for primary mission and command intelligence

requirements and to supplement Ops in providing realtime scientific data for command decisionmaking support.

• The ability to act as a command post for coordination of activities of various science laboratories and other departments, as well as for monitoring of secondary mission status.

• The ability to reconfigure and recalibrate sensor systems at a moment's notice for specific command intelligence requirements.

3.8.2 Science I and II aft station panels

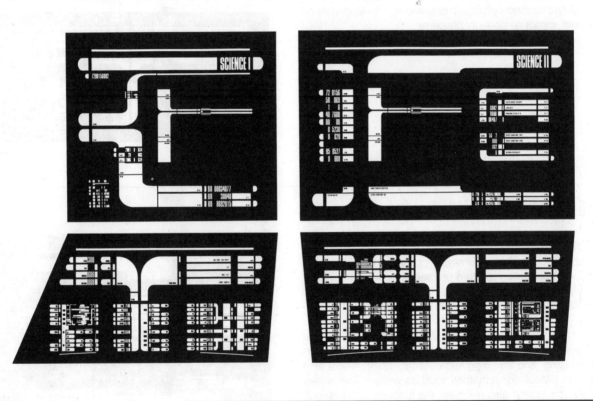

3.9 MISSION OPS

The third aft station is Mission Ops. This station provides additional support to the Operations Manager, and is specifically responsible for monitoring activity relating to secondary missions. In doing so, Mission Ops acts as an assistant to the Operations Manager, relieving him/her of responsibility for lower-priority tasks that must be monitored by a human operator.

Mission Ops is responsible for assignment of resources and priorities according to guidelines specified by the Operations Manager and by operating protocols. For example, Ops

may determine that a particular research project is to have usage of specific sensor elements, subject to priority usage of those same sensors by the bridge. Although the actual minute-to-minute assignment of resources will be automatically handled by the Ops panel software, Mission Ops will monitor the computer activity to ensure that such computer control does not unduly compromise any mission priorities. This is particularly important during unforeseen situations that may not fall within the parameters of preprogrammed decision-making software.

Mission Ops is responsible for resolving low-level conflicts, but will refer primary mission conflicts to the Operations Manager.

A Mission Ops tech generally serves as relief Operations Manager when the duty Ops officer is away from station.

OTHER MISSION OPS DUTIES

This station is responsible for monitoring telemetry from primary mission Away Teams. This includes tricorder data and any other mission-specific instrumentation.

Mission Ops is also responsible for monitoring the activities of secondary missions to anticipate requirements and possible conflicts. In cases where such conflicts impact on primary missions in progress, Mission Ops is required to notify the Operations Manager.

During Alert and crisis situations, Mission Ops also assists the Security Officer, providing information on Away Teams and secondary mission operations, with emphasis on possible impact on security concerns.

3.9.1 Mission Operations aft station panel

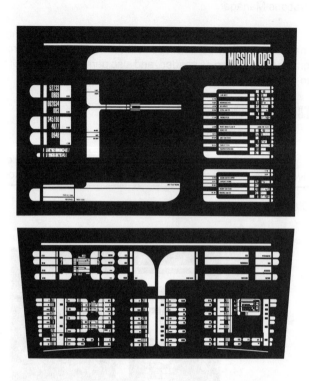

3.10 ENVIRONMENT

The Environmental Systems station permits monitoring and control of the life support systems aboard the *Enterprise*. Although this station is often unattended due to the highly automated nature of these systems, this station is of crucial importance during crisis and Alert situations.

This station is normally programmed to monitor status and performance for atmosphere, temperature, gravity, inertial damping, and shielding subsystems. Environment also monitors critical consumables such as oxygen and water. Finally, this station also oversees the function of the various recycling and reprocessing systems that insure a continuous supply of breathable air, water, food, and other consumables. When unattended, this station's programming will alert Ops of any situation requiring crew attention.

During Alert and crisis situations, Environment serves as a deputy Operations Manager, monitoring and allocating life support resources to maximize crew survivability. The Environmental Systems Officer (when required on the bridge) is authorized to initiate Yellow and Red Alert conditions and is responsible for execution of survival scenarios such as evacuation to environmental shelter areas.

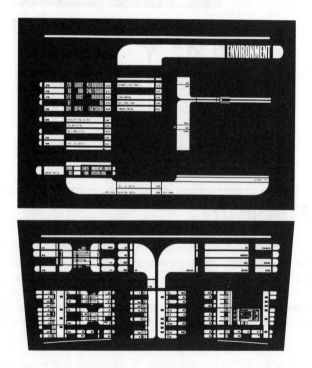

3.10.1 Environmental Systems aft station panel

3.11 ENGINEERING

The Engineering systems monitor duplicates in simplified form the Chief Engineer's primary status displays from Main Engineering. These displays include the warp propulsion system, impulse propulsion system, and related subsystems. The purpose of this station is to permit the Chief Engineer to maintain supervision over engineering systems while on the bridge. This is particularly critical during Alert situations that may require the Chief Engineer's presence on the bridge while simultaneously requiring that officer to maintain a close watch over the status of key systems. During most routine Cruise Mode operations, bridge monitoring of these systems is the responsibility of the Flight Control Officer and the Operations Manager.

Although this station is normally configured for passive systems status display, priority access by the Chief Engineer or senior staff can provide full control of virtually all engineering systems.

The console is linked to the engineering systems through the bridge's dedicated optical data network (ODN) trunks, but an additional measure of redundancy is provided by dedicated optical hardlines, which permit direct control of key systems in the event of major control systems failure. In such a case, the main computer cores would be assumed to be unavailable or unreliable, so manual control of systems would be enabled with support from the bridge Engineering subprocessor.

In Full Enable Mode, this station is capable of individually addressing each control and servo device (as well as Engineering command software) in all propulsion systems (subject to safety restrictions), giving the Chief Engineer enormous flexibility to reconfigure system operations in response to unforeseen situations.

This station is normally unattended, except by the Chief Engineer or key Engineering personnel, although most of its displays are readily accessible to both Ops and Conn through their respective control programs.

3.11.1 Engineering aft station panel

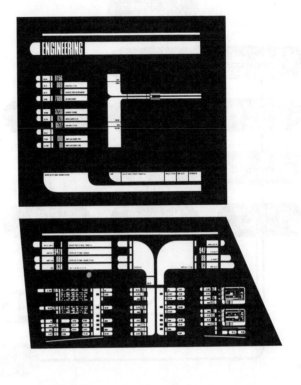

3.12 GUIDANCE AND NAVIGATION

Critical to the flight of any vehicle through interstellar space are the concepts of guidance and navigation. These involve the ability to control spacecraft motions, to determine the locations of specific points in three and four dimensions, and to allow the spacecraft to follow safe paths between those points.

The theater of operation for the USS *Enterprise* takes it through both known and unknown regions of the Milky Way galaxy. While the problems of interstellar navigation have been well-defined for over two hundred years, navigating about this celestial whirlpool, especially at warp velocities, still requires the precise orchestration of computers, sensors, active high-energy deflecting devices, and crew decision-making abilities.

SPACECRAFT GUIDANCE

The attitude and translational control of the USS *Enterprise* relative to the surrounding space involves numerous systems aboard both the Saucer Module and Battle Section. As the starship maneuvers within the volume of the galaxy, the main computers attempt to calculate the location of the spacecraft to a precision of 10 kilometers at sublight, and 100 kilometers during warp flight. The subject of velocity is important in these discussions, as different sensing and

3.12.1 Galactic navigational reference system

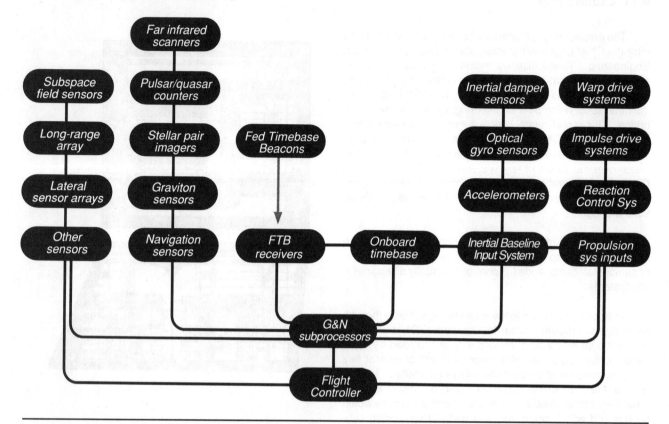

computation methods are employed for each flight regime. During extremely slow in-system maneuvering at sublight velocity, the main computers, coupled with the reaction control thrusters, are capable of resolving spacecraft motions to 0.05 seconds of arc in axial rotation, and 0.5 meters of single-impulse translation. During terminal docking maneuvers, accuracies of up to 2.75 cm can be maintained. Changes in spacecraft direction of flight, relative to its own center of mass, is measured in bearings, as shown in 3.4.2.

Internal sensing devices such as accelerometers, optical gyros, and velocity vector processors, are grouped within the inertial baseline input system, or IBIS. The IBIS is in realtime contact with the structural integrity field and inertial damping systems, which provide compensating factors to adjust *apparent* internal sensor values, allowing them to be compared with externally derived readings. The IBIS also provides a continuous feedback loop used by the reaction control system to verify propulsion inputs.

EXTERNAL SENSORS

The major external sensors employed at sublight include stellar graviton detectors, stellar pair coordinate imagers, pulsar/quasar counters, far infrared scanners, and Federation Timebase Beacon (FTB) receivers. These devices also communicate with the structural integrity field and inertial damping field processors, inertial sensors, and main computers to obtain an adjusted awareness of the ship's location.

The wide range of external sensors make it possible to obtain the greatest number of readings under many different conditions. The standard external sensor pallet has been designed to insure that coarse position calculations can be made under adverse operating conditions: e.g., magnetic fields, dense interstellar dust, and stellar flares.

While the network of FTBs operate on subspace frequencies to facilitate position calculations at warp, vehicles at sublight speed can, in fact, obtain more precise positioning data than ships at warp. In the absence of clear FTB signals, onboard timebase processors continue computing distance and velocity for later synchronization when FTB pulses are once again detected.

Guidance of the USS *Enterprise* at higher sublight velocities couples the impulse engines with those systems already mentioned. External sensor readings, distorted by higher relativistic speeds, necessitate adjustment by the guidance and navigation (G&N) subprocessors in order to accurately compute ship location and provide proper control inputs to the impulse engines. Extended travel at high sublight speed is not a preferred mode of travel for Federation vessels, due to the undesired time-dilation effects, but may be required occasionally if warp systems are unavailable.

In the *Galaxy* class starship, ongoing G&N system research tasks are handled by a mixed consultation crew of twelve *Tursiops truncatus* and *T. truncatus gilli*, Atlantic and

Pacific bottlenose dolphins, respectively. This crew is overseen by two additional cetaceans, *Orcinus orca takayai*, or Takaya's Whale. All theoretical topics in navigation are studied by these elite specialists, and their recommendations for system upgrades are implemented by Starfleet.

NAVIGATION

The whole of the galactic environment must be taken into account in any discussion of guidance and navigation. The Milky Way galaxy, with its populations of stars, gas and dust concentrations, and numerous other exotic (and energetic) phenomena, encompasses a vast amount of low-density space through which Federation vessels travel. The continuing mission segments of the USS *Enterprise* will take it to various objects within this space, made possible by the onboard navigation systems.

THE MILKY WAY GALAXY

The Milky Way galaxy would seem, by any scheme of mapping, to be a record-keeping nightmare created to thwart all who would attempt to traverse it. Not only is the entire mass rotating, but it is doing so at different rates, from its core to the outer spiral arms. Over time, even small-scale structures change enough to be a problem in navigation and mapping. A common frame of reference is necessary, however, in order to conduct exploration, establish trade routes, and perform various other Starfleet operations, from colony transfers to

rescue missions. The mapping and galactic heading system established by the Federation is shown in 3.12.1.

Celestial objects become known by planetary deep-space instrument scans and starship surveys, and are recorded within Starfleet's central galactic condition database. Locations and proper motions of all major stars, nebulae, dust clouds, and other stable natural objects are stored and distributed throughout the Federation. New objects are catalogued as they are encountered, and updated databases are regularly transmitted by subspace radio to Starfleet and allied Federation vessels.

During stops at Federation outposts and starbases, all detailed recordings of a ship's previous flight time are downloaded and sent on to Starfleet. Most of the information in the database concerns the present condition of an object, with "present" defined as real clock time measured at Starfleet Headquarters, San Francisco, Earth. The overall *visual* appearance of the galaxy from Earth or any planet is, of course, unreliable due to the limitation of the speed of light; so many additional sources (such as faster subspace readings) are needed to keep the database current. Where realtime object information is unavailable, predicted conditions are listed.

The main computers of the USS *Enterprise* apply the galactic condition database to the task of plotting flight paths between points in the galaxy. Objects lying along the flight

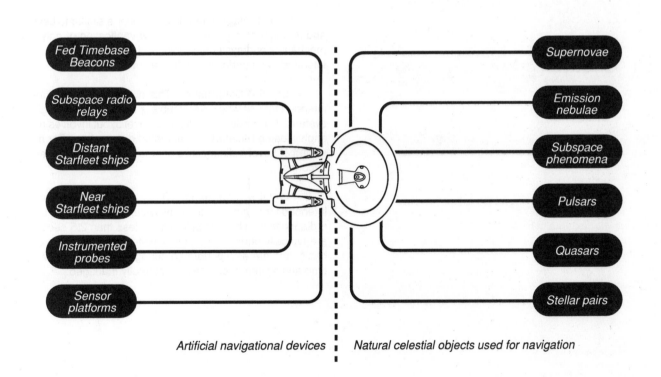

Artificial navigational devices | Natural celestial objects used for navigation

3.12.2 Navigational reference aids

path, such as stellar systems or random large solid bodies, are avoided. At sublight as well as warp velocities, the external and internal sensors communicate with the computers and engine systems to perform constantly updated course corrections along the basic trajectory.

DEFLECTION OF LOW-MASS PARTICLES

Lighter mass materials such as interstellar gas and dust grains are translated away from the ship's flight path by the main navigational deflector. During low-sublight travel, a number of nested parabolic deflector shields are projected by the main emitter dish. These shields encounter distant oncoming particles, imparting a radial velocity component to them, effectively clearing the space ahead of the vehicle for a short time. Higher sublight velocities require the additional use of precision-aimed deflector beams directed at specific targets in the projected flight path.

Control of the deflector power output is available in a number of modes, from simple deflection to predictive-adaptive subspace/graviton; a series of high-speed algorithms analyzes the ship's velocity and the density of the interstellar medium, and commands changes in the navigational deflector system.

3.13 SYSTEM DIAGNOSTICS

All key operating systems and subsystems aboard the *Enterprise* have a number of preprogrammed diagnostic software and procedures for use when actual or potential malfunctions are experienced. These various diagnostic protocols are generally classified into five different levels, each offering a different degree of crew verification of automated tests. Which type of diagnostic is used in a given situation will generally depend upon the criticality of a situation, and upon the amount of time available for the test procedures.

• **Level 1 Diagnostic.** This refers to the most comprehensive type of system diagnostic, which is normally conducted on ship's systems. Extensive automated diagnostic routines are performed, but a Level 1 diagnostic requires a team of crew members to physically verify operation of system mechanisms and to system readings, rather than depending on the automated programs, thereby guarding against possible malfunctions in self-testing hardware and software. Level 1 diagnostics on major systems can take several hours, and in many cases the subject system must be taken off-line for all tests to be performed.

• **Level 2 Diagnostic.** This refers to a comprehensive system diagnostic protocol which, like a Level 1, involves extensive automated routines, but requires crew verification of fewer operational elements. This yields a somewhat less reliable system analysis, but is a procedure that can be conducted in less than half the time of the more complex tests.

• **Level 3 Diagnostic.** This protocol is similar to Level 1 and 2 diagnostics but involves crew verification of only key mechanics and systems readings. Level 3 diagnostics are intended to be performed in ten minutes or less.

• **Level 4 Diagnostic.** This automated procedure is intended for use whenever trouble is suspected with a given system. This protocol is similar to Level 5, but involves more sophisticated batteries of automated diagnostics. For most systems, Level 4 diagnostics can be performed in under 30 seconds.

• **Level 5 Diagnostic.** This automated procedure is intended for routine use to verify system performance. Level 5 diagnostics, which usually require less than 2.5 seconds, are typically performed on most systems on at least a daily basis, and are also performed during crisis situations when time and system resources are carefully managed.

3.14 BATTLE BRIDGE

A second major facility for starship operational control is the Battle Bridge. This facility, located on Deck 8 at the top of the Battle Section, serves as a command and control center for tactical operations during Separated Flight Mode (See: 15.8). The Battle Bridge incorporates the standard Conn and Ops panels for starflight operations, but includes enhanced tactical analysis and weapons control stations, as well as communications and engineering. As with other control facilities, software-definable workstations permit consoles to be reconfigured as necessary to handle specific situations (See: 11.5).

In addition to its tactical role, the Battle Bridge is capable of serving as an auxiliary control center as a backup to the Main Bridge. The Battle Bridge computer subprocessors are able to control all major ship's systems, even in the event of total Main Bridge incapacity and partial main computer core failure.

The Battle Bridge is directly accessible from the Main Bridge by means of a dedicated emergency turboelevator shaft. Access is also possible by means of the regular turbolift system through a corridor on Deck 8.

3.15 MAIN ENGINEERING

The Main Engineering control center on Deck 36 serves as a master control for the ship's warp propulsion system, as well as the impulse propulsion system and other engineering systems.

Main Engineering also serves as a backup control center in the event of failure of the Main Bridge and the Battle Bridge. Workstations at this location can be reconfigured to emulate Conn, Ops, Tactical, and other command operations. This is a desirable site for such functions because of its protected location within the Engineering section and its proximity to key warp propulsion system components. Optical data network hardlines provide protected backup communications to other major systems.

Principal control consoles available to the engineering staff in Main Engineering include:

• **Master systems display.** This large tabletop display panel permits duty engineers to gain an overall understanding of the "health" of the spacecraft. This display incorporates two small workstations that permit individual engineers to perform specific tasks, leaving the larger displays for the remaining staff. This console can be configured for limited flight control functions in emergency situations.

3.15.1 Main Engineering, aft view

• **Warp propulsion systems status display.** This wall display incorporates a schematic of the warp propulsion system and shows performance of all key system elements.

• **Impulse propulsion systems status display.** This wall display incorporates a schematic of the impulse propulsion system and shows performance of all key system elements.

• **Master situation monitor.** This large wall display features a cutaway of the starship, showing the location of key systems and hardware, highlighting any elements that are currently experiencing any condition out of nominal. This display also incorporates two sets of user controls to permit use of this station for troubleshooting.

• **Chief Engineer's office.** This control room includes smaller-scale repeater versions of most key displays in Main Engineering, as well as workstations for the Chief Engineer and two assistants. It also includes emergency control stations, and the primary isolinear control chip panels for Main Engineering. This office is located immediately adjacent to the matter/antimatter reaction assembly. A reinforced optical window permits the Chief Engineer to directly observe the visible reaction patterns within the core without the need for sensor display.

• **Duty engineer's console.** Adjacent to the Chief Engineer's office is a smaller workstation available for the use of the duty engineer. This console incorporates master systems display repeater panels.

This facility is located immediately adjacent to the matter/antimatter reaction chamber. For safety reasons, two section isolation doors are available to protect the Main Engineering control center from the matter/antimatter reaction core chamber in case of serious malfunction or plasma breach. These isolation doors can be triggered automatically. Further protection is provided by a system of containment forcefields which can be activated in the event of a warp core breach or similar contingency (See: 5.10).

The tablelike master systems display console in the middle of Main Engineering is actually the same unit, refurbished, that was used by Admiral Cartwright and company in Starfleet Command in the movie Star Trek IV: The Voyage Home. *Most* Star Trek *production staffers have taken to informally referring to it as "the pool table."*

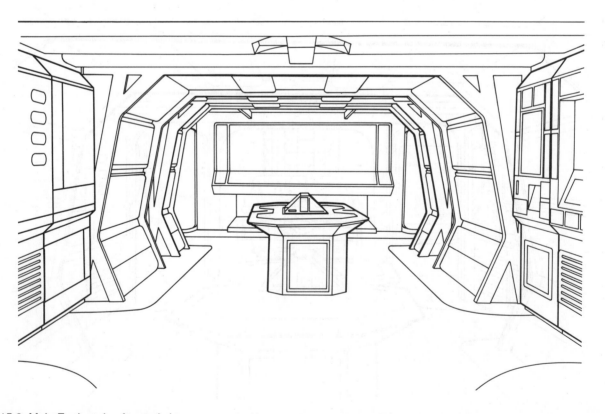

3.15.2 Main Engineering forward view

4.0 COMPUTER SYSTEMS

4.1 COMPUTER SYSTEM

The main computer system of the *Enterprise* is probably the most important single operational element of the starship next to the crew. The computer is directly analogous to the autonomic nervous system of a living being, and is responsible in some way for the operation of virtually every other system of the vehicle.

Crew interface for the main computer is provided by the Library Computer Access and Retrieval System software, usually abbreviated as LCARS. LCARS provides both keyboard and verbal interface ability, incorporating highly sophisticated artificial intelligence routines and graphic display organization for maximum crew ease-of-use (See: 3.3).

COMPUTER CORES

The heart of the main computer system is a set of three redundant main processing cores. Any of these three cores is able to handle the primary operational computing load of the entire vessel. Two of these cores are located near the center of the Primary Hull between Decks 5 and 14, while the third is located between Decks 30 and 37 in the Engineering Hull. Each main core incorporates a series of miniature subspace field generators, which creates a symmetrical (nonpropulsive) field distortion of 3350 millicochranes within the faster-than-light (FTL) core elements. This permits the transmission and

processing of optical data within the core at rates significantly exceeding lightspeed.

The two main cores in the Primary Hull run in parallel clock-sync with each other, providing 100% redundancy. In the event of any failure in either core, the other core is able to instantly assume the total primary computing load for the ship with no interruption, although some secondary and recreational functions (such as holodeck simulations) may be suspended. The third core, located in the Engineering Hull, serves as a backup to the first two, and also serves the Battle Section during separated flight operations.

Core elements are based on FTL nanoprocessor units arranged into optical transtator clusters of 1,024 segments. In turn, clusters are grouped into processing modules composed of 256 clusters controlled by a bank of sixteen isolinear chips. Each core comprises seven primary and three upper levels, each level containing an average of four modules.

CORE MEMORY

Memory storage for main core usage is provided by 2,048 dedicated modules of 144 isolinear optical storage chips. Under LCARS software control, these modules provide average dynamic access to memory at 4,600 kiloquads/sec. Total storage capacity of each module is about 630,000 kiloquads, depending on software configuration.

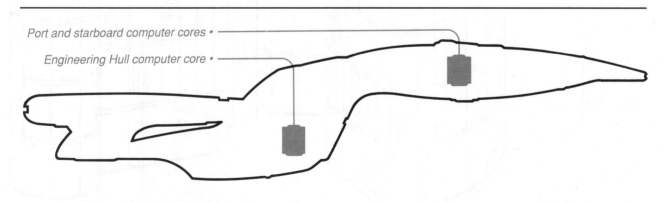

Port and starboard computer cores •

Engineering Hull computer core •

4.1.1 Location of main computer cores

The main cores are tied into the ship's optical data network by means of a series of MJL junction links which bridge the subspace boundary layer. There is a 12% Doppler loss in transmission rate across the boundary, but the resulting increase in processing speed from the FTL core elements more than compensates.

SUBPROCESSORS

A network of 380 quadritronic optical subprocessors is distributed throughout both ship's sections, augmenting the main cores. Within the habitable volume of the ship, most of these subprocessors are located near main corridor junctions for easy access. While these subprocessors do not employ FTL elements, the distributed processing network improves

overall system response and provides redundancy in emergency situations. Each subprocessor is linked into the optical data network, and most also have a dedicated optical link to one or more of the main cores.

The Main Bridge and the Battle Bridge each have seven dedicated and twelve shared subprocessors, which permit operations even in the event of main core failure. These bridge subprocessors are linked to the main cores by means of protected optical conduits, which provide alternate control linkages in the event of a primary optical data network failure. Further redundancy is provided by dedicated short-range radio frequency (RF) links, providing emergency data communications with the bridge. Additional dedicated subproces-

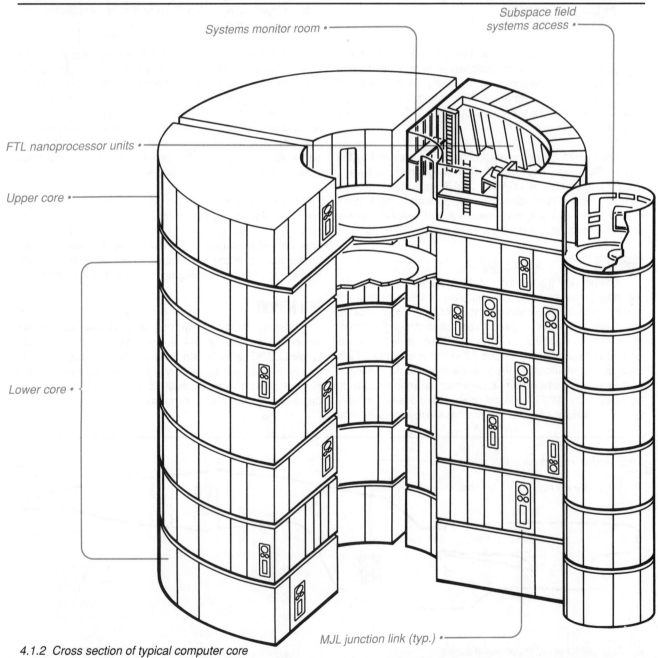

Systems monitor room •

Subspace field systems access •

FTL nanoprocessor units •

Upper core •

Lower core •

MJL junction link (typ.) •

4.1.2 Cross section of typical computer core

4.1.3 Optical data network interconnects between computer cores, main bridge, and other key systems

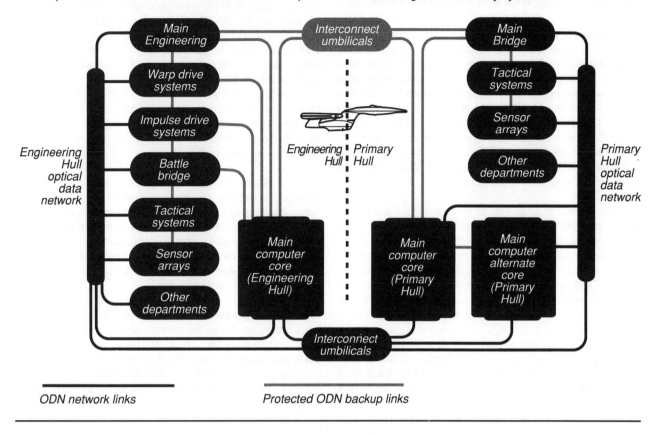

ODN network links   Protected ODN backup links

sors can be installed as needed to support mission-specific operations.

Virtually every control panel and terminal within the ship is linked to a subprocessor or directly into the optical data network. Each active panel is continually polled by LCARS at 30 millisecond intervals so that the local subprocessor and/or the main core is informed of all keyboard or verbal inputs. Each polling inquiry is followed by a 42 nanosecond compressed data stream, which provides panel update information. This data stream includes any requested visual or audio information for panel output.

Short-range RF data links are available throughout the ship to provide information transmission to portable and handheld devices such as tricorders and personal access display devices (PADD).

This integrated network of computers, subprocessors, and panels forms the "nervous system" of the ship and permits continuous realtime analysis of the ship's operating status.

The network is specifically designed to permit independent operation of remaining system elements in the event of a wide variety of partial system failures.

We realize quite well that the Enterprise *computer system is definitely overpowered in terms of twentieth-century computing applications. On the other hand, the history of computer technology has shown that each time a faster, more powerful computer becomes available, useful applications quickly follow to take advantage of the new machines, which in turn spurs computer designers to build still more powerful machines. One might expect that such trends will yield enormously powerful computers, which one might reasonably hope may significantly enhance the quality of life, as they apparently do for the men and women of the* Enterprise.

4.2 PERSONAL ACCESS DISPLAY DEVICE (PADD)

In its primary role aboard a starship, the personal access display device (PADD) is a handheld control and display terminal. Small, easily managed terminals and computers are in daily use throughout Starfleet, as a natural response to crew members' needs to (1) execute hardware functions in a variety of locations, and (2) manipulate visual information and communicate that information to others aboard ship. Access to the *Enterprise* computers and other pieces of equipment can be accomplished through the usual control displays and larger terminal screens, of course, but the PADD has become a convenient adjunct to those panels.

The standard small PADD is 10 x 15 x 1 cm and is constructed from three basic layers of imbedded circuit-composite material. All primary electronics, including multi-layer display screen, are bonded to the casing, a boronite whisker epoxy. If dropped accidentally, even from a height of 35 m, a PADD will remain undamaged. Replaceable components are limited to three, the sarium power loop, isolinear memory chip, and subspace transceiver assembly (STA).

In normal daily use, the power supply remains installed and is induction recharged. A full charge will last sixteen hours; if a PADD is about to exhaust its battery, it can set a memory flag in the main computer to transfer tasks to a working unit, or suspend them until a later time. The total memory capacity of the isolinear chips is 4.3 kiloquads. Like the tricorder, the PADD can transfer its total memory to the main computers in less than one second if the need arises. The STA is used to maintain data channels between the PADD and the *Enterprise* computers. If taken on an away mission, the PADD can also perform uplink/downlink operations and function as a transporter lock-on node. Data transmissions and computing functions can be shared with any other Starfleet device supporting the STA com protocols. As with the personal communicator, transmissions are encrypted for security purposes.

The display screen, 4.25 times larger than that of a tricorder, allows for the manipulation of control graphics, numerical data, and images by touch. Electrosensitive areas of the casing (colored brown on the standard engineering PADD) are designed for specific data movement and storage functions. They can also be used to personalize the default setup and single–crew member security restriction. An audio pickup sensor permits voice input.

The PADD's control functions mimic those of any multi-layer panel, insofar as the security restrictions for individual crew members are concerned. Properly configured with the Conn position bridge controls, a crew member can theoretically fly the *Enterprise* from a PADD while walking down a corridor. While this would be an impractical exercise due to

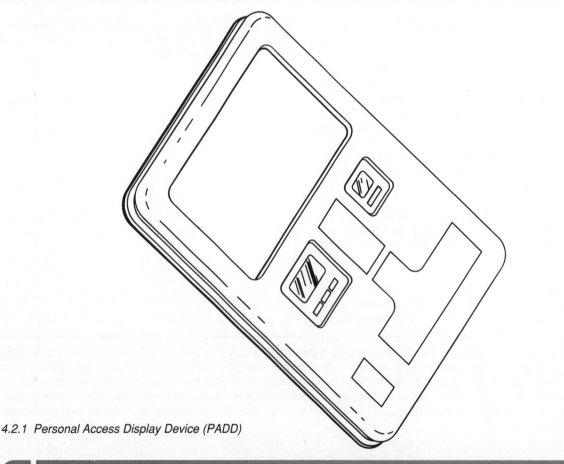

4.2.1 Personal Access Display Device (PADD)

PADD memory limitations and the relatively small diplay screen, it is an example of the overall multiple-option philosophy established in the *Galaxy* class starship design objectives by Starfleet's Advanced Starship Design Bureau.

This philosophy treats the starship as an integrated organism in which each component can be regarded as a cell in a body directed by a central brain, but with processing capabilities distributed throughout the neural network. Because of this, PADDs and many other handheld data devices are capable of accessing any data file or command program to which the user has authorized access.

Custom PADD configurations can be fabricated aboard the *Enterprise* or in any starship hardware replication facility equipped with custom isolinear circuit programming capabilities.

Guy Vardaman, who among other things occasionally plays a crew member seen in the background of scenes in the Enterprise *corridors, says that he and his fellow extras sometimes refer to PADDs as "hall passes." The acronym PADD was suggested by* Star Trek *research consultant Richard Arnold during the early days of the series.*

4.3 ISOLINEAR OPTICAL CHIPS

Isolinear optical chips are the primary software and data storage medium employed throughout the *Enterprise* computer systems. These nanotech devices represent a number of significant advances over the crystal memory cards used in earlier systems.

These new chips make use of single-axis optical crystal layering to achieve subwavelength switching distances. Nanopulse matrix techniques yield a total memory capacity of 2.15 kiloquads per chip in standard holographic format.

Like earlier crystal memory devices, isolinear chips optimize memory access by employing onboard nanoprocessors. In these new devices, however, higher processing speeds permit individual chips to manage data configuration independent of LCARS control, thus reducing system access time by up to 7%. Additionally, the chip substrate is infused with trace quantities of superconductive platinum/irridium, which permits FTL optical data transmission when energized by the core's subspace flux. This results in a dramatic 335% increase in processing speed when used in one of the main computer cores.

Isolinear chips can be ruggedized with the application of a protective tripolymer sealant over the refractive interface surface. This allows the chip to be handled without protective gloves. When so treated, isolinear chips are used as a convenient form of information transport. Many portable data-handling devices such as tricorders, PADDs, and optical chip readers are able to read and write to standard format isolinear chips.

4.3.1 Isolinear optical chip

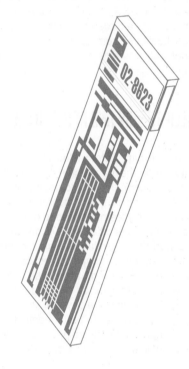

Isolinear optical chips were invented by veteran Star Trek *writer Dorothy Fontana for the episode "The Naked Now." The design of the prop is intended to reflect the original "microtape" data cartridges used in the original series, but in a much more compact and powerful form. Ironically, those original props are about the same size as the 3.5-inch Macintosh diskettes which we used when writing this book.*

5.0 WARP PROPULSION SYSTEMS

If one were to consider any of the ship's major components as its heart, the warp propulsion system would have to be the logical choice. The WPS, the single most complex and energetic element of the USS *Enterprise*, is the latest version of the device that at last afforded humanity access to deep interstellar space, facilitated contact with other lifeforms, and profoundly changed all preeminent technological civilizations in the Milky Way.

5.1 WARP FIELD THEORY AND APPLICATION

Like those before him, Zefram Cochrane, the scientist generally credited with the development of modern warp physics, built his work upon the shoulders of giants. Beginning in the mid-twenty-first century, Cochrane, working with his legendary engineering team, labored to derive the basic mechanism of continuum distortion propulsion (CDP). Intellectually, he grasped the potential for higher energies and faster-than-light travel, which signified practical operations beyond the Sol system. The eventual promise of rapid interstellar travel saw his team take on the added task of an intensive review of the whole of the physical sciences. It was hoped that the effort would lead to better comprehension of known phenomena applicable to warp physics, as well as the possibility of "left field" ideas influenced by related disciplines.

Their crusade finally led to a set of complex equations, materials formulae, and operating procedures that described the essentials of superluminal flight. In those original warp drive theories, single (or at most double) shaped fields, created at tremendous energy expenditure, could distort the space/time continuum enough to drive a starship. As early as 2061, Cochrane's team succeeded in producing a prototype field device of massive proportions. Described as a fluctuation superimpeller, it finally allowed an unmanned flight test vehicle to straddle the speed of light *(c)* "wall," alternating between two velocity states while remaining at neither for longer than Planck time, 1.3×10^{-43} second, the smallest possible unit of measurable time. This had the net effect of maintaining velocities at the previously unattainable speed of light, while avoiding the theoretically infinite energy expenditure which would otherwise have been required.

Early CDP engines — which were only informally dubbed "warp" engines — met with success, and were almost immediately incorporated into existing spacecraft designs with surprising ease. Although slow and inefficient by today's standards, these engines yielded a substantial reduction of undesired time dilation effects, paving the way for round-trip flights on the order of a few years, not decades. Cochrane and his team eventually relocated to the Alpha Centauri colonies (a move that took "only" four years because of CDP-powered space vehicles), and they continued to pioneer advances in warp physics that would eventually jump the wall altogether and explore the mysterious realm of subspace that lay on the other side.

The key to the creation of subsequent non-Newtonian methods, i.e., propulsion not dependent upon exhausting reaction products, lay in the concept of nesting many layers of warp field energy, each layer exerting a controlled amount of force against its next-outermost neighbor. The cumulative effect of the force applied drives the vehicle forward and is known as asymmetrical peristaltic field manipulation (APFM). Warp field coils in the engine nacelles are energized in sequential order, fore to aft. The firing frequency determines the number of field layers, a greater number of layers per unit time being required at higher warp factors. Each new field layer expands outward from the nacelles, experiences a rapid force coupling and decoupling at variable distances from the nacelles, simultaneously transferring energy and separating from the previous layer at velocities between $0.5c$ and $0.9c$. This is well within the bounds of traditional physics, effectively circumventing the limits of General, Special, and Transformational Relativity. During force coupling the radiated energy makes the necessary transition into subspace, applying an apparent mass reduction effect to the spacecraft. This facilitates the slippage of the spacecraft through the sequencing layers of warp field energy.

WARP POWER MEASUREMENT

The cochrane is the unit used to measure subspace field stress. Cochranes are also used to measure field distortion generated by other spatial manipulation devices, including tractor beams, deflectors, and synthetic gravity fields. Fields below Warp 1 are measured in millicochranes.

A subspace field of one thousand millicochranes or greater becomes the familiar warp field. Field intensity for each warp factor increases geometrically and is a function of the total of the individual field layer values. Note that the cochrane value for a given warp factor corresponds to the apparent velocity of a spacecraft traveling at that warp factor. For example, a ship traveling at Warp Factor 3 is maintaining a warp field of at least 39 cochranes and is therefore traveling at 39 times *c*, the speed of light. Approximate values for integer warp factors are:

Warp Factor 1 =   1 cochrane
Warp Factor 2 =   10 cochranes
Warp Factor 3 =   39 cochranes

Warp Factor 4 =   102 cochranes
Warp Factor 5 =   214 cochranes
Warp Factor 6 =   392 cochranes
Warp Factor 7 =   656 cochranes
Warp Factor 8 = 1024 cochranes
Warp Factor 9 = 1516 cochranes

The actual values are dependent upon interstellar conditions, e.g., gas density, electric and magnetic fields within the different regions of the Milky Way galaxy, and fluctuations in the subspace domain. Starships routinely travel at multiples of *c*, but they suffer from energy penalties resulting from quantum drag forces and motive power oscillation inefficiencies.

5.1.1 Warp speed/power graph

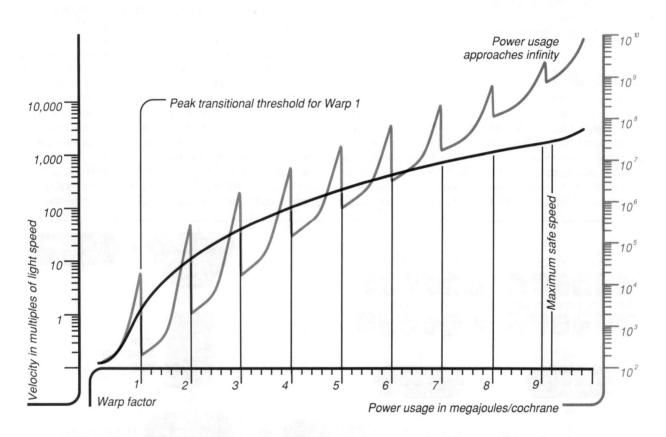

Figuring out how "fast" various warp speeds are was pretty complicated, but not just from a "scientific" viewpoint. First, we had to satisfy the general fan expectation that the new ship was significantly faster than the original. Second, we had to work with Gene's recalibration, which put Warp 10 at the absolute top of the scale. These first two constraints are fairly simple, but we quickly discovered that it was easy to make warp speeds TOO fast. Beyond a certain speed, we found that the ship would be able to cross the entire galaxy within a matter of just a few months. (Having the ship too fast would make the galaxy too small a place for the Star Trek format.) Finally, we had to provide some loophole for various powerful aliens like Q, who have a knack for tossing the ship millions of light years in the time of a commercial break. Our solution was to redraw the warp curve so that the exponent of the warp factor increases gradually, then sharply as you approach Warp 10. At Warp 10, the exponent (and the speed) would be infinite, so you could never reach this value. (Mike used an Excel spreadsheet to calculate the speeds and times.) This lets Q and his friends have fun in the 9.9999+ range, but also lets our ship travel slowly enough to keep the galaxy a big place, and meets the other criteria. (By the way, we estimate that in "Where No One Has Gone Before" the Traveler was probably propelling the Enterprise at about Warp 9.9999999996. Good thing they were in the carpool lane.)

The amount of power required to maintain a given warp factor is a function of the cochrane value of the warp field. However, the energy required to initially establish the field is much greater, and is called the peak transitional threshold. Once that threshold has been crossed, the amount of power required to maintain a given warp factor is lessened. While the current engine designs allow for control of unprecedented amounts of energy, the warp driver coil electrodynamic efficiency decreases as the warp factor increases. Ongoing studies indicate, however, that no new materials breakthroughs are anticipated to produce increased high warp factor endurance.

Warp fields exceeding a given warp factor, but lacking the energy to cross the threshold to the next higher level, are called fractional warp factors. Travel at a given fractional warp factor can be significantly faster than travel at the next lower integral warp, but for extended travel, it is often more energy-efficient to simply increase to the next higher integral warp factor.

THEORETICAL LIMITS

Eugene's Limit allows for warp stress to increase asymptotically, approaching but never reaching a value corresponding to Warp Factor 10. As field values approach ten, power requirements rise geometrically, while the aforementioned driver coil efficiency drops dramatically. The required force coupling and decoupling of the warp field layers rise to unattainable frequencies, exceeding not only the flight system's control capabilities, but more important the limit imposed by the aforementioned Planck time. Even if it were possible to expend the theoretically infinite amount of energy required, an object at Warp 10 would be traveling infinitely fast, occupying all points in the universe simultaneously.

WARP PROPULSION SYSTEM

As installed in the *Galaxy* class, the warp propulsion system consists of three major assemblies: the matter/antimatter reaction assembly, power transfer conduits, and warp engine nacelles. The total system provides energy for its primary application, propelling the USS *Enterprise* through space, as well as its secondary application, powering such essential high-capacity systems as the defensive shields, phaser arrays, tractor beam, main deflector, and computer cores.

The original propulsion system specifications, transmitted to the Utopia Planitia Fleet Yards on 6 July 2343, called for hardware capable of sustaining a normal cruising speed of Warp 5 until fuel exhaustion, a maximum cruising speed of Warp 7, and a maximum top speed of Warp 9.3 for twelve hours. These theoretical milestones had been modeled in computer simulations, based on a total vehicle mass of 6.5 million metric tonnes. In the following six months, however, well before the spaceframe designs had been finalized, Starfleet reevaluated the overall requirements of the *Galaxy* class, based upon a combination of factors. The driving influences were: (1) changing political conditions among members of the Federation, (2) intelligence forecasts describing improved Threat hardware, and (3) increasing numbers of

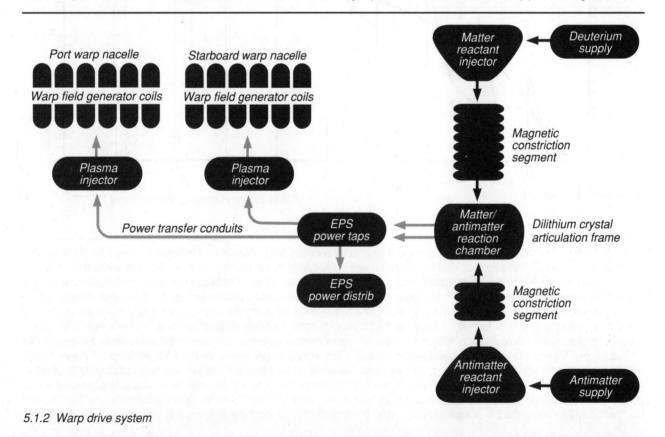

5.1.2 Warp drive system

scientific programs that could benefit from a vessel with superior performance.

Further computer modeling efforts by members of the structural, systems, and propulsion working groups resulted in revised specifications being sent to the Utopia Planitia designers on 24 December 2344. These specifications required the *Galaxy* class to sustain a normal cruising speed of Warp 6 until fuel exhaustion, a maximum cruising speed of Warp 9.2, and a maximum top speed of Warp 9.6 for twelve hours. The total estimated vehicle mass was reduced through materials improvements and internal rearrangements to 4.96 million metric tonnes.

Once the major designs were "frozen," prototype engine components were fabricated, using elements of past vehicles as reference points. Computer models of each major assembly were merged into a total system model in order to test theoretical performance characteristics. The first all-up system model test finally took place at UP on 16 April 2356, and was demonstrated to Starfleet two days later. As performance studies progressed, prototype hardware was fabricated. Materials failures plagued the initial development of the core of the system, the warp reaction chamber, which must contain the furious matter/antimatter reactions. These difficulties were eliminated with the introduction of cobalt hexafluoride to the inner chamber lining, which proved effective in reinforcing the core magnetic fields.

Similarly, materials problems slowed the construction of the warp engine nacelles. The key internal elements of the warp engines, the verterium cortenide 947/952 coils, which convert the core energy into the propulsive warp fields, could not be manufactured to flight tolerances in density and shape for the first half of the prototype construction phase. These problems were corrected with adjustments to a lengthy furnace cooling period.

Remarkably, work on the power transfer conduits between the warp core and the nacelles proceeded without incident. Detailed analysis of the prototype conduits revealed early on that they would easily bear the required structural and electrodynamic loads, and their basic function was little changed from their predecessors of a century earlier.

Once the prototype spaceframe test article was sufficiently complete to allow for it, engine installation was performed. The power transfer conduits, which had been imbedded within the nacelles support pylons as the spaceframe was built, awaited the docking of the nacelles and core assemblies. On 5 May 2356 the prototype starship NX-70637, as yet unnamed as the USS *Galaxy*, for the first time existed as a flyable space vessel.

5.2 MATTER/ANTIMATTER REACTION ASSEMBLY

As the warp propulsion system is the heart of the USS *Enterprise*, the matter/antimatter reaction assembly (M/ARA) is the heart of the warp propulsion system. The M/ARA is variously called the warp reactor, warp engine core, or main engine core. Energy produced within the core is shared between its primary application, the propulsion of the starship, and the raw power requirements of other major ship systems. The M/ARA is the principal power-generating system because of the 10^6 times greater energy output of the matter/antimatter reaction over that of standard fusion, as found in the impulse propulsion system.

The M/ARA consists of four subsystems: reactant injectors, magnetic constriction segments, matter/antimatter reaction chamber, and power transfer conduits.

REACTANT INJECTORS

The reactant injectors prepare and feed precisely controlled streams of matter and antimatter into the core. The matter reactant injector (MRI) accepts supercold deuterium from the primary deuterium tankage (PDT) in the upper bulge of the Engineering Hull and partially preburns it in a continuous gas-fusion process. It then drives the resulting gases through a series of throttleable nozzles into the upper magnetic constriction segment. The MRI consists of a conical structural vessel 5.2 x 6.3 meters, constructed of dispersion-strengthened woznium carbmolybdenide. Twenty-five shock attenuation cylinders connect it to the PDT and the major spacecraft framing members on Deck 30, maintaining 98% thermal isolation from the remainder of the Battle Section. In effect, the entire WPS "floats" within the hull in order to withstand 3x theoretical operational stresses.

Within the MRI are six redundant cross-fed sets of injectors, each injector consisting of twin deuterium inlet manifolds, fuel conditioners, fusion preburner, magnetic quench block, transfer duct/gas combiner, nozzle head, and related control hardware. Slush deuterium enters the inlet manifolds at controlled flow rates and passes to the conditioners, where heat is removed to bring the slush to just above the solid transition point. Micropellets are formed, preburned by magnetic pinch fusion, and sent down into the gas combiner, where the ionized gas products are now at 10^6K. The nozzle heads then focus, align, and propel the gas streams into the constriction segments. Should any of the nozzles fail, the combiner would continue to supply the remaining nozzles, which would dilate to accommodate the increased supply. Each nozzle measures 102 x 175 cm and is constructed of frumium-copper-yttrium 2343.

At the opposite end of the M/ARA lies the antimatter reactant injector (ARI). The internal design and operation of the ARI is distinctly different from that of the MRI, owing to the hazardous nature of the antimatter fuel. Every step in manipulating and injecting antihydrogen must be undertaken with magnetic fields to isolate the fuel from the spacecraft structure (See: 5.4). In some respects the ARI is a simpler device, requiring fewer moving components. However, the dangers inherent in handling antimatter necessitate uncompromising reliability in the mechanism. The ARI employs the same basic structural housing and shock attenuation struts as the MRI, with adaptations for magnetic-suspension fuel tunnels. The housing contains three pulsed antimatter gas flow separators, which break up the incoming antihydrogen into small manageable packets to boost up into the lower constriction segments. Each flow separator leads into an injector nozzle, and each nozzle cycles open in response to computer control signals. Nozzle firing can follow complex sequences, resulting from equally complex equations governing reaction pressures, temperatures, and desired power output.

MAGNETIC CONSTRICTION SEGMENTS

The upper and lower magnetic constriction segments (MCS) constitute the central mass of the core. These components work to structurally support the matter/antimatter reaction chamber, provide a pressure vessel to maintain the proper core operating environment, and align the incoming matter and antimatter streams for combining within the matter/antimatter reaction chamber (M/ARC.) The upper MCS measures 18 meters in length, the lower unit 12 meters. Both are 2.5 meters in diameter. A typical segment comprises eight sets of tension frame members, a toroidal pressure vessel wall, twelve sets of magnetic constrictor coils, and related

5.2.2 Magnetic constriction segments

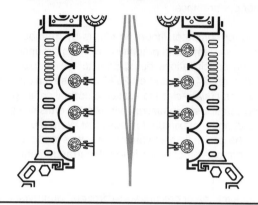

power feed and control hardware. The constrictor coils are high-density, forced-matrix cobalt-lanthanide-boronite, with thirty-six active elements configured to provide maximum field strength only within the pressure vessel and permitting little or no field spillage into Engineering. The pressure vessel toroids are alternating layers of vapor-deposited carbonitic ferracite and transparent aluminum borosilicate. The vertical tension members are machined tritanium and cortenite reinforcing whiskers, and are phase transition-bonded in place as the vehicle frame is being assembled to produce a single unified structure. All engine frame members possess integral conduits for structural integrity field energy reinforcing under normal operation. The outermost transparent layer serves as

5.2.1 Matter/antimatter reaction system

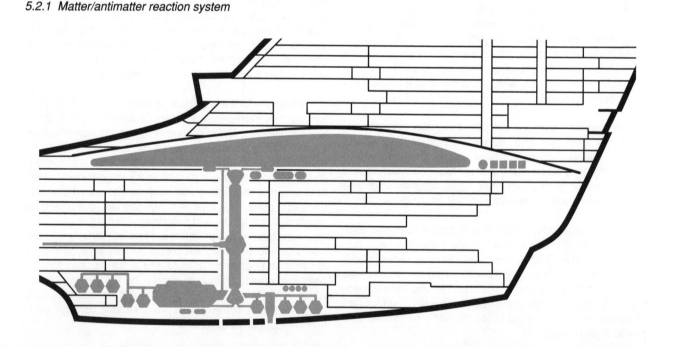

The studio initially thought that very little use would be made of the engine room in this new Enterprise. In fact, we originally did not plan to build this set for the first episode, "Encounter at Farpoint." The problem was that the nature of television production made it very likely that if this major set was not built for the pilot, it would probably never be done. When Gene Roddenberry discovered this omission, he immediately wrote a scene in the engine room, thus justifying the very large expenditure to build it for "Farpoint."

5.2.3 Matter/antimatter reaction assembly (M/ARA)

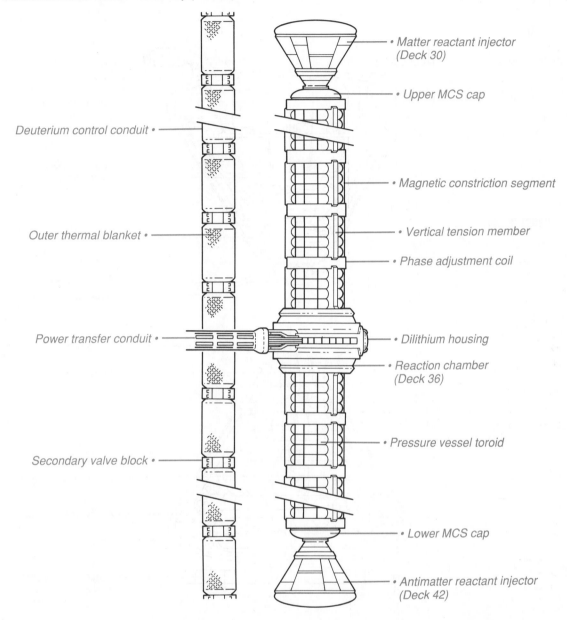

- Matter reactant injector (Deck 30)
- Upper MCS cap
- Magnetic constriction segment
- Vertical tension member
- Phase adjustment coil
- Dilithium housing
- Reaction chamber (Deck 36)
- Pressure vessel toroid
- Lower MCS cap
- Antimatter reactant injector (Deck 42)

Deuterium control conduit •

Outer thermal blanket •

Power transfer conduit •

Secondary valve block •

one observable gauge of engine performance, as harmless secondary photons are emitted from the inner layers, providing a visible blue glow. The peristaltic action and energy level of the constrictor coils can be readily seen by the Chief Engineer and/or deputy personnel.

As the streams of matter and antimatter are released from their respective nozzles, the constrictor coils compress each stream in the Y axis and add between 200 and 300 m/sec velocity. This insures proper alignment and collision energy for them each to land on target within the M/ARC at the exact center of the chamber. It is at this spot that the M/A reaction is mediated by the dilithium crystal articulation frame.

MATTER/ANTIMATTER REACTION CHAMBER

The matter/antimatter reaction chamber (M/ARC) consists of two matched bell-shaped cavities which contain and redirect the primary reaction. The chamber measures 2.3 meters in height and 2.5 meters in diameter. It is constructed from twelve layers of hafnium 6 excelion-infused carbonitrium, phase-transition welded under a pressure of 31,000 kilopascals. The three outer layers are armored with acrossenite arkenide for 10x overpressure protection, as are all interface joints to other pressure-bearing and energy-carrying parts of the system.

The equatorial band of the chamber contains the housing for the dilithium crystal articulation frame (DCAF). An ar-

5.2.4 Matter/antimatter reaction injectors

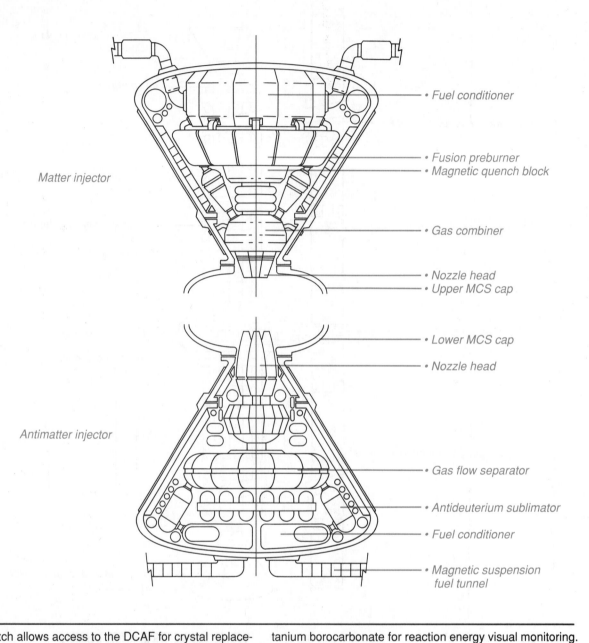

Matter injector

Antimatter injector

• Fuel conditioner

• Fusion preburner
• Magnetic quench block

• Gas combiner

• Nozzle head
• Upper MCS cap

• Lower MCS cap

• Nozzle head

• Gas flow separator

• Antideuterium sublimator

• Fuel conditioner

• Magnetic suspension
  fuel tunnel

mored hatch allows access to the DCAF for crystal replacement and adjustment. The DCAF consists of an EM-isolated cradle to hold approximately 1200 cm³ of dilithium crystal, plus two redundant sets of three-axis crystal orientation linkages. The crystal must be manipulated with six degrees of freedom to achieve the proper angles and depths for reaction mediation.

Connecting the equatorial band to the upper and lower halves of the chamber are twenty-four structural pins. These pins are hafnium 8 molyferrenite and are reinforced in tension, compression, and torsion, and are continuous with the engine structural integrity field. Running along the center of the equatorial band are two layers of diffused transparent tri-

tanium borocarbonate for reaction energy visual monitoring.

THE ROLE OF DILITHIUM

The key element in the efficient use of M/A reactions is the dilithium crystal. This is the only material known to Federation science to be nonreactive with antimatter when subjected to a high-frequency electromagnetic (EM) field in the megawatt range, rendering it "porous" to antihydrogen. Dilithium permits the antihydrogen to pass directly through its crystalline structure without actually touching it, owing to the field dynamo effect created in the added iron atoms. The longer form of the crystal name is the forced-matrix formula 2<5>6 dilithium 2<:>1 diallosilicate 1:9:1 heptoferranide. This highly complex atomic structure is based on simpler forms discovered in naturally occurring geological layers of certain planetary systems. It was for many years deemed irreproducible by known or predicted vapor-deposition methods, until breakthroughs in nuclear epitaxy and antieutectics allowed the formation of pure, synthesized dilithium for starship and conventional powerplant use, through theta-matrix compositing techniques utilizing gamma radiation bombardment.

M/ARC POWER GENERATION

The normal power-up sequence of the engine, as managed by the MCPC, is as follows:

1. From a cold condition, the total system temperature and pressure is brought up to 2,500,000K using a combination of energy inputs from the electro plasma system (EPS) and the MRI, and a "squeeze" from the upper magnetic constrictors.

2. The first minute amounts of antimatter are injected from below by the ARI. The lower MCS array squeezes the antimatter stream and matches its aim with the MRI above, so that both streams land at exactly the same XYZ coordinates within the M/ARC. The largest reaction cross-section radius is 9.3 cm, the smallest 2.1 cm. The stream cross-sections of the upper and lower MCS can vary, depending on the power level setting.

There are two distinct reaction modes. The first involves the generation of high levels of energy channeled to the electro plasma system, much like a standard fusion reaction, to provide raw energy for ship function while at sublight. In the DCAF, the crystal alignment cradle positions the dilithium so that the edge of two facets lies parallel to the matter/antimatter streams, coincident with the core's XYZ_B 0, 0, 125, where 125 is the reactant cross section radius. The reaction is mediated by the dilithium, forcing the upper limit of the resulting EM frequencies down, below 10^{20} hertz, and the lower limit up, above 10^{12} hertz.

The second mode makes full use of dilithium's ability to cause a partial suspension of the reaction, creating the critical pulse frequency to be sent to the warp engine nacelles. In this mode the XYZ coordinates are driven by the three-axis adjustments made by the DCAF and place the exact mathematical collision point 20 angstroms above the upper dilithium crystal facet (See: 5.2.2). The optimum frequency range is continuously tuned for specific warp factors and fractional warp factors. Regardless of the mode employed, the annihilation effect takes place at chamber centerpoint. The M/A ratio is stabilized at 25:1, and the engine is considered to be at "idle."

3. The engine pressure is slowly brought up to 72,000 kilopascals, roughly 715 times atmospheric pressure, and the normal operating temperature at the reaction site is 2×10^{12}K. The MRI and ARI nozzles are opened to permit more reac-

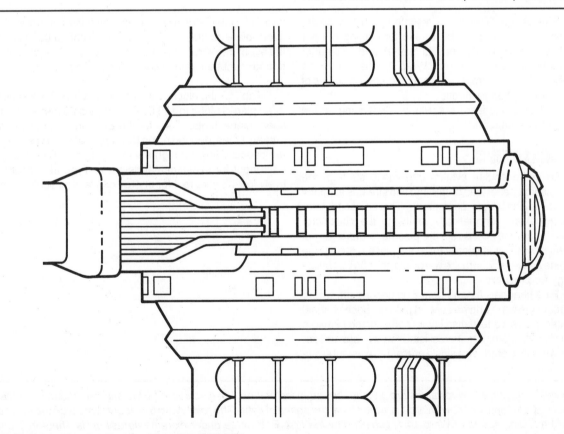

5.2.5 Matter/antimatter reaction chamber (M/ARC)

5.2.6 Dilithium crystals are used to regulate and control the matter-antimatter reaction.

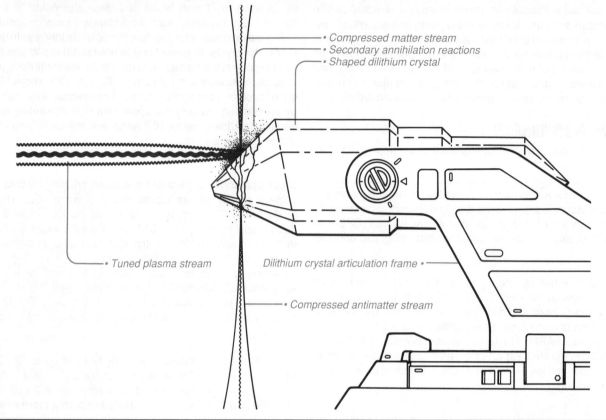

• *Compressed matter stream*
• *Secondary annihilation reactions*
• *Shaped dilithium crystal*

• *Tuned plasma stream*

Dilithium crystal articulation frame •

• *Compressed antimatter stream*

tants to fill the vessel. The ratio is adjusted to 10:1 for power generation. This is also the base ratio for making Warp 1 entry. The relative proportions of matter and antimatter change as warp factors rise until Warp 8, where the ratio becomes 1:1. Higher warp factors require greater amounts of reactants, but no change in ratio.

Other start-up modes are available, depending on the specifics of the situation.

POWER TRANSFER CONDUITS

As the entire engine system undergoes start-up, the energetic plasma generated is split into two streams at nearly right angles to the ship's centerline. The power transfer conduits (PTC) are magnetically similar to the constrictor segments, in that they constrain the plasma to the center of each channel and peristaltically force the plasma toward the warp engine nacelles, where the warp field coils (WFC) utilize the energy for propulsion.

The PTC channels extend from Engineering aft, where they intercept the warp engine support pylons. Each channel is fabricated from six alternating layers of machined tritanium and transparent aluminum borosilicate, which are phase-transition welded to produce a single pressure-resistant struc-

ture. The interfaces with the reaction chamber are explosive shear-plane joints that can separate within 0.08 seconds in the event the warp core must be jettisoned. The joints are set during manufacture and cannot be reused.

Taps for the electro plasma system (EPS) are located at three places along the PTC, at 5, 10, and 20 meters aft of the shear-plane joints. Taps for the EPS are available in three primary types, depending on their application. Type I accepts 0.1 capacity flow for high-energy systems. Type II accepts 0.01 input for experimental devices. Type III accepts relatively low-power input for energy conversion applications.

Oh, very well: The current warp values are presumably much faster than those achieved by the original Enterprise *in the first series, but the "old" and the "new" Warp 1 are the same, the speed of light. The "old" Warp 6 is about Warp 5 on the new scale. The (then) amazing speed of Warp 14.1, achieved by the first* Enterprise *under extreme duress in "Is There in Truth No Beauty?" now works out to around Warp 9.7, which the new ship achieved while fleeing Q during "Encounter at Farpoint."*

5.3 WARP FIELD NACELLES

The energetic plasma created by the M/ARC, and passed along the power transfer conduits, quickly arrives at the termination point, the warp engine nacelles. This is where the actual propulsion work is done. Each nacelle consists of a number of major assemblies, including the warp field coils (WFC), plasma injection system (PIS), emergency separation system (ESS), and maintenance docking port.

The basic structure of the nacelles is similar to that of the remainder of the starship. Titanium and duranium framing members are combined with longitudinal stiffeners, and overlaid with 2.5 meters of gamma-welded titanium hull skinning. The addition of three inner layers of directionally strengthened cobalt cortenide provides protection against high levels of warp-induced stress, particularly at the attachment hardpoints on the support pylons. All framing and skinning of the nacelles and the support pylons accommodates triply redundant conduits for SIF and IDF systems. Attached to the inner framing members are shock attenuation cylinders for the warp field coils, as well as thermal isolation struts for the plasma injection system.

The emergency separation system would be used in the event that a catastrophic failure occurred in the PIS, or if a nacelle damaged in combat or other situation could not be safely retained on its support pylon. Ten explosive structural latches can be fired, driving the nacelle up and away at 30 m/sec.

During starbase layovers and low-sublight travel, with the M/ARC powered down, the maintenance docking port allows any work pod or shuttle equipped with a standard docking collar to attach, permitting engineering crews and hardware rapid access to the interior of the nacelle. Normal monitoring visits from within the starship are made by single-occupant turbolift through the support pylon.

PLASMA INJECTION SYSTEM

At the terminus of each PTC is the plasma injection system, a series of eighteen valved magnetic injectors linked to the warp engine controllers. There is one injector for each warp field coil, and the injectors may be fired in variable sequences, depending on the warp flight function being executed. The injectors are constructed of arkenium duranide and single-crystal ferrocarbonite, with magnetic constriction toroids of nalgetium serrite. Control inputs and feedback are handled by twelve redundant links to the optical data network (ODN). Small timing discrepancies between the computer and the injectors exist during any initial startup of the coils or change in warp factors, due to the physical distance from the computer to the engines. These are rapidly smoothed out by predictive phase-synchronization software routines, thereby achieving as close to realtime operation of the engines as possible.

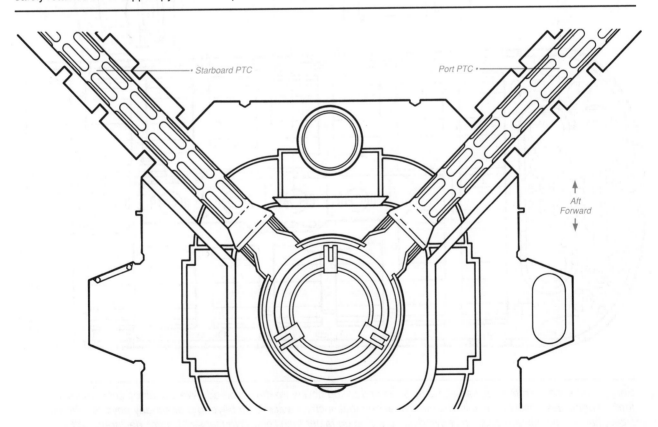

5.3.1 *Port and starboard warp power transfer conduits*

The injector open-close cycle is variable, from 25 ns to 50 ns. Each firing of an injector exposes its corresponding coil to a burst of energy to be converted into the warp field. At Warp Factors 1–4, the injectors fire at low frequencies, between 30 Hz and 40 Hz, and remain open for short periods, between 25 ns and 30 ns. At Warp Factors 5–7, the firing frequencies rise from 40 Hz to 50 Hz, and the injectors remain open for longer periods, 30 ns to 40 ns.

At Warp Factors 8–9.9, the injector firing frequencies rise to 50 Hz, but there is a tailoff of the injector cycle time, owing to limitations of residual charges in the magnetic valves, potential conflict with the energy frequencies from the M/ARC, and input/feedback control reliability. The longest safe cycle time for high warp is generally accepted to be 53 ns.

WARP FIELD COILS

The energy field necessary to propel the USS *Enterprise* is created by the warp field coils and assisted by the specific configuration of the starship hull. The coils generate an intense, multilayered field that surrounds the starship, and it is the manipulation of the shape of this field that produces the propulsive effect through and beyond the speed of light, *c*.

The coils themselves are split toroids positioned within the nacelles. Each half-segment measures 9.5 x 43 meters

5.3.2 Warp field nacelle

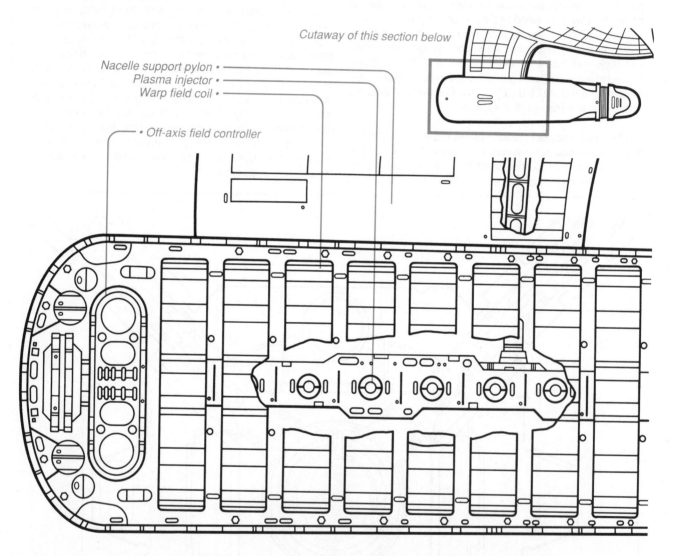

Cutaway of this section below

Nacelle support pylon •
Plasma injector •
Warp field coil •

• Off-axis field controller

Early in the series, Patrick Stewart came up to us and asked how warp drive worked. We explained some of the hypothetical principles described in this volume, but added that such a device is far beyond present-day physics. We emphasized that no one has any real idea how to make a ship go faster than light. "Nonsense," Patrick declared. "All you have to do is say, 'Engage.'" And he was right....

and is constructed from a core of densified tungsten-cobalt-magnesium for structural stiffening, and imbedded within a casting of electrically densified verterium cortenide. A complete pair measures 21 x 43 meters, with a mass of 34,375 metric tonnes. Two complete sets of eighteen coils each masses 1.23×10^6 metric tonnes, accounting for close to 25% of the total starship mass. The casting process, as discussed previously in 5.1, proved to be somewhat difficult to repeat reliably during the early phases of the *Galaxy* Class Project. Improvements in materials and procedures led to more exact copies for use in the spacecraft, though the installation of closely matched pairs of coils within a nacelle is still practiced. During coil refurbishment at a major starbase yard, the maximum time between the youngest and oldest coil should be no more than six months.

When energized, the verterium cortenide within a coil pair causes a shift of the energy frequencies carried by the plasma deep into the subspace domain. The quantum packets of subspace field energy form at approximately 1/3 the distance from the inner surface of the coil to the outer surface, as the verterium cortenide causes changes in the geometry of space at the Planck scale of 3.9×10^{-33} cm. The converted field energy exits the outer surface of the coil and radiates away from the nacelle. A certain amount of field energy recombination occurs at the coil centerline, and appears as a visible light emission.

WARP PROPULSION

The propulsive effect is achieved by a number of factors working in concert. First, the field formation is controllable in a fore-to-aft direction. As the plasma injectors fire sequentially, the warp field layers build according to the pulse frequency in the plasma, and press upon each other as previously discussed. The cumulative field layer forces reduce the apparent mass of the vehicle and impart the required velocities. The critical transition point occurs when the spacecraft appears to an outside observer to be traveling faster than c. As the warp field energy reaches 1000 millicochranes, the ship appears driven across the c boundary in less than Planck time, 1.3×10^{-43} sec, warp physics insuring that the ship will never be precisely at c. The three forward coils of each nacelle operate with a slight frequency offset to reinforce the field ahead of the Bussard ramscoop and envelop the Saucer Module. This helps create the field asymmetry required to drive the ship forward.

Second, a pair of nacelles is employed to create two balanced, interacting fields for vehicle maneuvers. In 2269, experimental work with single nacelles and more than two nacelles yielded quick confirmation that two was the optimum number for power generation and vehicle control. Spacecraft maneuvers are performed by introducing controlled timing differences in each set of warp coils, thereby modifying the total warp field geometry and resultant ship heading. Yaw motions (XZ plane) are most easily controlled in this manner.

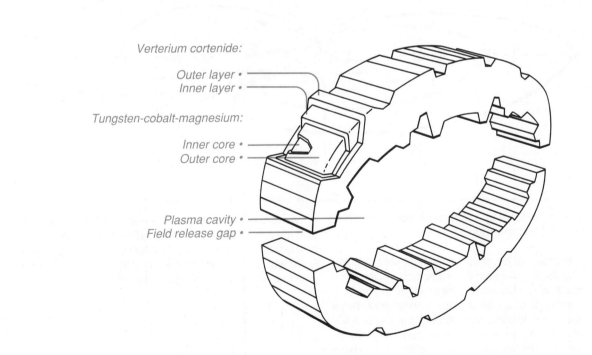

Verterium cortenide:
Outer layer •
Inner layer •

Tungsten-cobalt-magnesium:
Inner core •
Outer core •

Plasma cavity •
Field release gap •

5.3.3 Warp field coil segment (typical)

5.3.4 Subspace field geometry of Galaxy class starship

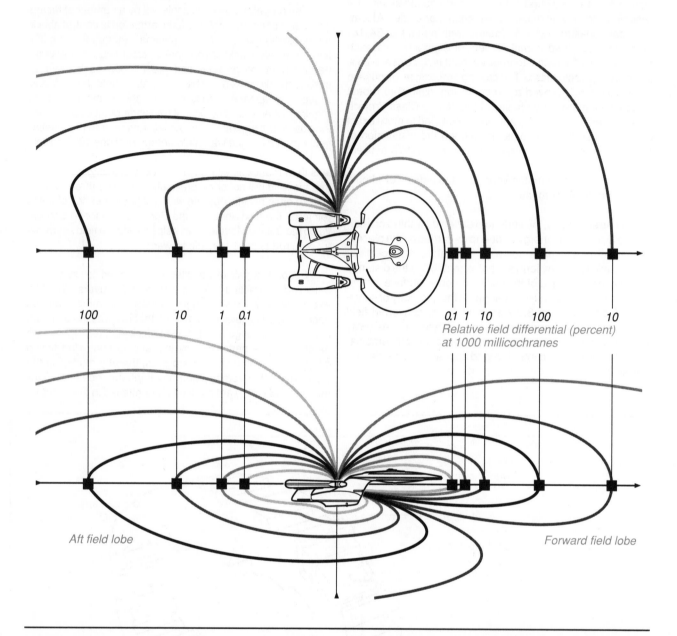

100   10   1   0.1

0.1 1 10   100   10

*Relative field differential (percent)
at 1000 millicochranes*

Aft field lobe

Forward field lobe

Pitch changes are affected by a combination of timing differences and plasma concentrations.

   Third, the shape of the starship hull facilitates slippage into warp and imparts a geometric correction vector. The Saucer Module, which retains its characteristic shape from the original concept of an emergency landing craft, helps shape the forward field component through the use of a 55° elliptical hull planform, found to produce superior peak transitional efficiency. The aft hull undercut allows for varying degrees of field flow attachment, effectively preventing pinwheeling, owing to the placement of the nacelles off the vehicle Y-axis center of mass. During Saucer Module separation and independent operation of the Battle Section, inter-

active warp field controller software adjusts the field geometry to fit the altered spacecraft shape (See: 5.1). In the event of accidental loss of one or both nacelles, the starship would linearly dissociate, due to the fact that different parts of the structure would be traveling at different warp factors.

5.4 ANTIMATTER STORAGE AND TRANSFER

5.4.1 Location of antimatter pods

Since its confirmed existence in the 1930s, the concept of a form of matter with the same mass but reversed charge and spin has intrigued scientists and engineers as a means to produce unprecedented amounts of energy, and to apply that energy to drive large space vehicles.

Cosmological theory maintains that all constituent parts of the universe were created in pairs; that is, one particle of matter and one particle of antimatter. Why there seems to be a propensity toward matter in our galactic neighborhood is, to this day, a topic of lively discussion. All of the basic antiparticles have been synthesized, however, and are available for continued experimental and operational use.

When, for example, an electron and an antielectron (or positron) are in close proximity, they mutually annihilate, producing energetic gamma rays. Other particle-antiparticle pairs annihilate into different combinations of subatomic particles and energy. Of particular interest to spacecraft engineers were the theoretical results presented by deuterium, an isotope of hydrogen, and its antimatter equivalent. The problems encountered along the way to achieving a working M/A engine, however, were as daunting as the possible rewards were glorious. Antimatter, from the time of its creation, could neither be contained by nor touch any matter. Numerous schemes were proposed to contain antihydrogen by magnetic fields. This continues to be the accepted method. Appreciable amounts of antihydrogen, in the form of liquid or, better yet, slush, posed significant risks should any portion of the magnetic containment fail. Within the last fifty years, reliable superconducting field sustainers and other measures have afforded a greater degree of safety aboard operational Starfleet vessels.

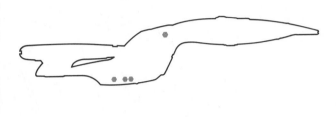

As used aboard the USS *Enterprise*, antimatter is first generated at major Starfleet fueling facilities by combined solar-fusion charge reversal devices, which process proton and neutron beams into antideuterons, and are joined by a positron beam accelerator to produce antihydrogen (specifically antideuterium). Even with the added solar dynamo input, there is a net energy loss of 24% using this process, but this loss is deemed acceptable by Starfleet to conduct distant interstellar operations.

The antimatter is kept contained by magnetic conduits and compartmentalized tankage while aboard the fueling facility. Early starships were also constructed with compartmentalized tankage in place, though this method proved less desirable from a safety standpoint in a ship subjected to high stresses. During normal refueling, antimatter is passed through the loading port, a 1.75 meter–wide circular probe-and-drogue device equipped with twelve physical hard-dock latches and magnetic irises. Surrounding the antimatter loading port on Deck 42 are thirty storage pods, each measuring 4 x 8 meters and constructed of polyduranium, with an inner magnetic field layer of ferric quonium. Each pod

---

Most privileged visitors to our main engine room set are duly impressed with the sense of "really being on the Enterprise." *Even so, there is still something missing. That "something" is the almost subliminal ambience added through background sound effects. The viewer is rarely consciously aware of it, but the characteristic low thrumming sound of the engine room or the instrument sounds of the bridge are a powerful part of "being there." Sound effects on* Star Trek: The Next Generation *are the province of associate producer Wendy Neuss. Under the supervision of co-producer Peter Lauritson, Wendy oversees the Emmy award–winning sound effects wizardry of supervising sound editor Bill Wistrom, sound effects editor Jim Wolvington, and assistant sound effects editor Tomi Tomita. (The original development of many* Enterprise *sound effects was also overseen by series creator Gene Roddenberry, along with Rick Berman, Bob Justman, and Brooke Breton.)*

These sound effects are usually the product of extensive digital processing, but many are built from surprisingly mundane sources. Despite the advanced technology available, our sound people generally prefer to start with acoustically recorded "natural" sounds because they feel the resulting harmonics are much more rich and interesting than purely synthesized tones. The bridge background sound includes the highly processed sound of an air conditioner's rumble. The characteristic "swoosh" of the doors opening is based on the sound of a flare gun with a bit of the squeak of Jim Wolvington's sneaker on the floor at Modern Sound.

Most Enterprise *sound effects are deliberately reminiscent of the sounds from the original* Star Trek *television series, but with a high-tech twist. Some, like the communicators and the ship's phasers, are actually derived from the first show's sounds. Alien sounds can come from a wide variety of sources such as the voices of the Bynars (from "11001001") which was built by programming brief "samples" of the actresses' voices into a Synclavier, then playing them back with a cadence much faster than normal human speech. The sound of "Tin Man's" interior was actually based on the sound of Wolvington's stomach, recorded through a stethoscope. Notes Wolvington, "I didn't tell anyone where that noise came from until after the show was done because I didn't want anyone to get sick!"*

5.4.2 Antimatter storage pod assembly (typical)

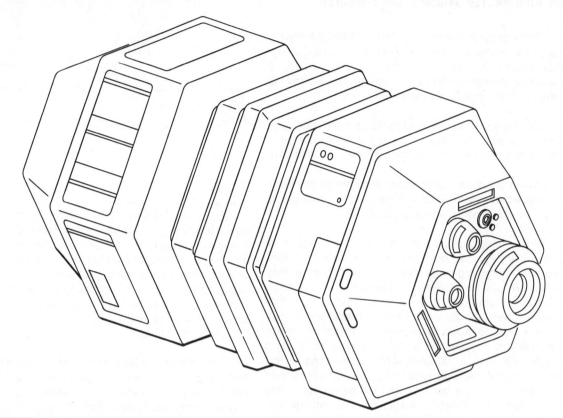

contains a maximum volume of 100 m^3 of antimatter, giving a 30-pod total starship supply of 3000 m^3, enough for a normal mission period of three years. Each is connected by shielded conduits to a series of distribution manifolds, flow controllers, and electro plasma system (EPS) power feed inputs. In rapid refueling conditions, reserved for emergency situations, the entire antimatter storage pod assembly (ASPA) can be drawn down on jackscrews and replaced in less than one hour.

In the event of loss of magnetic containment, this very same assembly can be ejected by microfusion initiators at a velocity of 40 m/sec, pushing it clear of the ship before the fields decay and the antimatter has a chance to react with the pod walls (See: 5.9). While small groups of pods can be replaced under normal conditions, the magnetic pump transfer method is preferred.

Antimatter, even contained within storage pods, cannot be moved by transporter without extensive modifications to the pattern buffer, transfer conduits, and transporter emitters for safety reasons due to the highly volatile nature of antimatter. (Specific exceptions apply for small quantities of antimatter stored in approved magnetic containment devices, normally used for specialized engineering and scientific applications.)

Refueling while in interstellar space is possible through the use of Starfleet tanker craft. Tanker transfers run considerable risks, not so much from hardware problems but because refined antimatter is a valuable commodity, and vulnerable to Threat force capture or destruction while in transit. Starfleet cruiser escorts are standard procedure for all tanker movements.

5.5 WARP PROPULSION SYSTEM FUEL SUPPLY

The fuel supply for the warp propulsion system (WPS) is contained within the primary deuterium tank (PDT) in the Battle Section. The PDT, which also feeds the IPS (impulse propulsion system), is normally loaded with slush deuterium at a temperature of -259°C, or 13.8K. The PDT is constructed of forced-matrix 2378 cortanium and stainless steel, with foamed vac-whisker silicon-copper-duranite insulation laid down in alternating parallel/biased layers and gamma-welded.

Penetrations for supply vessels, vent lines, and sensors are made by standard precision phaser cutters. There are a total of four main fuel feed manifolds from the PDT to the matter reactant injector, eight cross-feed conduits to the Saucer Module auxiliary tanks, and four feeds to the main impulse engine.

The total internal volume, which is compartmentalized against losses due to structural damage, is 63,200 m³, though the normal total deuterium load is 62,500 m³. As with the volume of antimatter loaded for a typical multimission segment, a full load of deuterium is rated to last approximately three years.

As with any constructed tank, a certain percentage of deuterium molecules is expected to migrate through the tank walls over time. The PDT leak rate has been measured at <.00002 kg/day. Proportionate values hold for all auxiliary tanks as well.

Slush deuterium is created by standard electro-centrifugal fractioning of a variety of materials, including seawater, outer planet satellite snows and ices, and cometary nuclei, and chilling down the fractioned liquid. Each will result in different proportions of deuterium and tailings, but can be handled by the same Starfleet hardware. Deuterium tanker craft are far more numerous than their antimatter counterparts, and can provide emergency reactants on a few days' notice. Two deuterium loading ports are located along the structural spine of the Battle Section, aft of the "tail" of the tank. The loading port interface contains structural connections for firm docking within a starbase or free-floating maintenance dock, as well as pressure relief, purge inlet and outlet fittings, and optical data network hardlines to the starbase computers.

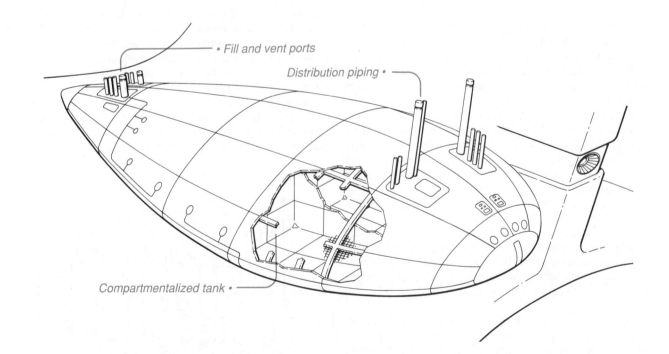

• Fill and vent ports

Distribution piping •

Compartmentalized tank •

5.5.1 Primary deuterium tank

5.6.1 Bussard ramscoop collection field

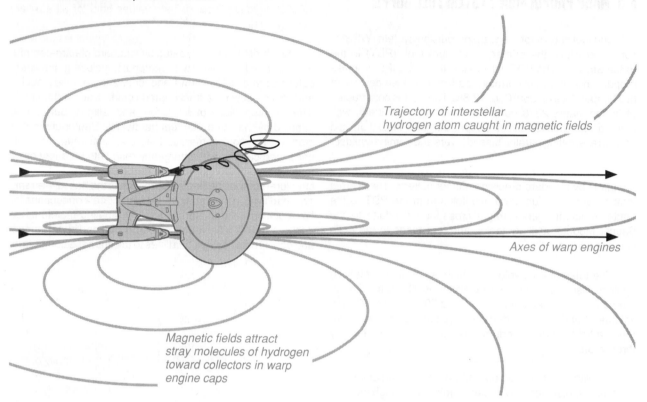

*Trajectory of interstellar
hydrogen atom caught in magnetic fields*

Axes of warp engines

*Magnetic fields attract
stray molecules of hydrogen
toward collectors in warp
engine caps*

5.6 BUSSARD RAMSCOOP FUEL REPLENISHMENT

In the event a deuterium tanker cannot reach a *Galaxy* class starship, the capability exists to pull low-grade matter from the interstellar medium through a series of specialized high-energy magnetic coils known collectively as a Bussard ramscoop. Named for the twentieth-century physicist and mathematician Robert W. Bussard, the ramscoop emanates directional ionizing radiation and a shaped magnetic field to attract and compress the tenuous gas found within the Milky Way galaxy. From this gas, which possesses an average density of one atom per cubic centimeter, may be distilled small amounts of deuterium for contingency replenishment of the matter supply. At high relativistic speeds, this gas accumulation can be appreciable, though the technique is not recommended for long periods for time-dilation reasons (See: 6.2). At warp velocities, however, extended emergency supplies can be gathered. While matching supplies of anti-matter cannot be recovered from space in this manner, minute amounts of antimatter can be generated by an onboard quantum charge reversal device (See: 5.7).

It is an accepted fact that a starship in distress will continue to deplete its energy supplies; however, systems such as this have been included to afford at least a small additional chance at survival.

A Bussard collector can be found at the forward end of

each warp engine nacelle. It consists of three main assemblies, an ionizing beam emitter (IBE), magnetic field generator/collector (MFG/C), and continuous cycle fractionator (CCF). The curved nacelle endcap, the largest single cast structure of the spacecraft, is formed from reinforced polyduranide and is transparent to a narrow range of ionizing energies produced by the emitter. It is the function of the emitter to impart a charge to neutral particles in space for collection by the magnetic field. At warp velocities, the ionizing energies are transitioned into subspace frequencies so that the beam components can project out ahead of the starship, decay to their normal states, and produce the desired effect.

Behind and supporting the endcap is the MFC/G, a

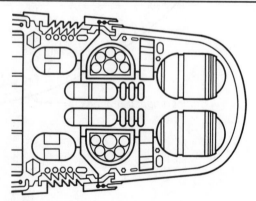

5.6.2 Bussard ramscoop

compact set of six coils designed to cast a magnetic "net" ahead of the starship and pull in the charged particles toward the intake grills. These coils are constructed from cobalt-lanthanide-boronite and obtain their power from either the power transfer conduits directly, or the general electro plasma system. At sublight velocities, the coils sweep forward normally. At warp velocities, however, the coil operation is reversed to *slow down* the incoming matter. This system works in close connection with the main navigational deflector. In normal operation, of course, the job of the deflector is to *prevent* any interstellar material from contacting the ship. Small field "holes" are manipulated by the deflector and MFG/C to permit usable amounts of rarified gas through.

Tucked within the MFG/C is the CCF, which continuously separates the incoming gas into different grades of matter considered "burnable" within the warp engine. The separated gases are compressed, and pressure-fed to holding tanks within the Battle Section.

5.7 ONBOARD ANTIMATTER GENERATION

As mentioned, there exists in the *Galaxy* class the ability to generate relatively small amounts of antimatter during potential emergency situations. The process is by all accounts incredibly power- and matter-intensive, and may not be advantageous under all operational conditions. As with the Bussard ramscoop, however, the antimatter generator may provide critical fuel supplies when they are needed most.

The antimatter generator resides on Deck 42, surrounded by other elements of the WPS. It consists of two key assemblies, the matter inlet/conditioner (MI/C), and the quantum charge reversal device (QCRD). The entire generator measures some 7.6 x 13.7 meters, and masses 1400 metric tonnes. It is one of the heaviest components, second only to the warp field coils. The MI/C utilizes conventional tritanium and polyduranide in its construction, as it handles only cryogenic deuterium and similar fuels. The QCRD, on the other hand, employs alternating layers of superdense, forced-matrix cobalt-yttrium-polyduranide and 854 kalinite-argium.

The Bussard ramscoop was featured in at least two episodes, "Samaritan Snare" and "Night Terrors." In both cases, the system was backflushed so that hydrogen gas or plasma flowed out of the scoops (rather than into them as would normally occur). In the first usage, it resulted in a spectacular (but harmless) pyrotechnic display. During "Night Terrors," the hydrogen stream was used to attempt to seal a dangerous spatial rift. The concept of using electromagnetic fields to collect interstellar hydrogen for fuel use was proposed by physicist Dr. Robert W. Bussard back in 1960.

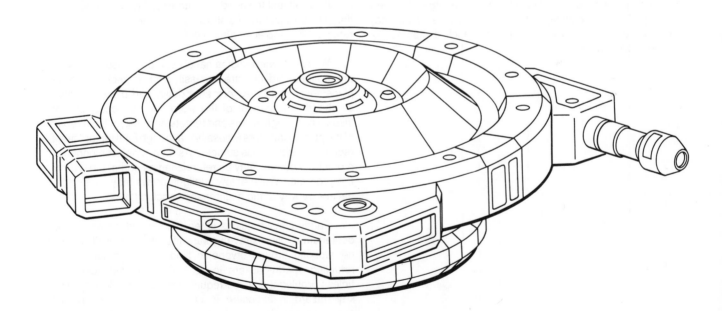

5.7.1 Antimatter generator

This is necessary to produce the power amplification required to hold collections of subatomic particles, reverse their charge, and collect the reversed matter for storage in the nearby anti-matter pods.

The technology that has given rise to the QCRD is similar to that of the transporter, SIF, IDF, and other devices that manipulate matter on the quantum level. The conversion process sees the inlet of normal matter, stretched out into thin rivulets no more than 0.000003 cm across. The rivulets are pressure-fed into the QCRD under magnetic suspension, where groups of them are chilled to within 0.001 degree of absolute zero, and exposed to a short-period stasis field to further limit molecular vibration. As the stasis field decays, focused subspace fields drive deep within the subatomic structure to flip the charges and spins of the "frozen" protons, neutrons, and electrons. The flipped matter, now antimatter, is magnetically removed for storage. The system can normally process 0.08 m^3/hr.

It can be said that the total potential energy contained in a given quantity of deuterium can drive a starship for some considerable distance. Applying this energy at sublight speeds will be next to useless in a desperate scenario. Interstellar flight at warp speeds requires tens of thousands of times greater velocities than those afforded by impulse power, and so antimatter generation will sometimes be necessary. One disadvantage imposed by the process is that it requires ten units of deuterium to power the generator, and the generator will produce only one unit of antimatter. Put another way, the law of conservation of energy dictates that the power required for this process will exceed the usable energy ultimately derived from the resulting antimatter fuel. However, this may provide a needed survival margin to reach a starbase or tanker rendezvous.

5.8 ENGINEERING OPERATIONS AND SAFETY

All warp propulsion system (WPS) hardware is maintained according to standard Starfleet mean time between failures (MTBF) monitoring and changeout schedules. Owing to the high usage rate of the matter/antimatter reaction assembly (M/ARA), all of its major components have been designed for maximum reliability and high MTBF values. Standard in-flight preventative maintenance is not intended for the warp engine, since the core and the power transfer conduits can be serviced only at a Starfleet yard or starbase equipped to perform Class 5 engineering repairs. While docked at one of these facilities, the core can be removed and dismantled for replacement of such components as the magnetic constrictor coils, refurbishment of interior protective coatings, and automated inspection and repair of all critical fuel conduits. The typical cycle between major core inspections and repairs is 10,000 operating hours.

While the WPS is shut down, the matter and antimatter injectors can be entered by starship crew for detailed component inspection and replacement. Accessible for preventative maintenance (PM) work in the MRI are the inlet manifolds, fuel conditioners, fusion preburner, magnetic quench block, transfer duct/gas combiner, nozzle head, and related control hardware. Accessible parts within the ARI are the pulsed antimatter gas flow separators and injector nozzles. A partial disassembly of the dilithium crystal articulation frame is possible in flight for probing by nondestructive testing (NDT) methods. Protective surface coatings may be removed and reapplied without the need for a starbase layover. Inboard of the reactant injectors, the shock attenuation cylinders may be removed and replaced after 5,000 hours.

Within the warp engine nacelles, most sensor hardware and control hardlines are accessible for inspection and replacement. With the core shut down and plasma vented overboard, the interior of the warp coils is accessible for inspection by flight crews and remote devices. In-flight repair of the plasma injectors is possible, although total replacement requires starbase assistance. As with other components, protective coatings may be refurbished as part of the normal PM program. While at low sublight, crews may access the nacelle by way of the maintenance docking port.

Safety considerations when handling slush and liquid deuterium involve extravehicular suit protection for all personnel working around cryogenic fluids and semisolids. All refueling operations are to be handled by teleoperators, unless problems develop requiring crew investigation. The key hazard in exposure to cryogenics involves material embrittlement, even in the case of cryoprotective garments. Care should always be taken to avoid direct contact, deferring close-quarters handling to specialized collection tools and emergency procedures.

5.9 EMERGENCY SHUTDOWN PROCEDURES

Operational safety in running the warp propulsion system (WPS) is strictly observed. Limits in power levels and running times at overloaded levels could be easily reached and exceeded. The system is protected by computer intervention, part of the overall homeostasis process. Starfleet human-factors experts designed the operational WPS software to make "overprotective" decisions in the matter of the health of the warp engine. Command overrides are possible at reduced action levels.

The intent was not to create human-computer conflicts; rather, command personnel are trained to use the software routines to their best effect for maximum starship endurance. Emergency shutdowns are commanded by the computer when pressure and thermal limits threaten the safety of the crew. The normal shutdown of the WPS involves valving off the plasma to the warp field coils, closing off the reactant injectors, and venting the remaining gases overboard. The impulse propulsion system (IPS) would continue providing ship power. In one shutdown scenario, the injectors would be closed off and the plasma vented simultaneously, the system achieving a cold condition within ten minutes. High external forces, either from celestial objects or combat damage, will cause the computer to perform risk assessments for "safe" overload periods before commanding a system throttleback or shutdown.

5.10 CATASTROPHIC EMERGENCY PROCEDURES

Under certain stress conditions, the WPS may sustain various degrees of damage, usually from external sources, and much of this may be repaired to bring the systems back to flight status. Complete, irreparable, and rapid failure of one or more WPS components, however, constitutes a catastrophic failure. Standard procedures for dealing with major vehicle damage apply to WPS destruction and include but are not limited to safing any systems that could pose further danger to the ship, assessing WPS damage and collateral damage to ship structures and systems, and sealing off hull breaches and other interior areas that are no longer habitable.

Fuel and power supplies are automatically valved off at points upstream from the affected systems, according to computer and crew damage control assessments. Where feasible, crews will enter damaged areas in pressure suits to assure that damaged systems are rendered totally inert, and perform repairs on related systems as necessary. If the WPS is damaged in combat, crews can augment their normal pressure suits with additional flexible multilayer armor for protection against unpredictable energy releases. Engineering personnel may elect to delay effecting system inerting until the ship can avoid further danger. Exact repair actions dealing with damaged WPS hardware will depend on the specifics of the situation.

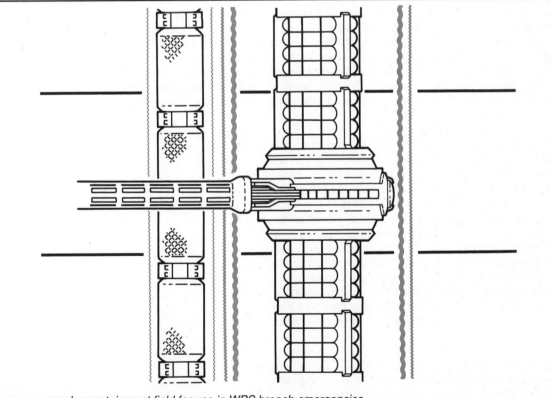

5.9.1 Emergency annular containment field for use in WPS breach emergencies

5.10.1 In an extreme emergency, both the warp core and antimatter pods can be ejected.

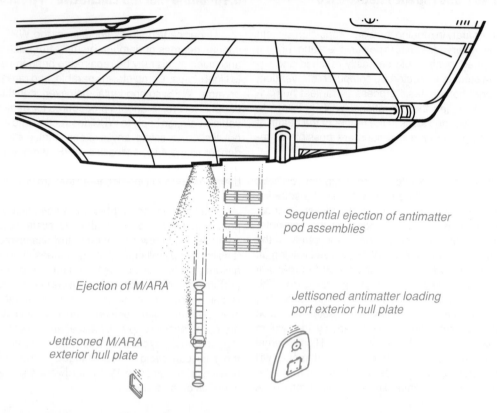

Sequential ejection of antimatter pod assemblies

Ejection of M/ARA

Jettisoned antimatter loading port exterior hull plate

Jettisoned M/ARA exterior hull plate

In some cases, damaged hardware is jettisoned, although security considerations will require the retention of the equipment whenever possible. In the event that all normal emergency procedures fail to contain massive WPS damage, including a multilayer safety forcefield around the core, two final actions are possible. Both involve the ejection of the entire central WPS core, with the added possible ejection of the antimatter storage pod assembly. The first option is deliberate manual sequence initiation; the second, automatic computer activation.

Core ejection will occur when pressure vessel damage is severe enough to breach the safety forcefield. Ejection will also occur if the damage threatens to overwhelm the structural integrity field system enough to prevent the safe retention of the core, whether or not the WPS continues to provide propulsive energy. The survival of the crew and the remainder of the starship is deemed in most cases to take priority over continued vessel operations. If the impulse propulsion system is operable, vessel movement may be possible to enhance survival prospects. Scenario-specific procedures within the main computer will suggest the proper actions leading to personnel rescue. During combat operations, the core will be commanded to self-destruct once a safe distance has been achieved.

Damage sustained by the antimatter storage pod assembly may require its rapid ejection from the Engineering Hull. Since the antimatter reactant supply possesses the energy

potential to vaporize the entire starship, multiply-redundant safety systems are in place to minimize the failure conditions of the pod containment devices. Structural or system failures would be analyzed by the computer as with the warp core, and the complete pod assembly would be propelled away from the ship. A manual ejection option, while retained in the emergency computer routines, is not generally regarded as workable in a crisis situation, due mainly to timing constraints related to magnetic valve and transfer piping purge events.

6.0 IMPULSE PROPULSION SYSTEMS

6.1 IMPULSE DRIVE

The principal sublight propulsion of the ship and certain auxiliary power generating operations are handled by the impulse propulsion system (IPS). The total IPS consists of two sets of fusion-powered engines: the main impulse engine, and the Saucer Module impulse engines. During normal docked operations the main impulse engine is the active device, providing the necessary thrust for interplanetary and sublight interstellar flight. High impulse operations, specifically velocities above 0.75c, may require added power from the Saucer Module engines. These operations, while acceptable options during some missions, are often avoided due to relativistic considerations and their inherent time-based difficulties (See: 6.2).

During the early definition phase of the *Ambassador* class, it was determined that the combined vehicle mass of the prototype NX-10521 could reach at least 3.71 million metric tons. The propulsive force available from the highest specific-impulse (I_{sp}) fusion engines available or projected fell far short of being able to achieve the 10 km/sec² acceleration required. This necessitated the inclusion of a compact space-time driver coil, similar to those standard in warp engine nacelles, that would perform a low-level continuum distortion without driving the vehicle across the warp threshold. The driver coil was already into computer simulation trials during the *Ambassador* class engineering phase and it was determined that a fusion-driven engine could move a larger mass than would normally be possible by reaction thrust alone, even with exhaust products accelerated to near lightspeed.

Experimental results with exhaust products temporarily accelerated beyond lightspeed yielded disappointing results, due to the lack of return force coupling to the engine frame. The work in this area is continuing, however, in an effort to increase powerplant performance for future starship classes.

In the time between the *Ambassador* and the *Galaxy* classes, improvements in the internal arrangement and construction of impulse engines proceeded, while continuing the practice of using a single impulse engine to perform both propulsion and power generation functions like its larger cousin, the warp engine. Magnetohydrodynamic (MHD) and electro plasma system (EPS) taps provide energy for all ship systems in a shared load arrangement with the warp reaction core.

IPS FUEL SUPPLY

The fuel supplies for the IPS are contained within the primary deuterium tank (PDT) in the Battle Section and a set of thirty-two auxiliary cryo tanks in the Saucer Module. Redundant cross-feeds within both spacecraft and fuel management routines in the main computers perform all fuel handling operations during flight and starbase resupply stopovers. While the PDT, which also feeds the WPS, is normally loaded with slush deuterium at a temperature of 13.8K, the cryo reactants stored within the Saucer Module tanks are in liquid form. In the event that slush deuterium must be transferred from the main tank, it is passed through a set of heaters to raise the temperature sufficiently to allow proper fuel flow with minimal turbulence and vibration.

As with the PDT, the auxiliary tanks are constructed of forced-matrix cortanium 2378 and stainless steel, laid down in alternating parallel/biased layers and gamma-welded. Penetrations for supply vessels, vent lines, and sensors are made by standard precision phaser cutters. They are installed by Fleet Yard transporters and may be transporter-removed for servicing at Starfleet maintenance docks. The internal volume of each auxiliary tank is 113 cubic meters and each is

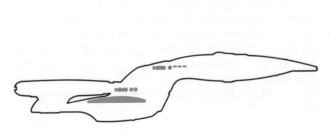

6.1.1 Impulse drive systems

6.1.2 Main impulse engine located on aft dorsal

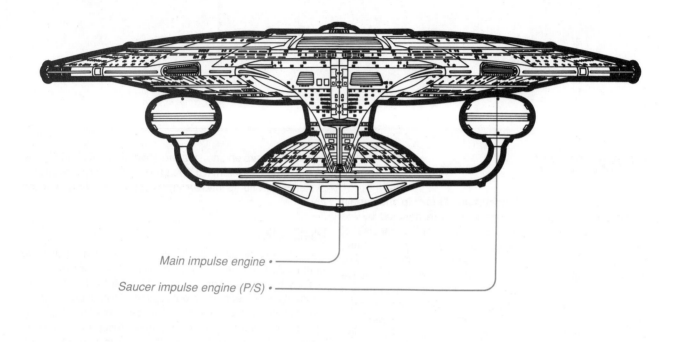

Main impulse engine •————

Saucer impulse engine (P/S) •————

capable of storing a total of 9.3 metric tonnes of liquid deuterium.

Emergency flight rules allow for the injection of minute amounts of antimatter into the impulse reaction chamber in the event that short periods of overthrust or increased power generation are required. The main impulse engine is supplied by the Battle Section's antimatter storage facility on Decks 41 and 42. The Saucer Module impulse engines are supplied by two dedicated antimatter storage pods on Deck 10. There is no transfer capability of antimatter between the two vehicles (See: 5.4).

IMPULSE ENGINE CONFIGURATION

The main impulse engine (MIE) is located on Deck 23 and thrusts along the centerline of the docked spacecraft. During separated flight mode, the engine thrust vectors are adjusted slightly in the +Y direction; that is, pointed slightly up from center to allow for proper center-of-mass motions (See: 6.3). The Saucer Module impulse engines are located on Deck 10 on the vehicle XZ plane and thrust parallel to the vehicle centerline.

Four individual impulse engines are grouped together to form the MIE, and two groups of two engines form the Saucer Module impulse engines. Each impulse engine consists of three basic components: impulse reaction chamber (IRC, three per impulse engine), accelerator/generator (A/G), driver

coil assembly (DCA), and vectored exhaust director (VED). The IRC is an armored sphere six meters in diameter, designed to contain the energy released in a conventional proton-proton fusion reaction. It is constructed of eight layers of dispersion-strengthened hafnium excelinide with a total wall thickness of 674 cm. A replaceable inner liner of crystalline gulium fluoride 40 cm thick protects the structural sphere from reaction and radiation effects. Penetrations are made into the sphere for reaction exhaust, pellet injectors, standard fusion initiators, and sensors.

The *Galaxy* class normally carries four additional IRC modules primarily as backup power generation devices, though

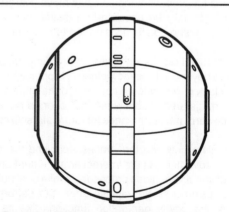

6.1.3 Typical impulse fusion reactor

these modules may be channeled through the main system exhaust paths to provide backup propulsion.

Slush deuterium from the main cryo tank is heated and fed to interim supply tanks on Deck 9, where the heat energy is removed, bringing the deuterium down to a frozen state as it is formed into pellets. Pellets can range in size from 0.5 cm to 5 cm, depending on the desired energy output per unit time. A standing pulsed fusion shock front is created by the standard initiators ranged about the forward inner surface of the sphere. The total instantaneous output of the IRC is throttleable from 10^8 to 10^{11} megawatts.

High-energy plasma created during engine operation is exhausted through a central opening in the sphere to the accelerator/generator. This stage is generally cylindrical, 3.1 meters long and 5.8 meters in diameter, constructed of an integral single-crystal polyduranium frame and pyrovunide exhaust accelerator. During propulsion operations, the accelerator is active, raising the velocity of the plasma and passing it on to the third stage, the space-time driver coils. If the engine is commanded to generate power only, the accelerator is shut down and the energy is diverted by the EPS to the ship's overall power distribution net. Excess exhaust products can be vented nonpropulsively. The combined mode, power generation during propulsion, allows the exhaust plasma to pass through, and a portion of the energy is tapped by the MHD system to be sent to the power net.

The third stage of the engine is the driver coil assembly (DCA). The DCA is 6.5 meters long and 5.8 meters in diameter and consists of a series of six split toroids, each manufactured from cast verterium cortenide 934. Energy from the accelerated plasma, when driven through the toroids, creates the necessary combined field effect that (1) reduces the apparent mass of the spacecraft at its inner surface, and (2) facilitates the slippage of the continuum past the spacecraft at its outer surface.

The final stage is the vectored exhaust director (VED). The VED consists of a series of moveable vanes and channels designed to expel exhaust products in a controlled manner. The VED is capable of steerable propulsive and nonpropulsive modes (simple venting).

IMPULSE ENGINE CONTROL

The impulse propulsion system is commanded through operational software routines stored within the spacecraft main computers. As with the warp propulsion system command processors, genetic algorithms learn and adapt to ongoing experiences involving impulse engine usage and

---

Extremely close examination of the impulse drive system schematic panel in Main Engineering might reveal that one of the components is labeled "Infinite Improbability Generation," a tip of the hat to Douglas Adams's Hitchhiker's Guide to the Galaxy.

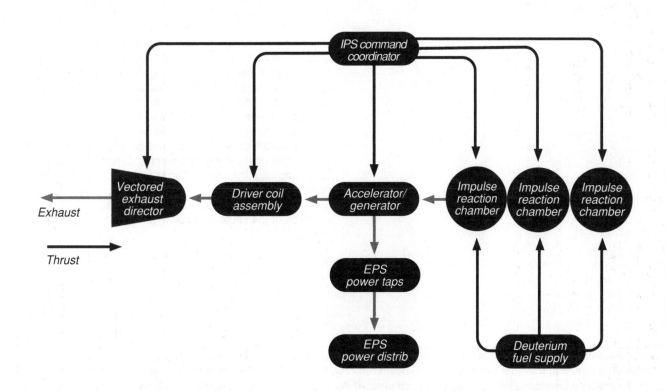

6.1.4 Impulse engine system

make appropriate modifications in handling both voluntary external commands and purely autonomic operations. Voice commands and keyboard inputs are confirmed and reconciled by the current active main computer, and then handed off to the IPS command coordinator for routing to the engines for execution. The IPS command coordinator is cross-linked with its counterpart in the WPS for flight transitions involving warp entry and exit. Specific software routines react to prevent field energy fratricide (unwanted conflicts between warp fields and impulse engine fields). The command coordinator is also crosslinked with the reaction control system (RCS) for attitude and translational control at all speeds.

6.2 RELATIVISTIC CONSIDERATIONS

While the *Galaxy* class starship is the most advanced space vehicle in Starfleet's inventory, it is perhaps ironic that one of its most sophisticated systems can actually cause a number of annoying problems with extended use.

As fledgling journeys were made by fusion starships late in the twenty-first century, theoretical calculations concerning the *tau* factor, or time dilation effect encountered at appreciable fractions of lightspeed, rapidly crossed over into reality. Time aboard a spacecraft at relativistic velocities slowed according to the "twin paradox." During the last of the long voyages, many more years had passed back on Earth, and the time differences proved little more than curiosities as mission news was relayed back to Earth and global developments were broadcast to the distant travelers. Numerous other spacefaring cultures have echoed these experiences, leading to the present navigation and communication standards within the Federation.

Today, such time differences can interfere with the requirement for close synchronization with Starfleet Command as well as overall Federation timekeeping schemes. Any extended flight at high relativistic speeds can place mission objectives in jeopardy. At times when warp propulsion is not available, impulse flight may be unavoidable, but will require lengthy recalibration of onboard computer clock systems even if contact is maintained with Starfleet navigation beacons. It is for this reason that normal impulse operations are limited to a velocity of 0.25c.

Efficiency ratings for impulse and warp engines determine which flight modes will best accomplish mission objectives. Current impulse engine configurations achieve efficiencies approaching 85% when velocities are limited to 0.5c. Current warp engine efficiency, on the other hand, falls off dramatically when the engine is asked to maintain an asymmetrical peristaltic subspace field below lightspeed or an integral warp factor (See: 5.1). It is generally accepted that careful mission planning of warp and impulse flight segments, in conjunction with computer recommendations, will minimize normal clock adjustments. In emergency and combat operations, major readjustments are dealt with according to the specifics of the situation, usually after action levels are reduced.

The use of stardates is, among other things, intended to suggest a timekeeping system that takes into account relativistic time dilation as well as any temporal effects of warp speeds. In actual practice, Star Trek *script coordinator Eric Stillwell (co-writer of "Yesterday's* Enterprise*") is the keeper of stardates. At the beginning of each season, Eric compiles a memo listing the estimated range of stardates available for each planned episode. The writers then use this as a guide to help the good captain keep track of his log entries.*

6.3.1 IPS fusion reactor replacement

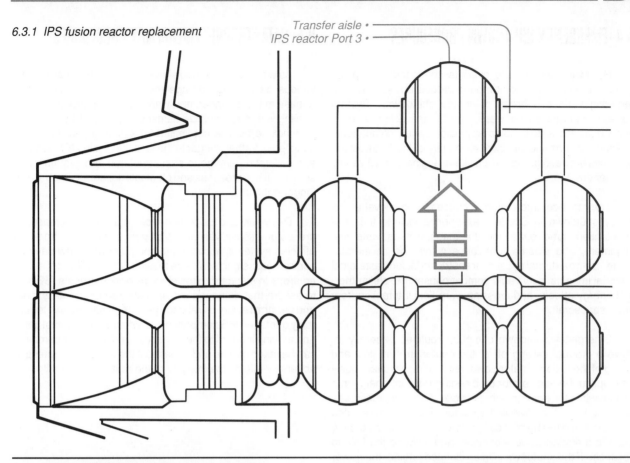

Transfer aisle •
IPS reactor Port 3 •

6.3 ENGINEERING OPERATIONS AND SAFETY

All main impulse engine (MIE) and saucer module impulse engine (SMIE) hardware is maintained according to standard Starfleet MTBF monitoring and changeout schedules. Those components in the system exposed to the most energetic duty cycles are, of course, subject to the highest changeout rate. For example, the gulium fluoride inner liner of the impulse reaction chamber (IRC) is regularly monitored for erosion and fracturing effects from the ongoing fusion reaction, and is normally changed out after 10,000 hours of use, or after 0.01 mm of material is ablated, or if ≥2 fractures/cm³ measuring 0.02 mm are formed, whichever occurs first. The structural IRC sphere is replaced after 8,500 flight hours, as are all related subassemblies. Deuterium and antimatter injectors, standard initiators, and sensors can be replaced during flight or in orbit without the assistance of a starbase.

Downstream, the accelerator/generator (A/G) and driver coil assembly (DCA) are changed out after 6250 hours, or if accelerated wear or specific structural anomalies occur. In the A/G, the normal need for changeout is brittle metal phenomenon resulting from radiation effects. During flight, only the accelerator assemblies may be demounted for nondestructive testing (NDT) analysis.

Similarly, the DCA is subject to changeout after 6,250 flight hours. Normal replacement is necessitated by EM and thermal effects created by the driver coils. None of the DCA assemblies may be replaced in flight and all repair operations must be handled at a dock-capable starbase. The vectored exhaust director (VED) is serviceable in flight, requiring the least attention to deteriorating energy effects. All directional vanes and actuators may be replicated and replaced without starbase assistance.

Operational safety is as vital to the running of the IPS as it is to the WPS. While hardware limits in power levels and running times at overloaded levels are easily reached and exceeded, the systems are protected through a combination of computer intervention and reasonable human commands. No individual IPS engine can be run at >115% energy-thrust output, and can be run between 101% and 115% only along a power/time slope of $t=p/3$.

The IPS requires approximately 1.6 times as many man-hours to maintain as the WPS, primarily due to the nature of the energy release in the fusion process. The thermal and acoustic stresses tend to be greater per unit area, a small penalty incurred to retain a small engine size. While warp engine reactions are on the order of one million times more energetic, that energy is created with less transmitted structural shock. The major design tradeoff made by Starfleet R&D is evident when one considers that efficient matter/antimatter power systems that can also provide rocket thrust cannot be reduced to IPS dimensions.

6.4 EMERGENCY SHUTDOWN PROCEDURES

Hardware failures and override commands can place abnormal stress on the total impulse propulsion system (IPS), requiring various degrees of engine shutdown. System sensors, operational software, and human action work in concert to deactivate impulse propulsion system components under conditions such as excessive thermal loads, thrust imbalances between groups of individual engines, and a variety of other problems.

The most common internal causes for low-level emergency shutdown in Starfleet experience include fuel flow constriction, out-of-phase initiator firings, exhaust vane misalignment, and plasma turbulence within the accelerator stage. Some external causes for shutdown include asteroidal material impacts, survivable combat phaser fire, stellar thermal energy effects, and crossing warp field interaction from other spacecraft.

Emergency shutdown computer routines generally involve a gradual valving off of the deuterium fuel flow and safing of the fusion initiator power regulators, simultaneously decoupling the accelerator by bleeding residual energy into space or into the ship's power network. As these procedures are completed, the driver coil assembly (DCA) coils are safed by interrupting the normal coil pulse order, effectively setting them to a neutral power condition, and allowing the field to collapse. If the shutdown is in an isolated engine, the power load distribution is reconfigured at the first indication of trouble.

Variations on these procedures are stored within the main computer and IPS command coordinators. Crew monitoring of a shutdown is a Starfleet requirement, although many scenarios have seen engines being safed before reliable human reactions could be incorporated. Voluntary shutdown procedures are dependable and accepted by the main computer in 42% of the recorded incidents.

6.5 CATASTROPHIC EMERGENCY PROCEDURES

As with the warp propulsion system, the IPS may sustain various degrees of damage requiring repair or deliberate release of the damaged hardware. Standard procedures for dealing with major vehicle damage apply to IPS destruction and include but are not limited to: safing any systems that could pose further danger to the ship, assessing IPS damage and collateral damage to ship structures and systems, and sealing off hull breaches and other interior areas which are no longer habitable.

Deuterium and fusion-enhancement antimatter reactants are automatically valved off at points upstream from the affected systems, according to computer and crew damage control assessments. Where feasible, crews will enter affected areas in standard extravehicular work garments (SEWG) to assure that damaged systems are rendered totally inert, and perform repairs on related systems as necessary. Irreparably damaged IPS components, starting with the thrust vents and moving inboard to the drive coils and reaction chambers, can be taken off-line and released if their continued retention adversely affects the integrity of the rest of the starship.

The Galaxy *class starship* Enterprise *has a lot of windows that look out into space, giving many of our sets a wonderful sense of "really" being on a starship. This requires us to do a lot of bluescreen shots to show streaking "warp stars" whenever the ship is traveling faster than light. Naturally, these visual effects are very expensive. The result is that there have been a few times when budget considerations have forced our producers to find an excuse — any excuse — to have the captain take the ship down to impulse so that we can avoid the extra expense.*

7.0 UTILITIES AND AUXILIARY SYSTEMS

7.1 UTILITIES

The *Galaxy* class *Enterprise* internal distribution infrastructure includes a number of related systems whose purpose is the distribution of vital commodities throughout the spacecraft. Although these commodities vary widely in the nature of distribution hardware, all require complex interconnections throughout the volume of the spacecraft, and nearly all are of sufficient criticality to require one or more redundant backup distribution networks.

MAJOR UTILITIES NETWORKS

These utilities distribution networks include:

• **Power.** Power transmission for onboard systems is accomplished by a network of microwave power transmission waveguides known as the electro plasma system (EPS). Major power supplies derive microwave power from the warp propulsion power conduits and the main impulse engines. Additional feeds draw power from the saucer module impulse engines as well as a number of auxiliary fusion generators. A secondary power distribution system provides electrical power for specialized requirements.

• **Optical Data Network (ODN).** Data transmission is accomplished with a network of multiplexed optical monocrystal microfibers. A series of five redundant major optical trunks link the two main computer cores in the primary hull, and an additional set of trunks link these to the third core in the engineering section. Any individual trunk is designed to be able to handle the total data load of the ship's basic operating systems. Major ODN trunks also provide information links to the 380 optical subprocessors located throughout the ship. These subprocessors improve system response time by distributing system load and provide a measure of redundancy in case of major system failure. From these subprocessors, additional ODN links connect to each individual control panel or display surface. Two secondary optical data networks provide protected linkages to key systems and stations; these backup systems are physically separated from the primary system and from each other.

• **Atmosphere.** Breathable atmosphere is distributed throughout the habitable volume of the ship by means of two independent networks of air-conditioning ducts that recirculate the breathable atmosphere after reprocessing. Switching nodes permit alternate system segments to be employed in the event part of one primary system is unavailable.

• **Water.** Potable water for drinking and cooling is distributed by two independent conduit networks. These networks run in parallel with wastewater return conduits to the four water recycling and reprocessing facilities located on Decks 6, 13, and 24.

• **Solid waste disposal.** Linear induction utility conduits are used to convey solid waste to reprocessing facilities on Decks 9, 13, and 34. Such waste is automatically separated into mechanically and chemically recyclable material, with the remainder stored for matter synthesis (replicator) recycling. Hazardous wastes are immediately reprocessed.

• **Transporter beam conduits.** A series of high energy waveguides serves to connect each transporter chamber to its associated pattern buffer tank and then to the various external transporter emitter arrays. Because any given personnel or cargo transporter may need to be linked to any of the seventeen external emitter arrays, this network must provide for any interconnection permutation.

• **Replicator and food service conduits.** Similar to the transporter beam conduits, these waveguides connect the food service and general replicator headends to replicator terminals throughout the ship.

• **Structural integrity field (SIF) power conduits.** Force field generators for the structural integrity field are located on Decks 11 and 32. Two parallel molybdenum-jacked triphase waveguide conduit networks distribute the field energy to the SIF conductivity elements built into the spacecraft framework. Crossovers between the Saucer Module and Engineering Section permit field generators in one hull to feed the entire spacecraft if necessary.

• **IDF power conduits.** Inertial damping field generators are located on Decks 11 and 33. Two parallel molybdenum-

7.1.1 Major utilities trunks

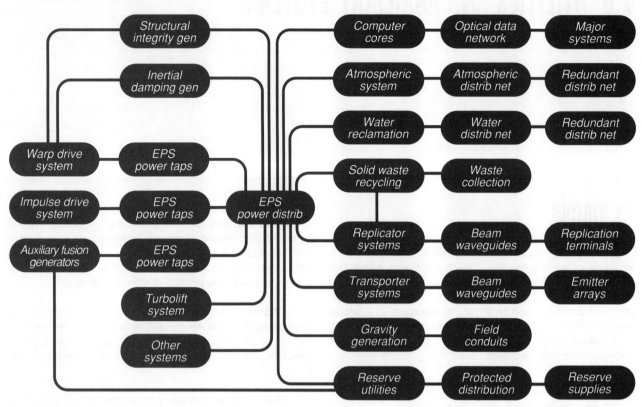

jacked triphase waveguide conduit networks, similar to the SIF network, distribute the field energy throughout the vehicle. Crossovers between the Saucer Module and Battle Section permit field generators in one hull to feed the entire spacecraft if necessary.

• **Synthetic gravity field bleed.** Although the ship's synthetic gravity field is created by the gravity generators located thoughout the ship, a network of forcefield conduits is employed to allow translation of excess inertial potential to other parts of the ship. This process is computer controlled to optimize gravitational stability and subspace field differential. Any inertial potential in excess of system capacity is automatically bled off into the structural integrity field system.

• **Cryogenic fluid transfer.** This refers to a number of insulated piping trunks that provide for intraship transfer of such cryogenic fluids as liquid helium. Oxygen for breathing gas replenishment is transferred to atmospheric processing modules in liquid form by means of the cryogenic fluid transfer system.

• **Deuterium fuel transfer.** Two 45 cm insulated conduits provide for transfer of liquid deuterium between the primary deuterium tank and the impulse propulsion system. Additional insulated conduits connect the primary deuterium tank with the warp propulsion system, and the Saucer Module impulse engines and its associated fuel storage tankage (using a cross-feed conduit connecting the two sections). Smaller 18.5 cm insulated conduits connect various auxiliary storage tanks and the auxiliary fusion power generators.

• **Turboelevator personnel transport system.** This includes the actual turboshaft tubes through which the inductively driven turbolift cars travel throughout the habitable volume of the ship, as well as the dedicated EPS power trunks and ODN links that support the system.

• **Reserve utilities distribution.** This refers to a low-capacity, independent system of atmosphere, power, data, and water distribution networks. These systems serve as backups for use in the event service is disrupted from primary systems. Depending on load factors, this reserve system has a capacity of approximately thirty-six hours.

• **Protected utilities distribution.** Another set of redundant utilities trunks, this system provides limited atmosphere, power, and data to critical areas of the ship as well as

---

Dick Brownfield, Star Trek *special mechanical effects whiz whose work on the* Enterprise *dates back as far as* Star Trek's *first pilot episode in 1964, tells us that some of the conduits and pipes seen on the original* Enterprise *sets were labeled with the term GNDN. Dick tells us that this was a joke with him and set decorator John Dwyer (another veteran of both versions of* Star Trek) *to inform the discerning starship crew member that a dummy pipe "Goes Nowhere and Does Nothing."*

to emergency environmental support shelter areas. Also incorporated into this network are low-capacity superconductive electrical power distribution cables for critical backup systems.

ADDITIONAL UTILITIES SYSTEMS

Additional utilities systems provide support for the ship's service infrastructure. These include:

• **Umbilical resupply connect ports and associated systems.** Principal among these are the resupply umbilical connect clusters located along the spine of the Engineering section. These include provisions for deuterium fuel loading, cryogenic oxygen resupply, gaseous atmospheric support, fresh water, wastewater off-loading, EPS external support, external synthetic gravity support, and external SIF/IDF support. Some of these umbilicals are used for resupply, the remainder allow external support systems (such as those available at a starbase) to carry the load of key systems, allowing the ship's systems to be shut down for servicing (See: 15.7).

• **Jefferies Tubes.** This refers to a system of access tunnels and utilities corridors that carry much of the various utilities conduits and waveguides. The Jefferies Tube network covers the entire volume of the ship, providing access to utilities trunks and circuitry. Also located within these tubes are a variety of maintenance and testing points that allow the performance of various systems to be physically measured at key points throughout the ship.

• **Corridor access panels.** Additional utilities distribution is provided by a network of passageways located within (and running parallel to) the personnel corridor walls. These corridor utility paths are accessible from within the corridor by removing the wall panels. Also located within certain corridor access panels are various emergency support packages, including emergency atmospheric and power supply modules, firefighting equipment, disaster medical supply kits, and environment suits (See: 13.4).

• **Auxiliary fusion generators.** Utilities systems include a number of small auxiliary fusion generators that provide power when the warp and impulse reactors are inactive. These fusion generators also provide supplemental power when needed and are a key element of contingency operations.

Jefferies Tubes are named in honor of Matt Jefferies, art director of the first Star Trek *series and the original designer of the starship* Enterprise. *The term is a carryover from the original series.*

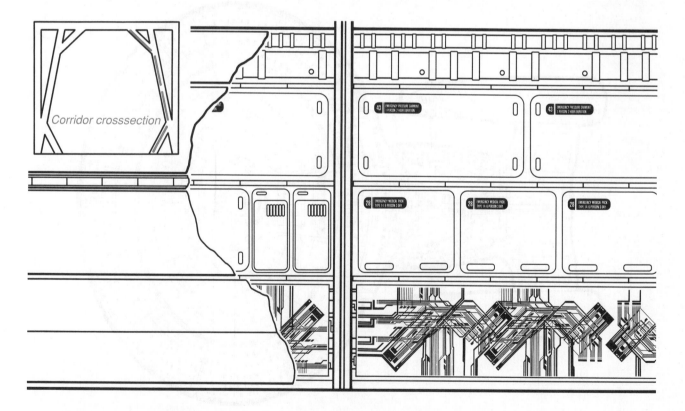

7.1.2 Corridor utilities and equipment lockers

7.2 EXTERIOR CONNECT HARDPOINTS

During its predicted one-hundred-year operational life-time, a *Galaxy* class starship is expected to put in for maintenance and upgrade layovers at starbases and repair docks approximately two hundred times. A typical starbase visit will include periodic component swapouts, structural scans by nondestructive testing methods, systems upgrades, and consumables resupply. Many of these functions are carried out though a series of dedicated umbilicals, loading bays, and access hatches located over the entire vehicle.

The exterior connections were designed into the starship to take advantage of certain existing docking mechanisms originally created for the *Ambassador* class and integrate new automated arm and end effector devices. Most of the consumables supplied to the ship are accepted through twenty-four transfer ports located along the structural spine of the Battle Section. Distinct one-way-fit supply tunnels mate with the spine ports, assuring that fluids, gases, and dried solids remain separate and are routed to the proper storage compartments. Most raw materials destined for eventual replicator reassembly are transferred in this manner and placed in large bulk holding tanks (See: 7.1).

Exterior connections for numerous other ship systems are located within the spine, including the electro plasma system, optical data network, main computers, structural integrity field, inertial damping field, and aft torpedo launcher. Much of the general "health" of the *Enterprise* can be gauged through these links, and appropriate preventative maintenance can be performed to bring the ship into homeostasis.

Fill, vent, and purge lines to the primary deuterium tankage is accessed through eight connectors in the spine. Complete tank cleaning and inspection are accomplished by starbase-assisted pumps, followed by deuterium refilling. Complete antimatter tankage refurbishment is performed only at certain starbases with refining or tanker transport capabilities. The antimatter ports and warp engine core access panel are located exterior to Deck 42 on the ventral surface of the Battle Section.

Bulk cargo is loaded through six large iris and flexible-planar bay doors located in the aft hull undercut, the forward ventral surface of the Battle Section, and the ventral surface of the Saucer Module. These doors open onto eighteen cargo holding and distribution spaces; materiel is routed to smaller storage bays for later use during flight. Certain internal cargo bays not serviced by exterior doors or cargo turbolifts are accommodated by large cargo transporter pads. Items requiring special handling, such as medical supplies, can be stored in these bays for rapid dispersal by transporter and antigrav pallets.

Personnel transfers are accomplished through four pressurized gangways. Two large elliptical tunnel connectors can

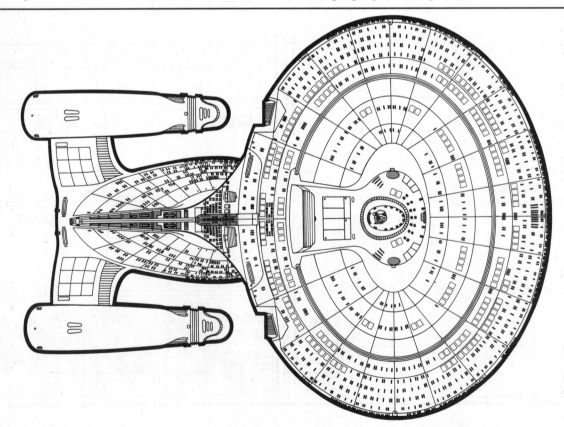

7.2.1 Exterior connect hardpoints

be deployed vertically from the dorsal surface of the Saucer Module. Most large-scale crew movements take place at these points, plus two docking collars on Deck 25, aft of the forward photon torpedo launcher. Starbase gangways are standardized with adaptable docking collar interfaces. There are two additional crossover points to starbase spacedock facilities in the form of turbolift pass-throughs, allowing turbolift modules to move directly to the base from the ship.

7.3 REACTION CONTROL SYSTEM

In its normal docked configuration, the USS *Enterprise* achieves low-velocity attitude and translational control through the use of six main and six auxiliary reaction control engines for fine adjustments. The reaction control system (RCS) is designed primarily for sublight operations involving station-keeping, drift-mode three-axis stabilization, and space dock maneuvering.

The RCS is divided into two parts corresponding to the two sections of the total starship. The Saucer Module RCS consists of four main and four auxiliary engines located on the hull edge; the two remaining main engines and ten venier thrusters make up the Battle Section RCS and are located outboard of the main deflector dish. In the docked configuration, both systems are cross-commanded by the main computer propulsion controller (MCPC) to provide the required guidance and navigation inputs. In separated flight modes, the Saucer Module continues to run modified MCPC routines, while the Battle Section switches over to its single computer core guidance and navigation (G&N) software.

Each main RCS engine consists of a gas-fusion reaction chamber, a magnetohydrodynamic (MHD) energy field trap, and upper and lower vectored-thrust exhaust nozzles. Deuterium fuel for each fusion chamber is stored in six immedi-

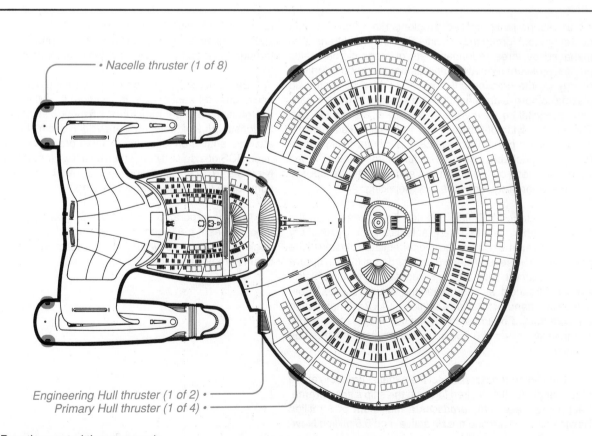

• *Nacelle thruster (1 of 8)*

Engineering Hull thruster (1 of 2) •
Primary Hull thruster (1 of 4) •

7.3.1 Reaction control thruster quads

7.3.2 RCS thruster quad assembly

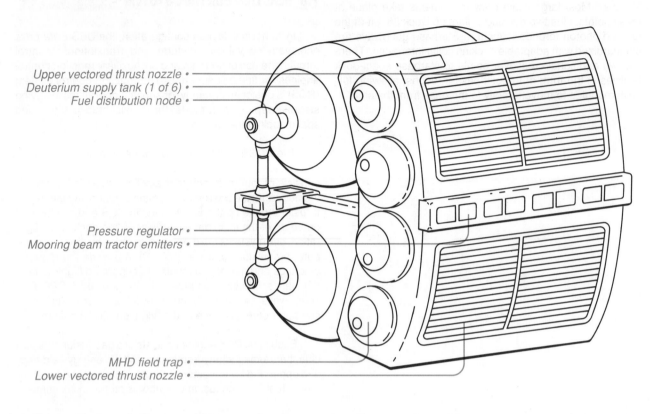

Upper vectored thrust nozzle •
Deuterium supply tank (1 of 6) •
Fuel distribution node •

Pressure regulator •
Mooring beam tractor emitters •

MHD field trap •
Lower vectored thrust nozzle •

ate-use supply tanks and tied to replenish lines from the main deuterium tank group in the Battle Section. Fuel transfer is managed by three redundant sets of magnetic-peristaltic pumps, pressure regulators, and distribution nodes. Ignition energy for the reaction chamber is provided by a step-up plasma compression generator, and supplied through a standard capacitance tap by the ship's power distribution net. The reaction chamber measures 3.1 meters in diameter and is constructed of hafnium carbide 0.2 meters thick, with a 0.21 cm replaceable inner wall of duranium tritanide. It can withstand a total of 400,000 firings and 5,500 hours' operating time before requiring inner wall servicing.

A two-stage MHD field trap lies downstream from the fusion chamber. The first stage acts as an energy recovery device and returns some of the undifferentiated plasma to the power net. The second stage performs partial throttle operations, in concert with fuel flow regulators, to control the exhaust products as they enter the thrust nozzle. Both stages are manufactured as a single unit 4 x 2 x 2 meters and are constructed of tungsten bormanite. The plasma return channels are rated at 6,750 hours before the inlets must be replaced.

The vectored nozzles direct the exhaust products at the proper angle for the desired force on the ship's spaceframe. Each nozzle assembly produces a maximum of 3 million Newtons thrust with one nozzle active, and 5.5 million New-

tons with both nozzles active. Kreigerium plate valves regulate the relative proportions of exhaust products flowing through the upper and lower nozzle components.

Each auxiliary engine consists of a microfusion chamber and vectored-thrust nozzle, but without the MHD trap. The microfusion chamber measures 1.5 meters in diameter and is constructed of hafnium duranide 8.5 cm thick. Each auxiliary engine channels its exhaust products through the main RCS nozzle and can generate a total thrust of 450,000 Newtons. The auxiliary engines are rated for 4,500 hours' cumulative firing time before servicing.

Also incorporated into the RCS quads are precision mooring beam tractor emitters used for close-quarters and docking maneuvers when starbase-equivalent mooring beams are not available.

7.4 NAVIGATIONAL DEFLECTOR

Although the density of the interstellar medium is extremely low, significant hazards to navigation exist, especially for a starship traveling at relativistic or warp velocities. Among these are micrometeoroid particulates, as well as the much rarer (but more hazardous) larger objects such as asteroids. Even the extremely tenuous stray hydrogen atoms of the interstellar medium itself can be a dangerous source of friction at sufficient velocities.

HARDWARE

The heart of the navigational deflector system is three redundant high power graviton polarity source generators located on Deck 34. Each of these generators consists of a cluster of six 128 MW graviton polarity sources feeding a pair of 550 millicochrane subspace field distortion amplifiers. The flux energy output of these generators is directed and focused by a series of powerful subspace field coils.

The main deflector dish consists of a duranium framework onto which is attached the actual emitter array, constructed of a series of molybdenum-duranium mesh panels that radiate the flux energy output. The dish is steerable under automatic computer control by means of four high-torque electrofluidic servos capable of deflecting the dish up to 7.2° from the ship's Z axis. Phase-interference techniques are used to achieve fine aiming of the deflector beam, using modulation control of the emitter array. Subspace field coils just upstream of the actual deflector emitter dish are used to shape the deflector beam into two primary components. First, a series of five nested parabolic shields extend nearly two kilometers ahead of the ship. These low-power fields are relatively static and are used to deflect the stray hydrogen atoms of the interstellar medium as well as any submicron particulates that may have escaped the deflector beam. The navigational deflector, also controlled by the subspace field coils, is a powerful tractor/deflector that sweeps thousands of kilometers ahead of the ship, pushing aside larger objects that may present a collision hazard.

LONG-RANGE SENSORS

Because the main deflector dish radiates significant amounts of both subspace and electromagnetic radiation, it can have detrimental effects on the performance of many sensors. For this reason, the long-range sensor array is located directly behind the main deflector, so that the primary axis of both systems are nearly coincident. This arrangement permits the long-range sensors to "look" directly through the axis of the fields.

The long-range sensor array is a key element of the navigational deflector system because it is used to provide detection and tracking of objects in the ship's flight path. The forward sensor array can also be used to provide this informa-

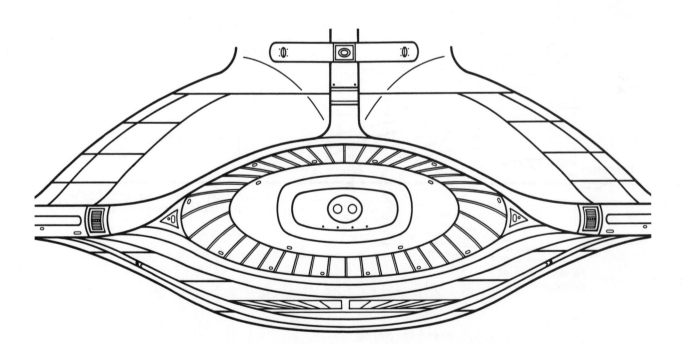

7.4.1 Navigational deflector

tion, but doing so results in lesser detection ranges and may use sensor elements better assigned to scientific use.

The molybdenum-duranium mesh of the main deflector emitters is designed with areas of 0.52 cm perforation patterns so as to be transparent to the long-range sensor array. Note that certain instruments, notably the subspace field stress and gravimetric distortion sensors, will not yield usable data when deflector output exceeds a certain level (typically 55%, depending on sensor resolution mode and field-of-view. See: 10.2).

OPERATIONAL CONSIDERATIONS

At normal impulse speeds (up to 0.25c), navigational deflector output can usually be kept at about 27 MW (with momentary surge reserve of 52 MW). Warp velocities up to Warp 8 require up to 80% of normal output with surge reserve of 675,000 MW. Velocities exceeding Warp Factor 8 require the use of two deflector generators operating in phase sync, and velocities greater than Warp 9.2 require all three deflector generators in order to maintain adequate surge reserve.

Navigational deflector operation is somewhat more complex when the Bussard ramscoop is in use because the navigational deflector actually pushes away the interstellar hydrogen that the collector seeks to attract (See: 5.6). In such cases, field manipulation is employed to create small "holes" in the navigational deflector shields, permitting the rarefied

7.4.3 Saucer deflector

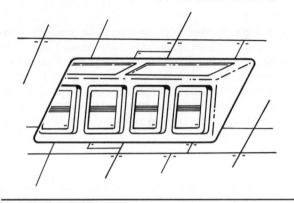

interstellar hydrogen to be directed into the ramscoop's magnetic fields.

SAUCER DEFLECTOR

When the *Enterprise* is operating in Separated Flight Mode, the main deflector obviously services the Battle Section. The Saucer Module is equipped with four fixed-focus navigational deflectors for use in such cases. These medium power units also serve as a backup to the main deflector when the ship is connected, and are located on the underside of the Saucer Module, just fore of the lower transporter emitter arrays.

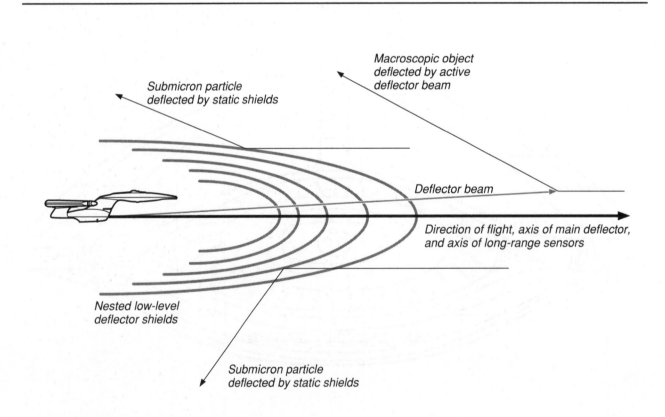

7.4.2 Navigational deflector shield configuration

7.5 TRACTOR BEAMS

Starfleet missions sometimes require direct manipulation of relatively large objects in proximity to a starship. Such operations can take the form of towing another ship, modifying the speed or trajectory of a small asteroid, or holding a piece of instrumentation at a fixed position relative to the ship. The execution of such missions generally requires the use of tractor beam remote manipulators.

Tractor emitters employ superimposed subspace/graviton force beams whose interference patterns are focused on a remote target, resulting in significant spatial stress being applied on the target. By controlling the focal point and interference patterns, it is possible to use this stress pattern to draw an object toward the ship. Conversely, it is also possible to invert the interference patterns and move the focal point to actually push an object.

EMITTERS

Tractor beam emitters are located at key positions on the ship's exterior hull, permitting objects at almost any relative bearing to be manipulated. Key among these are the two main tractor beam emitters, located fore and aft along the keel of the Engineering Hull as well as a third main emitter located on the forward surface of the interconnecting dorsal. Additional emitters are located near each shuttlebay for use in shuttle

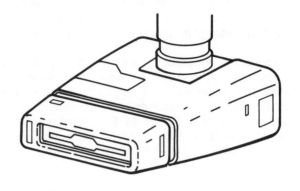

7.5.2 Typical tractor emitter

landing maneuvers. Mooring tractor beam emitters, used when the ship is in dock, are located at each reaction control thruster quad.

The main tractor beam emitters are built around two variable phase 16 MW graviton polarity sources, each feeding two 450 millicochrane subspace field amplifiers. Phase accuracy is within 2.7 arc-seconds per millisecond, necessary for precise interference pattern control. Secondary tractor beam emitters have lesser performance ratings. Main tractor beam emitters are directly mounted to primary structural members of the ship's framework. This is because of the significant mechanical stress and inertial potential imbalance

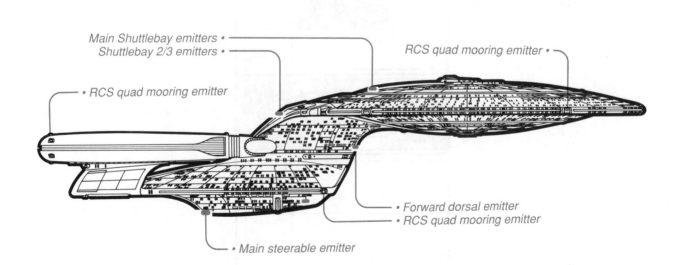

Main Shuttlebay emitters •
Shuttlebay 2/3 emitters •

RCS quad mooring emitter •

• RCS quad mooring emitter

• Forward dorsal emitter
• RCS quad mooring emitter

• Main steerable emitter

7.5.1 Tractor beam emitters

created by tractor beam usage. Additional structural reinforcement and inertial potential cancellation is provided by tying the tractor emitter into the structural integrity field (SIF) network by means of molybdenum-jacketed waveguides.

Effective tractor beam range varies with payload mass and desired delta-v (change in relative velocity). Assuming a nominal 5 m/sec^2 delta-v, the primary tractor emitters can be used with a payload approaching 7,500,000 metric tonnes at less than 1,000 meters. Conversely, that same delta-v can be imparted to an object massing about one metric tonne at ranges approaching 20,000 kilometers.

The original design of the new Enterprise *showed only one tractor beam emitter, at the base of the Engineering Section's fantail. At the time the location made sense, since the main application of tractor beams is to tow other ships. As the show progressed, however, we had more than one episode in which that emitter location was not visible in ship exterior scenes calling for tractor beams to be used. As a result, our visual effects staff has "added" a number of additional emitters to the ship. With hindsight, the new emitters do seem to make sense given the fact that the* Enterprise *sometimes needs to move objects that are not directly below and astern. Our television starship, like its imaginary counterpart, continues to evolve.*

7.6 REPLICATOR SYSTEMS

Recent advances in transporter-based molecular synthesis have resulted in a number of significant spinoff technologies. Chief among these are transporter-based replicators. These devices permit replication of virtually any inanimate object with incredible fidelity and relatively low energy cost.

There are two main replication systems on board the *Enterprise.* These are the food synthesizers and the hardware replicators. The food replicators are optimized for a finer degree of resolution because of the necessity of accurately replicating the chemical composition of foodstuffs. Hardware replicators, on the other hand, are generally tuned to a lower resolution for greater energy efficiency and lower memory matrix requirements. A number of specially modified food replication terminals are used in sickbay and in various science labs for synthesis of certain pharmaceuticals and other scientific supplies.

These replicator system headends are located on Deck 12 in the Saucer Module and on Deck 34 in the Engineering Section. These systems operate by using a phase-transition coil chamber in which a measured quantity of raw material is dematerialized in a manner similar to that of a standard transporter. Instead of using a molecular imaging scanner to determine the patterns of the raw stock, however, a quantum

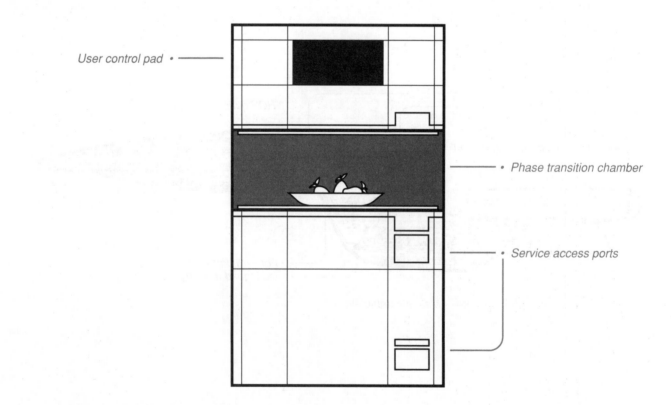

User control pad •

• Phase transition chamber

• Service access ports

7.6.1 Food replicator terminal (typical)

geometry transformational matrix field is used to modify the matter stream to conform to a digitally stored molecular pattern matrix. The matter stream is then routed through a network of waveguide conduits that direct the signal to a replicator terminal at which the desired article is materialized within another phase transition chamber.

In order to minimize replicator power requirements, raw stock for food replicators is stored in the form of a sterilized organic particulate suspension that has been formulated to statistically require the least quantum manipulation to replicate most finished foodstuffs (See: 13.5).

REPLICATION VERSUS STORAGE

The use of replicators dramatically reduces the requirement for carrying and storing both foodstuffs and spare parts. The limiting factor is the energy cost of molecular synthesis versus the cost of carrying an object onboard the ship. In the case of foodstuffs, the cost of maintaining a large volume of perishable supplies becomes prohibitive, especially when the cost of food preparation is included. Here, the energy cost of molecular synthesis is justified, especially when one considers the dramatic mass savings involved with extensive recycling of organic material.

On the other hand, certain types of commonly used spare parts and supplies are not economical for replication. In such cases, the items in question are used in sufficient quantity that it is more economical to store finished products than to spend the energy to carry raw materials and synthesize the finished product on demand. Additionally, significant stores of critical spares and consumables are maintained for possible use during Alert situations when power for replication systems may be severely restricted or unavailable.

REPLICATION LIMITS

The chief limitation of all transporter-based replicators is the resolution at which the molecular matrix patterns are stored. While transporters (which operate in realtime) recreate objects at quantum-level resolution suitable for lifeforms, replicators store and re-create objects at the much simpler molecular-level resolution, which is not suitable for living beings.

Because of the massive amount of computer memory required to store even the simplest object, it is impossible to record each molecule individually. Instead, extensive data compression and averaging techniques are used. Such techniques reduce memory storage required for molecular patterns by factors approaching 2.7×10^9. The resulting single-bit inaccuracies do not significantly impact the quality of most reproduced objects, but preclude the use of replicator technology to re-create living objects. Single-bit molecular errors could have severely detrimental effects on living DNA molecules and neural activity. Cumulative effects have been shown to closely resemble radiation-induced damage.

The data themselves are subject to significant accuracy limits. It is not feasible to record or store quantum electron-state information, nor can Brownian motion data be accurately re-created. Doing so would represent another billion-fold increase in the memory required to store a given pattern. This means that even if each atom of every molecule were reproduced, it is not feasible to accurately re-create the electron shell activity patterns or the atomic motions that determine the dynamics of the biochemical activity of consciousness and thought.

8.0 COMMUNICATIONS

8.1 INTRASHIP COMMUNICATIONS

Communications aboard the USS *Enterprise* take two basic forms, voice and data transmissions. Both are handled by the onboard computer system and dedicated peripheral hardware nodes. Though those sections of the computer normally allocated to communications tasks are named the communications system, the metaphor of the human central nervous system is more applicable in this situation. The sheer mass of adaptable links radiating outward from the main computers virtually assures that all information within the spacecraft will be rapidly transmitted to the correct destination, and will be received with little or no detectable loss of that information. While the multitude of communications functions are directly traceable to the same hardware, the operating modes and protocols around which they are based are distinctly different and are worth noting.

SYSTEM CONFIGURATION

The hardware configuration for dedicated intraship communications involves a minimum of 12,000 allocated data line sets and terminal node devices distributed throughout the starship, in parallel with the pure hardware telemetry links of the optical data network (ODN). This is the primary route for voice and data signals. An equal number of radio frequency (RF)-based terminal node devices are distributed throughout the ship as a first backup layer. A second backup layer runs parallel to the electro plasma system and consists of 7,550 kilometers of copper-yttrium-barium superconducting strands. This layer utilizes the same terminal node devices.

Each terminal node device is a disk measuring 11.5 cm in diameter and 2 cm thick. The casing is constructed of molded polykeiyurium, the internal arrangement consisting of a voice section and a data relay section. The voice section contains an analog-to-digital voice pickup/speaker wafer, preprocessor amplifier, optical fiber modulation input/output subcircuit, and digital-to-analog return processor. The data relay section contains two nested circuits consisting of a standard subspace transceiver assembly (STA), found most prominently in Starfleet-issue communicator badges, and short-range RF pickup and emitter. Handheld devices and transportable devices not hardwired to the ODN send and receive data via this part of the terminal node. While duplicate RF pickups exist in the backup system, their function in the primary system is to manipulate data signals for transmission over the optical fibers.

OPERATION

During voice operations, the normal procedure involves a crew member stating his or her name, plus the party or ship area being called, in a form that can be understood by the computer for proper routing. Examples: "Dr. Selar, this is the captain," or "Ensign Nelson to Engineering." The artificial intelligence (AI) routines in the main computer listen for intraship calls, perform analyses on the message opening content, attempt to locate the message recipient, and then activate the audio speakers at the recipient's location.

During the initial message routing, there may be a slight processing delay until the computer has heard the entire name of the recipient and located same. From that point on, all transmissions are realtime. When both parties have concluded their conversation, the channel may be actively closed with the word "out," which will be detected in context by the computer. If both parties discontinue without formally breaking the channel, and no other contextual cues have been offered to keep the line open, the computer will continue listening for ten seconds, and then close the line. When using the communicator badge to initiate a call aboard ship, the computer will consider the badge-tap to be force of habit, or simply a confirmatory signal.

In the event that the recipient is unavailable for a routine voice call, a system flag will be set in the computer and will alert the recipient that a waiting message has been stored. Emergency voice transmissions are prioritized and controlled by command authority instructions within the computer, and can be redefined by command personnel according to the situation.

During most Alert conditions, the communications system is automatically switched over to high-speed operations optimized to afford the Bridge uninterruptable links to the rest of the ship for contact with other departments and assessment

8.1.1 Intraship communications

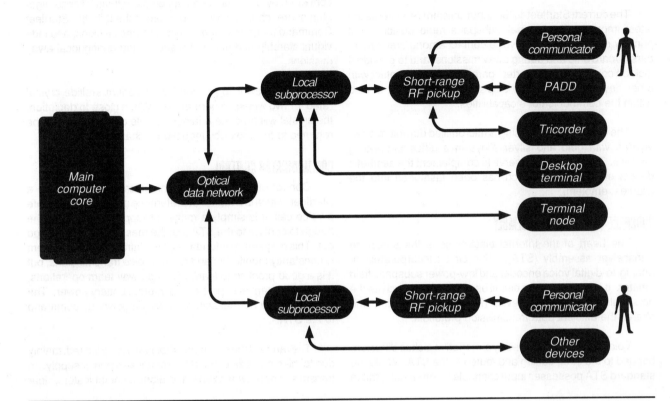

of possible damage. At this time, routine channel operations are disabled (See: 8.2).

Data transmissions may be established between any standard Starfleet hardware units equipped with RF or STA devices, either by manual keypresses or by vocally commanding the computer to handle the data transfers. In most cases, the computer will automatically execute the desired functions; on occasion, the computer may request identification keypresses for specific pieces of hardware, usually for verification of device type, data transmission protocols, or sequencing of multiple devices.

During both voice and data transmissions, channels may be secured by either manual inputs or vocal request, depending on the respective locations of the parties or devices involved.

8.2 PERSONAL COMMUNICATOR

The current Starfleet-issue communicator represents the latest improvement in small subspace radio devices. Its primary role is to maintain voice contact among crew members aboard ship and during away missions, and to provide a lock-on contact for transporter operations. Voice contact with other devices, such as the ship's main computers, is also within the communicator's capabilities.

The communicator casing is micromilled duranium over-layered with gold and silver alloys in a diffusion-bonding process. The metal alloys serve to complement the aesthetic design of the device, which has been fashioned into the Starfleet emblem.

SUBSPACE TRANSCEIVER ASSEMBLY

The heart of the internal electronics is the subspace transceiver assembly (STA). This circuit incorporates an analog-to-digital voice encoder and low-power subspace field emitter. It is also the same circuit used in devices such as the personal access display device (PADD) and tricorder, and shares the efficient data transmission protocols.

Voice inputs are received by a monofilm pickup diffusion-bonded to the inner casing and routed to the STA. While the standard STA possesses input channels for other data, these are not active in the communicator. As all Starfleet communications are normally encrypted, the voice signal pulses are converted by a series of encryption algorithms. These algorithms are changed on a random schedule by Starfleet Command for galaxywide subspace transmissions, and individual starship codes may be substituted during local away missions.

Battery power is provided by a sarium krellide crystal rated for two weeks in normal use. When close to depletion, the crystal will produce a faintly audible oscillation; it can be returned to full power by induction recharging.

COMMUNICATOR CONTROL

Control of the personal communicator while aboard a Starfleet vessel is a matter of preference and habit. To initiate a voice call, it is simply a matter of tapping the front of the badge to confirm to the STA that the message is meant to go out. This may seem redundant, as the intraship comm system is constantly monitoring and routing voice transmissions, but it is a good practice to learn. During away team operations, the tap is essential to preserving internal battery power. The tap activates a dermal sensor to relay a power up command to the STA.

The range of the communicator is severely limited, mainly due to the small size of the STA emitter and power supply. In transmissions between two stand-alone communicators, clear

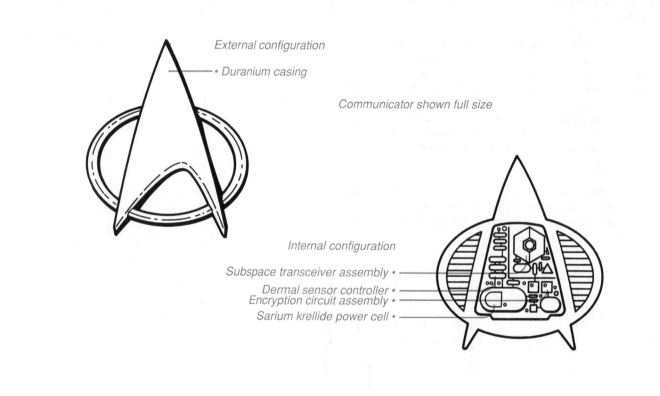

External configuration
• Duranium casing

Communicator shown full size

Internal configuration

Subspace transceiver assembly •
Dermal sensor controller •
Encryption circuit assembly •
Sarium krellide power cell •

8.2.1 Personal communicator assembly

8.2.2 Personal communicator schematic

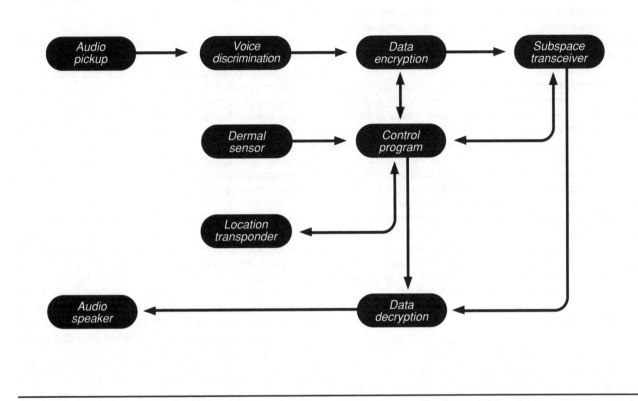

voice signals will propagate only 500 kilometers. This is a tiny fraction of the 40,000 km required to contact an orbiting spacecraft, so it is the spacecraft that must become the active partner in order to receive the communicator's lower-power signals, and transmit correspondingly high-power signals to the communicator's receiver.

The communicator is a line-of-sight device during away missions. Its planetside range may be improved if the magnetic field value is below 0.9 gauss, or mean geologic density is less than 5.56 g/cc.

Various EM factors will affect voice and transporter lock. Most remedies to comm interference will take place on the spacecraft side, as there are few user-adjustable controls within the communicator. In the event of loss of transporter lock, other ship sensors can be brought into play to locate Starfleet crew members, though the process can take longer to complete.

USER ID SECURITY

For security purposes, the communicator is a personalized Starfleet device that can be programmed to respond to the individual crew member's bioelectrical field and temperature profiles using the built-in dermal sensor. If an attempt is made to operate an appropriately programmed device by another crew member without security override authority, the

communicator will fail to activate. During benign situations, security codes are changed every five days. During emergency situations, or when Away Team members are involved in planetside operations, codes are changed on a random schedule at least once every twenty-four hours.

8.3 SHIP-TO-GROUND COMMUNICATIONS

The next higher organizational level for the overall communications system involves contact and information exchange between the starship and planetside personnel and remote equipment.

Communications external to the spacecraft are routed from the main computers to the radio frequency (RF) and subspace radio system nodes. While the term "radio" is something of an anachronism, since Starfleet communications more often than not involve visual information, it nevertheless continues to describe the basic function of the system. Normal radio frequencies are set aside as backups to the primary subspace bands, though RF is in continued use by numerous cultures maintaining relations with the Federation, and Starfleet vessels must sometimes rely on this older system when subspace bands prove unusable due to stellar or geological phenomena, or when hardware difficulties arise with either the host or remote sides. Such space-normal radio communications are, of course, restricted by the speed of light, resulting in severe time and distance limitations.

INSTALLED HARDWARE

The RF section consists of a network of fifteen triply redundant transceiver assemblies cross-connected by ODN and copper-yttrium 2153 hardlines and linked to the main computer comm processors. All are partially imbedded within the structural hull material at degree and distance intervals about the starship for maximum antenna coverage and manageable antenna timesharing loads.

Each transceiver assembly is a hexagonal solid measuring three meters across the faces and one-half meter in thickness. Each consists of separate voice and data subprocessors, eight six-stage variable amplifiers, realtime signal analysis shunts, and input/output signal conditioners at the hull antenna level. RF section power is obtained from Type III taps from the electro plasma system. The basic limitations of the RF section stem from the c velocity limit, and a normal useful range at moderate power on the order of 5.2 Astronomical Units (A.U.). RF frequencies directed through

the steerable central component of the main deflector can extend the useful range to some 1000 A.U., though no practical applications of this power have yet been demonstrated.

The subspace transceiver specifications, in proportion, are roughly akin to the warp propulsion system being compared to its less powerful impulse cousin. Approximately one hundred times more energy is required to drive voice and data signals across the threshold into the faster subspace frequencies, and even when applied to relatively short distances, the transmission reliability climbs dramatically. As with the RF section, small transceivers such as the standard subspace transceiver assembly (STA) in the personnel communicators need not emit great amounts of power if the large transmitters and receivers remain on the starship.

A series of twenty medium-power subspace transceivers are imbedded within the starship hull at various locations to provide communications coverage similar to that of the RF units. Each triply redundant device is contained within a trapezoidal solid measuring 1.5 x 2 meters by 1 meter in thickness. The system is powered by Type II electro plasma system (EPS) taps with a total maximum power load across the twenty nodes of 1.43×10^2 MW. Each transceiver consists of voice and data processors, EPS power modulation conditioners, subspace field coil subassemblies and directional focusing arrays, and related control hardware. Signal handoff from the optical data network is done with a combination of realtime and sequence anticipation AI routines for maximum intelligibility, given the FTL nature of the outgoing and incoming subspace signals.

APPLICATIONS

Communications between the starship and a destination typically 38,000 km to 60,000 km away from the antennae are handled by the above-mentioned radio systems. Situations encountered cover a broad range, but most notably include discussions with planetside governments, communication and control of Away Team operations, local and regional crisis management, data collection from remote and active occupied research stations, shuttlecraft departure and approach terminal guidance, and Starfleet search and rescue. The

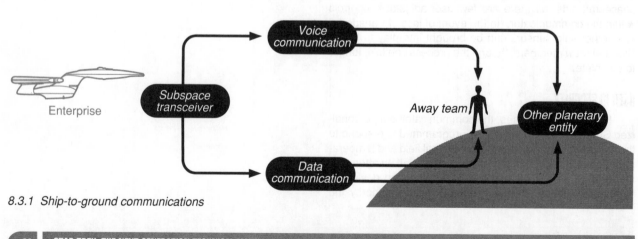

8.3.1 Ship-to-ground communications

subspace transceiver network is the active system linked to the transporter for personnel locator and coordinate lock-on functions. A minimum of three transceivers covering a given portion of the spacecraft sky coverage must be available for reliable transporter lock. The maximum reliable distance for routine transport is 40,000 km, owing to the median matter stream blooming tolerance of 0.005 arc-seconds, though subspace communications by the medium-power network can extend to some 60,000 km.

Normal contact with the starship, if externally initiated, is divided into two basic types: Starfleet personnel, especially those persons directly assigned to the ship, and non-Starfleet agents. Away Team members will call directly to the Bridge or other active departments during the course of their work. Normal contact from outside agents will be held by Security for presentation to the captain or other senior officers. Emergency transmissions will usually be passed without computer delay for appropriate action.

Standard encryption/decryption, plus enhanced security encryption protocols, are handled by FTL processors within the main computers. Starfleet encryption algorithms are rotated and updated on a random schedule. Multiple private key portions are retained with the starship computers, and the public portions are transmitted to Starfleet-issue hardware, such as handheld instrumentation, communicators, personal access display devices, and other pieces of expendable gear vulnerable to possible capture by Threat forces. Calling for a secure channel on either the spacecraft or remote side will be detected by the main computer, which will place higher encryption schemes in standby mode to await confirmation by command personnel.

With certain non-Starfleet subspace transmission protocols, particularly for data burst receiving, protocol matching delays may be forced by the computer until matrix translation values are calculated and applied in realtime. True Starfleet burst modes, as designed into the standard and medical tricorders, allow rapid emergency transmissions of stored information via the subspace system. Single antenna coverage is acceptable, though the physical layout of the antenna groups assures at least two arrays will be visible if the spacecraft is in line-of-sight of a transmitter.

8.4 SHIP-TO-SHIP COMMUNICATIONS

The most energetic and far-reaching communications possible from the USS *Enterprise* encompass ship-to-ship and ship-to-starbase transmissions. These will typically span from hundreds of Astronomical Units to tens of light years, far beyond the capabilities of the lower-power subspace transceiver units already described.

The communications system designed into the starship comprises ten ultra-high power subspace transceivers. Each is a trapezoidal solid 6 x 4 meters by 3 meters thick, set below the hull skin layer. The antenna array is the only device imbedded within the outer 11.34 cm of the skin. It is tied to the rest of the transceiver by a direct field energy waveguide.

Since the operation of the long-range units can take place at both sublight and warp velocities, the internal arrangement of the transceiver allows for a greater number of major assemblies, including a sublight signal preprocessor, a warp velocity signal preprocessor, an adaptive antenna radiating element steering driver, Doppler and Heisenberg compensators, a combined selectable noise/clutter eliminator and amplifier stage, and a passive ranging determinator. As with the short-range system, signal encryption/decryption is handled by the main computer.

All Starfleet starships are able to transmit and receive voice and data via subspace, at a maximum transfer rate of 18.5 kiloquads/second. Calls between ships during low-action levels are usually initiated by a hailing signal packet, which contains all pertinent information relating to the calling ship. The call, usually directed toward upper-tier command personnel, can be held for routing to the proper destination by Security or Ops. Routine voice and data exchanges between scientific, technical, and operational departments aboard both vessels can be cleared by Security once contact has been established.

Crisis action levels, especially during Red Alert, can see normal hailing signals circumvented, depending on the exact situation. As with the other communications modes, calls can be closed out by either active controls, direct voice commands, or the aural monitoring functions of the main computer as it processes contextual cues.

STARBASE CONTACTS

Communications with starbases are handled in a similar manner. Depending on the action level and distance from the starship, voice contact with a starbase can be routed through numerous Starfleet Command tiers. As face-to-face exchanges take place, information is constantly moving along hundreds of other high-speed subspace channels. Starship logs are downloaded along with volumes of collected information, including vehicle hardware and crew performance, sensor scans, strategic and tactical analyses, experiment results, and many other areas. Uploads to the starship include new

8.4.1 Ship-to-ship communications

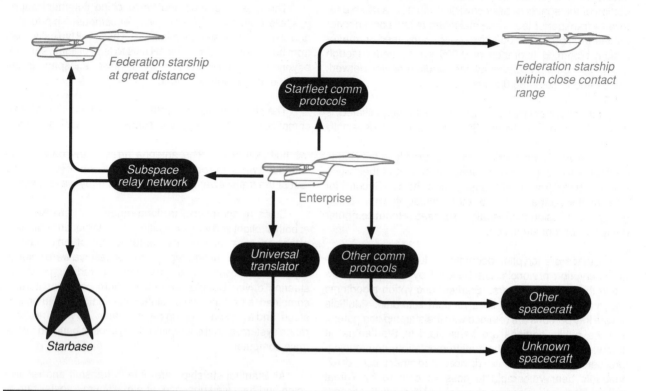

additions to the galactic condition database, Starfleet clock synchronization values, compilations of other starship downloads, flight advisories, mission orders, and other information necessary to the smooth running of a starship. While docked at a major starbase, voice and data are normally transferred by the ODN.

NON-STARFLEET CONTACTS

Most of the key interstellar-capable cultures in the Milky Way have come to use subspace frequencies in the interest of rapid communication. To echo an old saying, it's the only game in town. As such, even those that have had dealings with the Federation but are not members usually have gone some way toward adopting some common protocols, if only to interact with Starfleet vessels. Those who do not use standard voice and data translation routines, especially newly encountered races, can nevertheless be dealt with if the *Enterprise* main computers can perform adequate signal analyses and produce viable algorithms for use with the universal translator.

In many cases, however, dedicated survey and contact ships will precede starships as large as the *Galaxy* class, performing pathfinder missions, making cultural contacts, and compiling the required communication information. The possibility always exists, however, that a certain small percentage of true first contacts will be made by the *Enterprise*, activating a series of events designed to insure adherence to

the Prime Directive by all concerned departments. Pending Federation policy determinations on the specific contact, Starfleet's traditionally conservative interpretation of the Prime Directive's noninterference requirements may result in subspace channels being closed down or set to higher encryption, if it has been determined that a new contact is using subspace radio.

8.5 SUBSPACE COMMUNICATIONS NETWORK

The speed of propagation of a subspace signal continues to be the limiting factor in any long-range communications. Subspace radio signals, even those highly focused and radially polarized, will decay over time, as the energies forced across the subspace threshold will tend to "surface" to become normal slower EM. As this decay occurs, enormous amounts of information are lost, since the modulated signal does not decay evenly.

The propagation speed under ideal galactic conditions is equivalent to Warp Factor 9.9997. This places subspace radio about sixty times faster than the fastest starship, either existing or predicted. The phenomenon, which occurs at distances proportional to the peak radiated power of the outgoing beam with an upper distance limit of 22.65 light years, has necessitated the placement of untended relay booster beacons and small numbers of crew-tended communications bases at intervals of twenty light years, forming irregular strings of cells along major trade lanes and areas of ongoing exploration. Within the Federation, Starfleet's subspace communications network is supplemented by the Federation's civil communications system, as well as by various local networks.

New relay beacons are placed as areas of the galaxy are charted; small expendable beacons are carried aboard the Enterprise and other starships as temporary devices until permanent units can be placed. Already the extended exploration and patrol range of Starfleet vessels is so great that over 500 new subspace relays are made operational each year.

Starfleet is continuing to conduct experiments with higher energy levels in an attempt to drive communications signals into "deeper" layers of subspace, where it is thought the signal will travel farther prior to decay. If this is indeed feasible, it may someday be possible to eliminate up to 80% of the installed boosters.

Long-range subspace communications are vital to the continued effective operations of starships and their attendant planetside and free-flying base stations. Federation policy is formulated and carried out based on the rapid and accurate conveyance of orders, analyses, opinions, and scientific and technical information.

While the hardware and processes have been thoroughly described, the basic concept of communications is more important than the preceding sections might imply. In a very real sense, the unceasing beat of life in the galaxy is dependent upon communications. Multiple levels of organization exist in the Milky Way, ranging from 10^{-33} cm to 10^{14} km. Quarks and subatomic particles populate the lower end and lead to larger structures, through molecules, organic chemicals, and bioforms. At the higher end, atoms assemble into planets, solar systems, stellar clusters, and density waves in

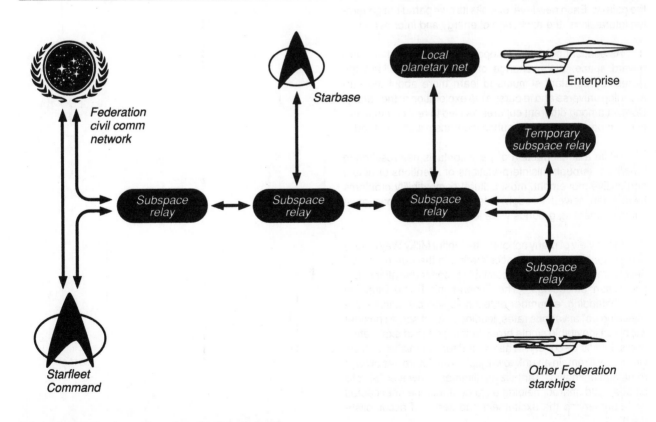

8.5.1 Starfleet subspace communications network

8.5.2 Automated subspace radio relay platform

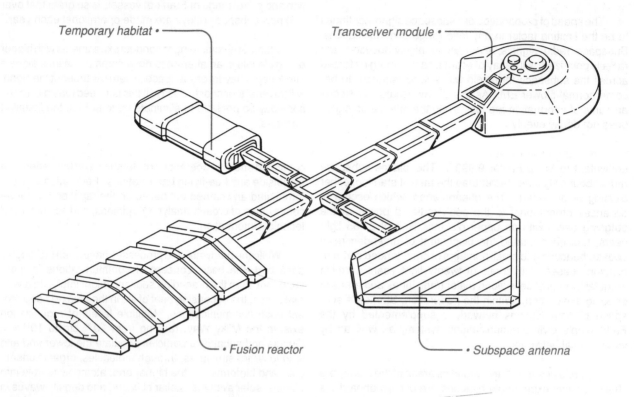

Temporary habitat •

Transceiver module •

• Fusion reactor

• Subspace antenna

the galaxy. Each new level exhibits its own paradigm governing interactions, the exchange of energy and information.

As sentient beings developed and progressed outward toward space, the exchange of information provided the necessary constant stimulus to learn more about the surrounding universe and to pursue the exploration of the galaxy. Contact among different cultures has led to real communications, in part facilitated by subspace transmission methods.

While a small fraction of early contacts has resulted in hostilities, through misinterpretations of intentions or actual aggressive movement, most cultural compatibility problems have been solved through determined negotiations once common meeting grounds were found.

In the view of many scholars, the entire Milky Way galaxy is experiencing a gradual acceleration in the rate of overall development because of continuing communications between sentient beings. The Federation's Prime Directive notwithstanding, a number of technological civilizations are "catching up" at various rates, leading to what some consider will be an inevitable single broad leading edge of exploration and scientific discovery. The exact direction this wave front will take will remain an unknown, just as the future has always remained unknown. Tantalizing glimmers, however, will still be seen and shared, helping us to deal with the unexpected while preserving the excitement and sense of accomplishment.

8.6 UNIVERSAL TRANSLATOR

The technical ability to exchange data is not in itself sufficient to permit communication. A common set of symbols and concepts — a language — is equally important before communications can occur. This is difficult enough on a planet where individuals of the same species speak different languages, but it becomes a formidable task indeed when dealing with individuals from different planets who may share neither biology, culture, nor concepts.

The Universal Translator is an extremely sophisticated computer program that is designed to first analyze the patterns of an unknown form of communication, then to derive a translation matrix to permit realtime verbal or data exchanges. Although the Universal Translator is primarily intended to work with spoken communications, it has been used successfully for translation with a wide range of language media.

DERIVING A TRANSLATION MATRIX

The first step in deriving a translation matrix is to obtain as large a sample as possible of the unknown communication. Wherever possible, this sample should include examples of at least two native speakers conversing with each other. Extensive pattern analysis yields estimates on symbology, syntax, usage patterns, vocabulary, and cultural factors. Given an adequate sample, it is usually possible to derive a highly simplified language subset in only a few minutes, although Federation policy generally requires a much more extensive analysis before diplomatic usage of the Universal Translator is permitted.

In the case where the individual lifeform communicated with has a similar language translation technology, it is sometimes useful to translate outgoing messages into the Linguacode language form, since this is specifically designed as a culturally neutral "antiencrypted" language medium.

LIMITATIONS

The accuracy and applicability of the translation matrix is only as good as the language sample on which the matrix is based. A limited sample will generally permit a basic exchange of concepts, but can lead to highly distorted translations when concepts, vocabulary, or usage vary too far from the sample. Since the Universal Translator constantly updates the translation matrix during the course of usage, it is often useful to allow the program to accumulate a larger linguistic sample by exchanging simple subjects before proceeding to the discussion of more complex or sensitive subjects.

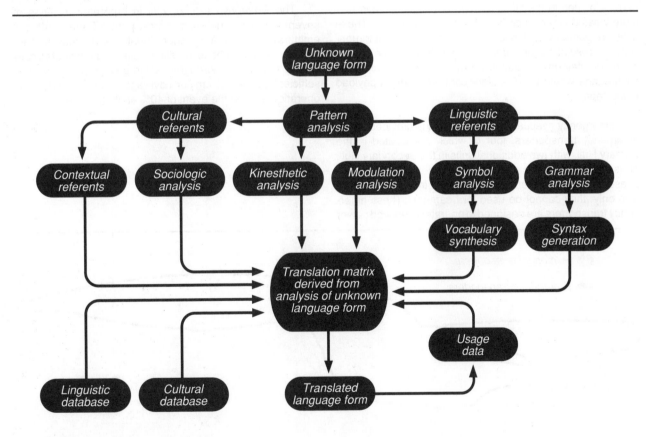

8.6.1 Universal Translator

9.0 TRANSPORTER SYSTEMS

9.1 TRANSPORTER SYSTEMS INTRODUCTION

Extravehicular transport to and from the ship is accomplished by a number of transporter systems, which allow personnel or equipment to be transported at ranges up to 40,000 kilometers.

Transport for crew and guests is provided by four personnel transporters located on Deck 6 of the Saucer Section. Two additional personnel transporters are located on Deck 14 in the Engineering Section.

Cargo transport is provided by four low-resolution transporters located in the Deck 4 cargo bay complex, and four more located in the Deck 38/39 cargo bay complex. These units are primarily designed for operation at molecular (non-lifeform) resolution for cargo use, but they can be set for quantum (lifeform) resolution transport if desired, although such usage would entail a significant reduction in payload mass capacity.

Emergency evacuation from the ship is provided by six emergency transporters, four of which are located in the Primary Hull, with two additional units in the Secondary Hull. These transporters are equipped with high-volume scan-only phase transition coils and are capable of transport from the ship only; they cannot be used for beam-up. These emergency transporters are designed to operate at reduced power

levels compared to standard units, but have therefore reduced range and Doppler compensation capabilities. Typical range is about 15,000 km, depending on available power.

Each pair of transporters is designed to share a single pattern buffer tank, generally located on the deck directly below the actual transport chambers. The emergency transporters are designed to access the pattern buffers from the primary personnel transporters to supplement their own buffers. This doubling of hardware results in only a 31% reduction in payload capacity of the shared pattern buffers, but yields nearly a 50% increase in system throughput in emergency situations.

The *Enterprise* exterior hull incorporates a series of seventeen transporter emitter array pads. These conformal emitters incorporate long-range virtual-focus molecular imaging scanners and phase transition coils, and are strategically located to provide 360-degree coverage in all axes. There is sufficient overlap of emitter coverage to provide adequate operation even in the event of 40% emitter failure.

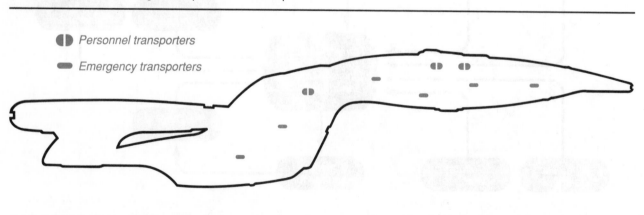

◑ *Personnel transporters*

▬ *Emergency transporters*

9.1.1 *Location of personnel transporters*

9.2.1 Personnel transporter (typical)

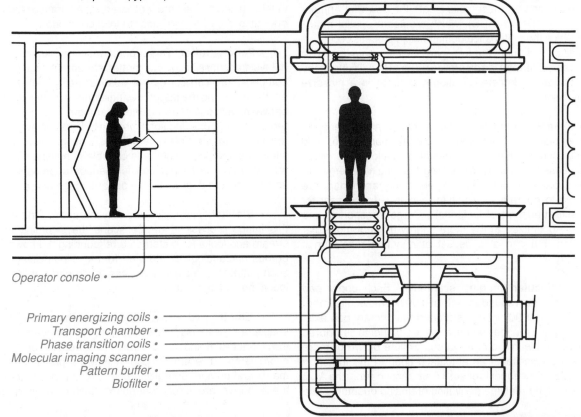

Operator console •

Primary energizing coils •
Transport chamber •
Phase transition coils •
Molecular imaging scanner •
Pattern buffer •
Biofilter •

9.2 TRANSPORTER SYSTEMS OPERATION

Transporter operations can be broken into five major stages. Because of the criticality of this system, normal operating rules require a transporter chief to supervise and monitor system operation. (Note: This section describes a beam-down sequence from the transport chamber to a remote destination. The beam-up sequence from a remote site to the transport chamber involves the same system elements in a somewhat different configuration.)

• **Target scan and coordinate lock.** During this initial step, the destination coordinates are programmed into the transporter system. Targeting scanners verify range and relative motion, as well as confirming suitable environmental conditions for personnel transport. Also during this stage, a battery of automated diagnostic procedures assures that the transporter system is functioning within operational standards for personnel use.

• **Energize and dematerialize.** The molecular imaging scanners derive a realtime quantum-resolution pattern image of the transport subject while the primary energizing coils and the phase transition coils convert the subject into a subatomically debonded matter stream.

• **Pattern buffer Doppler compensation.** The matter stream is briefly held in the pattern buffer, which allows the

system to compensate for the Doppler shift between the ship and the transport destination. The pattern buffer also acts as a safety device in case of system malfunction, permitting transport to be aborted to another chamber.

• **Matter stream transmission.** The actual point of departure from the ship is one of seventeen emitter pad arrays that transmit the matter stream within an annular confinement beam to the transport destination.

SYSTEM COMPONENTS

Major components for the transporter system include:

• **Transport chamber.** This is the protected volume within which the actual materialize/dematerialize cycle occurs. The chamber platform is elevated above the floor to reduce the possibility of dangerous static discharge, which sometimes occurs during the transport process.

• **Operator's console.** This control station permits the Transporter Chief to monitor and control all transporter functions. It also permits manual override of autosequencer functions and other emergency abort options.

• **Transporter controller.** This dedicated computer subprocessor is located to one side of the chamber itself. It manages the operation of transporter systems, including autosequence control.

• **Primary energizing coils.** Located at the top of the transport chamber, these coils create the powerful Annular Confinement Beam (ACB), which creates a spatial matrix within which the materialize/dematerialize process occurs. A secondary field holds the transport subject within the ACB; this is a safety feature, as disruption of the ACB field during the early stages of dematerialization can result in a massive energy discharge.

• **Phase transition coils.** Located in the transport chamber platform. These wideband quark manipulation field devices accomplish the actual dematerialization/materialization process by partially decoupling the binding energy between subatomic particles. All personnel transporters are designed to operate at quantum resolution (necessary for successful transport of lifeforms). Cargo transporters are generally optimized at the more energy-efficient molecular resolution, but can also be set at quantum resolution if necessary.

• **Molecular imaging scanners.** Each upper pad incorporates four redundant sets of 0.0012μ molecular imaging scanners at $90°$ intervals around the primary pad axis. Error-checking routines permit any one scanner to be ignored if it disagrees with the other three. Failure of two or more scanners necessitates an automatic abort in the transport process. Each scanner is offset 3.5 arc seconds from the ACB axis, permitting realtime derivation of analog quantum state data using a series of dedicated Heisenberg compensators. Quantum state data are not used when transporters are operating in cargo (molecular resolution) mode.

• **Pattern buffer.** This superconducting tokamak device delays transmission of the matter stream so that Doppler compensators can correct for relative motion between the emitter array and the target. A single pattern buffer is shared between each pair of transporter chambers. Operating rules require at least one additional pattern buffer to be available in the system for possible emergency shunting. In emergency situations, the pattern buffer is capable of holding the entire matter stream in suspension for periods approaching 420 seconds before degradation in pattern image occurs.

• **Biofilter.** Normally used only in transport to the ship, this image processing device scans the incoming matter stream and looks for patterns corresponding to known dangerous bacteriological and viral forms. Upon detection of such patterns, the biofilter excises these particles from the incoming matter stream.

• **Emitter pad array.** Mounted on the exterior of the spacecraft, these assemblies transmit the components of the transporter ACB and matter stream to or from the destination coordinates. The emitter pad includes a phase transition matrix and primary energizing coils. Also incorporated into these arrays are three redundant clusters of long-range

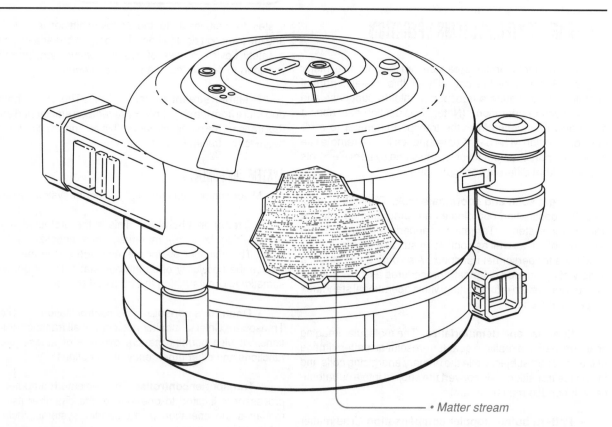

• *Matter stream*

9.2.2 Pattern buffer tank

virtual-focus molecular imaging scanners used during the beam-up process. Using phase inversion techniques, these emitters can also be used to transport subjects to and from coordinates within the habitable volume of the ship itself.

• **Targeting scanners.** A set of fifteen partially redundant sensor clusters located in the lateral, upper, and lower sensor arrays, these devices determine transporter coordinates, including bearing, range, and relative velocity to remote transport destinations. The targeting scanners also provide environmental information on the target site. Transport coordinates can also be determined using navigational, tactical, and communications scanners. For site-to-site intraship beaming, coordinates can be derived from interior sensors. Ship's personnel can be located for transport using communicators.

TRANSPORTER OPERATION TIMELINE

Transport operations require a large number of highly intricate procedures to be performed within milliseconds of one another, with extremely small margins for error. For this reason, much of the actual transport process is highly automated, although operating protocols generally require the supervision of a Transporter Chief. The operator will generally verify the coordinate lock and system readiness. The actual transport sequence is conducted by the autosequence programs of the transporter controller, under supervision of the operator.

Transporter autosequence major events for beamdown program (times are typical and vary with range and payload mass):

Time (seconds)	Device	Event
00.000	Op console	Autosequence initiation.
00.001	Transporter controller	Automatic diagnostic sequence begins.
00.007	Transporter controller	Transport system query for verification of signal routing and pattern buffer availability. Also verify assignment of backup pattern buffer.
00.046	Transporter controller	Diagnostic verification of controller logic states.
00.057	Transporter controller	Diagnostic verification of targeting scanners and Doppler compensation.
00.063	Transporter controller	Diagnostic verification of pattern buffer.
00.072	Transporter controller	Diagnostic verification of backup pattern buffer.
00.085	Pattern buffer	Pattern buffer initialize. Also initialize backup buffer.
00.097	Transporter controller	Diagnostic verification of phase transition coils.
00.102	Phase transition coils	Reference signal activated.

Time (seconds)	Device	Event
00.118	Op console	Verification of emitter array assignment.
00.121	Transporter controller	Diagnostic verification of emitter array and waveguide conduits.
00.138	Transporter controller	Diagnostic verification of molecular imaging scanners and Heisenberg compensators.
00.140	Targeting scanners	Target scan verification of beamdown coordinates.
00.142	Op console	Panel indicates system readiness.
00.145	Primary energizing coils	Begin emission of annular confinement beam in chamber.
00.151	Phase transition coils	Energize to 1.7 MeV. Initial frequency set at 10.2 GHz.
00.236	Pattern buffer	Superconducting tokamak to operating capacity.
00.259	Emitter array	Energize ACB elements to 1.7 MeV.
00.327	Pattern buffer	Synchronize with phase transition coils.
00.332	Molecular scanners	Reset scanners to null.

Time (seconds)	Device	Event
00.337	Molecular imaging scanners	Quark resolution enhancement enabled.
00.338	Primary energizing coils	ACB to 12.5 MeV (initial operating level).
00.341	Op console	Panel indicates beginning of energizing sequence. This process can be controlled manually at operator's discretion.
00.359	Molecular imaging scanners	Begin scan sequence. Reference beam frequency lock.
00.363	Primary energizing coils	ACB modulation lock.
00.417	Phase transition coils	Begin ramp-up to 162.9 GHz, energize to 32 MeV.

Time (seconds)	Device	Event
00.432	Molecular imaging scanner	Begin transmission of analog image data to pattern buffer.
00.464	Transporter controller	Verification of image data integrity.
00.523	Pattern buffer	Frequency sync with phase transition coils.
00.596	Phase transition coils	Frequency locked at 162.9 GHz. Begin dematerialization cycle.
00.601	Transporter controller	Transport ID trace stored to provide record of transporter activity.
00.998	Pattern buffer	Begin acceptance of matter stream.
01.027	Transporter controller	Verification of matter stream integrity.

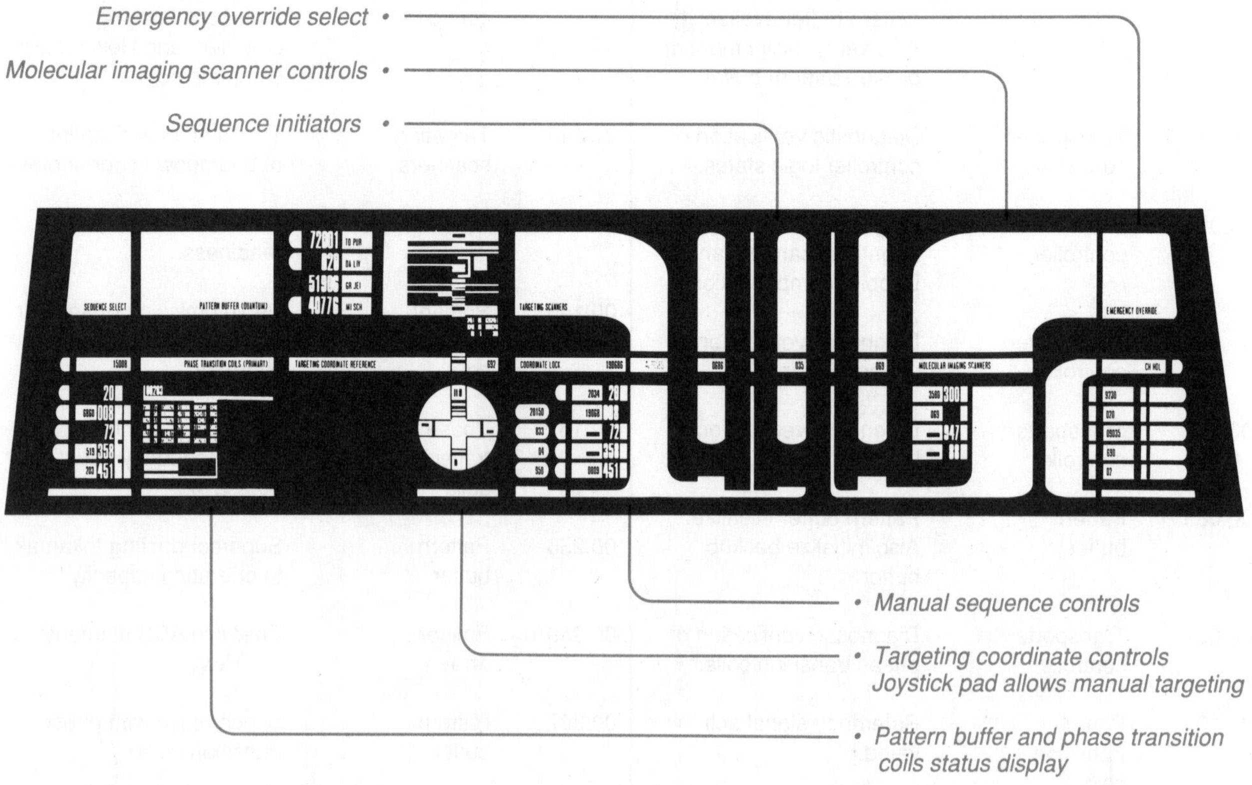

Emergency override select •

Molecular imaging scanner controls •

Sequence initiators •

• Manual sequence controls

• Targeting coordinate controls
Joystick pad allows manual targeting

• Pattern buffer and phase transition
coils status display

9.2.3 Transporter control console

Time (seconds)	Device	Event
01.105	Phase transition coils	Increase input power to 37 MeV.
01.132	Emitter array	ACB to 1.9 MeV. Reference beam phase lock.
01.190	Targeting scanners	Reverify target coordinates, range, and relative velocity.
01.204	Transporter controller	Reverify integrity of pattern buffer operation. Option to switch to backup buffer or abort sequence.
01.216	Targeting scanners	Target lock. Begin continuous scan of target coordinates.
01.221	Emitter array	Begin transmission of annular confinement beam to target coordinates.
01.227	Emitter array	First detected return of ACB reflection. Doppler compensation sync with pattern buffer.
01.229	Transporter controller	Ground level correction determination for target coordinates.
01.230	Emitter array	ACB to full power.
01.237	Pattern buffer	Begin transmission of matter stream to emitter array.
01.240	Emitter array	Begin transmission of image data through ACB.
01.241	Emitter array	Begin transmission of matter stream through ACB. Begin materialization cycle.

Time (seconds)	Device	Event
02.419	Transporter controller	Verify materialization sequence underway. Option to abort to alternate transporter pad.
02.748	Phase transition coils	Begin ramp down to 25.1 GHz. (Typical. Actual ramp-down start varies with payload mass.)
03.069	Pattern buffer	50% benchmark in matter stream reached. Abort to alternate pad option canceled.
04.077	Primary energizing coils	Dematerialization cycle complete. Hold ACB power level.
04.185	Phase transition coils	Hold at 25.1 GHz.
04.823	Emitter array	Materialization cycle complete.
04.824	Transporter controller	Verify pattern integrity.
04.947	Phase transition coils	Power down to standby.
04.949	Primary energizing coils	Release ACB lock.
04.951	Pattern buffer	Tokamak power down to standby.
04.973	Emitter array	Release ACB lock.
05.000	Op console	Signal successful transport.

The transporter console has three touch-sensitive light bars, which control the transport process. This was intended as an homage to the transporter in the original Star Trek *series, which had three sliders that Scotty always used.*

9.3 OTHER TRANSPORTER FUNCTIONS

• **Beam up.** This process is very much as described above except that the emitter array serves as the primary energizing coil and that the signal is usually processed through the transporter biofilter.

• **Site-to-site transport.** This refers to a double-beaming procedure in which a subject is dematerialized at a remote site and routed to a transporter chamber. Instead of being materialized in the normal beam-up process, however, the matter stream is then shunted to a second pattern buffer and then to a second emitter array, which directs the subject to the final destination. Such direct transport consumes nearly twice the energy of normal transport and is not generally employed except during emergency situations. Site-to-site transport is not employed during emergency situations that require the transport of large numbers of individuals because this procedure effectively halves the total system capacity due to minimum duty cycle requirements (See: 9.4).

• **Hold in pattern buffer.** A transport subject that has not yet begun the materialization cycle can be held in the pattern buffer without image degradation for up to 420 seconds, depending on payload mass. Although it is normal procedure to direct the matter stream immediately to the emitter array once Doppler compensation has been synchronized, this "hold" option can be exercised in the event that any problems are detected with the emitter array or waveguide conduits. This option is also available at operator discretion for security situations when it is desired to detain a transport subject for a brief time until security officers are available.

• **Molecular resolution transport.** Living objects are always transported at quantum resolution. In the interests of power conservation, many cargo objects are transported at the lesser molecular resolution. Although personnel transporters are optimized for the higher quantum resolution level, they can be set to operate for cargo transport if desired.

• **Dispersal.** Disengaging the annular confinement beam will cause the materializing matter stream to have no reference matrix against which to form. In such a case, the transport subject will form in a random fashion, usually taking the form of randomly dissociated gases and microscopic particulates. Operator override of the transport autosequence can cause the ACB to be deactivated in order to allow the harmless dispersal of a highly dangerous transport subject such as an explosive device. Two safety interlocks prevent this option from being accidentally activated. Such dispersal is usually accomplished by transporting the subject into space.

• **Near-warp transport.** Transporting through a low-level subspace field (less than 1,000 millicochranes) requires a series of adjustments to the transport sequence including a 57 MHz upshifting of the ACB frequency to compensate for subspace distortion.

• **Transport at warp.** Transporting through a warp field requires a similar 57 MHz ACB frequency upshift; it also requires the ship and the remote site to be contained within warp fields of the same integral value. Failure to maintain warp field equivalence will result in severe loss of ACB and pattern integrity. Such loss of pattern integrity is fatal to living transport subjects.

• **Biofilter scan.** Incoming transporter signals are automatically scanned for patterns corresponding to a wide variety of known hazardous bacteriological and viral forms. When such patterns are detected, limited quantum matrix manipulation is employed to render the offending forms inert.

We suggested the idea of transporters being unable to function in warp back in the second-season episode "The Schizoid Man." We realized, however, that laying down such an absolute rule would get some future writers into trouble, so we took the precaution of suggesting a loophole, namely that you could indeed beam at warp, just as long as both the ship and the target were at the same warp factor. Sure enough, that very situation came up in "The Best of Both Worlds," and Transporter Chief O'Brien has a line in which he confirms that we have indeed "matched warp velocity for transport." (There probably are occasions where we have indeed broken this rule, but we do try to get things right.)

9.4 LIMITATIONS OF USE

The personnel and cargo transport systems are enormously useful for starship operations, but are nevertheless subject to significant limitations. Some key limitations of operation include:

• **Range.** Normal operating range is approximately 40,000 km, depending on payload mass and relative velocity. Emergency evacuation transporters have more limited capabilities and are limited to approximately 15,000 km, again depending on available power.

• **Interference from deflector shields.** When deflector shields are raised to defensive configuration, it is impossible for the ACB to propagate normally across the required EM and subspace bandwidth. In addition, spatial distortion from the shields can seriously disrupt pattern integrity. For this reason, transport is not possible when shields are in place.

• **Duty cycle.** Although the transport autosequence lasts approximately five seconds, pattern buffer cooldown and reset takes an average of eighty-seven seconds, yielding an average duty cycle of just over ninety-two seconds. Since the transport beam conduits permit the matter stream to be routed to any pattern buffer, any given chamber can be reused immediately without waiting for cooldown by switching to another pattern buffer. Since there are only three pattern buffers normally used for personnel transport, this process can be repeated twice before waiting for pattern buffer reset. This translates into an average of about 1.9 six-person transports per minute, resulting in a total system capacity of about seven hundred persons per hour.

• **Transport while at warp.** Warp fields produce severe spatial distortion in transporter beams, making it impossible to transport when the ship is traveling at warp speeds. The only exception is when both the ship and the target site are traveling at the same integral warp velocity.

• **Replication limits.** Personnel transport is accomplished at quantum-level resolution using analog image data. By contrast, food and hardware replication (which employs transporter technology) employs digital image data at the much more limited molecular-level resolution. Because of this crucial limitation, replication of living beings is not possible.

9.5 TRANSPORTER EVACUATION

The transporter systems are enormously useful during missions that require bringing large numbers of individuals to or from the ship in short timeframes. The use of transporter systems imposes specific requirements on evacuation mission profiles.

EVAC TO SHIP

In case of emergency evacuation to the ship, all six personnel transporters would be brought into use. Maximum beam-up rate is limited by the minimum duty cycle of the transporter systems (See: 9.4). Utilizing all six personnel transporters results in a maximum beam-up rate of approximately seven hundred persons per hour.

In such scenarios, however, the personnel transporters would be supplemented with the eight cargo transporters. Although the cargo transporters are normally optimized for operation at molecular (nonlifeform) resolution, they can be reset for quantum (lifeform-safe) transport at a significant reduction in payload mass, yielding an additional beam-up capacity of three hundred persons per hour for a total system capacity of one thousand persons per hour.

EVAC FROM SHIP

Emergency evacuation from the *Enterprise* can be accomplished at a significantly greater rate than transport to the ship due to the availability of six emergency evacuation transporters capable of transporting twenty-two persons at a time off the ship. These units, which are incapable of transport to the ship, share the personnel transporters' pattern buffers, but employ high-volume scan-only phase transition coils, yielding a 370% increase in payload mass over the standard units, although their range is limited to 15,000 km (compared to 40,000 km for the standard units). As a result, when emergency transporters are used to supplement the personnel and cargo transporters, the rate is nearly doubled to some 1,850 persons an hour.

The emergency transporters have another significant operating advantage, that of lesser power requirements. This can be of great importance during crisis situations when available power is limited. In such cases, transport can be restricted to emergency transporters only, yielding an evacuation rate of about one thousand persons per hour, owing to the longer degauss time for the lower-power phase transition coils.

The transporter is one of the most brilliant dramatic concepts in Star Trek. *It allows our characters to move quickly and cleanly into the midst of a story. In* Star Trek: The Next Generation, *transporter technology is further postulated to have been advanced to the point where it can be used to replicate objects. This is a nifty idea, but we must be careful to limit the ability of the replicator, lest it become able to re-create any rare or valuable object, and perhaps even to bring dead people back to life. Such abilities would be quite detrimental to dramatic storytelling. The idea of replicated objects being stored at "molecular resolution" instead of the "quantum resolution" necessary to re-create living beings is a result of this concern. (Actually, there have been a couple of occasions where the transporter has been improperly used to save the day, but our writers have become more careful about such things.)*

10.0 SCIENCE AND REMOTE SENSING SYSTEMS

10.1 SENSOR SYSTEMS

The *Galaxy* Class *Enterprise* features one of the most sophisticated and flexible sensor packages ever developed for a Federation starship. These sensors make the *Enterprise* one of the most capable scientific research vessels ever built.

There are three primary sensor systems aboard the *Enterprise*. The first is the long-range sensor array located at the front of the Engineering Hull. This package of high-power devices is designed to sweep far ahead of the ship's flight path to gather navigational and scientific information.

The second major sensor group is the lateral arrays. These include the forward, port, and starboard arrays on the rim of the Primary Hull, as well as the port, starboard, and aft arrays on the Secondary Hull. Additionally, there are smaller upper and lower sensor arrays located near Decks 2 and 16 on the Primary Hull, providing coverage in the lateral arrays' blind spots.

The final major group is the navigational sensors. These dedicated sensors are tied directly into the ship's Flight Control systems and are used to determine the ship's location and velocity. They are located on the forward, upper port, upper starboard, aft, and upper and lower arrays.

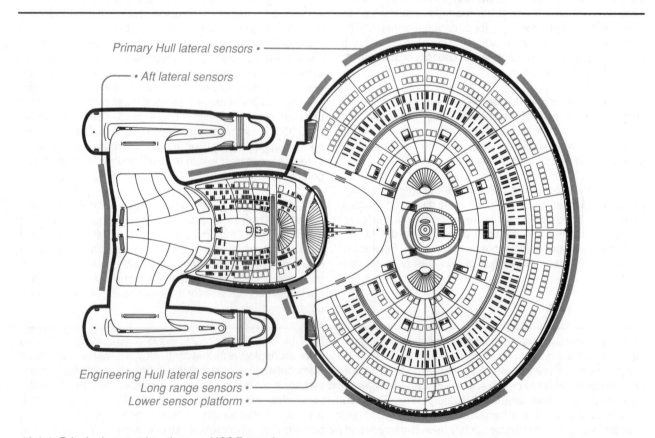

Primary Hull lateral sensors •

• Aft lateral sensors

Engineering Hull lateral sensors •
Long range sensors •
Lower sensor platform •

10.1.1 Principal sensor locations on USS Enterprise

In addition, there are several packages of special-purpose and engineering sensors such as the subspace flow sensors located at various points on the ship's skin.

The sensor systems provide the *Enterprise* and its crew with extensive capabilities in areas including:

• **Astronomical observation.** This includes optical and wideband EM scanning capabilities for the study of stellar objects and other phenomena across light year range. Capabilities include wide-angle scan ability for automated star-mapping functions and a wide range of individually controllable instruments for mission-specific studies.

• **Planetary surface analysis.** A broad range of short-range sensors provide extensive mapping and survey capabilities from planetary orbit. Besides high-resolution optical and EM scanning, virtual neutrino spectrometers and short-range quark resonance scanners provide detailed geologic structure analysis.

• **Remote lifeform analysis.** A sophisticated array of charged cluster quark resonance scanners provide detailed biological data across orbital distances. When used in conjunction with optical and chemical analysis sensors, the lifeform analysis software is typically able to extrapolate a bioform's gross structure and deduce the basic chemical composition.

10.2 LONG-RANGE SENSORS

The most powerful scientific instruments aboard the USS *Enterprise* are probably those located in the long-range sensor array. This cluster of high-power active and passive subspace frequency sensors is located in the Engineering Hull directly behind the main deflector dish.

The majority of instruments in the long-range array are active scan subspace devices, which permit information gathering at speeds greatly exceeding that of light. Maximum effective range of this array is approximately five light years in high-resolution mode. Operation in medium-to-low resolution mode yields a usable range of approximately 17 light years (depending on instrument type). At this range, a sensor scan pulse transmitted at Warp 9.9997 would take approximately forty-five minutes to reach its destination and another forty-five minutes to return to the *Enterprise*. Standard scan protocols permit comprehensive study of approximately one adjacent sector per day at this rate. Within the confines of a solar system, the long-range sensor array is capable of providing nearly instantaneous information.

Primary instruments in the long-range array include:

• Wide-angle active EM scanner
• Narrow-angle active EM scanner

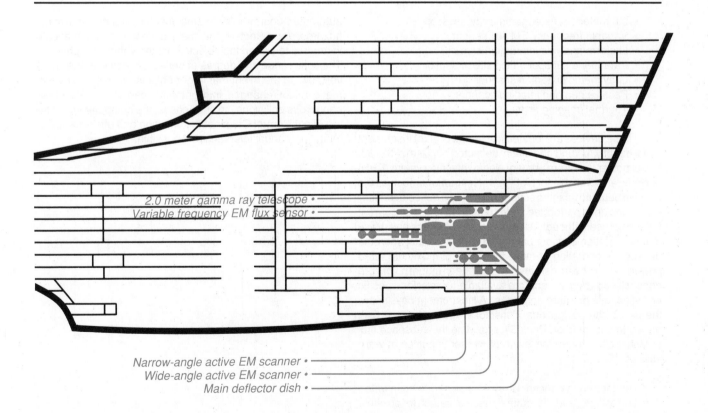

2.0 meter gamma ray telescope •
Variable frequency EM flux sensor •

Narrow-angle active EM scanner •
Wide-angle active EM scanner •
Main deflector dish •

10.2.1 Long-range sensor array

10.2.2 Long-range sensor preprocessors

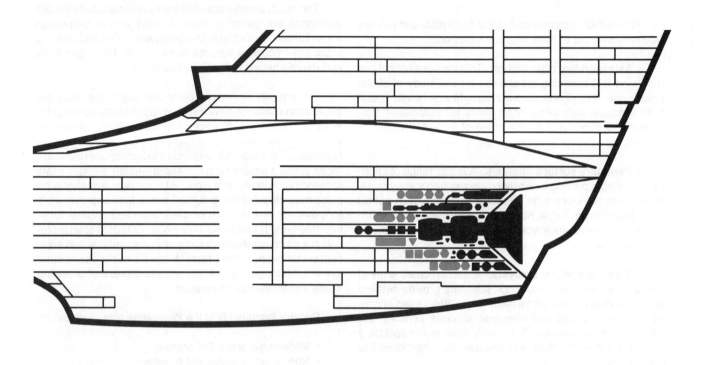

- 2.0 meter diameter gamma ray telescope
- Variable frequency EM flux sensor
- Lifeform analysis instrument cluster
- Parametric subspace field stress sensor
- Gravimetric distortion scanner
- Passive neutrino imaging scanner
- Thermal imaging array

These devices are located in a series of eight instrument bays directly behind the main deflector on Decks 32–38. Direct power taps from primary electro plasma system (EPS) conduits are available for high-power instruments such as the passive neutrino imaging scanner. The main deflector emitter screen includes perforated zones designed to be transparent for sensor use, although the subspace field stress and gravimetric distortion sensors cannot yield usable data when the deflector is operating at more than 55% of maximum rated power. Within these instrument bays, fifteen mount points are nominally unassigned and are available for mission-specific investigations or future upgrades. All instrument bays share the use of the navigational deflector's three subspace field generators located on Deck 34, providing the subspace flux potential allowing transmission of sensor impulses at warp speeds (See: 7.4).

The long-range sensor array is designed to scan in the direction of flight, and it is routinely used to search for possible flight hazards such as micrometeoroids or other debris. This operation is managed by the Flight Control Officer under automated control. When small particulates or other minor hazards are detected, the main deflector is automatically instructed to sweep the objects from the vehicle's flight path. The scan range and degree of deflection vary with the ship's velocity. In the event that larger objects are detected, automatic minor changes in flight path can avoid potentially dangerous collisions. In such cases, the computer will notify the Flight Control Officer of the situation and offer the opportunity for manual intervention if possible.

10.3 NAVIGATIONAL SENSORS

A terrestrial bird, a living organism, is aware of its surroundings and uses its senses to find its way from one point to another, frequently guided by stars in the night sky. The comparison of the USS *Enterprise* to the bird here is an apt one. In much the same way, the *Enterprise* system constantly processes incoming sensor data and routinely performs billions of calculations each second, in an effort to mimic the biological solution to the problem of navigation. While an equivalent number of *Enterprise* sensors and simulated neurons (and their interconnections) within the main computers are still many orders of magnitude less efficiently designed than the avian brain, nonetheless the *Enterprise* system is more than adequate to the task of traversing the galaxy.

Sensors provide the input; the navigational processors within the main computers reduce the incessant stream of impulses into usable position and velocity data. The specific navigational sensors being polled at any instant will depend on the current flight situation. If the starship is in orbit about a known celestial object, such as a planet in a charted star system, many long-range sensors will be inhibited, and short-range devices will be favored. If the ship is cruising in interstellar space, the long-range sensors are selected and a majority of the short-range sensors are powered down. As with an organic system, the computers are not overwhelmed by a barrage of sensory information.

The 350 navigational sensor assemblies are, by design, isolated from extraneous cross-links with other general sensor arrays. This isolation provides more direct impulse pathways to the computers for rapid processing, especially during high warp factors, where minute directional errors, in hundredths of an arc-second per light year, could result in impact with a star, planet, or asteroid. In certain situations, selected cross-links may be created in order to filter out system discrepancies flagged by the main computer.

Each standard suite of navigational sensors includes:

- Quasar Telescope
- Wide-Angle IR Source Tracker
- Narrow-Angle IR-UV-Gamma Ray Imager
- Passive Subspace Multibeacon Receiver
- Stellar Graviton Detectors
- High-Energy Charged Particle Detectors
- Galactic Plasma Wave Cartographic Processor
- Federation Timebase Beacon Receiver
- Stellar Pair Coordinate Imager

The navigational system within the main computers accepts sensor input at adaptive data rates, mainly tied to the ship's true velocity within the galaxy. The subspace fields within the computers, which maintain faster-than-light (FTL) processing, attempt to provide at least 30% higher proportional energies than those required to drive the spacecraft, in order to maintain a safe collision-avoidance margin. If the FTL

processing power drops below 20% over propulsion, general mission rules dictate a commensurate drop in warp motive power to bring the safety level back up. Specific situations and resulting courses of action within the computer will determine the actual procedures, and special navigation operating rules are followed during emergency and combat conditions.

Sensor input processing algorithms take two distinct forms, baseline code and rewritable code. The baseline code consists of the latest version of 3D and 4D position and flight motion software, as installed during starbase overhauls. This code resides within the protected archival computer core segments and allows the starship to perform all general flight tasks. The *Enterprise* has undergone three complete reinstallations of its baseline code since its first dock departure. The rewritable code can take the form of multiple revisions and translations of the baseline code into symbolic language to fit new scenarios and allow the main computers to create their own procedure solutions, or add to an existing database of proven solutions.

These solutions are considered to be learned behaviors and experiences, and are easily shared with other Starfleet ships as part of an overall spacecraft species maturing process. They normally include a large number of predictive routines for high warp flight, which the computers use to compare predicted interstellar positions against realtime observations, and from which they can derive new mathematical formulae. A maximum of 1,024 complete switchable rewrite versions can reside in main memory at one time, or a maximum of 12,665 switchable code segments. Rewritable navigation code is routinely downloaded during major starbase layovers and transmitted or physically transferred to Starfleet for analysis.

Sensor pallets dedicated to navigation, as with certain tactical and propulsion systems, undergo preventative maintenance (PM) and swapout on a more frequent schedule than other science-related equipment, owing to the critical nature of their operation. Healthy components are normally removed after 65–70% of their established lifetimes. This allows additional time for component refurbishment, and a larger performance margin if swapout is delayed by mission conditions or periodic spares unavailability. Rare detector materials, or those hardware components requiring long manufacturing lead times, are found in the quasar telescope (shifted frequency aperture window and beam combiner focus array), wide angle IR source tracker (cryogenic thin-film fluid recirculator), and galactic plasma wave cartographic processor (fast Fourier transform subnet). A 6% spares supply exists for these devices, deemed acceptable for the foreseeable future, compared to a 15% spares supply for other sensors.

10.4 LATERAL SENSOR ARRAYS

The *Enterprise* is equipped with the most extensive array of sensor equipment available. The spacecraft exterior incorporates a number of large sensor arrays providing ample instrument positions and optimal three-axis coverage.

Each sensor array is composed of a continuous rack in which are mounted a series of individual sensor instrument pallets. These sensor pallets are modules designed for easy replacement and updating of instrumentation. Approximately two-thirds of all pallet positions are occupied by standard Starfleet science sensor packages, but the remaining positions are available for mission-specific instrumentation. Sensor array pallets provide microwave power feed, optical data net links, cryogenic coolant feeds, and mechanical mounting points. Also provided are four sets of instrumentation steering servo clusters and two data subprocessor computers.

The standard Starfleet science sensor complement consists of a series of six pallets, which include the following devices:

Pallet #1
Wide-angle EM radiation imaging scanner
Quark population analysis counter
Z-range particulate spectrometry sensor

Pallet #2
High-energy proton spectrometry cluster
Gravimetric distortion mapping scanner

Pallet #3
Steerable lifeform analysis instrument cluster

Pallet #4
Active magnetic interferometry scanner
Low-frequency EM flux sensor
Localized subspace field stress sensor
Parametric subspace field stress sensor
Hydrogen-filter subspace flux scanner
Linear calibration subspace flux sensor

Pallet #5
Variable band optical imaging cluster
Virtual aperture graviton flux spectrometer
High-resolution graviton flux spectrometer
Very low energy graviton spin polarimeter

Pallet #6
Passive imaging gamma interferometry sensor
Low-level thermal imaging sensor
Fixed angle gamma frequency counter
Virtual particle mapping camera

The standard Starfleet sensor complement comprises twenty-four semi-redundant suites of these six standard sen-

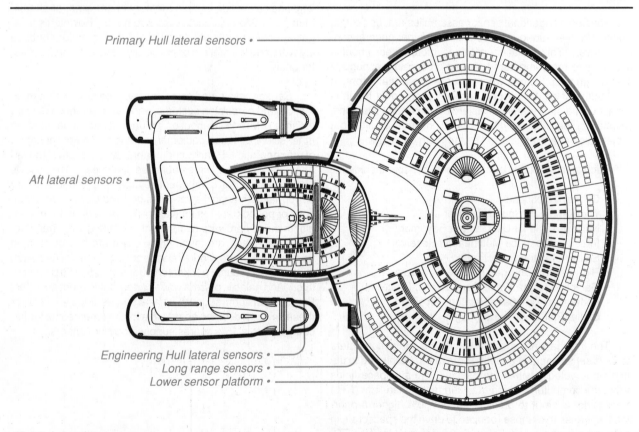

Primary Hull lateral sensors •

Aft lateral sensors •

Engineering Hull lateral sensors •
Long range sensors •
Lower sensor platform •

10.4.1 Lateral sensor arrays

10.4.2 Individual sensor pallet (typical)

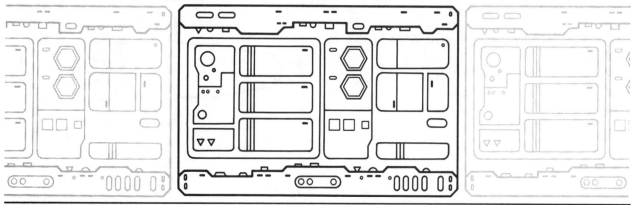

sor pallets. These 144 pallets are distributed on the Primary Hull and Secondary Hull lateral arrays. The instrumentation is located to maximize redundant coverage. A total of 284 pallet positions are available on both hulls.

The upper and lower sensor platforms provide coverage in very high and very low vertical elevation zones. These arrays employ a more limited subset of the standard Starfleet instrument package.

In addition to standard Starfleet instruments, mission-specific investigations frequently require nonstandard instruments that can be installed into one or more of the 140

nondedicated sensor pallets. When such devices are relatively small, such installation can be accomplished from service access ports inside the spacecraft.

Installation of larger devices must be accomplished by extravehicular activity. A number of personnel airlocks are located in the sensor strip bays for this purpose. If a device is sufficiently large, or if installation entails replacement of one or more entire sensor pallets, a shuttlepod can be used for extravehicular equipment handling.

10.5 INSTRUMENTED PROBES

The detailed examination of many objects and phenomena in the Milky Way galaxy can be handled routinely by the ship's onboard sensor arrays, up to the resolution limits of the individual instruments and to the limits of available data extraction algorithms used in extrapolating values from combinations of instrument readings. Greater proportions of high-resolution data of selected sites can be gathered using close approaches by instrumented probe spacecraft. These probes are generally sized to fit the fore and aft photon torpedo launchers, providing rapid times-to-target. Three larger classes of autonomous probes are based upon existing shuttlecraft spaceframes that have been stripped of all personnel support systems and then densely packed with sensor and telemetry hardware.

GENERAL USE PROBES

The small probes are divided into nine classes, arranged according to sensor types, power, and performance ratings. The features common to all nine are spacecraft frames of gamma molded duranium-titanium and pressure-bonded lufium boronate, with certain sensor windows of triple layered transparent aluminum. Sensors not utilizing the windows are affixed through various methods, from surface blending with the hull material to imbedding the active detectors within the hull itself. All nine classes are equipped with a standard suite

of instruments to detect and analyze all normal EM and subspace bands, organic and inorganic chemical compounds, atmospheric constituents, and mechanical force properties. While all are capable of at least surviving a powered atmospheric entry, three are designed to function for extended periods of aerial maneuvering and soft landing.

Many probes include varying degrees of telerobotic operation capabilities to permit realtime control and piloting of the probe. This permits an investigator to remain on board the *Enterprise* while exploring what might otherwise be a dangerously hostile or otherwise inaccessible environment.

The following section lists the specifications of each class. The higher class numbers are not intended to imply greater capabilities, but rather different options available to the command crew when ordering a probe launch. General use probes readied for immediate launching are stored adjacent to the photon torpedo reactant loading area on Deck 25. Other standby probes are stored on Deck 26 on standard torpedo transfer pallets. All probes are accessible to Engineering crews for periodic status checks and modifications for unique applications.

10.5.1 Class I Sensor Probe *Range: 2 x 10⁵ km Delta-v limit: 0.5c Powerplant: Vectored deuterium microfusion propulsion. Sensors: Full EM/Subspace and interstellar chemistry pallet for in-space applications. Telemetry: 12,500 channels at 12 megawatts.*

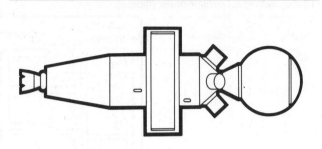

10.5.2 Class II Sensor Probe *Modified Class I. Range: 4 x 10⁵ km Delta-v limit: 0.65c Powerplant: Vectored deuterium microfusion propulsion; extended deuterium fuel supply. Sensors: Same instrumentation as Class I with addition of enhanced long-range particle and field detectors and imaging system. Telemetry: 15,650 channels at 20 megawatts.*

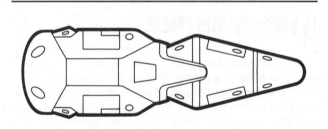

10.5.3 Class III Planetary Probe *Range: 1.2 x 10⁶ km Delta-v limit: .65c Powerplant: Vectored deuterium microfusion propulsion. Sensors: Terrestrial and gas giant sensor pallet with material sample and return capability; on-board chemical analysis submodule. Telemetry: 13,250 channels at ≈15 megawatts. Additional data: Limited SIF hull reinforcment. Full range of terrestrial soft landing to subsurface penetrator missions; gas giant atmosphere missions survivable to 450 bar pressure. Limited terrestrial loiter time.*

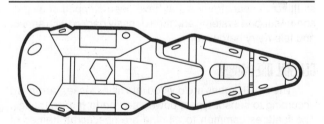

10.5.4 Class IV Stellar Encounter Probe *Modified Class III. Range: 3.5 x 10⁶ km Delta-v limit: 0.60c Powerplant: Vectored deuterium microfusion propulsion supplemented with continuum driver coil; extended maneuvering deuterium supply. Sensors: Triply redundant stellar fields and particles detectors, stellar atmosphere analysis suite. Telemetry: 9,780 channels at 65 megawatts. Additional data: Six ejectable/ survivable radiation flux subprobes. Deployable for nonstellar energy phenomena.*

10.5.5 *Class V Medium-Range Reconnaissance Probe*
Range: 4.3 x 10¹⁰ km Delta-v limit: Warp 2. Powerplant: Dual-mode matter/antimatter engine; extended duration sublight plus limited duration at warp. Sensors: Extended passive data-gathering and recording systems; full autonomous mission execution and return system. Telemetry: 6,320 channels at 2.5 megawatts. Additional data: Planetary atmosphere entry and soft landing capability. Low observability coatings and hull materials. Can be modified for tactical applications with addition of custom sensor countermeasure package.

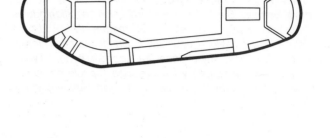

10.5.6 *Class VI Comm Relay/Emergency Beacon* Modified Class III. Range: 4.3 x 10¹⁰ km Delta-v limit: 0.8c Powerplant: Microfusion engine with high-output MHD power tap. Sensors: Standard pallet. Telemetry/comm: 9,270 channel RF and subspace transceiver operating at 350 megawatts peak radiated power. 360° omni antenna coverage, 0.0001 arc-second high-gain antenna pointing resolution. Additional data: Extended deuterium supply for transceiver power generation and planetary orbit plane changes.

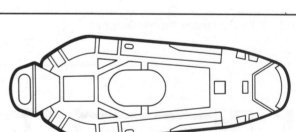

10.5.7 *Class VII Remote Culture Study Probe* Modified Class V. Range: 4.5 x 10⁸ km Delta-v limit: Warp 1.5. Powerplant: Dual-mode matter/antimatter engine. Sensors: Passive data gathering system plus subspace transceiver. Telemetry: 1,050 channels at 0.5 megawatts. Additional data: Applicable to civilizations up to technology level III. Low observability coatings and hull materials. Maximum loiter time: 3.5 months. Low-impact molecular destruct package tied to antitamper detectors.

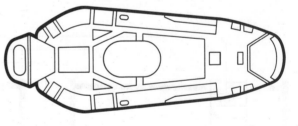

10.5.8 *Class VIII Medium-Range Multimission Warp Probe* Modified photon torpedo casing. Range: 1.2 x 10² l.y. Delta-v limit: Warp 9. Powerplant: Matter/antimatter warp field sustainer engine; duration 6.5 hours at Warp 9; MHD power supply tap for sensors and subspace transceiver. Sensors: Standard pallet plus mission-specific modules. Telemetry: 4,550 channels at 300 megawatts. Additional data: Applications vary from galactic particles and fields research to early-warning reconnaissance missions.

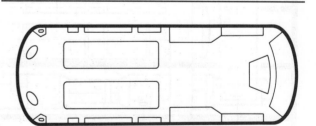

10.5.9 *Class IX Long-Range Multimission Warp Probe*

Modified photon torpedo casing. Range: 7.6 x 10² l.y. Delta-v limit: Warp 9. Powerplant: Matter/antimatter warp field sustainer engine; duration twelve hours at Warp 9; extended fuel supply for Warp 8 maximum flight duration of fourteen days. Sensors: Standard pallet plus mission-specific modules. Telemetry: 6,500 channels at 230 megawatts. Additional data: Limited payload capacity; isolinear memory storage 3,400 kiloquads; fifty-channel transponder echo. Typical application is emergency log/message capsule on homing trajectory to nearest starbase or known Starfleet vessel position.

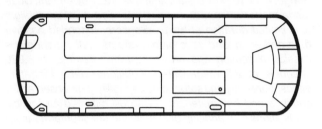

10.5.10 *Forward probe/torpedo launcher*

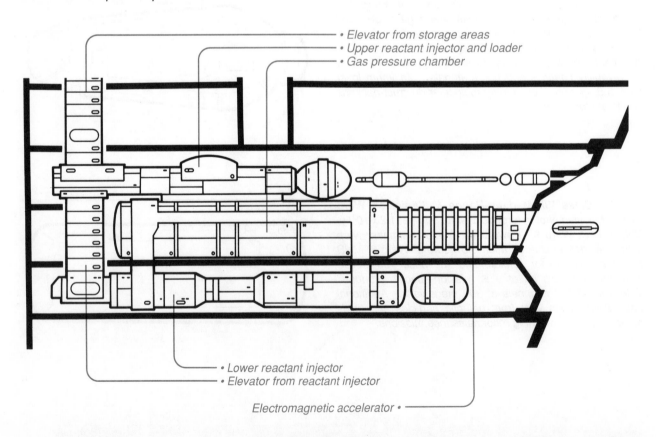

• *Elevator from storage areas*
• *Upper reactant injector and loader*
• *Gas pressure chamber*

• *Lower reactant injector*
• *Elevator from reactant injector*

Electromagnetic accelerator •

10.6 TRICORDER

The standard tricorder is a portable sensing, computing, and data communications device developed by Starfleet R&D and issued to starship crew members. It incorporates miniaturized versions of those scientific instruments found to be most useful for both shipboard and away missions, and its capabilities may be augmented with mission-specific peripherals. Its many functions may be accessed by touch-sensitive controls or, if necessary, voice command.

MAIN FEATURES

The standard tricorder measures 8.5 x 12 x 3 cm and masses 353 grams. The case is constructed of micromilled duranium foam, and is divided into two hinged sections for compact storage. The control surfaces consist of ruggedized positive-feedback buttons and a 2.4 x 3.6 cm display screen. While a full personal access display device–type multilayer control screen would have afforded the user with a wider range of preferences in organizing commands and visual information, the simplified button arrangement was chosen for greater ease of use in the field. The internal electronics, on the other hand, were designed to provide the greatest number of possible options in managing sensor data, visual images, and multichannel communications, in all incoming, outgoing, or recorded modes.

The major electronic components include the primary power loop, sensor assemblies, parallel processing block, control and display interface, subspace communication unit, and multiple memory storage units.

Power is provided to the total system through a rechargeable sarium crystal rated for eighteen hours of full instrument activity. True power usage rate and maximum useful time is, of course, dependent on which subsystems are active, and is continuously computed for call-up on the display. Typical power usage is 15.48 watts.

The sensor assemblies incorporate a total of 235 mechanical, electromagnetic, and subspace devices mounted about the internal frame as well as imbedded in the casing material as conformal instruments. One hundred and fifteen of these are clustered in the forward end for directional readings, with a field-of-view (FOV) lower limit of 1/4 degree. The other 120 are omnidirectional devices, taking measurements of the surrounding space. The deployable hand sensor incorporates seventeen high-resolution devices for detailed readings down to an FOV of one minute of arc. Within these FOV limits, both active and passive scans can provide readings approaching the theoretical limits of the EM radiation of physical process under study. By combining readings from different sensors, the tricorder computer processors can synthesize images and numerical readouts to be acted upon by the crew member.

10.6.1 Standard tricorder (deployed)

10.6.2 Tricorder user interface

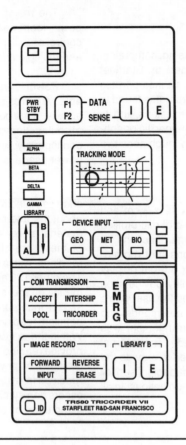

The computer capabilities of the standard tricorder are distributed throughout the device as preprocessors attached to the various sensors and twenty-seven polled main computing segments (PMCS). Each PMCS contains subsections dedicated to rapid management of the sensor assemblies, prioritizing of processing tasks, routing of processed data, and management of control and power systems. The PMCS chips supplied with the TR-580 and TR-595H(P) standard tricorders are rated at 150 GFP calculations per second.

The control and display interface (CDI) routes commands from both the panel buttons and display screen to the PMCS for execution of tricorder functions. Multiple functions can be run simultaneously, limited only by PMCS speed. In practice, crew members usually carry out no more than six separate scanning tasks.

Communications functions are carried out by tricorder through the subspace transceiver assembly (STA). Voice and data are uplink/downlinked along standard communicator frequencies. Transmission data rates are variable, with a maximum speed in Emergency Dump Mode of 825 TFP. Communication range is limited to 40,000 km intership, similar to the standard communicator badge.

The data storage sections of the standard tricorder include fourteen wafers of nickel carbonitrium crystal for 0.73 kiloquads of interim processor data storage, and three built-in isolinear optical chips, each with a capacity of 2.06 kiloquads, for a total of 6.91 kiloquads. The swappable library crystal chips are each formatted to hold 4.5 kiloquads. In Emergency Dump Mode, all memory devices are read in sequence and transmitted, including any library chips in place. In practice, the total time to dump a standard tricorder's memory to a starship can be as long as 0.875 seconds.

GENERAL DESCRIPTION OF CONTROLS AND INDICATORS

When stowed, the only visible control is the power switch. It shows a red power-on light and a green power level indicator (See: 10.6.2). When deployed, all of the available controls are visible.

• **PWR STBY** — Power standby light. If the tricorder is not used for more than ten minutes, this indicator will illuminate, and the tricorder goes into low-power mode. Any new touch of any control will bring the device back up to full power. When the tricorder is stowed but performing ongoing tasks, low-power mode does not occur.

Actor Gates McFadden (who plays Dr. Beverly Crusher) has always been a stickler for getting medical procedure as accurate as possible. Rick developed this tricorder guide partially because of her request for a set of consistent operating guidelines for our props.

10.6.3 Handheld sensor

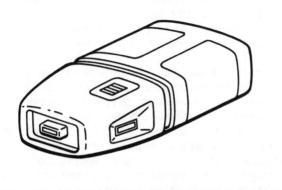

• **F1/F2** — Control function select switch. Most buttons on the tricorder have more than one function. This is a convenient toggle for often-repeated function changes and may be preprogrammed by the individual crew member. The F1/F2 switch is active during data operations only.

• **I and E** — These two controls manage the source of sensory information, either the tricorder itself (Internal), or remote device (External), or both sources simultaneously. The remote device can be any sensor platform that uses the same data collection machine language. The term "platform" denotes a vehicle operating on or above another planetary body, including the USS *Enterprise* or other spacecraft.

• **DISPLAY SCREEN** — This screen is capable of showing any realtime, stored, or computed image. The display area is similar in construction and function to Starfleet control panels and display screens, although the layering technique is simplified and the default image size is naturally smaller. Selected areas of an image may be enlarged by touch; many other screen functions may be customized using the standard tricorder's stored setup programs.

• **LIBRARY A/B** — The standard tricorder contains a read/write drive to record information onto small crystal memory chips for later retrieval, or to load previously recorded information into the tricorder's main memory. Each chip has a maximum capacity of 4.5 kiloquads.

• **ALPHA BETA DELTA GAMMA** — These indicators denote which data recording or retrieval activity is taking place in the tricorder library section. A more detailed readout of data operations can be called up on the display screen.

• **DEVICE INPUT** — Each of these three keys can be assigned to manage up to nine remote devices, for a total of twenty-seven different information sources. For a routine away mission, the default settings on power-up are GEO, MET, and BIO, covering geological, meteorological, and biological functions.

• **COMM TRANSMISSION** — This section controls the transmission of data and images to and from the tricorder

through the STA. ACCEPT toggles the tricorder to accept one-way transmissions from a designated remote source. POOL allows for networking of the tricorder and one or more designated remote sources. INTERSHIP sets up a special tricorder-to-ship data link employing multiple high-capacity channels. TRICORDER sets up a similar high-capacity link, but to other tricorders. While all four modes can be active simultaneously, the system will slow down significantly. In practice, no more than two modes are usually necessary at one time.

• **EMRG** — This is the emergency "dump everything to the ship" button. It provides for non-error-checking burst mode data transmission in critical situations. In practice, this function can be used no more than two times before the standard tricorder's primary power is exhausted. All sensing tasks are suspended and power is maximized to the STA.

• **IMAGE RECORD** — This section manages single or sequential image files recorded by the standard tricorder. The control has four divisions: FORWARD, REVERSE, INPUT, and ERASE. When used in concert with other tricorder functions, relatively complete documentation of an away mission can be achieved. At standard imaging resolution, at a normal recording speed of 120 Area View Changes (AVC)/sec, the tricorder can store a total of 4.5 hours of sequential images. Higher speeds yield a proportionately lower total recording time.

• **LIBRARY B** — Library B is the primary storage area for sequential images, though the memory configuration may be changed to include other storage areas, depending on the application. I and E control the image source.

• **ID** — This touchpad may be used to personalize a tricorder for default power-up settings, or as a security device for single–crew member operation.

10.7 SCIENCE DEPARTMENT OPS

The *Enterprise* is equipped to support a number of research teams whose assignments are designed to take advantage of the fact that the ship is a mobile research platform whose assignments will take it through a very large volume of space. Such secondary research missions typically include stellar mapping and observation projects, planetary surveys, interstellar medium studies, cultural and lifeform studies.

These secondary mission teams must necessarily focus their work on stars and planets near primary mission sites, but the broad operating range of the *Enterprise* makes this an extraordinary opportunity to study a large number of celestial objects. As with other investigation teams, secondary research projects are generally developed by Starfleet researchers or affiliated university and industrial scientists, and assigned to the *Enterprise* for either short-term or ongoing investigations.

The *Galaxy* class starship in extended mission configuration includes facilities to support approximately twenty specialized mission teams, depending on team sizes and types of investigations being conducted. These facilities include living accommodations for up to 225 people, as well as nonspecialized laboratory and work spaces that can be configured for specific investigator requirements. Addition-ally, some forty sensor pallet assignments on the lateral arrays are reserved for mission-specific instrumentation, which can be installed and modified as needed. Similarly, some fifteen instrument mounting positions within the long-range array cluster are available for mission-specific investigations.

Each individual department or investigation team is responsible for the operation of its own observations and experiments. Because secondary mission investigations are by definition subordinate to primary mission requirements, these teams must remain flexible in their operations. Nonetheless, each department or team is responsible for providing a regular update of operational preferences to the Operations Manager so that daily mission profiles can be designed to satisfy as many departmental needs as possible.

Our property masters, Joe Longo and Alan Sims, and their assistant Charlie Russo, have come up with a fairly amazing array of scientific hand tools. Many of these have been designed by Rick, but one that was not was the "spectral analyzer" used in the geology laboratory in "Pen Pals." Fans of the movie Buckaroo Banzai *may have recognized it as the oscillation overthruster, still eluding the clutches of the evil red Lectroids. Another Buckaroo reference in* Star Trek *was the bridge dedication plaque on the starship* Excelsior *in* Star Trek VI, *which bore the motto, "No matter where you go, there you are."*

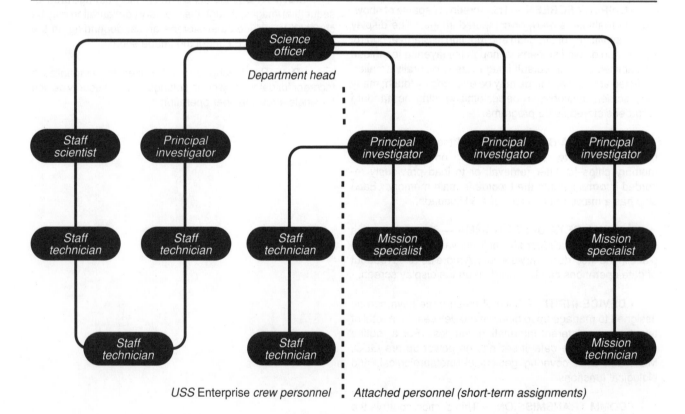

USS *Enterprise crew personnel* : *Attached personnel (short-term assignments)*

10.7.1 Organization of a typical science department

11.0 TACTICAL SYSTEMS

11.1 PHASERS

Even before the development of true interstellar space-craft by various cultures, it was clear that directed-energy devices would be necessary to assist in clearing gas, dust, and micrometeoroid material from vehicle flight paths. Emerging space-faring races are continuing to employ this method as an excellent maximizer of shipboard energy budgets, because a relatively small energy expenditure produces a large result. Material in space can be vaporized, ionized, and eliminated as a hazard to spaceflight. It did not take an enormous leap of imagination, of course, to realize that directed energy could also prove to be an effective weapon system.

The lead defensive system maintained by Starfleet Command for sublight use for the last century is the phaser, the common term for a complicated energy release process developed to replace pure EM devices such as the laser, and particle beam accelerators. Phaser is something of a hold-over acronym, PHASed Energy Rectification, referring to the original process by which stored or supplied energy entering the phaser system was converted to another form for release toward a target, without the need for an intermediate energy transformation. This remains essentially true in the current phaser effect.

Phaser energy is released through the application of the

rapid nadion effect (RNE). Rapid nadions are short-lived subatomic particles possessing special properties related to high-speed interactions within atomic nuclei. Among these properties is the ability to liberate and transfer strong nuclear forces within a particular class of superconducting crystals known as *fushigi-no-umi*. The crystals were so named when it appeared to researchers at Starfleet's Tokyo R&D facility that the materials being developed represented a virtual "sea of wonder" before them.

SHIPBOARD PHASERS

As installed in the *Galaxy* class, the main ship's phasers are rated as Type X, the largest emitters available for starship use. Individual emitter segments are capable of directing 5.1 megawatts. By comparison, the small personal phasers issued to Starfleet crew members are Type I and II, the latter being limited to 0.01MW. Certain large dedicated planetary defense emitters are designated as Type X+, as their exact energy output remains classified. The *Galaxy* class supports twelve phaser arrays in two sizes, located on both dorsal and ventral surfaces, as well as two arrays for lateral coverage.

A typical large phaser array aboard the USS *Enterprise*, such as the upper dorsal array on the Saucer Module, consists of two hundred emitter segments in a dense linear arrangement for optimal control of firing order, thermal effects, field halos, and target impact. Groups of emitters are supplied by redundant sets of energy feeds from the primary trunks of

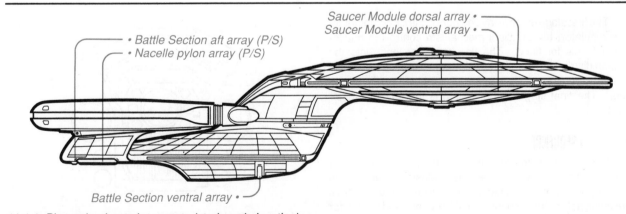

• Battle Section aft array (P/S)
• Nacelle pylon array (P/S)

Saucer Module dorsal array •
Saucer Module ventral array •

Battle Section ventral array •

11.1.1 *Phaser bank emplacements (starboard elevation)*

11.1.2 Phaser bank emplacements (dorsal view)

Dorsal phaser array •
Battle Section upper array (P/S) •

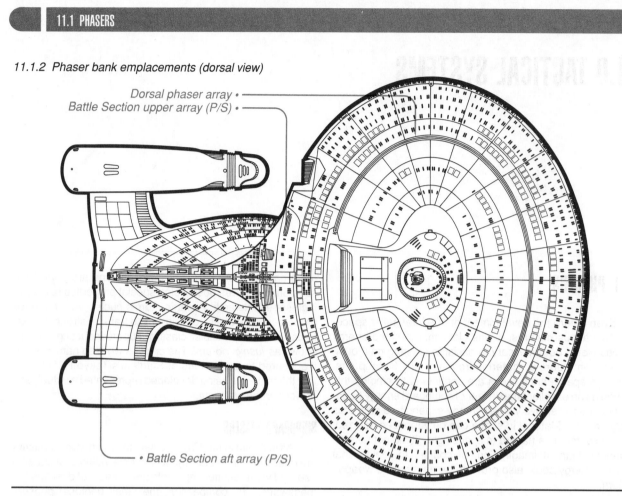

• Battle Section aft array (P/S)

the electro plasma system (EPS), and are similarly interconnected by fire control, thermal management, and sensor lines. The visible hull surface configuration of the phaser is a long shallow raised strip, the bulk of the hardware submerged within the vehicle frame.

In cross section, the phaser array takes on a thickened **Y** shape, capped with a trapezoidal mass of the actual emitter crystal and phaser-transparent hull antierosion coatings. The base of an array segment sits within a structural honeycomb channel of duranium 235 and supplied with supersonic regenerative LN_2 cooling. The complete channel is thermally isolated by eight hundred link struts to the titanium vehicle frame.

The first stage of the array segment is the EPS submaster flow regulator, the principal mechanism controlling phaser power levels for firing. The flow regulator leads into the plasma distribution manifold (PDM), which branches into two hundred supply conduits to an equal number of prefire chambers. The final stage of the system is the phaser emitter crystal.

ACTIVATION SEQUENCE

Upon receiving the command to fire, the EPS submaster flow regulator manages the energetic plasma powering the phaser array through a series of physical irises and magnetic switching gates. Iris response is 0.01 seconds and is used for

gross adjustments in plasma distribution; magnetic gate response is 0.0003 seconds and is employed for rapid fine-tuning of plasma routing within small sections of an array. Normal control of all irises and gates is affected through the autonomic side of the phaser function command processor, coordinated with the Threat assessment/tracking/targeting system (TA/T/TS). The regulator is manufactured from combined-crystal sonodanite, solenogyn, and rabium tritonide, and lined with a 1.2 cm layer of paranygen animide to provide structural surface protection.

Energy is conveyed from each flow regulator to the PDM, a secondary computer-controlled valving device at the head

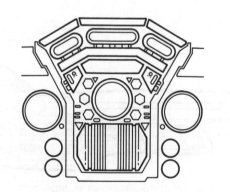

11.1.3 Typical phaser bank element

11.1.4 Phaser bank emplacements (ventral view)

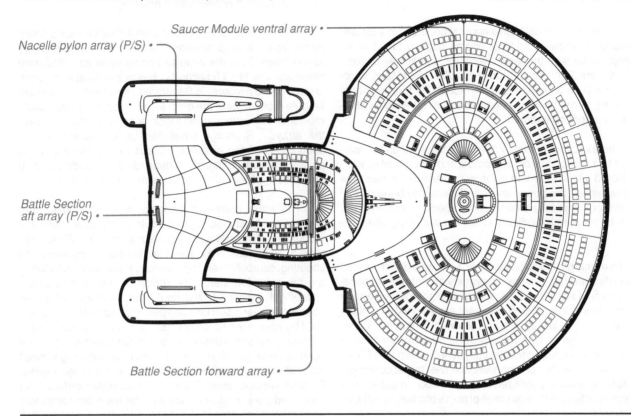

Saucer Module ventral array •

Nacelle pylon array (P/S) •

Battle Section
aft array (P/S) •

Battle Section forward array •

end of each prefire chamber. The manifold is a single crystal boronite solid, and is machined by phaser cutters. The prefire chamber is a sphere of LiCu 518 reinforced with wound hafnium tritonide, which is gamma-welded. It is within the prefire chamber that energy from the plasma undergoes the handoff and initial EM spectrum shift associated with the rapid nadion effect (RNE). The energy is confined for between 0.05 and 1.3 nanoseconds by a collapsible charge barrier before passing to the LiCu 518 emitter for discharge. The action of raising and collapsing the charge barrier forms the required pulse for the RNE. The power level commanded by the system or voluntarily set by the responsible officer determines the relative proportion of protonic charge that will be created and pulse frequency in the final emitter stage.

BEAM EMISSION

The trifaceted crystal that constitutes the final discharge stage is formed from LiCu 518 and measures 3.25 x 2.45 x 1.25 meters for a single segment. The crystal lattice formula used in the forced-matrix process is Li><Cu>>:Si::Fe>:>:O. The collimated energy beam exits one or more of the facets, depending on which prefire chambers are being pumped with plasma. The segment firing order, as controlled by the phaser function command processor, together with facet discharge direction, determines the final beam vector.

Energy from all discharged segments passes direction-ally over neighboring segments due to force coupling, con-

verging on the release point, where the beam will emerge and travel at *c* to the target. Narrow beams are created by rapid segment order firing; wider fan or cone beams result from slower firing rates. Wide beams are, of course, prone to marked power loss per unit area covered.

11.2 PHASER OPERATIONS

In their primary defensive application, the ship's phaser arrays land single or multiple beams upon a target in an attempt to damage the target structure, sometimes to complete destruction. As with other Starfleet-developed hardware, the Type X phaser is highly adaptable to a variety of situations, from active low-energy scans to high-velocity ship-to-ship combat operations.

The exact performance of most phaser firings is determined by an extensive set of practical and theoretical scenarios stored within the main computers. Artificial intelligence routines shape the power levels and discharge behaviors of the phaser arrays automatically, once specific commands are given by responsible officers to act against designated targets.

Low-energy operations provide a valuable direct method of transferring ship's energy for a variety of controlled applications, such as active sensor scanning. In high-energy weapon firings, several interrelated computer systems work to place the beam on the target, all within a few milliseconds. Long- and short-range sensor scans provide target information to the Threat assessment/tracking/targeting system (TA/T/TS), which drives the phaser arrays with the best target coverage. Multiple targets are prioritized and acted upon in order. The maximum effective tactical range of ship's phasers is 300,000 kilometers.

Targets protected by defensive EM shields and surface absorptive-ablative coatings may still be dealt with, but with a commensurate increase in power to defeat the shields. Phasers may be fired one-way through the ship's own shields due to EM polarization, with a small acceptable drag force penalty at the inner shield interface.

Threat vessels will be encountered with a wide variety of shields that act upon phaser emissions to reduce their effectiveness; the type most often confronted spreads the beam cross section, redirecting the energy around the shields and back into space. Higher power levels will usually overburden the shields and allow the phaser to hit the target directly, although more sophisticated adversaries possess highly resistant shield generators. It has been the experience of some starship tactical officers that rapid-firing volleys at different parts of a shield bubble can weaken it. The phaser arrays on a *Galaxy* class ship are located to achieve maximum beam dwell time on a target.

Generally speaking, regardless of the actual beam type, pulse or continuous, or the specific Threat situation, the most effective tactic is to maintain *contact* between the beam and the Threat shield or physical hull. Computer sequencing of the arrays will always attempt to expose the target, even while the arrays are recharging. Conversely, the best tactics for minimizing disabling return phaser fire are to present the smallest visible ship cross section to the Threat weapons, and continue changing attitude so as to deny the beams any sites on which to inflict concentrated energies.

In Cruise Mode, all phaser arrays receive their primary power from the warp reaction chamber, with supplementary fusion power from the impulse engine systems. Recharge times are kept to ≤0.5 seconds. Full power firing endurance is rated at ≈45 minutes. In Separated Flight Mode, the Saucer Module is cut off from the main electro plasma system, and it must then rely on increased fusion generator output to power the arrays. Recharge times can be maintained at ≤0.5 seconds, but firing endurance drops to <15 minutes at full power. Survival during crises depends on the understanding by Tactical officers of the constraints of both modes.

The actual number of variables involved in spacecraft defense can be staggering and would quickly overwhelm any manual efforts to adequately protect a starship. While ship-to-ship operations may seem as simple as pointing and shooting, computers and semiautonomous weapon systems are the accepted standards, driven by the realities of the spaceflight regime. In the total Starfleet history of armed spacecraft, over 3,500 unique spacecraft combat maneuvers (SCMs) have been recorded, too numerous to present more than a tiny fraction in detail (see descriptions following). Since combat conditions can change within seconds, high-speed calculations and tactical choices will also change rapidly. General result-oriented firing and movement orders from command personnel are translated by the main computers and scripted into "trees" of possible sequences, along with a prioritization of the best paths for the current time, and influenced by the predictions of Threat assessment routines.

As with the navigation system, which is directly linked to the tactical system within the main computers, phaser algorithms take two distinct forms, baseline code and self-rewritable code. Both code types cover all known advantages and weaknesses of Threat vessels, including simulated adversaries used for training purposes, and analysis routines for new Threat types. The rewritable symbolic code performs primarily high-speed autonomic functions related to the defense of the *Enterprise*, quickly reacting to danger from outside and repairing internal damage. Only 10% of the rewritable code is needed for weapon fire control routines; they are fairly straightforward and are complicated only by firing sequences, precise timings, and unusual targeting requirements. All stored rewritable code is routinely transferred to Starfleet Headquarters and remote sites by secure means for high-level analysis.

SPACECRAFT TACTICAL MANEUVERS INVOLVING PHASERS

The following three cleared excerpts from the overall Starfleet SCM database describe general *Galaxy* class ship maneuver variations utilizing Type X phaser banks only. Photon torpedo firings in combination with phasers are treated as specialized SCMs.

CATNO.SCMDB GAL/ENT/PHA/LS 142-01-40274/TTM
VAR/ROM/TD'D/1

Two vessel scenario, low sublight, ≤0.01*c* relative, ≤0.01*c* absolute, Cruise Mode. Romulan Warbird Threat vessel (mobile), closes on *Galaxy* class (stationary) along bearing 0°, ±10°, mark 0°, range ≈5000 km. Threat vessel discharges 20 GW phaser pulses toward *Galaxy* class. *Galaxy* class shields energize within 550 ns to minimum phaser dispersion level, rise to full within 2,000 ns. *Galaxy* class maneuvers to minimum aspect on thruster or impulse power if possible. General return fire procedure, if implemented: Determine Threat passing side, yaw *Galaxy* class through same direction at matching rate minus 15%, pitch to 5° relative to Threat XY centerline, auto-adjust *Galaxy* class YZ plane. PROG 532 sequential follow-fire arrays: Upper Forward Main, Lower Forward Main, P/S Lateral, Upper Aft Main.

CATNO.SCMDB GAL/ENT/PHA/HS 339-54-40274/TTM
VAR/FER/T23/2

Three vessel scenario, high sublight, ≤0.02*c* relative, ≤.75*c* absolute, Cruise Mode. Ferengi Marauder Threat vessels (mobile), closes on *Galaxy* class (mobile) along bearings 240° and 120°, ±10°, marks 40° and 280°, range ≈800 km. Threat vessels simultaneously discharge 500 MW electro plasma waves toward *Galaxy* class. *Galaxy* class shields fully energized, reactive outboard pulsing to hot standby. General return fire procedure, if implemented: Determine Threat evasive pattern, maintain *Galaxy* class relative attitude centerline divided between both Threat vessels. Yaw 90° to combined plasma wavefront if possible prior to phaser discharge. PROG 14 continuous fire arrays: Upper Aft Main, Lower Aft Main, P/S Lateral.

CATNO.SCMDB GAL/ENT/PHA/MS 565-11-40274/TTM
VAR/CAR/HAC/1

Two vessel scenario, mid-sublight, ≤0.001*c* relative, ≤0.60*c* absolute, Separated Flight Mode, Saucer Module only. Cardassian Enhanced Penetrator Threat vessel (mobile), exchanges fire with *Galaxy* class (mobile) along bearing 280°, mark 300°, range 15 km at closest approach. *Galaxy* class shields fully energized, reactive outboard pulsing to full active. General return fire procedure, if implemented: Predict table of possible Threat trajectories and attach required targeting vectors. Break 45° –Z/30° +X to present maximum number of ventral array elements to Threat. PROG 3401 pulsed fire, broad spectrum to blind Threat sensors: Lower Main Aft, P/S Lateral. Follow with PROG 245 continuous fire, narrow spectrum: Lower Aft Main, P/S Lateral.

Virtually all phaser-related scenarios deal with sublight starship velocities, and for good reason. Space vessels operating at warp are protected, to a large degree, simply by the limitations of lightspeed physics. Phaser energy dissipates quickly in the vicinity of moving warp fields, especially when those fields are accompanied by active deflectors. This remains true even if the targets are motionless relative to each other (in comparison, subspace emission devices such as tractor beams and transporters are less adversely affected). Computational simulations suggest that an extremely narrow Type X phaser discharge, if released at full power *and* aligned along an oncoming target's velocity vector, has a 25% chance of disrupting the target's hull integrity. Other position and velocity combinations are subjects of continued research, since some small tactical advantages may yet be extracted for future use.

11.3 PHOTON TORPEDOES

The tactical value of phaser energy at warp velocities, and indeed high relativistic velocities, is close to none. As greater numbers of sentient races were encountered in the local stellar neighborhood, some of which were classified as definite Threats, the need for a warp-capable defensive weapons delivery method was recognized as an eventual necessity. Rudimentary nuclear projectiles were the first to be developed in the mid-2000s, partly as an outgrowth of debris-clearing devices, independent sensor probes, and defensive countermeasures technology.

Fusion explosives continued to be deployed throughout the latter half of the twenty-second century, as work progressed on lighter and faster ordnance. Late in the development of the first true photon torpedoes, a reliable technique for detonating variable amounts of matter and antimatter had continued to elude Starfleet engineers, while the casing and propulsion system were virtually complete. On the surface, the problem seemed simple enough to solve, especially since some early matter/antimatter reaction engines suffered regular catastrophic detonations. The exact nature of the problem lay in the rapid *total* annihilation of the torpedo's warhead. While most warp engine destructions due to failure of antimatter containment appeared relatively violent, visually, the actual rate of particle annihilation was quite low.

Two torpedo types were being developed simultaneously, beginning in 2215. The first was a simple 1:1 matter/antimatter collision device consisting of six slugs of frozen deuterium which were backed up by carbon-carbon disks and driven by microfusion initiators into six corresponding magnetic cavities, each holding antideuterium in suspension. As the slugs drove into the cavities, the annihilation energies were trapped briefly by the magnetic fields, and then suddenly released. The annihilation rate was deemed adequate to serve as a defensive weapon and was deployed to all deep interstellar Starfleet vessels. While a torpedo could coast indefinitely after firing, the maximum effective tactical range was 750,000 kilometers because of stability limits inherent to the containment field design.

The device Starfleet was waiting for was the second type, made operational in 2271. The basic configuration is still in use and deployed on the *Galaxy* class with a maximum effective tactical range of 3,500,000 kilometers for midrange detonation yield. Variable amounts of matter and antimatter are broken into many thousand minute packets, effectively increasing the annihilation surface area by three orders of magnitude. The two components are both held in suspension by powerful magnetic field sustainers within the casing at the time of torpedo warhead loading. They are held in two separate regions of the casing, however, until just after torpedo launch, as a safety measure. The suspended component packets are mixed, though they still do not come into

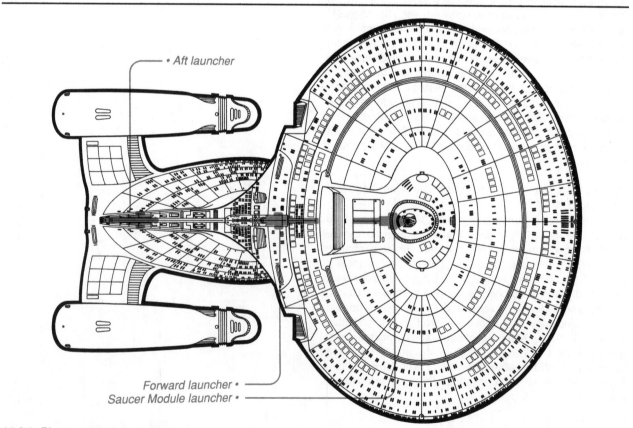

• Aft launcher

Forward launcher •
Saucer Module launcher •

11.3.1 *Photon torpedo launchers*

11.3.2 *Photon torpedo (typical)*

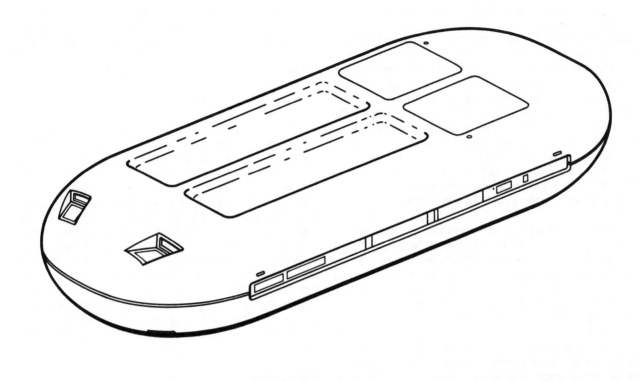

direct contact with one another because of the fields surrounding each packet. At a signal from the onboard detonation circuitry, the fields collapse and drive the materials together, resulting in the characteristic release of energy. While the maximum payload of antimatter in a standard photon torpedo is only about 1.5 kilograms, the released energy per unit time is actually greater than that calculated for a *Galaxy* class antimatter pod rupture.

TORPEDO CONFIGURATION

The standard photon torpedo carried by the *Galaxy* class is an elongated elliptical tube constructed of molded gamma-expanded duranium and a plasma-bonded terminium outer skin. The completed casing measures 2.1 x 0.76 x 0.45 meters and masses 247.5 kilograms dry weight. The finished casing is split equatorially by phaser cutters, which also provide penetrations for warhead reactant loading, hardline optical data network connections, and propulsion system exhaust grills. Within the casing are installed deuterium and antideuterium holding tanks, central combiner tank, and their respective magnetic suspension components; target acquisition, guidance, and detonation assemblies; and warp sustainer engine. The holding and combiner tank shells are gamma-welded hafnium titanide. The tank liners, as well as the warp sustainer engine coils, are all constructed from directionally cast silicon-copper carbide to maximize field efficiency.

The multimode sustainer engine is not a true warp engine due to its small physical size, one-twelfth the minimum matter/antimatter (M/A) reaction chamber size. Rather, it is a miniature M/A fuel cell, which powers the sustainer coils to grab and hold a hand-off field from the launcher tube, to continue at warp if launched during warp flight by the starship. The cell, a cylinder 20 cm in diameter and 50 cm in length, is limited to a narrow warp field frequency range and cannot add more than a slight amount of power to the original hand-off field. The maximum cruising velocity will follow the formula $v_{max} = v_l + 0.75 v_l / c$, where v_l is the launch velocity. Other flight modes are triggered according to initial launch conditions. If launched during low-impulse flight, the coils will drive the torpedo up to a 75% higher sublight velocity. If launched at high sublight, the sustainer will not cross the threshold into warp, but will continue to drive the torpedo at high relativistic velocities. If required, the maximum effective range can be extended, but with a loss of detonation yield, as the sustainer engine draws reactants from the M/A tanks.

Once given direct prelaunch trajectory instructions by the optical data network, and optionally updated in flight by subspace radio link, the torpedo's targeting and guidance systems communicate with the sustainer to produce the optimum travel time to the target. This allows the arming circuitry a minimum of 1.02 seconds to combine the warhead fuels. Trajectory changes are made by differentially constricting the sustainer exhaust grills.

The actual firing operation occurs in the two launcher tubes, one forward within the connecting dorsal on Deck 25, and one aft above the support pylon wing on Deck 35. The launcher is downstream from four loader stages, where the M/A fuels are injected into four torpedoes at one time. Each loader can place a torpedo into the launcher for volley firing. In each position, the launcher tube, 30 meters in length, is constructed from machined tritanium and sarium farnide. It is strung with sequential field induction coils and launch assist gas generators to provide initial power to the sustainer and propel the casing away from the starship. Once fired, the launcher tube is purged of surface residues by flash steriliz-ers, the coil charges are neutralized, and the firing sequencer is reset to await a new load of torpedoes. In the event a set of casings is loaded, and the ship then stands down from Red Alert, the warhead fuels are off-loaded and returned to stor-age, and the launcher system is powered down.

Both launchers can be loaded with as many as ten torpedoes at one time for simultaneous launch. In such cases, all torpedo devices are ejected from the tube in a single impulse and remain together for approximately 150 meters. At this point, individual control programs assume flight and targeting control for each torpedo. This is an effective means for simultaneous delivery of torpedoes to multiple targets.

The same technologies that produced high-velocity de-fensive weapons have also produced advanced warp-ca-pable remote sensor probes. One quarter of the 275 basic casings normally stored aboard the ship can be packed with sensor arrays, signal processors, and telemetry systems for launch toward nearby targets. Applications will typically include stellar and planetary studies, as well as strategic reconnaissance.

11.4 PHOTON TORPEDO OPERATIONS

The uses of photon torpedoes against natural and con-structed targets are as varied as those devised for the *Galaxy* class shipboard phaser arrays. A complete examination of defensive and productive applications would require addi-tional volumes dealing with specific celestial objects and Spacecraft Combat Maneuvers (SCMs), though the funda-mentals are included here.

Photon torpedoes are directed against Threat force tar-gets at distances from 15 to nearly 3,500,000 kilometers from the starship. In docked flight, targeting data is gathered from the ship's various sensor systems and processed at FTL speeds in the main computers, then relayed through the Tactical bridge station to the forward and aft torpedo launch-ers. The automated reactant handling and torpedo loading into the launcher are managed by the tactical situation control-ler (TSC), in concert with the TA/T/TS. This dedicated section of the computer maintains regularly updated files of actual and simulated Threat tracking algorithms, firings, and battle damage reports, plus adaptive algorithms for new Threat targets. Tactical inputs determine the desired results from a list of basic menu choices, including nonstandard instructions, such as the option of computer-assisted manual torpedo flight control.

WEAPONS CONTROL

In Separated Flight Mode, the main computer in the Battle Section accepts a total handoff of control from the Saucer Module main computers, switching the duplicate situation controller to full active status. This allows uninter-rupted control of the two launcher tubes. With the Battle Section no longer occupying the docking cavity, the single aft-firing torpedo launcher in the Saucer Module is open to space. The main computer tactical situation controller manages the firing of this launcher, designed to defend the Saucer Module in the event of attack away from the Battle Section.

Since photon torpedoes are classified as semi-autono-mous weapons, initial firing direction is not a major concern. Most firings involve direct fore or aft vectors, within ten degrees of the vehicle centerline. When required, rapid trajectory changes may be executed following launch to achieve target acquisition, cruise tracking, and terminal guid-ance. This is utilized with numerous preprogrammed starship maneuvers, momentarily disabling Conn bridge station atti-tude and translational panel inputs. Targets within twenty-five kilometers involve launch followed immediately by a fast breakaway to guarantee that the starship will remain outside the explosion hazard radius, which is variable with yield. Sensor blinding of pursuing Threat vessels can be attempted by aft volley firings of four or more weapons. Combinations of many factors, including warp or impulse velocity changes, volley firing spread angles, and warhead yield are sorted and matched to Threat vehicles.

Targeting is directed by the Tactical Officer following command authorization. Target detection and prioritization are orchestrated by the Tactical Officer with interactive prompts and responses from the computers. Torpedo sensors and guidance circuits are configured by the tactical situation controller to sense specific EM and subspace energies, and will perform homing maneuvers most suitable to the scenario. While Threat defenses exist against photon torpedoes, including high-energy deflector shields and active torpedo countermeasures, improvements in tactical algorithm creation routines are constantly being applied. Phaser "dimpling" of a Threat shield can sometimes allow torpedo penetration for detonation *within* the outer shield layers, constraining the explosion and causing almost total vaporization of the Threat rather than vessel fragmentation.

OTHER APPLICATIONS

Photon torpedoes, being general energy release devices, have found their way into many other specialized applications. Reinforced torpedo casings are able to penetrate geologic formations for deep explosive modifications in terraforming and planetary engineering projects. Torpedoes are detonated as long-range sensor calibrators at both warp and sublight speeds. They are often used to divert or dissociate asteroidal materials designated as hazards to spacecraft and planets.

11.5 BATTLE BRIDGE

Due to the unique nature of vehicle configurations designed into the USS *Enterprise*, a separate command and control center is necessary for the Stardrive, or Battle Section, from which operations may be conducted when in Separated Flight Mode. The Battle Bridge, while duplicating most of the functions of the Main Bridge, concentrates on dedicated piloting, support, and defense systems stations. Early long-range starships lacking separation systems relied upon an auxiliary bridge, usually located deep within the Primary Hull structure, in the event the Main Bridge was disabled.

DESIGN VARIATIONS

Two main variants of the *Galaxy* class Battle Bridge have been installed on the USS *Enterprise* since the starship was constructed. Each has been designed as a replaceable module; swapout is accomplished through a series of electrohydraulic jackscrews in the Battle Section head and structural locking clamps around the base and periphery of the module. Periodic upgrades will be tested out during the entire operational cycle in an effort to maintain adequate defensive capabilities; each *Galaxy* class starship will always exhibit some minor differences when compared with its dockmates.

Similar design philosophies drove the internal arrangement of the Main Bridge and Battle Bridge. The latter main-

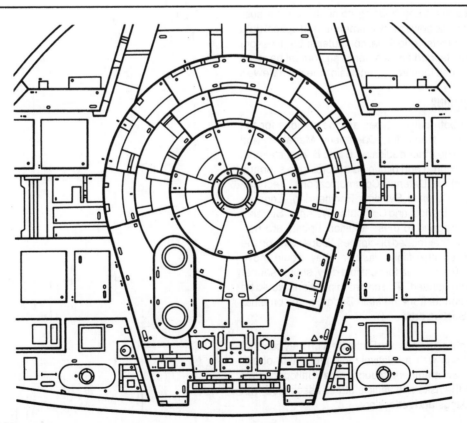

11.5.1 Battle Bridge

11.5.2 Battle Bridge control stations

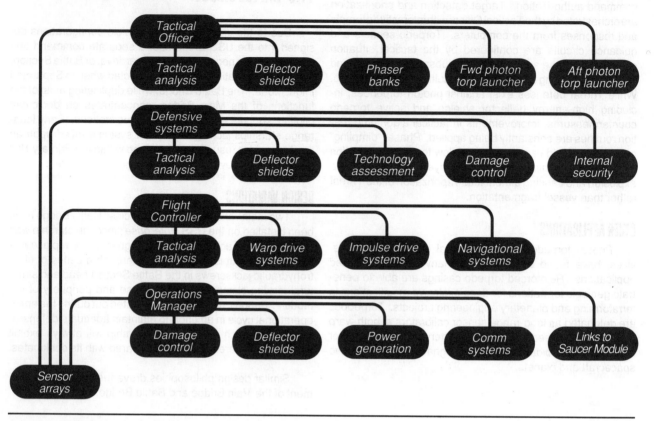

tains an aft equipment bay housing computer optical sub-processors, as well as power, environmental, and optical data network trunk connects. Additional computer subprocessors are located in smaller port and starboard equipment bays, as well as in the armored forward bay enclosing the main viewer.

BATTLE BRIDGE STATIONS

Common to both current types are the stations for the ship captain, Flight Controller, Operations Manager, and Tactical Officer. The other dedicated Battle Bridge stations, which will be configured and occupied according to scenario requirements, include Defense Communications, Technology Assessment, Defense Systems Engineering, Engagement Damage Intelligence, and Computer Systems. Starship crew members assigned to these additional posts are normally assigned to other related disciplines. Depending on the Alert status and specific flight situation, they would move toward the Battle Bridge area for possible duty, should saucer separation be commanded. The common positions would be occupied by personnel from the Main Bridge, or in combination with Battle Section crew.

In benign flight situations, the Battle Section may conduct separate operations with a relatively low proportion of defense-oriented crew members, though the actual options list is limited due to the risks and vehicle stress associated with repeated undockings and redockings.

11.6 TACTICAL POLICIES

Starfleet draws proudly upon the traditions of the navies of many worlds, most notably those of Earth. We honor our distinguished forebears in many ceremonial aspects of our service, yet there is a fundamental difference between Starfleet and those ancient military organizations. Those sailors of old saw themselves as warriors. It is undeniably true that preparedness for battle is an important part of our mission, but we of Starfleet see ourselves foremost as explorers and diplomats. This may seem a tenuous distinction, yet it has a dramatic influence on the way we deal with potential conflicts. When the soldiers of old pursued peace, the very nature of their organizations emphasized the option of using force when conflicts became difficult. That option had an inexorable way of becoming a self-fulfilling prophecy.

Today, peace is no easier than it was in ages past. Conflicts are real, and tensions can escalate at a moment's notice between adversaries who command awesome destructive forces. Yet we have finally learned a bitter lesson from our past: When we regard force as a primary option, that option *will* be exercised. Starfleet's charter, framed some two centuries ago after the brutal Romulan Wars, is based on a solemn commitment that force is *not* to be regarded as an option in interstellar relations unless all other options have been exhausted.

RULES OF ENGAGEMENT

Although starships are fully equipped with sophisticated weaponry and defenses, Starfleet teaches its people to use every means at their disposal to anticipate and defuse potential conflict before the need for force arises. This, according to Federation mandate, is Starfleet's primary mode of conflict resolution. Starfleet's rules of engagement are firmly based on these principles. Due to the extended range of Starfleet's theater of operations, it is not uncommon for starships to be beyond realtime communications range of Starfleet Command. This means a starship captain often has broad discretionary powers in interpreting applicable Federation and Starfleet policies. The details of these rules are classified but the basics are as follows.

A starship is regarded as an instrument of policy for the United Federation of Planets and its member nations. As such, its officers and crew are expected to exhaust every option before resorting to the use of force in conflict resolution. More important, Federation policy requires constant vigilance to anticipate potential conflicts and to take steps to avert them long before they escalate into armed combat.

Perhaps the most dangerous conflict scenario is that of the unknown, technically sophisticated Threat force. This refers to a confrontation with a spacecraft or weapons system from an unknown culture whose spacefaring and/or weapons capability is estimated to be similar or superior to our own. In such cases, the lack of knowledge about the Threat force is a severe handicap in effective conflict resolution and in tactical planning. Complicating matters further, such conflicts are often First Contact scenarios, meaning cultural and sociologic analysis data are likely to be inadequate, yet further increasing the import of the contact in terms of future relationships with the Federation. For these reasons, Starfleet requires cultural and technologic assessment during all First Contact scenarios, even those that occur during combat situations in deep space. Rules of engagement further require that adequate precaution be taken to avoid exposure of the ship and its crew or Federation interests to unnecessary risk, even when a potential Threat force has not specifically demonstrated a hostile intent. There are, however, specific diplomatic conditions under which the starship will be considered expendable.

More common than the unknown adversary is conflict with a known, technically sophisticated Threat force. This refers to confrontation with a spacecraft or weapons system from a culture with which contact has already been made, and whose spacefaring and/or weapons capability is similar or superior to our own, even if the specific spacecraft or weapons system is of an unknown type. In such cases, tactical planning has the advantage of at least some cultural and technologic background of the Threat force, and the ship's captain will have detailed briefings of Federation policies toward the Threat force. In general, starships are not permitted to fire first against any Threat force, and any response to provocation must be measured and in proportion to such provocation. Here again, Starfleet requires adequate precaution be taken to avoid excessive risk to the ship or other Federation interests.

Much more limiting are conflicts with spaceborne Threat forces estimated to be substantially inferior in terms of weapons systems and spaceflight potential. Here again, the use of cultural and technologic assessment is of crucial importance. Prime Directive considerations may severely restrict tactical options to measured responses designed to reduce a Threat force's ability to endanger the starship or third parties. Typically, this means limited strikes to disable weapons or propulsion systems only. Rules of engagement prohibit the destruction of such spacecraft except in extreme cases where Federation interests, third parties, or the starship itself are in immediate jeopardy.

Even more difficult are conflicts in which a Starfleet vessel or the Federation itself is considered to be a third party. Such scenarios include civil and intrasystem conflicts or terrorist situations. In evaluating such cases, due care must be taken to avoid interference in purely local affairs. Still, there are occasionally situations where strategic or humanitarian considerations will require intervention. Starfleet personnel are expected to closely observe Prime Directive considerations in such cases.

11.7 PERSONAL PHASERS

The primary defensive arms carried by Starfleet crew members are two types of small phasers, Type I and Type II. Both are high-energy devices sized for personal use and can be stowed in or attached to one's uniform. As with the larger ship-mounted arrays, the Type I and II phasers convert stored energy into tightly controllable beams for a variety of applications. Type III phaser rifles are also available for special situations, although these are rarely necessary on normal Starfleet away missions and are therefore not incuded in the ship's standard inventory.

Phasers operate on a modified version of the rapid nadion effect, previously described in 11.1. Rapid nadions produce a pulsed protonic charge in the heart of the device, a stabilized LiCu 521 superconducting crystal (lattice formula $Li<>Cu><Si::Fe<:>O$). LiCu 521 is an advanced version of the 518 crystal mass-produced for the ship's Type X Main Phaser and exhibits a 3% improvement in thermodynamic efficiency at 92.65%.

HARDWARE ARRANGEMENT AND OPERATION

Most features of personal phaser internal configuration are common to Type I and Type II (See: 11.7.1). Energy is stored within a replenishable sarium krellide cell. Sarium krellide holds a maximum of 1.3×10^6 megajoules per cubic

centimeter, at a maximum leak rate of no more than 1.05 kilojoules per hour. When one considers that the total stored energy of even the Type I phaser, if released all at once, is enough to vaporize three cubic meters of tritanium, it is reassuring to know that a full storage cell cannot be discharged accidentally. Sarium krellide must be coupled with the LiCu 521 crystal for discharge to occur. Cell charging can be accomplished aboard ship through standard power taps of the electro plasma system, and in the field through portable bulk sarium krellide units. The Type I cell measures 2.4 x 3.0 cm and holds 7.2×10^6 MJ; the Type II cell measures 10.2 x 3.0 cm and holds 4.5×10^7 MJ.

Downstream from the power cell are three interconnected control modules: the beam control assembly, safety interlock, and subspace transceiver assembly (STA). The beam control assembly includes tactile interface buttons for configuring the phaser beam width and intensity, and a firing trigger. The safety interlock is a code processor for safing the power functions of the phaser and for personalizing a phaser for limited personnel use. Key-press combinations of beam width and intensity controls are used to configure the phaser's safety condition. The STA is used as part of the safety system while aboard Starfleet vessels. It maintains contact between the phaser and the ship computers to assure that power levels are automatically restrained during shipboard firings, usually limited to heavy stun. Emergency override commands may be keyed in by the beam controls. The STA adapted for phaser use is augmented with target sensors and processors

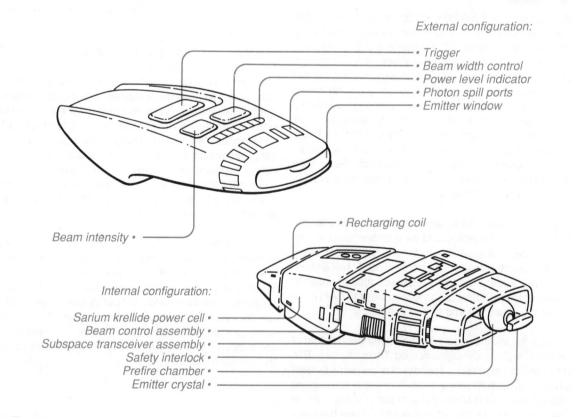

External configuration:
- Trigger
- Beam width control
- Power level indicator
- Photon spill ports
- Emitter window

Beam intensity •

• Recharging coil

Internal configuration:

Sarium krellide power cell •
Beam control assembly •
Subspace transceiver assembly •
Safety interlock •
Prefire chamber •
Emitter crystal •

11.7.1 Type I personal phaser

11.7.2 Type II personal phaser

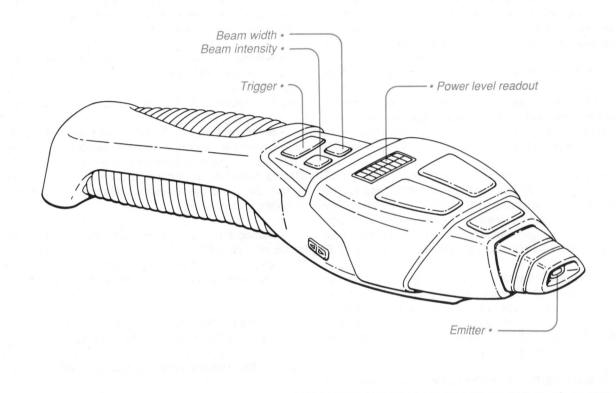

Beam width •
Beam intensity •
Trigger •
• Power level readout
Emitter •

for distant aiming functions.

Energy from the power cell is controlled by all three modules and routed by shielded conduits to a prefire chamber, a 1.5 cm diameter sphere of LiCu 521 reinforced with gulium arkenide. Here the energy is held temporarily by a collapsible charge barrier before passing to the actual LiCu 521 emitter for discharge out of the phaser, creating a pulse. As with the larger phaser types, the power level set by the user determines the pulse frequency and relative proportion of protonic charge created in the final emitter stage. The Type I contains a single prefire chamber; the Type II contains four.

At triggering, the charge barrier field breaks down in 0.02 picoseconds. Through the rapid nadion effect the LiCu 521 segmented emitter converts the pumped energy into a tuned phaser discharge. As with the ship's main phasers, the greater the energy pumped from the prefire chamber, the higher will be the percentage of nuclear disruption force (NDF) created. At low to moderate settings, the nuclear disruption threshold will not be crossed, limiting the phaser discharge to stun and thermal impact resulting from simple electromagnetic (SEM) effects.

At the higher settings, as an override precaution for the user, the discharge will take a distance of approximately one meter to decay and recombine to form full-lethality emissions. In the Type I, the emitter crystal is an elliptical solid measuring 0.5 x 1.2 cm. In the Type II, it is a regular trapezoid 1.5 x 2.85 cm.

AVAILABLE POWER SETTINGS AND EFFECTS

The power levels available to both the Type I and Type II phasers are designated 1 to 8. The Type II has an additional eight levels, from 9 to 16, all involving high proportions of nuclear disruption energy. The Type III phaser rifle has power levels similar to the Type II personal phaser, except that its power reserve is nearly 50% greater. The following list describes the effects associated with each level:

• **Setting 1:** Light Stun; discharge energy index 15.75 for 0.25 seconds, SEM:NDF ratio not applicable. This setting is calibrated for base humanoid physiology, and causes temporary central nervous system (CNS) impairment. Subjects remain unconscious for up to five minutes. Higher levels of reversible CNS damage result from repeated long exposures. The discharge energy index is related to RNE protonic charge levels. Standard median-density composite structural material samples are not permanently affected, although small vibrational warming will be detected. A standard composite sample consists of multiple layers of tritanium, duranium, cortenite, lignin, and lithium-silicon-carbon 372. A standardized damage index is derived for setting comparisons; each whole number represents the number of cm of material penetrated or molecularly damaged. The damage index for this setting is zero.

• **Setting 2:** Medium Stun; discharge energy 45.30 for

0.75 seconds, SEM:NDF ratio not applicable. Base-type humanoids are rendered unconscious for up to fifteen minutes, resistant humanoids up to five minutes. Long exposures produce low levels of irreversible CNS and epithelial damage. Structural materials are not affected, though higher levels of vibrational warming are evident. The damage index is zero.

• **Setting 3:** Heavy Stun; discharge energy 160.65 for 1.025 seconds, SEM:NDF ratio not applicable. Base humanoids remain in a sleep state for approximately one hour, resistant bioforms for fifteen minutes. Single discharges raise 1cc of liquid water by 100°C. Structural samples experience significant levels of thermal radiation. The damage index is 1.

• **Setting 4:** Thermal Effects; discharge energy 515.75 for 1.5 seconds, SEM:NDF ratio not applicable. Base humanoids experience extensive CNS damage and epidermal EM trauma. Structural materials exhibit visible thermal shock. Discharges of longer than five seconds produce deep heat storage effects within metal alloys. The damage index is 3.5.

• **Setting 5:** Thermal Effects; discharge energy 857.5 for 1.5 seconds, SEM:NDF ratio 250:1. Humanoid tissue experiences severe burn effects but, due to water content, deep layers will not char. Simple personnel forcefields are penetrated after five seconds. Large Away Team fields will not be affected. The damage index is 7.

• **Setting 6:** Disruption Effects; discharge energy 2,700 for 1.75 seconds, SEM:NDF ratio 90:1. Organic tissues and structural materials exhibit comparable penetration and molecular damage effects as higher energies cause matter to dissociate rapidly. Familiar thermal effects begin decreasing at this level. The damage index is 15.

• **Setting 7:** Disruption Effects; discharge energy 4,900 for 1.75 seconds, SEM:NDF ratio 1:1. Organic tissue damage causes immediate cessation of life processes, since disruption effects become widespread. The damage index is 50.

• **Setting 8:** Disruption Effects; discharge energy 15,000 for 1.75 seconds, SEM:NDF ratio 1:3. Cascading disruption forces cause humanoid organisms to vaporize, as 50% of affected matter transitions out of the continuum. The damage index is 120; all unprotected matter is affected and penetrated according to depth/time.

• **Setting 9:** Disruption Effects; discharge energy 65,000 for 1.5 seconds, SEM:NDF ratio 1:7. The damage index is 300; medium alloy or ceramic structural materials over 100 cm thickness begin exhibiting energy rebound prior to vaporization.

• **Setting 10:** Disruption Effects; discharge energy 125,000 for 1.3 seconds, SEM:NDF ratio 1:9. The damage index is 450; heavy alloy structural materials absorb or rebound energy, 0.55 sec delay before material vaporizes.

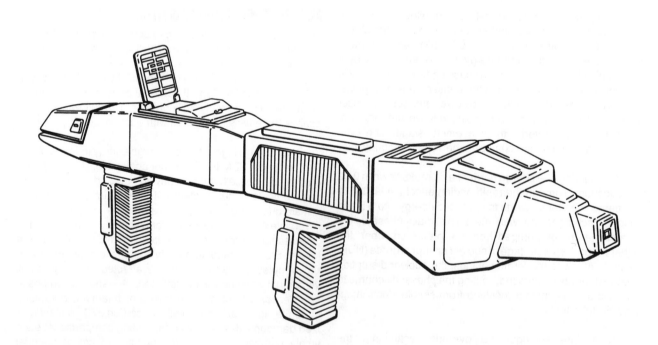

11.7.3 Type III phaser rifle

• **Setting 11:** Explosive/Disruption Effects; discharge energy 300,000 for 0.78 seconds, SEM:NDF ratio 1:11. The damage index is 670; ultradense alloy structural materials absorb/rebound energy, 0.20 sec delayed reaction before material vaporizes. Light geologic displacement; $\leq$10 m^3 rock/ore of 6.0 g/cm^3 explosively uncoupled per discharge.

• **Setting 12:** Explosive/Disruption Effects; discharge energy 540,000 for 0.82 seconds, SEM:NDF ratio 1:14. The damage index is 940; ultradense alloy structural materials absorb/rebound energy, 0.1 sec delayed reaction before material vaporizes. Medium geologic displacement; $\leq$50 m^3 rock/ore of 6.0 g/cm^3 explosively uncoupled per discharge.

• **Setting 13:** Explosive/Disruption Effects; discharge energy 720,000 for 0.82 seconds, SEM:NDF ratio 1:18. The damage index is 1,100; shielded matter exhibits minor vibrational heating effects. Medium geologic displacement; $\leq$90 m^3 rock/ore of 6.0 g/cm^3 explosively uncoupled per discharge.

• **Setting 14:** Explosive/Disruption Effects; discharge energy 930,000 for 0.75 seconds, SEM:NDF ratio 1:20. The damage index is 1,430; shielded matter exhibits medium vibrational heating effects. Heavy geologic displacement; $\leq$160 m^3 rock/ore of 6.0 g/cm^3 explosively uncoupled per discharge.

• **Setting 15:** Explosive/Disruption Effects; discharge energy 1.17 x 10^6 for 0.32 seconds, SEM:NDF ratio 1:25. The damage index is 1,850; shielded matter exhibits major vibrational heating effects. Heavy geologic displacement; $\leq$370 m^3 rock/ore of 6.0 g/cm^3 explosively uncoupled per discharge.

• **Setting 16:** Explosive/Disruption Effects; discharge energy 1.55 x 10^6 for 0.28 seconds, SEM:NDF ratio 1:40. The damage index is 2,450; shielded matter exhibits light mechanical fracturing damage. Heavy geologic displacement; $\leq$650 m^3 rock/ore of 6.0 g/cm^3 explosively uncoupled per discharge.

SAFETY CONSIDERATIONS

As a result of the basic physics required to produce a phaser discharge, an undesirable but unavoidable process exists, namely that of phaser overload. The accepted methods employed for energy storage, flow, control, and discharge allow for an amplified rebounding to occur from the storage cell to the prefire chamber, and simultaneously back to the storage cell. While the total energy within the system remains the same, the flow pressure is elevated during the rebound, to the point where the storage cell cannot reabsorb the energy fast enough. The barrier field will be reinforced during this buildup, effectively preventing normal discharge through the emitter.

Conductive acoustic effects manifest themselves during overload, ranging from 6 kHz to over 20 kHz within thirty seconds. Explosive destruction of the phaser will occur when the energy level exceeds the prefire chamber's density and structural limits.

The safety interlock will prevent overload under most operating conditions, though the design specifications could not cope with some forms of tampering. This can become a priority security matter should a standard-issue phaser fall into the hands of a Threat force.

PERSONNEL TRAINING AND OPERATIONS

All Starfleet and attached personnel receive initial basic instruction on the operation and use of a low-power variant of the Type I phaser (limited to Setting 3). All Starfleet officers receive advanced training and are issued full-power Type I phasers as personal defensive arms. During Alert conditions aboard ship and during Away Missions, the Security Division will oversee the distribution of Type II units. Training for the use of Type III phaser rifles is available on starbases only.

Continued proficiency training in defensive techniques is maintained at four-month intervals for shipboard personnel, and at one-month intervals for Away Team candidates. Each Security Division officer's continuing phaser training progresses at varied rates, depending on individual specialties.

11.8 DEFLECTOR SHIELDS

The tactical deflector system is the primary defensive system of the *Galaxy* class starship. It is a series of powerful deflector shields that protect both the spacecraft and its crew from both natural and artificial hazards.

Like most forcefield devices, the deflector system creates a localized zone of highly focused spatial distortion within which an energetic graviton field is maintained. The deflector field itself is emitted and shaped by a series of conformal transmission grids on the spacecraft exterior, resulting in a field that closely follows the form of the vehicle itself. This field is highly resistive to impact due to mechanical incursions ranging from relativistic subatomic particles to more massive objects at lesser relative velocities. When such an intrusion occurs, field energy is concentrated at the point of impact, creating an intense, localized spatial distortion.

To an observer aboard the starship, it appears that the intruding object has "bounced off" the shield. A zero-dimensional observer on the intruding object would, however, perceive that his/her trajectory is unaffected, but that the location of the starship has suddenly changed. This is somewhat analogous to the spatial distortion created by a natural gravity well, and is typically accompanied by a momentary discharge of Cerenkov radiation, often perceived as a brief blue flash. The deflector is also effective against a wide range of electromagnetic, nuclear, and other radiated and field energies.

FIELD GENERATORS

The deflector system utilizes one or more graviton polarity source generators whose output is phase-synchronized through a series of subspace field distortion amplifiers. Flux energy for the Primary Hull is generated by five field generators located on Deck 10. Three additional generators are located on Deck 31 in the Secondary Hull. Two additional field generators are located in each of the warp nacelles, although the output of the Saucer Module grid can be boosted to include the nacelles if necessary. Each generator consists of a cluster of twelve 32 MW graviton polarity sources feeding a pair of 625 millicochrane subspace field distortion amplifiers. Cruise

Mode operating rules require one generator in each major section to be operational at all times, with at least one additional unit available for activation should an Alert condition be invoked. During Alert situations, all operational deflector generators are normally brought to full standby.

Nominal system output (Cruise Mode) of the deflector system is 1152 MW graviton load. Peak momentary load of a single generator can approach 473,000 MW for periods approaching 170 milliseconds. During Alert status, up to seven generators can be operated in parallel phase-lock, providing a continuous output of 2688 MW, with a maximum primary energy dissipation rate in excess of 7.3×10^5 kW.

Heat dissipation on each generator is provided by a pair of liquid helium coolant loops with a continuous-duty rating of 750,000 MJ. Four backup generators are located in each hull, providing up to twenty-four hours of service at 65% of nominal rated power. Normal duty cycle on primary generators is twelve hours on-line, with nominal twelve hours degauss and scheduled maintenance time. Graviton polarity sources are rated for 1,250 operating hours between routine servicing of superconductive elements.

SHIELD OPERATING FREQUENCIES

Providing shielding against the entire spectrum of electromagnetic radiation would prove far too energy-costly for normal Cruise Mode use. Additionally, a full-spectrum shielding system would prevent onboard sensors from gathering many types of scientific and tactical data. Instead, Cruise Mode operating rules allow for deflectors to operate at the relatively low level (approximately 5% of rated output) and at the specific frequency bands necessary to protect the spacecraft's habitable volume to SFRA-standard 347.3(a) levels for EM and nuclear radiation.

During Alert situations, shields are raised to defensive configuration by increasing generator power to at least 85% of rated output. Shield modulation frequencies and bandwidths are randomly varied to prevent a Threat force from adjusting the frequency of a directed energy weapon (such as a phaser) to penetrate shields by matching frequency and phase. Conversely, when the frequency characteristics of a

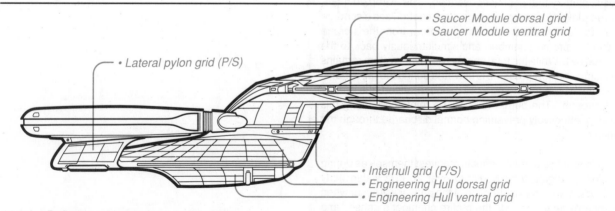

• Saucer Module dorsal grid
• Saucer Module ventral grid
• Lateral pylon grid (P/S)
• Interhull grid (P/S)
• Engineering Hull dorsal grid
• Engineering Hull ventral grid

11.8.1   *Deflector grids (starboard elevation)*

11.8.2 Deflector grids (dorsal view)

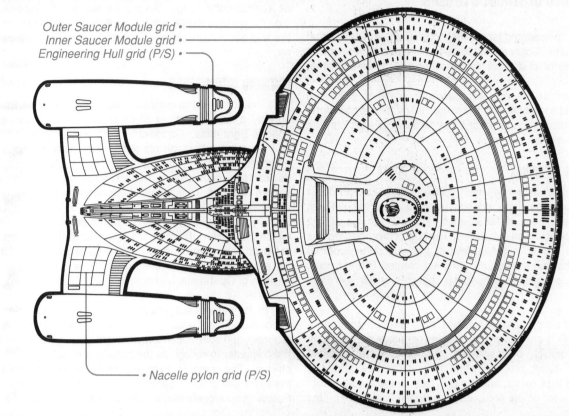

Outer Saucer Module grid •
Inner Saucer Module grid •
Engineering Hull grid (P/S) •

• Nacelle pylon grid (P/S)

directed energy weapon are known, it is possible to dramatically increase deflector efficiency by adjusting the shielding frequencies to match those of the incoming weapon. Similar techniques are used to protect the vehicle against various natural hazards, as when shielding is increased in the 10^{-10} meter band to protect against X rays generated by a supernova.

Raising shields to defensive configuration also triggers a number of special operating rules. First, active sensor scans are operated according to special protocols that are intended to minimize the interference due to the shielding effects. For certain types of scans, sensors are continually recalibrated to take advantage of any EM "windows" left open by rotation of shield frequencies. In other cases, the random variation of shield frequencies is modified slightly to allow a specific EM window at specific intervals necessary for data collection. Such sensor operation techniques generally result in substantially reduced data collection rates, so sensor usage is strictly prioritized during Alert situations. Further, most defensive scenarios require sensors to be operated in "silent running" mode during which the usage of active scan sensors is not permitted and only passive sensors may be used.

Also affected by deflector shield usage is operation of the transporter system. The annular confinement beam that

serves as the transmission medium for the transporter beam requires such a wide EM and subspace bandwidth that it is normally impossible to transport through shields. Additionally, the shields' spatial distortion effects can be severely disruptive of the transporter beam's pattern integrity.

Shield operation also has a significant impact on warp drive operation. Because of the spatial distortion inherent in the shielding generation process, there is a measurable effect on the geometry of the warp fields that propel the ship. Warp drive control software therefore includes a number of routines designed to compensate for the presence of deflector shields, which would otherwise cause (at maximum rated output) a 32% degradation in force coupling energy transfer. Simultaneously, shield generator output must be upshifted by approximately 147 kilohertz to compensate for translational field interaction.

The idea of frequency "windows" in the shields used for sensor scans was the basis of O'Brien's trick in "The Wounded" when he was able to beam onto the USS Phoenix, *even though that ship's shields were raised at the time.*

11.9 AUTO-DESTRUCT SYSTEMS

It is an accepted fact of life aboard Starfleet vessels that the ultimate sacrifice may have to be made to insure that neither the intact starship nor the technology contained therein will fall into the possession of Threat forces. The total destruction of the docked spacecraft or either of its two separated components can be executed by special command authorization procedures, and may be accomplished with two related systems.

DESTRUCT SCENARIOS

Most situations in which vehicle destruct would occur have been extensively modeled using computer simulations. As this is a tactic of extreme last resort, all other available options must first be exhausted. The bulk of the modeling has centered around potential loss of the ship during combat operations with known and computer-created Threat forces, although sophisticated hijacking schemes cannot be ruled out.

In the worst-case examples, all propulsion and defensive systems are irreversibly disabled or destroyed, and there is no possibility of assistance by other Starfleet or allied vessels. A high probability that the ship can be boarded or tractored then exists, and the activation of the auto-destruct sequence within the computer is to be the final event. To a lesser degree, certain scenarios judge a disabled starship to be a catastrophic danger to a greater number of living beings; e.g., the population of a planet, requiring the abandonment of the ship and its subsequent destruction to prevent the disaster.

COMMAND AUTHORIZATION

The command to activate auto-destruct can be issued only by a limited number of crew members according to specific flight rules. Conditional tests programmed into the main computers are distributed to key autonomous sub-processor nodes throughout the ship to allow the auto-destruct sequence to be carried out, even if the main computers are disabled. These tests check for the proper sequence activation inputs by command personnel, beginning with the captain and first officer. The programmed conditions check for the succession of command personnel; if either the captain or first officer is determined by the computer to be unavailable, the system will accept inputs from officers only down to the position of Operations Manager.

In the case of authorization issued by the captain and executive officer, the captain activates the destruct sequence program, and both officers provide verbal input, which permits the computer to recognize the identity and authority of both officers. The computer then requests verbal confirmation of the executive officer's concurrence with the destruct order. Following such confirmation, the computer will request the de-

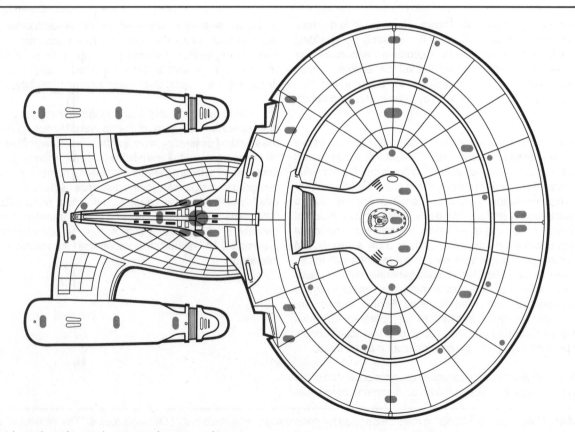

11.9.1 Location of auto-destruct ordnance packages

sired interval until destruct. At this point, the auto-destruct sequence will commence, counting down until scheduled destruct. Computer voice announcements and data graphic displays throughout the spacecraft provide time-remaining information.

The auto-destruct sequence can be aborted by voice command at any time prior to the actual activation of the ordnance packages at T − 0 seconds. Authority for cancellation of the auto-destruct sequence is vested with the captain and executive officer.

HARDWARE CONFIGURATION AND OPERATION

In the preferred configuration, the starship undergoes rapid vaporization from thermal and mechanical shock caused by a deliberate release of warp engine reactants. Remote computer system decryption algorithms generate one final set of cascade failure commands, and all engine safety interlocks are compromised. Matter from the primary deuterium tankage and the total supply of antimatter from the storage pods on Deck 42 are expelled simultaneously, producing an energy release on the order of 10^{15} megajoules, roughly equivalent to 1,000 photon torpedoes.

If the command links to the engine systems are severed, the secondary destruct system is automatically selected. Ordnance packages are located at key locations around the vehicle, including the antimatter storage pods. These are detonated in concert with intentional overloads of all fusion reaction chambers. The release yield of the secondary system is calculated to be 10^9 megajoules, roughly equivalent to 500 photon torpedoes. The secondary destruct system becomes the primary system for the Saucer Module in Separated Flight Mode.

12.0 ENVIRONMENTAL SYSTEMS

12.1 LIFE SUPPORT AND ENVIRONMENTAL CONTROL

Of all major ship's systems, life support and environmental control are among the most critical. Every key system element is designed with multiple redundancy to provide for maximum crew safety, even in the unlikely event of multiple system failure. Under normal operating conditions, the mean time between failure for the environmental systems should exceed five hundred operating years. Even under such a total failure, emergency backups should insure crew survival in most situations.

Major life support equipment facilities are located in the Primary Hull on Decks 6, 9, and 13. In the Engineering Hull, major life support equipment is located on Decks 11, 21, 24, and 34. The primary life support systems comprise two parallel systems, each serving as a backup to the other. Synthetic gravity generators are located throughout the habitable volume of the spacecraft.

Each major life support facility includes a tie-in to the reserve utilities distribution networks. These tie-ins include a limited supply of critical consumables, including breathable air, power supply, and water. The reserve utilities distribution network is designed to provide minimal life support and power in the event of complete disruption of both primary environmental support systems.

Other emergency provisions include distributed reserve life support systems, emergency support shelter areas, and contingency support modules intended to provide shipwide breathable atmosphere for up to thirty minutes in a major systemwide failure.

12.2 ATMOSPHERIC SYSTEM

The USS *Enterprise* environmental system maintains a Class M compatible oxygen-nitrogen atmosphere throughout the habitable volume of the spacecraft. Two independent primary atmospheric plenum systems deliver temperature and humidity controlled environmental gases throughout the vehicle. Additionally, a separate reserve system and emergency systems provide additional redundancy.

Atmospheric processing units for the primary system are located throughout the spacecraft at the rate of approximately two redundant primary units for every 50 m^3 of habitable ship's volume. These devices maintain a comfortable, breathable mixture by removing CO_2 and other waste gases and particulates, then replenishing the O_2 partial pressure. This is principally accomplished through the use of photosynthetic bioprocessing. The atmospheric processors also maintain temperature and humidity within prescribed limits. Once so processed, the breathing mixture is recirculated through the plenum network.

Cruise Mode operational rules specify a ninety-six-hour duty cycle for processing modules, although normal time between scheduled maintenance is approximately two thousand operating hours. At the end of each ninety-six-hour duty cycle, it is normal for the entire atmospheric processing load to be automatically switched to the alternate primary system. It is, however, possible to individually switch specific system elements as needed. Atmospheric plenum flow can be remotely switched at utilities junction nodes, so that breathing atmosphere can be rerouted to processors at other locations, offering an additional measure of redundancy.

The reserve system is a third redundant set of atmospheric processors, providing up to 50% of nominal system capacity for periods up to twenty-four hours, depending on system load. These are intended for use in the event of incapacity of major elements of the two primary atmospheric systems. The reserve system shares the plenum network of the two primary systems, and operates by computerized system analysis, which allows any damaged plenum sections or processors to be isolated and removed from service.

Additionally, emergency atmospheric supply systems provide breathing mixture to designated shelter areas for up to thirty-six hours in crisis situations. These systems draw on independent oxygen and power supplies, physically isolated from the primary systems and from each other. The emergency systems are not intended to provide shipwide atmospheric supply. The emergency atmospheric supply systems provide minimal recycling capacity (CO_2 scrubbing and O_2 replenishment only), but oxygen supply can be significantly extended by drawing on any available supplies from the three primary systems, or from any unused contingency supply modules.

In case of major failure of atmospheric supply necessitating use of the emergency system, contingency atmospheric supply modules, located at most corridor junctions, will maintain a breathable environment for approximately thirty minutes, sufficient for the crew to evacuate to shelters. Environmental suits would be provided to all personnel required to work in areas in which a breathable atmosphere is not maintained. Except in cases of large-scale explosive decompression, even a severe atmospheric supply failure is expected to permit upward of fifty minutes for evacuation of all personnel to designated shelter areas.

Nominal atmospheric values for Class M compatible conditions (per SFRA-standard 102.19) are 26°C, 45% relative humidity, with pressure maintained at 101 kilopascals (760 mmHg). Atmospheric composition is maintained at 78% nitrogen, 21% oxygen, 1% trace gases. Approximately ten percent of living accommodations can be switched to Class H, K, or L environmental conditions without major hardware swapout. An additional 2% of living accommodations are equipped for Class N and N(2) conditions. Atmospheric processing modules can be replaced at major starbase layover to permit vehiclewide adaptation to Class H, K, or L environmental conditions.

Believability (not to mention crew safety) demands that the Enterprise environmental support systems be extremely reliable with many redundant backups. The problem from a television standpoint is this makes it a little tough to create story situations in which our crew can be threatened by life support failure. In one episode, "Brothers," writer-producer Rick Berman needed all bridge atmospheric support systems to fail. He rationalized it by having Geordi express amazement that seven independent safety interlocks had been bypassed, thereby acknowledging that the ship is indeed designed to make such failures extremely improbable.

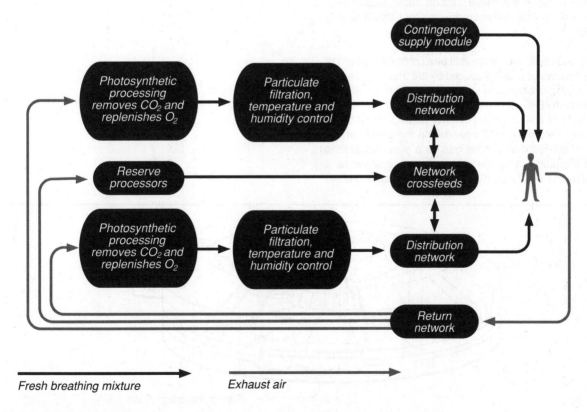

Fresh breathing mixture ➤

Exhaust air ➤

12.2.1 Atmospheric system

12.3 GRAVITY GENERATION

Since the time of the first orbital research stations in the Sol system, the difficulties as well as the benefits presented by microgravity situations have been exhaustively documented.

The crews of the first true human-built interstellar craft of the twenty-first century coped with acceleration and zero-*g* coasting mission segments through the use of rotating centrifuges, acceptable solutions for the day.

Humanoid organ systems require gravitational and electromagnetic fields to insure proper cellular growth and viability, simulating the natural conditions present on most Class M worlds. Low-level field devices simulated the planetary electrical and magnetic energy, and the descendants of many twenty- to thirty-year flights arrived in a healthy state.

The general planform of the *Galaxy* class starship returns to a more natural existence in that people are free to move about on planar surfaces with a constant gravity holding them to the deck. Aboard the starship, this is accomplished through the use of a network of small gravity generators. The network is divided into four regions, two within the Saucer Module and two within the Battle Section. All four work to maintain the proper sense of "down," and are also actively tied to the inertial damping field system to minimize motion shock during flight. The two Saucer Module gravity networks each support 400 generators; those in the Battle Section each support 200. Fields overlap slightly between devices, but this is barely noticeable.

The gravity field itself is created by a controlled stream of gravitons, much like those produced by the tractor beam. In fact, the basic physics is the same. Power from the electro plasma system (EPS) is channeled into a hollow chamber of anicium titanide 454, a sealed cylinder measuring 50 cm in diameter by 25 cm high. Suspended in the center of the cylinder, in pressurized chrylon gas, is a superconducting stator of thoronium arkenide. The stator, once set to a rotational rate above 125,540 rpm, generates a graviton field

with a short lifetime, on the order of a few picoseconds. This decay time necessitates the addition of the second layer of generators beyond 30 meters distance. The field is gentle enough to allow natural walking without a gravity gradient from head to foot, long a problem in brute-force physical centripetal systems.

The superconducting stator remains suspended from the time of manufacture, and requires only an occasional synchronizing energy pulse from the EPS, normally once each sixty minutes. In the event of EPS failure, the stator will continue to provide an attraction field for up to 240 minutes, though some degradation to about 0.8*g* will be detected. Any perceived ship motions that might disturb the stator gyroscopically are damped by sinesoidal ribs on the inner surface of the anicium titanide cylinder, effectively absorbing motions with an amplitude of less than or equal to 6 cm/sec. All higher-amplitude motions are relieved by the ship's inertial damping field.

Gravity generators are located throughout the habitable volume of the spacecraft. Because of this, inertial potential can vary from one location within the ship to another, especially during severe turning maneuvers. In order to allow translation of excess inertial potential from one part of the ship to another, the gravity generators are connected together by a network of small waveguide conduits that allow field bleed for gravitational stability.

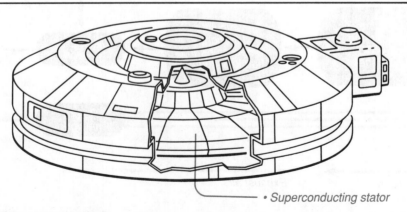

• *Superconducting stator*

12.3.1 Synthetic gravity generator (typical)

12.4 EMERGENCY ENVIRONMENTAL SYSTEMS

The basic design philosophy of the *Enterprise* environmental support systems is for extreme reliability coupled with multiple redundancy. Nevertheless, Starfleet recognizes the unknown hazards to which starships and their crews are often exposed, and has provided yet another layer of preparedness for potential environmental crisis situations.

The purpose of these emergency environmental support systems is to provide suitable life support for the crew for periods of time sufficient for the Engineering staff to restore normal function to either primary system or to the reserve system. The first element of this is an emergency backup system designed to provide shipwide lighting and atmospheric supply for approximately thirty minutes. This is intended to allow an orderly evacuation of all ship's personnel to emergency support shelters. These shelters are the second element of the emergency environmental support system.

CONTINGENCY ATMOSPHERIC AND POWER SUPPLY

Supplementing the two redundant primary atmospheric support systems and reserve backup system is the contingency atmospheric and power supply system. This system consists of 425 self-contained air supply and power modules located throughout the ship at many corridor junctions.

The principal elements of these modules include ventilation fans, cryogenic oxygen storage, CO_2 scrubbers, emergency lights, and batteries. In the event of a total failure of all primary and reserve systems, these units provide approximately thirty minutes of atmosphere and lighting throughout the ship, allowing all personnel to take sanctuary in designated environmental support shelters.

EMERGENCY SHELTERS

In the event of major shipwide failure of environmental support, personnel can be instructed to report to one of fifty-two emergency shelter areas located throughout the habitable volume of the vehicle. Each designated shelter area is designed to sustain up to sixty-five crew members for up to thirty-six hours, assuming a minimum level of external support. These areas receive priority life support from a series of dedicated, protected utilities trunks so that they can remain habitable even in the event of major system outages elsewhere in the spacecraft.

These shelters are also equipped with independent emergency breathing gas, water, food, and power supplies for up to twenty-four hours of operation, even with no support from other ship's systems. Emergency shelters are also equipped with at least two emergency pressure garment (EPG) environment suits, allowing crew personnel to travel through the unprotected portions of the vehicle for possible repair or rescue operations (See: 14.4).

OTHER SCENARIOS

A lesser environmental support failure may result in one or more areas being rendered uninhabitable. In such cases, the Commanding Officer may opt to evacuate the affected areas in order to protect crew personnel or to conserve life support capacity. Another option in the event of anticipated environmental systems failure is to evacuate personnel to shelter areas to minimize risk in the event that switchover to emergency backups is necessary.

A more severe failure could force the evacuation of either the entire Saucer Module or Stardrive Section, with the crew taking refuge in the unaffected section. In such cases, environmental engineering personnel could remain in the damaged section to attempt repairs.

In the episode "Night Terrors," the Ten Forward lounge was established to be a designated emergency environmental support shelter.

12.5 WASTE MANAGEMENT

The USS *Enterprise*, like most large deep-space vehicles, sustains a closed ecological system to maintain environmental support. Unlike a planetary biosphere, however, a starship must use technologic means to approximate the complex ecologic processes that sustain life. Among these processes aboard the *Enterprise* are the waste management systems, which make optimal reuse of waste products. Without such recycling, the ship would be unable to carry sufficient food and water for the extended voyages required by many Starfleet missions.

WATER AND SEWAGE RECYCLING

Each crew member aboard the *Enterprise* typically generates approximately 52 liters of wastewater and sewage per day. This wastewater is pumped to treatment and recycling units located in the environmental support complexes on Decks 6, 13, and 24. Preliminary treatment is accomplished by a series of mechanical filtration processes that remove solids and particulates. (The residue is conveyed to the organic waste processing system for further treatment and recycling.) Osmotic and electrolytic fractioning is then employed to remove dissolved and microscopic contaminants for treatment and recycling. The resulting water is superheated to 150°C for biological sterilization before being subjected to a final mechanical filtration stage, then it is returned to one of several freshwater storage tanks for reuse.

The various waste sludges recovered from the water recycling processes are a valuable resource. The organic waste processing system subjects the sludge to a series of sterilizing heat and radiation treatments. The waste is then electrolytically reprocessed into an organic particulate suspension that serves as the raw material for the food synthesizer systems. Remaining byproducts are conveyed to the solid waste processing system for matter replication recycling.

SOLID WASTE RECYCLING

Solid waste such as trash is conveyed to processing units on Decks 9, 13, and 34 by means of linear induction utility conduits. Incoming solid waste is automatically scanned and classified as to type and composition. Items that can be recycled with mechanical reprocessing are separated. Such items, which constitute approximately 82% of all solid waste, include articles of clothing, packaging and other discarded containers, and small personal articles. These items are conveyed to a series of dedicated processors that first sterilize the waste products, then reduce them to a recyclable form (such as the processed fiber packets from which uniforms and other garments are fabricated). Hazardous materials (such as toxic, biohazard, and radioactive substances) are separated, and the remaining unrecoverable material is stored for matter replication recycling.

MATTER REPLICATION RECYCLING

Material that cannot be directly recycled by mechanical or chemical means is stored for matter synthesis recycling. This is accomplished by molecular matrix replicators that actually dematerialize the waste materials and rematerialize them in the form of desired objects or materials stored in computer memory. While this process provides an enormous variety of useful items, it is very energy intensive and many everyday consumables (such as water and clothing) are recycled by less energy intensive mechanical or chemical means. Certain types of consumables (such as foodstuffs) are routinely recycled using matter replication because this results in a considerable savings of stored raw material (See: 13.5).

HAZARDOUS WASTE RECYCLING

Approximately 5% of all liquid and solid wastes are considered to be hazardous materials under toxicity, reactivity, biohazard, or radioactivity standards. Such materials are separated from other waste materials and are immediately diverted to a matter replicator, which converts them to inert carbon particles. This material is then stored for matter replication recycling.

The Star Trek *production company has been making its own efforts toward recycling the resources of planet Earth. Bins have been placed in the production offices as well as on the soundstages for the recycling of aluminum, paper, glass, and plastics, an effort spearheaded by* Star Trek *craft services person John Nesterowicz. (Particularly good use is made of our paper recycling bins, as a television company goes through a lot of paper to do its work.) The use of ozone-threatening, nondegradable plastic foam coffee cups has been abolished on our shooting stages, as well. During the filming of the movie* Star Trek VI, *director Nick Meyer ordered recycling bins placed on those stages, as well.* Star Trek *and Paramount Pictures have also embarked upon a major effort to reduce the creation of air pollutants by eliminating the use of certain types of spray lacquers for set painting and some types of special effects smoke and fog machines. Other environmentally conscious efforts offered by the studio include programs to encourage employee carpooling and company-sponsored discount bus passes. Some of these measures are quite costly in terms of finding acceptable substitutes, but all agree that the goal of protecting our environment is worth it.*

13.0 CREW SUPPORT SYSTEMS

13.1 CREW SUPPORT

Starfleet recognizes that its single most important system and most valuable resource is its people. The crew of a starship determines, far more than any technology or hardware, the success of any given mission. Accordingly, Starfleet has a long tradition of placing its personnel at the top of its priority list.

The long, exacting, and frequently hazardous nature of starship duty places a very considerable toll on its crew. Yet the nature of Starfleet missions requires each crew member to be continually operating at very near 100%. The success of a mission, the safety of the ship, or the fate of an entire planet can at any moment hinge on the performance of any crew member. Reconciling the demanding nature of starship duty with the need to maintain quality over extended periods is a difficult goal, but Starfleet's personnel policies make it a reality.

Starfleet personnel are well trained and highly motivated, but maintaining that motivation is an ongoing challenge. Starfleet's command structure is designed to support this philosophy and our officers understand the importance of nurturing and encouraging the efforts of each crew member. This ranges from ample opportunities for personnel to advance within Starfleet, to a policy of actively listening to the needs and concerns of all personnel. Each crew member is encouraged to be innovative in his/her job, and allowed to excel in his/her chosen area. Indeed, many of our most important technical and procedural advances have come from on-duty personnel who have suggested better ways to do their jobs.

Educational facilities range from training simulators, classrooms, and professional advancement programs to informal gatherings of crew members. Significant blocks of off-peak Holodeck usage time are typically reserved for training exercises — such simulations can often be counted as field experience toward promotions. Many starships have ongoing lecture programs featuring visiting mission specialists who are often at the forefront of their fields of study. All these permit interested individuals to advance at their own pace within their chosen specialty, or to gain the knowledge and experience to branch into other areas.

Part of Starfleet's support for its personnel is the attention lavished on living accommodations. All Starfleet personnel are provided with comfortable, spacious living quarters. Food service aboard the *Galaxy* class starship is provided by a sophisticated replicator system that provides a vast array of culinary selections from a hundred planets. Recreational facilities range from four holographic environment simulators, two fully equipped gymnasiums and other exercise and sports facilities, a concert hall and theater, an arboretum, and a variety of lounges for off-duty use.

Starfleet duty is extremely demanding, but the entire organization is devoted to supporting its people and allowing them to excel. Starfleet's extraordinary history of over two centuries of space exploration is ample testament to the success of that policy.

This section grew out of a discussion in which we realized that the greatest advance seen on Star Trek *is not warp drive or transporter technology, but in management. Keeping a thousand individuals performing at top efficiency for years at a time is something that most present-day groups can only dream about. Yet those few organizations that can demonstrate a successful "search for excellence" have shown the extraordinary value of treating your people with respect. We figure that Starfleet must have learned this lesson well.*

13.2 MEDICAL SYSTEMS

The Medical department onboard the USS *Enterprise* is charged with providing health care to the ship's company and all attached personnel. The extended nature of many starship voyages as well as the hazardous nature of Starfleet duty can make this a considerable challenge. Additionally, the diverse range of lifeforms both in Starfleet as well as on various destination planets dramatically increases the scope of the task.

FACILITIES

The Medical department, under the direction of the Chief Medical Officer, is principally located in two sickbay facilities on Deck 12. The primary facility, located on the port side of the ship, consists of two medical intensive-care wards, an attached laboratory, the CMO's office, and a small nursery. The second facility, located on the starboard side of Deck 12, is similar to the primary sickbay but features two dedicated surgery suites, a physical therapy facility, a nursery, and a null-grav therapy ward. Adjacent to the second facility is a dental care office and a full biohazard isolation unit.

These facilities provide the medical staff with an impressive complement of tools with which to handle an extraordinary range of medical problems for both known and presently unknown species. Capabilities include a fully equipped medical laboratory with advanced bio-assay and lifeform analysis hardware. Also available are nanotherapy, genetic sequence, and virotherapeutic equipment. Medical lab capabilities can be bolstered by employing the lab services of one or more shipboard science departments.

In a large-scale medical emergency situation, all three shuttlebays can be converted to medium- and intensive-care hospital facilities using quick-deploy emergency hospital modules. Additionally, lesser numbers of overflow patients can be handled by conversion of guest quarters on Decks 5 and 6 to medical intensive-care units (See: 16.3).

STAFF

Normal medical department staffing is four staff physicians (of which at least one must have training in emergency medicine), three medical technicians, and twelve registered nurses. Normal on-duty medical complement for first and second shifts is one staff physician, two nurses, and one medical technician. During the night shift, normal staffing drops to two nurses. These staffing figures are subject to upward adjustment, depending on patient load. In emergency situations, cross-trained personnel from other departments can be made available for medical duty. Approximately 40% of all crew personnel are cross-trained for various secondary medical functions.

A staff of eight to twelve additional research and laboratory personnel are also attached to the medical department.

13.2.1 Deck 12 sickbay intensive-care ward

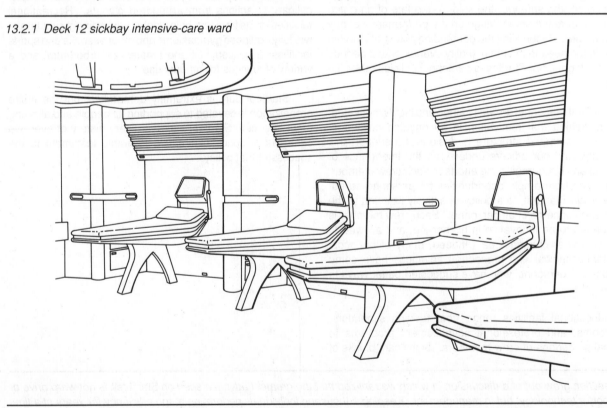

A close examination of one of the medical displays in sickbay shows that one of the patient status indicators is labeled Medical Insurance Remaining. (Don't bother trying to freeze-frame your VCR. It's another one of those things that are way too small to read on television.)

13.2.2 Biobed and surgical support frame

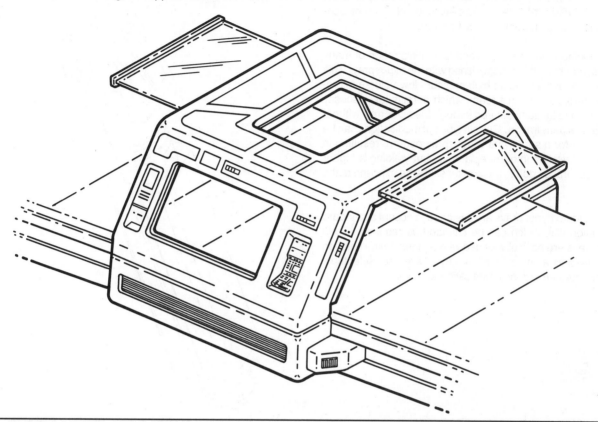

These individuals are typically attached to various research projects, but are available to assist with medical lab assignments on a priority basis as needed.

HARDWARE

A key element of the medical intensive-care unit is the biobed sensor and support unit. This orthopedically designed hospital bed incorporates a basic array of biofunction sensors that can be tied into a variety of remote medical instruments including the medical tricorder (See: 13.3). Also incorporated are a number of medical gas and fluid connect points for various devices, including the surgical support frame.

A vital tool in nearly all surgical procedures is the surgical support frame (SSF), or "clamshell" as it is sometimes called. The SSF not only maintains a sterile environment for most surgical procedures, but also incorporates several vital diagnostic and life support tools. These include a battery of biofunction sensors, supplementing those provided by the biobed and by the overhead medical equipment array. The SSF is capable of automated administration of intravenous medication as well as cardiovascular support and emergency defibrillation. A variety of surgical support frame types are available for different procedures, as well as for different lifeform types. Most biobed units are designed to accept surgical support frames.

Surgical procedures and other intensive-care proce-

dures are accomplished at the primary biobed, located at the center of each sickbay ward or surgical suite. Above this biobed is an overhead cluster of diagnostic and biofunction sensors. This array also incorporates a low level forcefield generator that can be used to reduce the chance of potentially harmful microorganisms entering or leaving the biobed area. Note that this forcefield is of relatively limited utility and is not adequate to maintain a totally sterile environment sufficient for surgical procedures or to satisfy biohazard protocols.

Medical personnel on Away Team missions or other assignments away from sickbay facilities are frequently issued any of a variety of medikits. These portable equipment

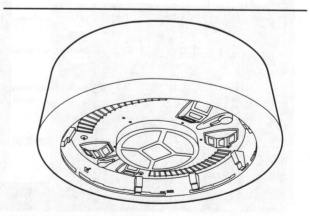

13.2.3 Overhead sensor cluster

packages typically include a medical tricorder, field hypospray, respirator, defib module, sample kit, and selection of bandages and drugs for emergency field use.

Subcutaneous and intravenous administration of many types of medication is accomplished with the hypospray. This device employs a pinpoint high-pressure low-volume microscopic aerosuspension stream, which permits low-viscosity medication to be administered through the epidermis without mechanical penetration. Certain types of medications can be formulated for a somewhat wider spray pattern, resulting in lesser penetration into the epidermis, but yielding a higher rate of absorption due to the greater skin area exposed to the drug.

Standard hyposprays are designed to accept a standard medication vial, which can be changed as required. Field hyposprays are normally loaded with an inert saline solution that serves as a vehicle fluid for any of five user-selectable concentrated emergency medication ampules.

13.2.5 Hypospray

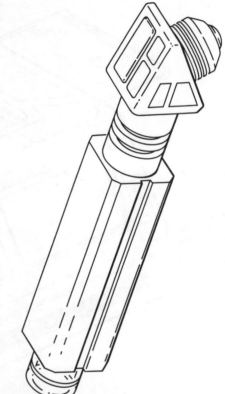

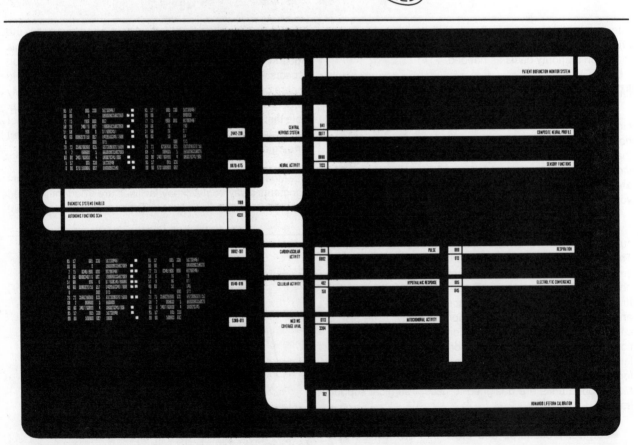

13.2.4 Main diagnostic display

13.3.1 Medical tricorder and scanner peripheral

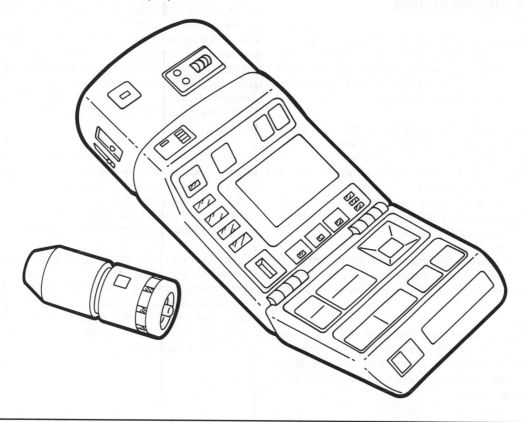

13.3 MEDICAL TRICORDER

The medical tricorder (MT) consists of a standard tricorder, to which is added a specialized medical peripheral (MP) device. This peripheral, one of a number of dedicated auxiliary computing options available to Starfleet crews, adds many powerful sensor and analysis functions to those used by sickbay personnel aboard the ship.

The MP comprises two components, the computing section and deployable high-resolution sensor. The MP works with the standard tricorder user interface to access all of the normal and added functions, in both shipboard and field operations. It measures 8.5 x 3.0 x 3.0 cm and masses 80 g, bringing the total tricorder length to 15 cm, and mass to 430 g. As with the standard tricorder, the case is constructed of micromilled duranium foam. The major components include an auxiliary sarium krellide power cell, sensor assemblies, peripheral processing block, and memory storage units. Power is not tapped from the main supply in the standard tricorder unless required, and cells in both sections can be recharged through the standard tricorder induction circuit. Total operation time is eighteen hours.

The peripheral sensors encompass 86 electromagnetic devices mounted about the internal frame, upper and side panels of the casing, and the forward section of the hand sensor receptacle. Each maintains an FOV lower limit of 1/4

degree. None are omnidirectional, but specialized for focused medical readings. The hand sensor incorporates fifteen high-resolution devices for readings down to thirty seconds of arc. Active and passive scans provide detailed diagnostic readings of total body mechanical processes, organ system function, disease organism infiltration, and body electromagnetic conditions. Combined readings can synthesize images and numerical readouts to aid sickbay personnel in identifying biological antagonists and determining courses of treatment.

The MP computer capabilities are contained in the medical database comparator/analysis subsection (MDC/AS) attached to 101 sensors. The MDC/AS manages incoming data, prioritizes processing tasks, routes processed data, and manages control and power systems. It is rated at 1.5×10^{10} calculations per second. In the field the database section draws upon an updatable file of known medical conditions for most humanoid types and 217 DNA-based nonhumanoids. When operating aboard ship, the MP can draw upon the entire medical database of the USS Enterprise as well as the files allocated to other disciplines.

A wide selection of tomographic and micrographic scans are included in the default device settings. The function controls of the standard tricorder may be used to configure custom scan modes for the case-mounted and hand sensors, with menu choices visible on the main display screen.

13.4 CREW QUARTERS SYSTEMS

Starfleet believes that providing comfortable living quarters to all crew and attached personnel to be of primary importance. Indeed, living accommodations are one of the most visible displays of Starfleet's commitment to caring for its single most important "system," its people.

Each person aboard the *Enterprise* is assigned approximately 110 square meters of personal living quarters space. These accommodations typically include a bedroom, living/work area, and a small bathroom. Families may request that their living quarters be combined to create a single larger dwelling. Living quarters decks are designed to be modular with movable walls to permit reconfiguration for such requests as crew load and structure change.

Other amenities available include food synthesizer terminals, sonic showers, standard showers, null-grav sleeping chambers, personal holographic viewers, and provisions for pets.

Individuals assigned to the *Enterprise* for periods more than six months are permitted to reconfigure their quarters within hardware, mass, and volume limits. Individuals assigned for shorter periods are generally restricted to standard quarters configurations.

The *Enterprise* in extended mission mode includes several large areas on Decks 9, 11, 33, and 35 that are configured and maintained as living quarters, but are normally unoccupied. These areas are held in reserve to allow the *Enterprise* to absorb large numbers of mission specialists or other guest and attached personnel (in various short-term mission configurations, use of these quarters can increase the ship's complement to as many as 6,500 individuals). These accommodations are in addition to normal guest and VIP accommodations.

Guest quarters on Decks 5 and 6 are convertible on short notice for medical extensive care use. These quarters include utility hookups for biomed telemetry and medical gases. Stored within these quarters are conversion kits providing necessary hardware and medical supplies. Lounge areas at corridor junctions can be converted to nursing stations.

Approximately 10% of all individual living quarters are equipped for immediate conversion to Class H, K, and L environmental conditions. An additional 2% of living quarters can be adapted to Class N and N(2) environments. Vehicle-wide adaptation to Class H, K, or L environmental conditions can be made by replacement of life support system modules during a major starbase layover.

13.4.1 Typical crew living accommodations

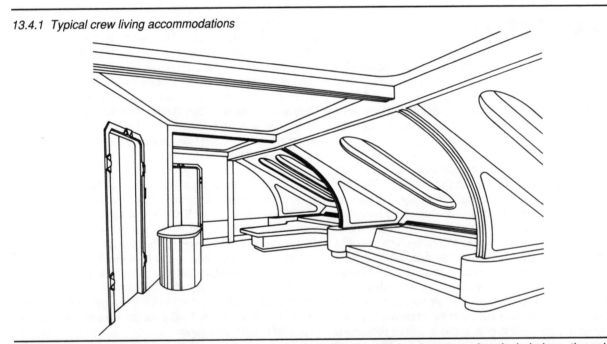

Most of the living quarters seen on the show feature an angled ceiling into which are set several vertical windows, through which one can see the stars. These windows match those seen on the upper surface of the ship's Saucer Module. Since there are many hundreds of such windows on the Enterprise *miniature, there are presumably hundreds of such living units on board the ship. The same five-room set is redressed with different furniture and divided up in different ways to serve as the living quarters of most of our regular characters. We also have a "junior officers' quarters" set, which does not have the dramatic ceiling windows. This set was originally built as Captain Kirk's quarters for the first* Star Trek *movie, and would seem to suggest that Starfleet has indeed upgraded its crew accommodations in the years between Kirk and Picard.*

13.5.1 Food replication system

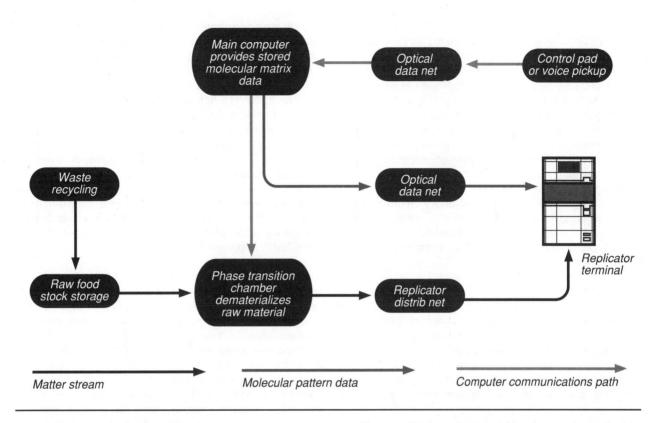

Matter stream   *Molecular pattern data*   *Computer communications path*

13.5 FOOD REPLICATION SYSTEM

Food service on board the *Enterprise* is provided by a molecular replication system that can instantly recreate any of thousands of food selections at a moment's notice. This system employs transporter-based matter replication which can produce, with almost total fidelity, nearly 4,500 types of foods, which are stored in computer memory.

The heart of the food replication system is a pair of molecular matrix matter replicators located on Decks 12 and 34. These devices dematerialize a measured quantity of raw material in a manner similar to that of a standard transporter. Unlike a standard transporter, however, no molecular imaging scanners are used to derive analog pattern data of the original material. Instead, a sophisticated quantum geometry transformational matrix field is used to modify the matter stream to conform to a digitally stored molecular pattern matrix.

The matter stream is then routed through a network of waveguide conduits to any one of hundreds of replicator terminals located throughout the spacecraft. Such terminals are located in most living quarters as well as in various lounges and common dining areas. The molecular pattern matrix controls the rematerialization process at the replication terminal, so that the finished product is a virtually identical copy of the original dish.

The raw food stock material is an organic particulate suspension, a combination of long-chain molecules that has been formulated for minimum replication power requirements. When dematerialized, using a slightly modified phase transition coil chamber, the resulting matter stream statistically requires the least quantum transformational manipulation to replicate most finished foodstuffs. This "transmutation" of matter is a modern scientific miracle, but the use of this raw material keeps the energy cost within reason.

Although the raw food stock is normally replaced at starbase resupply, osmotic and electrolytic fractioning of wastewater allows up to 82% of food stock to be reclaimed

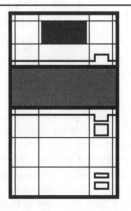

13.5.2 Food replication terminal (typical)

and reused. In a shortage, raw food stock can be replicated from general raw stock or waste material, but the energy cost is correspondingly higher, so this practice is to be avoided.

This system is relatively expensive to operate in terms of mass of the hardware involved and the energy cost of operation, but it is a significant savings over a traditional food storage and preparation system. Older techniques required the storage (either in refrigeration or stasis) of a large number of raw foodstuff types. The total mass of stored foodstuffs would have to be nearly twenty times greater in order to provide even a tenth of the menu items offered by the replicator system. Because food is stored as a single uniform staple, very little mass and storage penalty is incurred in providing an extremely wide range of menu choices. Extensive recycling of food stock permits an even more dramatic mass savings over extended voyages. Further, the labor involved even in automated food preparation (and the crew support costs thereby incurred) further increases the cost of traditional food service.

As with all transporter-based replication systems, the food replicators operate at molecular resolution. Because of this, there are significant numbers of single-bit errors in the resulting replicated materials. These errors are not nutritionally significant (although some individuals do claim to be able to taste differences in certain dishes), but certain types of Altarian spices have shown a tendency to become mildly toxic when replicated, so their use is avoided in replicated dishes.

An example of the limitations of the replicator system is a line in "Sins of the Father" in which Picard claims to find replicated caviar inferior to the real thing. (On the other hand, we wonder if the good captain could really tell the difference in a blind taste test.) Another example of replicator limits is the single-bit DNA errors that led Data and Beverly to suspect Romulan trickery in the episode "Data's Day."

13.6 TURBOLIFT PERSONNEL TRANSPORT SYSTEM

Intraship personnel transport is provided by the turboelevator system. This network of inductively powered transport tubes allows high-speed personnel movement throughout the habitable volume of the ship.

The turboshaft network consists of two parallel main vertical arteries, which provide service to hubs in horizontal networks located on each deck. Redundant horizontal links on Decks 8, 10, 25, and 31 connect the discontinuous vertical segments. The network is designed to provide alternate access routes to all decks, permitting alternate routing during times of heavy system usage. This design philosophy also minimizes the effect of any given single malfunction on overall system performance. Additionally, there is a single dedicated emergency turboshaft connecting the Main Bridge on Deck 1 to the Battle Bridge on Deck 8.

Each turbolift car consists of a lightweight duranium-composite framework supporting a cylindrical personnel cab fabricated from microfoamed duranium sheeting. Motive force is provided by three linear induction motors mounted longitudinally within the cab's exterior frame. These induction motors derive power from electromagnetic conduits located along the length of each turboshaft and are capable of accelerations approaching 10 m/sec^2. For crew comfort, an inertial damping matrix at the base of the cab reduces (but does not eliminate) the acceleration effects of turbolift motion.

An auditory pickup within the cab provides the ability for crew personnel to vocally command the operation of the turbolift. Upon receipt of destination instructions from a passenger, the individual lift car queries the network control computer and receives instructions on optimal route. Such route instructions take into account other turbolift cars currently active in the network. The voice pickup also allows automatic voiceprint identification of passengers, permitting inobtrusive screening of unauthorized personnel to restricted areas.

An average of ten turbolift cars are in service at all times

13.6.1 Turbolift car

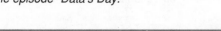

13.6.2 Turboshaft network

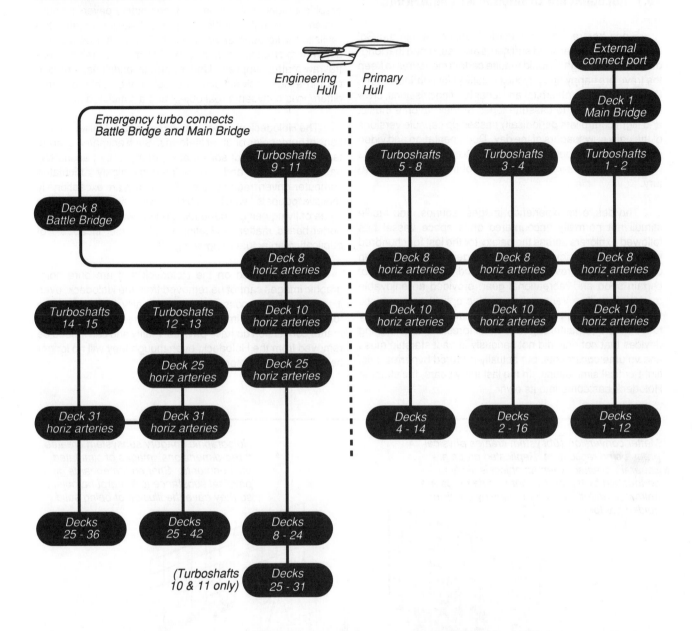

within the ship. During times of peak usage such as change-of-shift, this number can be doubled with only a 22% reduction in overall system response time. This is because the turbo-shaft network is designed with multiple access loops, permitting flexible routing to most in-ship destinations.

During Alert status and reduced power scenarios, turbolift usage may be restricted or completely prohibited at the discretion of the Commanding Officer. In such cases, person-nel movement among decks is still possible because of a secondary network of vertical ladder passageways and Jefferies Tubes.

While docked at a starbase, the turboelevator system

can be linked directly to the support facility's own turbolift system. This is accomplished by means of a connect point located at the upper terminus of turboshaft two, adjacent to the Main Bridge. When so linked, turbolift cars can travel freely between the starbase and the ship.

13.7 HOLOGRAPHIC ENVIRONMENT SIMULATORS

Since before the first satellite launches within the Sol system, fiction writers and engineers alike assumed that long-duration space flights would require certain measures to keep the travelers happy and psychologically fit for continued duty. During the first Earth orbital and lunar landing missions, crew members listened to cassette tapes of their favorite music, and flight controllers periodically passed up capsule versions of the daily newspapers of the day. Documentation and video recordings were routinely transmitted to orbital stations and planetary outposts into the early part of the twenty-first century.

The desire to experience images, sounds, and tactile stimuli not normally encountered on a space vessel has followed explorers across the galaxy for the last four hundred years. Computer-driven projection imagery has filled starship crews' needs for provocative spaces and, with the addition of certain sport and recreational gear, provided an enjoyable model of reality. Various holographic optical and acoustic techniques were applied through the years, finally giving way to a series of breakthroughs in small forcefield and imaging devices that not only did not seriously impact starship mass and volume constraints, but actually nurtured hyperrealistic, flight-critical simulations. In the last thirty years, the starship Holodeck has come into its own.

The Holodeck utilizes two main subsystems, the holographic imagery subsystem and the matter conversion subsystem. The holographic imagery subsection creates the realistic background environments. The matter conversion subsystem creates physical "props" from the starship's central raw matter supplies. Under normal conditions, a participant in a Holodeck simulation should not be able to detect differences between a real object and a simulated one.

The Holodeck also generates remarkably lifelike recreations of humanoids or other lifeforms. Such animated characters are composed of solid matter arranged by transporter-based replicators and manipulated by highly articulated computer-driven tractor beams. The results are exceptionally realistic "puppets," which exhibit behaviors almost exactly like those of living beings, depending on software limits. Transporter-based matter replication is, of course, incapable of duplicating an actual living being.

Objects created on the Holodeck that are pure holographic images cannot be removed from the Holodeck, even if they appear to possess physical reality because of the focused forcebeam imagery. Objects created by replicator matter conversion do have physical reality and can indeed be removed from the Holodeck, even though they will no longer be under computer control.

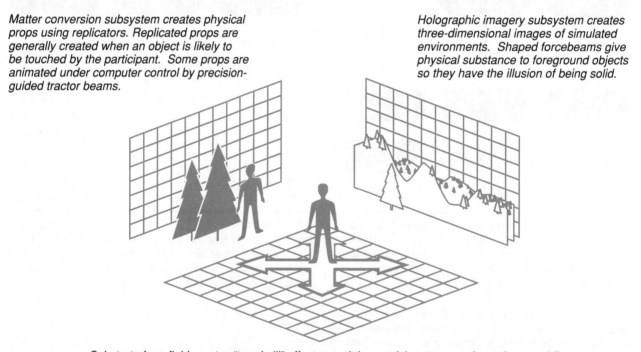

Matter conversion subsystem creates physical props using replicators. Replicated props are generally created when an object is likely to be touched by the participant. Some props are animated under computer control by precision-guided tractor beams.

Holographic imagery subsystem creates three-dimensional images of simulated environments. Shaped forcebeams give physical substance to foreground objects so they have the illusion of being solid.

Substrate forcefield creates "treadmill" effect, permitting participant to remain stationary while the simulated environment "scrolls" by, within the limits of the simulation program.

13.7.1 Holographic environment simulator system

13.7.2 Omnidirectional holo diode cluster (typical)

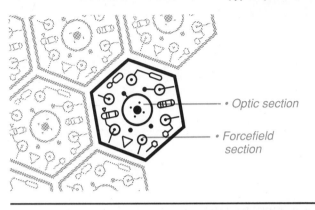

• Optic section

• Forcefield section

The basic mechanism behind the Holodeck is the omni-directional holo diode (OHD). The OHD comprises two types of microminiature device that projects a variety of special forcefields. The density of OHDs is 400 per cm², only slightly less than the active visual matrix of a multilayer display panel, and powered by standard medium-duty electro plasma taps. Entire walls are covered with OHDs, manufactured in an inexpensive wide-roll circuit printing process. A typical Holodeck surface comprises twelve subprocessing layers totaling 3.5 mm, diffusion bonded to a lightweight structural cooling tile averaging 3.04 cm thick. The primary subprocessor/emitter materials include keiyurium, silicon animide, and superconducting DiBe<2>Cu 732. Each single OHD measures 0.01mm. The optical data network mechanism by which OHDs are sent impulses is similar to that for smaller display screens, though complete walls are broken down into manageable high-speed segments, each 0.61 m². Dedicated high-speed subsections of the starship main computers drive these room-sized displays.

In addition to their ability to project full-color stereoscopic images, OHDs manipulate forcefields in three dimensions to allow Holodeck visitors to "feel" objects that aren't really there. This tactile stimulation provides the proper feedback one might expect from a rock on the ground or a tree growing in a forest. The only limiting factors to the numbers and kinds of objects described by the computers are memory and time to record or calculate from scratch the originals of the desired objects, whether real or imagined, such as a Klein bottle.

Other stimuli, such as sound, smell, and taste, are either simulated by more traditional methods, such as speakers or atomizers, or built into the created objects using replicator techniques.

The optic version of an OHD emits a complete image of an overall environment based on its location in the installed surface panel. The visitor, however, sees only a tiny portion of any one OHD, in much the same manner as a fly's eye operating in reverse. As one moves about, the visible portions of the OHDs change, altering the view. The actual energy emissions are unlike direct visible EM projections, but rather polarized interference patterns. The image is reconstructed where the patterns intersect at the lens of the eye or other visual receptor.

The forcefield version creates a tiny steerable forcefield. Its larger cousins are the more familiar tractor beams and navigational deflector. Under computer control, over a vast number of OHDs, the cumulative field effect is substantial. If the Holodeck is recreating, for example, a large mass of rock, the computer would first create the three-dimensional surface of the rock. This is accomplished by commanding certain OHDs to intersect their fields at the required polygon coordinates. If the field strength is tuned to provide the proper mineral hardnesses, the mass will feel like rock. A vast library of recorded real substances is available, and custom settings may be commanded for experimental purposes.

The shaped forcefields and background imagery allow the visitor to experience volumes and distances apparently larger than the Holodeck room could physically accommodate. The environment can be scrolled to continue if desired, or set for bounding limits indicated by soft wall contacts and audible reminders of wall proximity.

Within the USS *Enterprise*, crew members can visit four main Holodecks on Deck 11. In addition, a set of twenty smaller personal holographic simulator rooms are situated on Decks 12 and 33.

In a working environment like a Federation starship, safety is of prime importance and is engineered into every system. Because the starship living environment is so highly controlled, the emotional release associated with encounters with limited real physical hazards has been shown to be of significant value in maintaining the psychological well-being of many crew members. Simulated high velocities and forces are normally created by sensory illusions. While safeguards against critical bodily harm are programmed into the computers, certain scenarios can result in unavoidable sprains and bruises, even for experienced users. Hazards posed by "dangerous" lifeforms can seem exceedingly real and will fulfill most requirements.

14.0 AUXILIARY SPACECRAFT SYSTEMS

14.1 SHUTTLECRAFT OPERATIONS

The USS *Enterprise* is equipped with auxiliary shuttlecraft to support mission objectives.

Standard complement of shuttlecraft includes ten standard personnel shuttles, ten cargo shuttles, and five special-purpose craft. Additional special-purpose shuttles can be provided to a starship as necessary. The *Enterprise* also carries twelve two-person shuttlepods for extravehicular and short-range use.

Operating rules require that at least eleven shuttle vehicles be maintained at operational status at all times. Cruise Mode operating rules require one standard shuttlecraft and one shuttlepod to be at urgent standby at all times, available for launch at five minutes' notice. Four additional shuttlecraft are always available on immediate standby (thirty minutes to launch), and an additional six vehicles are maintained for launch with twelve hours' notice. Red Alert Mode operating rules require two additional shuttles to be brought to urgent standby, and all nine remaining operational vehicles to be maintained at immediate standby.

We did not have a shuttlecraft for much of our first season. The reason is that the expense of building all of the standing Enterprise *sets was so high that the studio wanted to defer the expense of the shuttle until the second season. What the studio didn't count on is that writer Sandy Fries wanted to show some parts of the ship that hadn't been shown yet. Upon discovering that we had not yet seen a shuttlecraft, Sandy was quick to write it into his first season script "Coming of Age." Ironically, this was somewhat similar to the situation that existed during the early days of the original* Star Trek *series when they, too, could not yet afford a shuttlecraft mockup. (This also explains why our heroes did not send a shuttle down to the planet to rescue Sulu and company in the original series' early first season episode "The Enemy Within.")*

14.2 SHUTTLEBAYS

The *Galaxy* class USS *Enterprise* has three major facilities intended for the support of auxiliary shuttlecraft operations from the ship.

The Main Shuttlebay, located in the center and aft sections of Deck 4 in the Primary Hull, includes launch support, recovery, and maintenance facilities for shuttle operations.

Two additional secondary shuttlebays are located in the center and aft sections (both port and starboard) of Deck 13 in the dorsal area of the Secondary Hull.

Shuttlebay exterior space doors are triple-layered compressible extruded duranium. Inner doors are composed of lightweight neofoam sheeting in an expanded tritanium framework. During active shuttlebay operations, atmospheric integrity is maintained by means of an annular forcefield, which permits both doors to remain open for vehicular ingress and egress without depressurizing the bay.

Shuttlebay Two also includes a dedicated maintenance bay for servicing sensor array pallets. Two shuttlepods are provided for extravehicular removal and replacement of these pallets. Additionally, two adjacent maintenance bays provide work facilities for preparation and servicing of mission-specific sensor instrumentation.

Shuttlebay Three includes hardware for short-term conversion to Class H, K, or L environmental conditions, intended for use in emergency evacuation situations.

Each shuttlebay has its own operations control booth, which is supervised by an on-duty Flight Deck Officer. Each Flight Deck Officer is responsible for operations within that particular shuttlebay, but must report to the main shuttlebay officer for launch and landing clearance. In turn, the main shuttlebay officer must seek clearance from the Operations Manager on the Main Bridge.

Launch maneuvers and landing approach piloting is managed by a number of precision short-range tractor beam

14.2.1 Location of shuttlebays

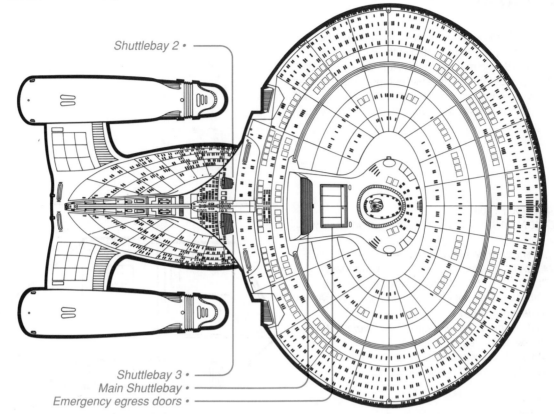

Shuttlebay 2 •

Shuttlebay 3 •
Main Shuttlebay •
Emergency egress doors •

emitters located in each shuttlebay and on the ship's exterior, just outside each set of space doors. These tractor beams are computer controlled under the direction of the Flight Deck Officer, permitting the safe maneuvering of shuttle vehicles within the bays and in the 350-meter approach zone.

Maintenance facilities include replacement parts sufficient for twelve months of normal starship operations. These normally include two complete replacement spaceframes, which can be used for refurbishment of severely damaged ships.

Note that replicator usage can allow fabrication of nearly any critical missing parts, but large-scale replication is not considered energy-efficient except in emergency situations. However, in such situations, power usage is usually strictly

limited, so it is unwise to depend upon the availability of replicated spare parts. This is another reason that the ship must maintain a significant stock of spare parts in inventory at all times.

We don't have a list of the names of all shuttlecraft and shuttlepods onboard the Enterprise. *The main reason is that this is one of those things you want to leave somewhat nebulous so that writers of future episodes have some room to play around with. Names established to date include:* Sakharov *(named after the late Soviet physicist and peace advocate),* El Baz *(for planetary geologist Farouk El Baz),* Onizuka *(for the* Challenger *astronaut),* Pike *(for Christopher Pike, early captain of the first starship* Enterprise*),* Feynman *(for the Nobel laureate physicist who was Mike's hero),* Hawking *(for physicist Stephen Hawking), and* Voltaire *(for the eighteenth-century French writer and philosopher). We've also seen a shuttlepod* Cousteau, *from the starship* Aries. *Most of these names were selected or approved by Rick Berman. We made a big status graphic in the shuttlebay control booth in which an unreadable display suggests that we might have shuttles with names like* Sam Freedle *(our unit production manager during the second season),* Indiana Jones *(after the noted archaeologist), and a few others we probably shouldn't mention. During the filming of the episode "In Theory," directed by* Star Trek *actor Patrick Stewart (who occasionally works as a spokesperson for Pontiac automobiles), some wag on the production crew relabeled the shuttlepod with the name* Pontiac-1701D.

14.3 SHUTTLECRAFT

The seven shuttle vehicles most often carried in the USS *Enterprise* inventory are represented in the views and specifications below. Single major uprated variants are included. As combinations of interchangeable components, such as cargo pallets, engines, and unique mission housings, will affect vehicle dimensions and performance figures, only base values are given.

14.3.1 Shuttlepod Type 15
PRODUCTION BASE: *Starbase 134 Integration Facility, Rigel VI.*
TYPE: *Light short-range sublight shuttle.*
ACCOMMODATION: *Two; pilot and systems manager.*
POWER PLANT: *Two 500 millicochrane impulse driver engines, eight DeFl 657 hot gas RCS thrusters. Three sarium krellide storage cells.*
DIMENSIONS: *Length, 3.6 m; beam, 2.4 m; height, 1.6 m.*
MASS: *0.86 metric tonnes.*
PERFORMANCE: *Maximum delta-v, 12,800 m/sec.*
ARMAMENT: *Two Type IV phaser emitters.*

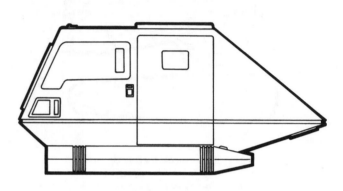

14.3.2 Shuttlepod Type 15A
PRODUCTION BASE: *Starbase 134 Integration Facility, Rigel VI.*
TYPE: *Light short-range sublight shuttle.*
ACCOMMODATION: *Two; pilot and systems manager.*
POWER PLANT: *Two 500 millicochrane impulse driver engines, eight DeFl 657 hot gas RCS thrusters. Three sarium krellide storage cells.*
DIMENSIONS: *Length, 3.6 m; beam, 2.4 m; height, 1.6 m.*
MASS: *0.97 metric tonnes.*
PERFORMANCE: *Maximum delta-v, 13,200 m/sec.*
ARMAMENT: *Two Type IV phaser emitters.*

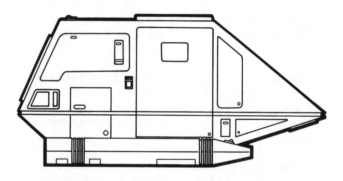

14.3.3 Shuttlepod Type 16
PRODUCTION BASE: *Starbase 134 Integration Facility, Rigel VI.*
TYPE: *Medium short-range sublight shuttle.*
ACCOMMODATION: *Two; pilot and systems manager.*
POWER PLANT: *Two 750 millicochrane impulse driver engines, eight DeFl 635 hot gas RCS thrusters. Four sarium krellide storage cells.*
DIMENSIONS: *Length, 4.8 m; beam, 2.4 m; height, 1.6 m.*
MASS: *1.25 metric tonnes.*
PERFORMANCE: *Maximum delta-v, 12,250 m/sec.*
ARMAMENT: *Two Type IV phaser emitters.*

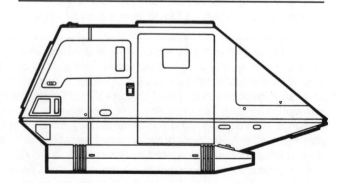

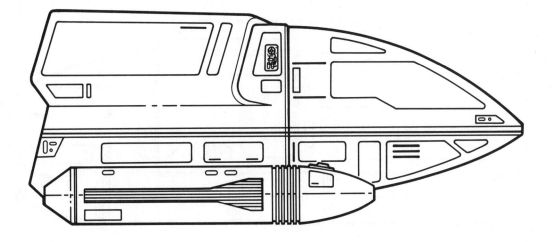

14.3.4 Personnel Shuttle Type 6
PRODUCTION BASE: ASDB Integration Facility, Utopia Planitia Fleet Yards, Mars.
TYPE: Light short-range warp shuttle.
ACCOMMODATION: Two flight crew. Passenger configurations: six (STD); two (diplomatic).
POWER PLANT: Two 1,250 millicochrane warp engines, twelve DeFl 3234 microfusion RCS thrusters (STD); two 2,100 millicochrane warp engines (UPRTD).
DIMENSIONS: Length, 6.0 m; beam, 4.4 m; height, 2.7 m.
MASS: 3.38 metric tonnes.
PERFORMANCE: Warp 1.2 for 48 hours (STD); Warp 2 for 36 hours (UPRTD).
ARMAMENT: None (STD); Two Type IV phaser emitters (special operations).

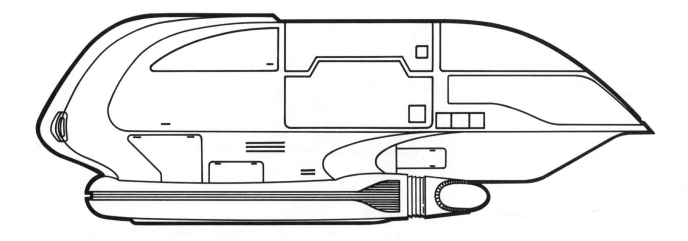

14.3.5 Personnel Shuttle Type 7
PRODUCTION BASE: ASDB Integration Facility, Utopia Planitia Fleet Yards, Mars.
TYPE: Medium short-range warp shuttle.
ACCOMMODATION: Two flight crew. Passenger configurations: six (STD); two (diplomatic).
POWER PLANT: Two 1,250 millicochrane warp engines, twelve DeFl 3234 microfusion RCS thrusters (STD); two 2,100 millicochrane warp engines (UPRTD).
DIMENSIONS: Length, 8.5 m; beam, 3.6 m; height, 2.7 m.
MASS: 3.96 metric tonnes.
PERFORMANCE: Warp 1.75 for 48 hours (STD); Warp 2 for 36 hours (UPRTD).
ARMAMENT: None (STD); two Type V phaser emitters (special operations).

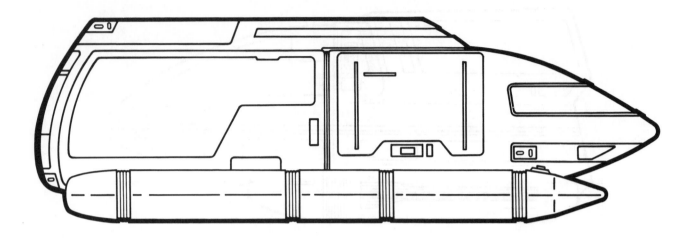

14.3.6 Cargo Shuttle Type 9A
PRODUCTION BASE: Starfleet Plant #24, Utopia Planitia Fleet Yards, Mars.
TYPE: Heavy long-range warp shuttle.
ACCOMMODATION: Two flight crew, one cargo specialist.
POWER PLANT: Two 2,150 millicochrane warp engines, twelve DeFl 2142 microfusion RCS thrusters (STD); two 2,175 millicochrane warp engines (UPRTD).
DIMENSIONS: Length, 10.5 m; beam, 4.2 m; height, 3.6 m.
MASS: 4.5 metric tonnes (empty). Maximum payload, 6.6 metric tonnes (STD); 8.9 metric tonnes (UPRTD).
PERFORMANCE: Warp 2 for 36 hours (STD); Warp 2.2 for 32 hours (UPRTD). ARMAMENT: None (standard); two Type V phaser emitters (special operations).

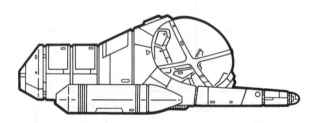

14.3.7 Sphinx Workpod Type M1 (Base Module/Sled Attachments)
PRODUCTION BASE: Starfleet Plant #2, Utopia Planitia Fleet Yards, Mars.
TYPE: Light industrial manipulator (Sphinx M1A), medium industrial manipulator (Sphinx M2A), and medium tug (Sphinx MT3D).
ACCOMMODATION: Pilot (M1A, M2A); pilot and cargo specialist (MT3D).
POWER PLANT: Two 4,600 Newton-second I_{sp} microfusion primary thrusters, sixteen DeBe 3453 hot gas RCS thrusters. Four alfinium krellide power storage cells.
DIMENSIONS: Length, 6.2 m; beam, 2.6 m; height, 2.5 m.
MASS: 1.2 metric tonnes.
PERFORMANCE: Maximum delta-v, 2,000 m/sec. Maximum manipulator mass, 2.3 metric tonnes. Maximum sled mass, 4.5 metric tonnes.
ARMAMENT: None.

14.4 EXTRAVEHICULAR ACTIVITY

Situations requiring one or more crew members to exit the starship in an airless or otherwise hostile environment are known collectively as extravehicular activity (EVA). These include detailed visual inspections, periodic maintenance, damage control, and unique hardware modifications. They may be done alone or in concert with teleoperator and automated systems.

Various degrees of protection are available for starship crews. While the actual configurations carried by Starfleet vessels will vary according to major mission segments and swapouts for improved models, typical suit types are presented here. The first, the low pressure environment garment (LPEG), is a close-fitting, lightweight suit, designed for benign airless operations. One use would be during an orbital starbase layover, where the spacecraft is in External Support Mode, well protected against radiation and micrometeoroid hazards. The suit features simplified multilayer construction, affording atmospheric integrity, gas exchange, and thermal and humidity control without sacrificing mobility. All consumables and circulation equipment are mounted within an integral backpack, with controls placed for 50 percentile humanoids on the chest and forearm areas. The suit allows for exterior operations, though time outside is limited to three hours. A variant of the LPEG is the emergency pressure garment (EPG), designed for long-term storage in starship emergency equipment lockers. The EPG is capable of supporting life for two hours in most ship abandonment or isolated hull breach scenarios while crews await rescue.

Starfleet's midlevel suit is the standard extravehicular work garment (SEWG). This type is reinforced with additional radiation and pressure layers for extended operations, and is configured with a sixteen-hour consumables supply, plus enhanced recycling devices. It is designed for most major industrial tasks and hazardous exploration assignments. Radiation and micrometeoroid protection is essentially unlimited. The suit controls are supplemented by advanced autonomic life support controllers within the suit computer.

The current high-level suit is the augmented personnel module (APM). This suit is a hybrid garment composed of both hard and flexible body segments, essentially a complete small spacecraft. The concept, still valid after four hundred years, allows the occupant to perform slightly longer duration missions than the SEWG, but with much greater relative comfort. A wide array of readily available tools and manipulator options is coupled with reaction control system thrusters, resulting in high productivity EVA returns.

All suit types are available in customized versions for nonhumanoid and handicapped crew members.

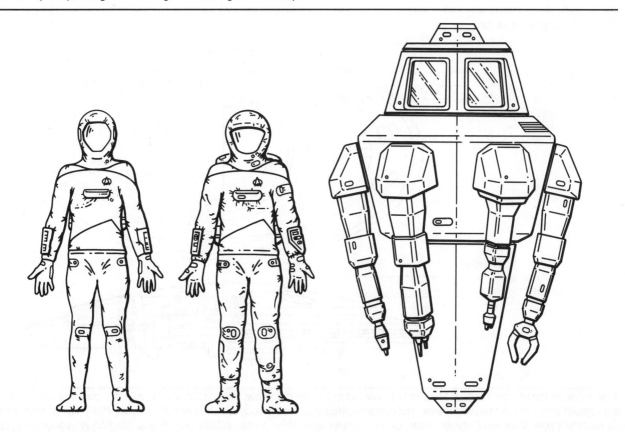

14.4.1 Extravehicular garment types

14.6 CAPTAIN'S YACHT

One of the specialized auxiliary spacecraft carried by the USS *Enterprise* is the captain's yacht. This spacecraft is characterized as multipurpose, though it normally functions to convey diplomatic personnel on special missions not normally accomplished by shipboard transporters.

The general planform is a flattened elliptical solid, designed for the space environment and extended atmospheric flight. It measures 10 m along the minor axis and 18 m in the major axis, and 8 m in height. The total loaded mass is rated at 95 metric tonnes. The structural framing comprises gammawelded tritanium and duranium members measuring an average 18.6 x 9.2 cm in cross section. Hull skinning is composed of eight alternating layers of keiyurium borocarbide and cortenium molybdenite, with major tiling sections averaging 6.02 cm thick.

The interior habitat volume is subdivided to form the flight deck, two modest staterooms, flight crew bunks, galley, and Engineering access. Surrounding the habitat are the imbedded impulse engine system, cryogenic reactant tanks, lenticular aerodyne atmosphere flight motors, and related subsystems. The spacecraft is normally piloted by a crew of two, supplemented by a service representative to assist diplomatic guests.

The yacht is capable of sustained sublight velocities approaching 0.65*c*. The impulse propulsion system (IPS) consists of six sequential beam-fusion reaction chambers feeding a central toroidal driver coil. Each chamber measures 1.3 m in diameter and is similar to its larger IPS cousins on the *Enterprise*. The reaction exhaust is vented through the driver coil and magnetohydrodynamic (MHD) accelerator for impulse travel. The MHD tap provides power to the navigational deflector grid for removal of interstellar dust and gas from the vehicle flight path. For atmosphere flight the exhaust is redirected after it exits the MHD tunnel and sent through the aerodyne engines around the ellipse equator. The normal atmosphere cruising velocity is Mach 6; maximum safe waverider velocity is Mach 20. Magnetic turbulence contour equalizers, variants of the navigational deflector, provide momentum conditioning at Mach transitions.

The *Enterprise* is designed to operate safely without the yacht in place, since its structural integrity field and inertial damping fields produce slightly modified fields in those areas to compensate for the concavity of the yacht docking structure. Yacht operational rules in the vicinity of the starship are generally the same as those for other auxiliary spacecraft, with the difference being that the yacht, during emergency undockings, may be safely deployed at velocities as high as Warp Factor 7. The yacht's systems are designed to afford the craft a smooth falloff of warp field, though the decaying field energy cannot be sustained for any appreciable time.

14.5.1 The captain's yacht

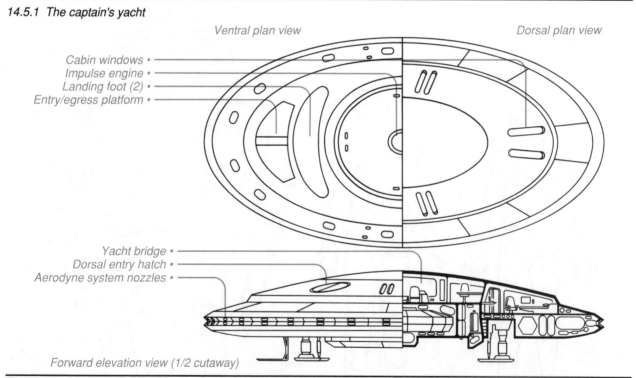

Ventral plan view   Dorsal plan view

Cabin windows •
Impulse engine •
Landing foot (2) •
Entry/egress platform •

Yacht bridge •
Dorsal entry hatch •
Aerodyne system nozzles •

Forward elevation view (1/2 cutaway)

This is one of those nifty things that we may never get to see on the show. We did briefly flirt with the idea of actually using the captain's yacht in "Samaritan Snare," but it was decided to use an "executive shuttlecraft" instead. Patrick Stewart informs us that the yacht is named Calypso, *after Jacques Cousteau's ship. Visual effects coordinator (and Navy veteran) Ron B. Moore points out that naval tradition would probably insist the craft be called the Captain's Gig.*

15.0 USS ENTERPRISE FLIGHT OPERATIONS

15.1 INTRODUCTION TO FLIGHT OPERATIONS

Operations aboard the USS *Enterprise* are divided into three general categories: flight operations, primary mission operations, and secondary mission operations.

Flight operations are those that relate directly to the function of the starship itself. These include power generation, propulsion, environmental support, utilities, and other systems that are required to maintain the spaceworthiness of the vehicle.

Mission operations are those tasks that have been assigned to the ship and its crew. Mission operations are divided into two categories, primary and secondary missions.

Primary missions are those whose execution is under current direct supervision of the Main Bridge. Primary missions often require flight control of the spacecraft, or use of significant fractions of the ship's sensors or other resources.

Secondary missions are those that are not under direct supervision of the Main Bridge. These operations are usually run in parallel with and are designed not to impact upon primary mission operations. Secondary missions are typically long-term scientific or cultural studies that are run semiautonomously by specialized mission teams.

It is not uncommon for a dozen secondary missions to be running concurrently. It is also not uncommon for a secondary mission to be designated as a primary mission for a specified period of time. For example, the launch of a specialized instrument probe is a primary mission when controlled by the Main Bridge, but the subsequent data collection phase, supervised by a specialized mission team, might be treated as a secondary mission.

15.2 MISSION TYPES

The multimission starship is by definition capable of performing a wide range of mission scenarios, offering autonomous capability of executing nearly any of Starfleet's objective. This capability is extremely valuable for vehicles operating near the frontier of Federation influence where additional Starfleet support may be unavailable.

Missions for the *Galaxy* class USS *Enterprise* generally fall into one of the following categories, utilizing the following spacecraft capabilities:

• **Deep-space exploration.** The *Enterprise* is equipped for long-range stellar survey and mapping missions, as well as a wide range of planetary exploration.

• **Ongoing scientific investigations.** The *Enterprise* has support capability for a number of ongoing scientific research projects. Many such projects are classified as secondary missions.

• **Contact with alien lifeforms.** Pursuant to the Starfleet Life Contact Policy Directive, facilities to support such missions include a full exobiology and cultural sociology staff, as well as a highly sophisticated complement of universal translation software.

• **Federation policy and diplomacy.** The *Enterprise* is frequently the sole Federation envoy during deep-space operations.

• **Tactical and defense.** Typical tactical and defensive missions might include patrol of the Romulan Neutral Zone, or protection of Federation interests in planetary or interstellar conflicts.

• **Emergency and rescue.** Typical rescue scenarios include rescue of Starfleet and non-Starfleet spacecraft in distress. Planetary rescue scenarios include medium-scale evacuation from planetary surfaces of humanoid and non-humanoid populations. Large-scale evacuation of planetary populations is not feasible.

15.3 OPERATING MODES

Normal flight and mission operations of the *Galaxy* class starship are conducted in accordance with a variety of operating rules, determined by the current operating mode of the vehicle. These operating modes are specified by the Commanding Officer, although in certain cases the computer can initiate Alert status upon detection of a potentially critical situation.

In brief, the major operating modes are:

• **Cruise Mode.** This refers to the normal operating condition of the spacecraft.

• **Yellow Alert Mode.** This is a condition of increased readiness in which key systems are brought to greater operating capacity in anticipation of potential crises.

• **Red Alert Mode.** This condition is invoked during actual or immediately imminent emergency conditions. It is also invoked during battle situations.

• **External Support Mode.** This is a state of reduced system operations typically invoked when the ship is docked at a starbase and is at least partially dependent on external power or environmental support systems.

• **Separated Flight Mode.** This is a set of operating protocols used when the Saucer Module has separated from the Stardrive Section. Note that many Red Alert operating rules apply, since such separation is typically for combat situations.

• **Reduced Power Mode.** These protocols may be activated when power availability or power usage is reduced to less than 26% of normal Cruise Mode load.

Note that while each operating mode has a distinct set of operating rules and protocols, the Commanding Officer has a wide latitude in responding to specific situations. This is especially critical during Alert situations. The Operations Manager is also heavily involved in making judgments regarding priority allocations for departments and systems at such times.

15.4 CRUISE MODE

This refers to the normal operating condition of the USS *Enterprise*. During Cruise Mode, ship's primary operational personnel are organized into three distinct working shifts. Each shift is assigned to duty status during one of three eight-hour work periods. Primary operations are defined as those functions that must be performed or enabled at all times. These are generally to insure the spaceworthiness of the vehicle, environmental support, propulsion systems operations, and the ability to perform primary missions.

Other support functions including secondary mission operations are not necessarily required to be maintained on a twenty-four-hour-a-day basis. Many such departments will confine themselves to one or two operational shifts to increase the interactivity among working personnel.

Cruise Mode operational rules include:

• Level 4 automated diagnostic series are run on all ship's primary and tactical systems at the beginning of each shift. (Key systems may require more frequent diagnostics per specific operational and safety rules.)

• At least one major power system to remain at operational status at all times. At least one additional power system to be maintained at standby. (For example, if the warp engines are currently providing propulsion and power, Cruise Mode operating rules require either the main impulse engines, the Saucer Module impulse engines, or an auxiliary fusion generator to be at standby.)

• Long-range navigational sensors to be active if the ship is traveling at warp speed. Lateral and forward sensor arrays to be maintained at ready status, although these instruments can be made available for secondary mission use at the discretion of Ops.

• Navigational deflector to be active as needed for protection of the spacecraft from unanticipated debris or drag from the interstellar medium.

• At least 40% of phaser bank elements and one photon torpedo launcher to be maintained at cold standby status, available for activation at two minutes' notice.

• One shuttlebay is maintained at launch readiness with at least one shuttle vehicle maintained at launch minus five minutes status.

15.5 YELLOW ALERT

This designates a shipwide state of increased preparedness for possible crisis situations. During Yellow Alert, all on-duty crew and attached personnel are informed of the potential crisis via panel display and are directed to prepare for possible emergency action. Second shift crew personnel are also alerted and those in key operational positions are directed to prepare for possible duty on five minutes' notice. Cross-trained second shift personnel are directed to prepare for possible duty in their secondary assignments. Specific systems preparations include:

• Level 4 automated diagnostic series run on all ship's primary and tactical systems to determine ship's current readiness status.

• If presently off-line, warp power core brought to full operating condition and maintained at 20% power output. Level 4 diagnostics provide a status report on warp capability including maximum available engine output.

• Main impulse propulsion system brought to full operating condition. At least one backup reactor element is brought to hot standby. In Yellow Alert status triggered by potential hostile action, Saucer Module impulse propulsion system is brought to partial standby.

• All tactical and long-range sensor arrays are brought to full operational status. Secondary mission use of any sensor elements can be overridden if required by bridge.

• Deflector systems brought to full standby. Secondary deflector generators brought to partial standby. All operational backup generators are energized to partial readiness.

• Phaser banks are energized to partial standby. Power conduits are enabled, and targeting scanners are activated. Level 4 automated diagnostics verify operational status.

• Photon torpedo launchers are brought to partial standby. One torpedo device is energized to partial launch readiness and primed with a standard antimatter charge, unless specifically overridden by Ops or Tactical. Level 4 automated diagnostics confirm operational status.

• The Battle Bridge is brought to partial standby status and backup bridge crews are notified for possible duty in the event of possible Saucer sep maneuvers.

• Two of the three shuttlebays are brought to launch readiness. The number of shuttlecraft at launch readiness is maintained at one.

• Onboard sensors record the location of all personnel and alert Security of any anomalous activity. Location and activity information is recorded for postmission analysis.

• Level 5 automated diagnostics are performed to verify readiness of autonomous survival and recovery vehicle systems (lifeboats).

Yellow Alert can be invoked by the Commanding Officer, Operations Manager, Chief Engineer, Tactical Officer, or by the supervisor of any current primary mission operation. Additionally, the main computer can automatically invoke Yellow Alert status in some cases upon detection of certain types of unknown spacecraft, as well as upon detection of certain types of malfunctions or system failures.

15.6 RED ALERT

This condition is invoked during actual states of emergency in which the vehicle or crew are endangered, immediately impending emergencies, or combat situations.

During Red Alert situations, crew and attached personnel from all three duty shifts are informed via alarm klaxons and annunciator lights. Key second shift personnel are ordered to report immediately to their primary duty stations, while other second shift personnel report to their secondary duty stations. Key third shift personnel (who are presumably on their sleep cycle) are ordered to report to their secondary duty stations (or special assignment stations) in fifteen minutes. Specific systems preparations include:

• Level 4 automatic diagnostic series run on all ship's primary and tactical systems at five-minute intervals. Bridge given immediate notification of any significant change in ship's readiness status.

• If presently off-line, warp power core to be brought to full operating condition and maintained at 75% power output. Level 3 diagnostics conducted on warp propulsion systems at initiation of Red Alert status, Level 4 series repeated at five-minute intervals.

• Main impulse propulsion system is brought to full operating condition. All operational backup reactor units are brought to hot standby. In actual or potential combat situations, Saucer Module impulse propulsion system is brought to full operating status.

• All tactical and long-range sensor arrays are brought to full operational status. Secondary mission use of sensor elements is discontinued, except with approval of Ops.

• Deflector systems are automatically brought to tactical configuration unless specifically overridden by the Tactical Officer. All available secondary and backup deflector generators are brought to hot standby.

• Phaser banks are energized to full standby. Power conduits are enabled, targeting scanners are activated. Level 3 diagnostics are performed to confirm operational status.

• Photon torpedo launchers are brought to full standby. One torpedo device in each launcher is energized to full launch readiness and primed with a standard antimatter charge of 1.5 kg.

• The Battle Bridge is brought to full standby status and backup bridge crews are notified for possible duty in the event of possible Saucer sep maneuvers.

• All three shuttlebays are brought to launch readiness. Two shuttlecraft are brought to launch minus thirty seconds' readiness.

• Onboard sensors record the location of all personnel and alert Security of any anomalous activity. Location and activity information is recorded for postmission analysis.

• Level 4 automated diagnostics are performed to verify readiness of autonomous survival and recovery vehicle systems (lifeboats). Readiness of ejection initiator servos is verified through a partial Level 3 semiautomated check. Security officers are assigned to insure that all passageways to lifeboat accesses are clear.

• Isolation doors and forcefields are automatically closed between sections to contain the effects of possible emergencies, including fire and decompression of habitable volume.

Red Alert situations, by their very nature, frequently involve unforeseeable variables and unpredictable circumstances. For this reason, Red Alert (even more than other operating states) requires the Commanding Officer and all personnel to remain flexible. All Red Alert operating rules, therefore, are subject to adaptation based on specific situations.

Red Alert can be invoked by the Commanding Officer, Operations Manager, Chief Engineer, or the Tactical Officer. Additionally, the main computer can automatically invoke Red Alert status in some cases upon detection of certain types of unknown spacecraft, as well as upon detection of certain types of critical malfunctions or system failures. In such cases, the automatic declaration of Red Alert status is subject to review by the Commanding Officer.

15.7 EXTERNAL SUPPORT MODE

This is a state of reduced activity that exists when the ship is docked at a starbase or other support facility. During External Support Mode, the ship will typically receive umbilical support for at least a portion of operating power and/or life support, thus enabling a partial or total shutdown of onboard power generation.

External Support Mode rules permit the spacecraft to conduct a cold shutdown of all primary power plants as long as sufficient umbilical support is provided for all remaining personnel and systems. These protocols are intended to permit maintenance of critical systems, which would otherwise be difficult to accomplish during normal service cycles.

External Support operational rules include:

• Spacecraft must be hard docked to support facility with umbilical connects providing electro plasma system power, environmental support, structural integrity field (SIF) power, and thermal and gravitational control. At least one hard gangway must provide direct shirtsleeve access between the spacecraft and the service facility.

• Cold shutdown of all primary power plants is permitted as long as sufficient umbilical support is provided for all onboard activity. It is preferred that at least one auxiliary fusion generator remain on-line, if possible.

• Partial shutdown of environmental support systems is permitted, allowing atmospheric and water processing to be handled by support facility through umbilical connects. Life support service must continue to be provided for all inhabited portions of the ship's interior. Onboard ventilator fans, air-conditioning, thermal control, and plumbing must be maintained, although specific areas may be shut down as needed for maintenance work.

• Gravitational power generation may be discontinued so long as field energy for synthetic gravity is provided through umbilical connects.

• Cold shutdown of both structural integrity field and inertial damping field is permitted so long as spacecraft remains hard docked to support facility. It is preferred that at least one SIF generator remain at hot standby.

• Cold shutdown of all navigational and tactical deflector systems is permitted so long as the spacecraft remains hard docked to the support facility. It is preferred that at least one SIF generator remain at hot standby.

15.8 SEPARATED FLIGHT MODE

Any time the two major components of the total starship must undock and perform different flight tasks, Separated Flight Mode is initiated. Benign situations involve a variation on Cruise Mode rules (See: 15.4), while emergency situations involve a follow-on subset of Red Alert rules (See: 15.6). Separation under benign conditions will most often occur during maintenance layovers and flight dynamics checkouts, when the risk to both spacecraft is negligible. Operational rules include:

• Level 4 automated diagnostic series are run on all ship's primary and tactical systems at the beginning of each shift. (Key systems may require more frequent diagnostics per specific operational and safety rules.)

• At least one major power system to remain at operational status at all times. At least one additional power system to be maintained at standby.

• One shuttlebay is maintained at launch readiness with at least one shuttle vehicle maintained at launch minus five minutes' status.

Emergency situations requiring separation generally require greatly increased activity and energy production, and personnel movements within each starship component. Once separation is ordered, the following special operational rules are observed:

• Warp power core to be brought to full operating condition and maintained at ≥90% power output. Level 3 diagnostics conducted on warp propulsion systems at initiation of Red Alert status, Level 4 series repeated at five-minute intervals.

• Main impulse propulsion system is brought to full operating condition. All operational backup reactor units are brought to hot standby. In actual or potential combat situations, Saucer Module impulse propulsion system is brought to full operating status.

• Saucer Module SIF/IDF systems are set to high output for all velocity regimes, including low warp or sublight velocities.

During benign situations, Separated Flight Mode may be initiated by the Commanding Officer, Operations Manager, Chief Engineer, or the Tactical Officer, depending on the exact nature of the vessel separation. In its emergency version, this mode may be invoked only by the Commanding Officer immediately following a transfer of control to the Battle Bridge. All automatic preparations, as initiated by the main computer, may be made without the actual call for separation, in order to prepare both components for rapid response times.

15.9 REDUCED POWER MODE

Reduced Power Mode refers to a number of operating states designed for maximum power conservation. These protocols can be invoked in case of a major failure in space-craft power generation, in case of critical fuel shortage, or in the event that a tactical situation requires severe curtailment of onboard power generation.

When Reduced Power Mode is invoked, a Level 5 systems analysis is performed for the entire spacecraft, with the results made available to the Commanding Officer, the Chief Engineer, and the Operations Manager. The purpose of this analysis is to determine an overall energy budget for the spacecraft, to help plan power allocations that will mini-mize operational compromises.

• If the spacecraft is not presently traveling at warp velocity, a cold shutdown of the entire warp propulsion system is to be performed. Exceptions to this rule include situations where the warp core is the only remaining power source for the spacecraft, or when failure of other sources are believed imminent, or when the Commanding Officer deter-mines the necessity for warp velocity travel.

• Main impulse propulsion system is to be brought to the minimum required to maintain onboard power usage. Backup fusion reactors are to be kept at standby, but should remain off-line unless necessary, at the discretion of the Chief Engi-neer.

• Hourly energy budget and consumption reports to be made by the Operations Manager to the Chief Engineer and the Commanding Officer.

• Spacecraft flight operations are to be conducted in a conservative manner. If warp travel is deemed necessary, speeds greater than integral warp factors are not allowed due to lesser efficiencies at fractional warp factors (i.e., it is permitted to travel at Warp 2.0 or Warp 3.0, but not Warp 2.5 or 3.4).

• Inertial damping system and structural integrity field to be operated at minimum levels. Only one of each generator to be operational, unless system failure is believed imminent or unless tactical situations dictate otherwise. Accordingly, changes in velocity are to be kept to a minimum.

• All use of tactical and lateral sensor arrays for second-ary missions to be discontinued, except where deemed essential by the Operations Manager.

• Deflector systems brought to minimum power. Sec-ondary deflector generators and backups brought to cold shutdown unless deemed necessary by the Commanding Officer, Flight Control Officer (Conn), or Tactical Officer. Navigational deflector to be operated at minimum power.

• Phaser banks brought to cold shutdown unless deemed necessary by the Commanding Officer.

• Photon torpedo launchers brought to cold shutdown unless deemed necessary by the Commanding Officer.

• Shuttlebay operations are suspended unless specifi-cally authorized by the Commanding Officer. Any use of shuttle vehicles is to be conducted from either secondary shuttlebay. Ingress and egress is to be minimized, with use of forcefield doors minimized.

• Crew status survey to be conducted by Security department with preparations made for contingency evacu-ation of part of the ship's habitable volume for environmental support conservation.

• Environmental systems to operate at no more than 50% of normal levels. Ship's compartments not in use to be sealed off for conservation of environmental resources.

• Transporter usage is not allowed unless specifically ordered by the Commanding Officer or department head.

• Turbolift system usage discouraged for all personnel. Activation of turbolift requires voice ID; computer may re-quest explanation of need.

• Energy-intensive recreational activities such as Holodeck usage not permitted.

• Food replicator usage is not allowed. Preserved food stores are made available to all personnel. In a lesser crisis, minimum replicator power can be made available for synthe-sis of TKL rations or similar.

16.0 EMERGENCY OPERATIONS

16.1 INTRODUCTION TO EMERGENCY OPERATIONS

The entire philosophy behind the integrated systems design of the *Galaxy* class starship is one of maximizing crew safety during all mission profiles and in all emergency situations. Starfleet has a long tradition of placing the safety of its people first. The extraordinary lengths to which Starfleet has gone in insuring crew safety in the design and operation of its ships is a persuasive demonstration of Starfleet's commitment to this tradition and philosophy.

The principle of automatic computer monitoring of ship operations to detect and correct system anomalies long before they become problems has long been a means of optimizing both crew safety and operational effectiveness. This process alone deals with over 87% of all potential problems with minimal crew intervention.

The *Galaxy* class starship, like its predecessors, incorporates a sophisticated array of redundant systems and backups, intended to assure continuous service of all key systems. Critical environmental support and engineering systems will generally employ at least one backup, which is physically separated from the primary and has power supplied by an independent source.

Supplementing these approaches are systems, protocols, trained personnel, and specialized hardware intended to cope with a wide range of potential emergency situations.

16.2 FIRE SUPPRESSION

The habitable volume of the *Galaxy* class starship is constructed of materials conforming to SFRA-standard 528.1(b) for inflammability in nitrogen-oxygen atmospheres. All shipboard equipment, furnishings, and personal effects onboard must conform to SFRA 528.5(c–f). The Chief Engineer is responsible for the observance of these policies by all departments and personnel.

Fire detection sensors are incorporated into the environmental monitoring sensors located throughout the habitable volume of the spacecraft. These sensors scan for changes in air temperature or ionization, and are also programmed to detect airborne particles or gases characteristic of combustion byproducts. Crew members can also signal the presence of a fire by use of personal communicator or comm panel.

In the event of fire, monitoring sensors would immediately notify Ops as well as Security. In the case of a relatively small fire, a containment forcefield would be generated around the burning area by the ship's computer. This field seals the fire off from the atmospheric oxygen supply, causing most fires to be rapidly extinguished. In the event of such an occurrence, crew personnel should remain at least two meters from the fire to avoid unnecessary exposure to either fire hazards or the forcefield.

Ceiling mounted detector cluster projects fire suppression forcefield

Forcefield contains flame, preventing atmospheric oxygen from feeding fire

Carbon dioxide exhaust is trapped inside, suffocating fire

16.2.1 Use of forcefields for fire suppression

To avoid spontaneous re-ignition of an extinguished fire, the computer will maintain containment field until the combustible material has cooled to below the ignition point.

Larger fires may require the activation of section isolation doors and forcefields to limit the possible spread of the fire. In such cases, extinguishing fields can be supplemented with handheld fire extinguishers and firefighting gear located in strategically placed corridor storage modules.

In extreme emergencies, isolated sections of the habitable volume can be vented to the vacuum of space. Since this procedure would be fatal to any crew member in those sections, such venting cannot be performed until the areas have been evacuated. The only exceptions to this protocol are if the Commanding Officer certifies that the fire poses an imminent danger to the entire spacecraft and crew.

16.3 EMERGENCY MEDICAL OPERATIONS

At first glance, it might appear that the *Galaxy* class USS *Enterprise* is overequipped for medical support. While the nominal mission of the medical department is to provide health care for the ship's crew and attached personnel, this is a relatively small task considering the standard long-term crew complement of about a thousand individuals. However, the Medical department must also be capable of responding to a wide range of medical and emergency situations. These scenarios include emergencies on other spacecraft, planetary disasters, and bacteriologic and other exobiological threats, as well as crises involving nonhumanoid patients.

One of the key provisions for emergency preparedness is the requirement that at least 40% of crew and attached personnel be cross-trained for various secondary assignments including emergency medical, triage, and other disaster response functions. (Other nonmedical support secondary assignments include Engineering and Security duties.) Yellow and Red Alert protocols call for cross-trained personnel with noncritical primary assignments to be available for their secondary assignments as necessary.

Emergency medical facilities are designed to significantly increase the patient-load capacity of the *Enterprise* sickbay. Depending on the severity and patient load, different options are available.

Large numbers of patients can be handled by emergency conversion of one or more shuttlebays into triage and treatment centers. The main shuttlebay is equipped with five portable emergency hospital modules, which can be set up in the flight deck area, providing up to five triage and surgery wards. Three additional emergency patient care modules can provide up to seventy-five intensive-care beds and 530 medium-care beds. Shuttlebays 2 and 3 are each equipped with one hospital and one emergency patient care module. These emergency care facilities are equipped for full biohazard protocol, minimizing exposure risk to *Enterprise* personnel.

Additionally, Shuttlebay 3 includes hardware for short-term conversion to Class H, K, or L environmental conditions, intended for nonhumanoid populations. Note that the use of shuttlebay facilities for medical service will necessarily impact shuttlecraft launch and recovery operations, a factor that can be significant during evacuation scenarios. For this reason, large-scale evacuation involving shuttlecraft support will generally make use of sickbay and other facilities first, before shuttlebay conversion procedures are invoked.

Fewer numbers of patients can be handled by conversion of other facilities. Guest quarters on Decks 5 and 6 are convertible to medical intensive-care use, and utility hookups

---

The idea of forcefields being used to extinguish shipboard fires was devised by writer Melinda Snodgrass in her episode "Up the Long Ladder." It was not only logical in terms of the ship's technology, but made for a pretty funny scene.

to those compartments include biomedical telemetry links and medical gas connections. The ship's cargo bays, gymnasiums, and other recreational facilities can also be converted to emergency medical use. All of these compartments are stocked with medical conversion kits, which provide necessary hardware and standard medical supplies. Additionally, during noncrisis situations, one or more Holodecks can be converted to patient care use. While this is a very convenient procedure, it is also very energy-intensive and is not normally employed for long-term care or during alert situations.

Supplementing emergency medical supplies, contingency preparedness scenarios include provisions for large-scale replication of supplies and hardware. Nevertheless, because energy availability for replication may be severely limited during crisis situations, emergency plans are designed to depend primarily upon the use of stored supplies.

A typical emergency situation might be a case where a severe explosion has injured 150 crew members on a starship. The *Enterprise* medical department response might be as follows:

After the determination of the existence of the emergency situation, the Chief Medical Officer would receive a report from the Main Bridge. The CMO would consult with the Commanding Officer as well as the Security Officer to determine that the accident site is sufficiently safe for *Enterprise* personnel to transport over. Such determination would generally be based on sensor scans of the accident site.

A survey and triage team would then be transported to the accident site. The CMO would normally lead this team, evaluating the extent of casualties and on-site requirements. Simultaneously, the medical staff on the *Enterprise* would be preparing sickbay and secondary treatment areas for the imminent arrival of patients.

At the accident site, the triage team would separate patients into one of three categories:

1. Individuals whose injuries are not immediately life-threatening and do not require immediate transport to the ship;

2. Individuals whose injuries are severe enough to require immediate attention but can be successfully treated; and

3. Individuals whose injuries are so severe that they are beyond help.

Individuals in the second category are prioritized for transport to the ship. The triage team does not administer any actual patient care (except for airway management) because to do so would slow triage processing to an unacceptable rate.

The CMO may opt to supplement the on-site triage team with an on-site treatment team, although treatment in a controlled on-ship environment is usually preferred.

Using all personnel transporters aboard the *Enterprise*, a maximum of approximately one thousand individuals per hour can be evacuated to the ship. If the number of casualties is relatively small, site-to-site transport can be used to beam the patients directly to the on-board treatment area. Otherwise, patients are beamed only to the transporter rooms and then shuttled to the treatment area by gurney. This is because site-to-site transport effectively halves the capacity of the transporter system.

While on-site triage is underway, conversion of secondary treatment areas would be prepared, using medical conversion kits. For major disasters, hospital and emergency patient care modules can be deployed, providing full-scale surgical and intensive-care facilities. If necessary, these conversions can include complete biohazard protocols.

Once patients are received onboard, treatment teams would include all available medical staff. The medical staff would be supplemented as needed by additional cross-trained personnel from other departments.

16.4 LIFEBOATS

The nature of its missions in the galaxy requires that the *Enterprise* carry a set of small spacecraft for dedicated escape and rescue operations. Located throughout both the Primary and Secondary Hulls, these ejectable lifeboats are designed to meet the short-term survival needs of the starship crew in the event of a catastrophic emergency.

As set down in the original Starfleet specifications, the standardized ASRV, or autonomous survival and recovery vehicle, is capable of the following operations:

• Rapid departure from its parent starship with a minimum velocity of 40 m/s.

• Independent maneuvering with a total delta-*v* of 3,600 m/sec.

• Life support for a total of eighty-six person-days.

• Recombination with other lifeboats after ejection to augment survivability.

• Subspace radio signaling for location and recovery.

• Atmosphere entry and landing.

The first group of ASRVs were delivered in 2337 in time to be fitted to the last *Renaissance* class starship, the USS *Hokkaido*, and with minimal hardware and software changes were chosen as the lifeboats for the *Galaxy* class. Automated facilities on Earth, Mars, Rigel IV, and Starbase 326 produce 85% of the ASRVs, with satellite facilities on Velikan V and Rangifer II acting as industry second-sources for the remaining 15%.

The ASRV measures 3 x 3 x 3 m and its shape is characterized as a truncated cube. The total mass is 1.35 metric tonnes. Its internal spaceframe is a standard beam and stringer arrangement, constructed from gamma-welded tritanium and frumium monocarbonite. The frame is skinned with single-crystal microfilleted tritanium, with umbilical pass-throughs, conformal emitters, and sensors doped with hafnium cobarate for passive thermal control during atmosphere entry.

Spacecraft propulsion is achieved through three distinct systems: ejection initiator, main impulse engine, and reaction control system. The ejection initiator is a single-pulse, buffered microfusion device that propels the lifeboat through the launch channel. Power is tapped from the fusion reaction to start the lifeboat's inertial damping field and spin up the gravity generator. Like its larger cousin aboard the *Enterprise*, the IDF protects the crew against acceleration forces. The main impulse engine, a low-power microfusion system for all pri-

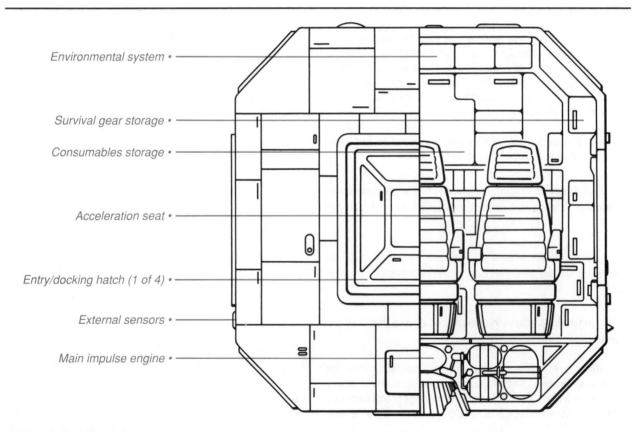

Environmental system •

Survival gear storage •

Consumables storage •

Acceleration seat •

Entry/docking hatch (1 of 4) •

External sensors •

Main impulse engine •

16.4.1 Typical lifeboat pod

mary spacecraft maneuvering, is rated at a maximum 950 kg thrust and is fed from a 75 kg deuterium fuel supply. The reaction control system performs all precise attitude and translation motions required for combined operations with other lifeboats and maneuvering during planetary landing.

Life support on the ASRV is maintained by its automatic environmental system, providing complete atmospheric composition, pressure, humidity, and temperature control. Stored food and water supplies as well as a waste management system are included. Lightweight environment suits are stowed with portable survival packs for planetside operation. The normal lifeboat crew capacity is four, with provisions for as many as six if necessary.

One important feature of the ASRV design, the in-line twin hatches, allows it to dock with other lifeboats to form larger clusters. This capability, nicknamed "gaggle mode" by experienced pilots, dramatically increases in-space survival rates by affording access to wounded crew members by medical personnel, combining consumables supplies, and adding propulsion options. Gaggle mode must be terminated prior to atmosphere entry, as the structural loads cannot be handled by the combined craft.

Out of four hundred ejectable lifeboats installed within the *Galaxy* class, eighty are specialized ASRVs with two additional docking ports to increase the packing density and

structural integrity of the gaggle. Computer simulations indicate that at least 25% of any total number of ejected ASRVs are likely to be the four-port version.

Crucial to the successful recovery of the ASRVs are the subspace communications systems and automatic distress beacons.

Lifeboats are yet another nifty idea that we may never actually get to see in an episode. On the other hand, model maker Greg Jein, who built some of the dead starships for the graveyard scene in "The Best of Both Worlds, Part II," put some open lifeboat hatches on the destroyed ships, thereby suggesting that lifeboats were indeed used. Careful examination of that scene shows several different starships, including the Nebula *class USS* Melbourne, *designed by Ed Miarecki.*

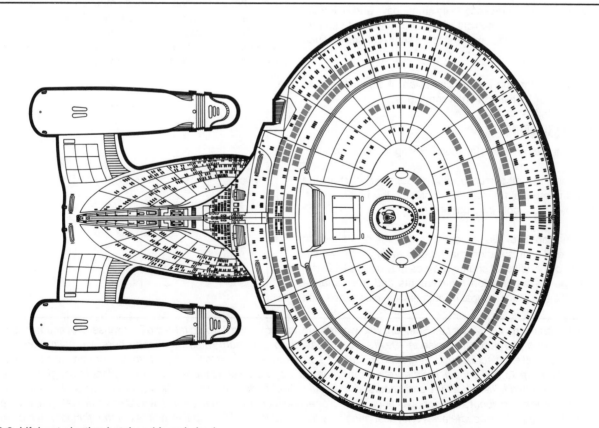

16.3.2 Lifeboat ejection hatches (dorsal view)

16.5 RESCUE AND EVAC OPERATIONS

Rescue and evacuation operations generally fall into two categories, rescue and evacuation to the ship, and evacuation from the ship. The former will generally involve transport from another ship or a planetary surface. The latter will generally involve removal of the ship's company to another ship, a planetary surface, or into space.

RESCUE SCENARIOS

Resources available for rescue and evacuation to the ship include:

• Ability to transport up to 1,000 persons per hour to the ship via personnel transporters.

• Availability of five personnel shuttlecraft on immediate standby and up to six additional shuttles available on twelve-hour notice. Additional shuttle vehicles may be available depending on other mission requirements and maintenance status. Total transport capacity of these vehicles varies with range and other factors, but averages 250 persons per hour from Class M planetary surfaces to standard orbit.

• Capacity to support up to 15,000 evacuees with conversion of shuttlebays and cargo bays to emergency living accommodations.

• Ability to convert secondary shuttlebays and Holodeck areas to emergency medical triage and treatment centers. Cross-training of sufficient starship personnel to handle such situations.

• Ability for short-term conversion of Shuttlebay 3 to Class H, K, or L environmental conditions.

ABANDON-SHIP SCENARIOS

Resources available for abandon-ship scenarios include:

• Ability to transport up to 1,850 persons per hour from the ship via personnel transporters, including the use of emergency beam-out-only transporters.

• Availability of five personnel shuttlecraft on immediate standby and up to six additional shuttles available on twelve-hour notice. Additional shuttle vehicles may be available depending on other mission requirements and maintenance status. Total transport capacity of these vehicles varies with

range and other factors, but averages 250 persons per hour from standard orbit to a Class M planetary surface.

• Abandon-ship protocols include use of ASRV (autonomous survival and recovery vehicle) lifeboats, which provide free space survival accommodations for up to 1,400 individuals for up to fourteen days. A total of four hundred ASRVs are available (See: 16.4).

• In a lesser emergency in either the Saucer Module or the Stardrive Section, the saucer separation maneuver is an option, with evacuation of the ship's company to whichever section is not affected by the crisis. Evacuation protocols include options to leave behind a team of engineering personnel or other specialists who will attempt to deal with the emergency situation.

• Environmental suits are available for evacuation into the space environment. In such scenarios, personnel may exit through any of the exterior airlocks, through the shuttlebays, or through the exterior turbolift couplings (assuming that the turbolift system has been disabled). Environmental suits are available in storage lockers at all exit ports and shuttlebays, as well as in emergency equipment lockers located in corridor storage modules located throughout the habitable volume of the spacecraft.

• Many exterior windows are also equipped with emergency release mechanisms that will permit direct exterior access. These emergency release mechanisms, located near the base of most windows, are enabled only in the event of atmospheric pressure loss, power loss, certain Red Alert scenarios, and only if personnel within that contiguous compartment are protected with environmental suits.

We were consulting with writer Lee Sheldon, who wanted to know how long it would take the Enterprise to evacuate the entire population of a planet for the episode "Devil's Due." Based on maximum rates mentioned here, we estimated that the transporters and shuttlecraft could bring approximately 1,250 persons per hour to the ship. It would therefore take about twelve hours to bring up 15,000 people, the theoretical maximum. If they were taking these people to a planet five light years away at Warp 9, it would take about forty-eight hours for the round trip. Adding twenty-four hours for loading and off-loading, this would average out to about 200 people an hour. If the planet had four billion inhabitants, it would therefore take the Enterprise about 1,900 years to evacuate everyone, assuming they lived that long. (Melinda Bell points out that things would be made even worse if they had children.)

17.0 CONCLUSION

17.1 PROJECTED UPGRADES

The *Galaxy* class USS *Enterprise* is not a static design. Rather, it is a dynamic system that is constantly being adapted to revised mission objectives and continuing technical advances. A key element of these adaptations is an ongoing program of upgrades and refits expected to continue throughout the projected hundred-year lifetime of the spacecraft. Starfleet expects numerous significant advances in technology during that time.

Minor system upgrades are often performed during routine starbase layovers. During the ship's early years, such upgrades are expected to take place with relatively great frequency — perhaps two to four times annually — as the spacecraft operating systems "mature" with flight experience. Later, upgrades and refits are expected to occur less frequently, but will often be for maintenance or mission-specific purposes. Currently anticipated system upgrades include annual replacement of the LCARS computer software and a major upgrade of the warp drive's matter/antimatter reaction assembly, scheduled for early in the vessel's sixth year of operation.

After the initial few years of shakedown, major upgrades are typically scheduled for twenty-year intervals, when the ship is removed from service for approximately one year so that work such as computer core swapout or warp coil replacement can be accomplished.

Other major system refits can be performed at the direction of Starfleet Command when it is necessary to reconfigure the spacecraft for another mission classification. Such major mission-related reconfigurations are not expected to be frequently required for the multimission *Galaxy* class starships, but the scope of Starfleet's objectives often require flexibility in mission philosophies.

17.2 FUTURE DIRECTIONS: THE ROAD TO 1701-E

Twenty years from now, the *Galaxy* class USS *Enterprise* will still be in the first phase of her operational lifetime. Crews will follow rotation cycles. New captains and senior officers will steer her into missions of vital importance to the preservation of peace in the Milky Way and the continued exploration of the unknown. Eventually, the *Galaxy* class will be superseded with a new space vehicle whose design will be as revolutionary as that of the *Enterprise* is today. One starship in the new class may even be the sixth to bear the name *Enterprise*, the NCC–1701-E.

Starfleet Command, through its Advanced Starship Design Bureau, is already considering concepts for the proposed *Nova* class. It is difficult to predict mission and technologic requirements for vehicles that are still in the early phases of planning, but even these preliminary concepts offer a fascinating glimpse into the future.

One proposed *Nova* concept calls for a ship with approximately 10% less total internal volume than the current *Galaxy* class, but which features a hybridized external shape. The overall curvilinear style of the 1701-D was shaped by an understanding of warp physics that is being refined. Research into materials, manufacturing processes, and the enhanced utilization of warp energies are driving toward a hybrid angular-curvilinear hull shape. Proponents of this design contend that the vehicle will require less fabrication time due to the simplified cross sections, and will also demand less major hull and frame rebuilding over its operational life. R&D facilities within the Federation assume that a new cycle of improved hardware efficiency and changing political conditions within the galaxy could allow for redefined missions with a down-sized vessel.

Another approach assumes that warp field control techniques will improve to the point where even greater Z-axis warp field compression will be possible than in the present *Galaxy* class ship. This concept would feature a primary hull described as a 24° ellipse for substantially greater peak transitional efficiency. Preliminary tests have been unable to maintain a stable warp envelope with this degree of Z-axis distortion, but advanced research in high-frequency subspace field modulation may lead to a breakthrough in this area.

Still another advanced starship concept would call for variable-geometry warp nacelle pylons permitting optimization of field stress during extended Warp 8+ flight, resulting in significantly improved engine efficiencies. This design study features a saucer section composed of wedge-shaped modular segments that could be easily replaced as mission demands change and new technology becomes available. This concept calls for an internal volume approximately 40% less than the present *Galaxy* class starship, but this design is expected to perform similar mission profiles within normal cruise ranges because of the relative ease of spacecraft segment swapout.

A fourth possible advanced starship design would completely abandon the traditional saucer and nacelle configuration in favor of a linear arrangement featuring forward mounted warp nacelles. Crew and mission-specific modules would be mounted along the spine of the spaceframe. This concept would require significant advances in warp geometry technologies, but it would permit tremendous flexibility in ship configuration with little structural modification to the basic spaceframe. Proponents of this design suggest that the additional R&D costs for this ship would be more than balanced by the savings realized through the adaptability of this design to a wide range of starship types.

Whatever the direction of future starship design, various vehicle planforms will be tested in thousands of hours of computer simulations and in the flight of testbed vessels, leading to the final design, in much the same process that led to the *Galaxy* class *Enterprise*. Theoretical engine designs will come and go, with each new type adding to the knowledge gained from its predecessors. Alloys and composites will be subjected to unimaginable stresses. The best of these will be chosen to form new shells to preserve living environments for those who travel among the stars.

Even with the remarkable assistance of thinking machines and industrial hardware, the task will still be accomplished by people, imagining and guiding. The desire to move ever outward will remain strong within many evolving civilizations, as they find purpose through the creation of vessels that carry us into the unknown.

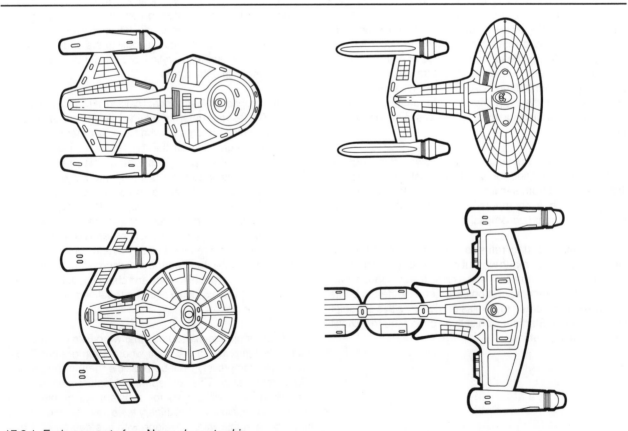

17.2.1 Early concepts for a Nova *class starship*

17.3 MISSION BACKGROUND

The role of the multimission starship in Starfleet's vehicle mix has undergone significant changes in recent years. Dramatic expansion of Federation territory and in the number of member cultures has led to increases in the demands on Starfleet operations within the Federation, as well as beyond the frontier. Further, recent experiences with the Romulans, the Cardassians, and the Borg as well as disturbing reports of unrest within the Klingon Empire illustrate the importance of maintaining a significant defensive capability.

As required research and patrol ranges increase annually, the number of spacecraft required increases dramatically. Accordingly, Starfleet vessel construction policies are increasingly based on the theory that it is more efficient to have a larger number of small, mission-specific starships, than to have a smaller number of large, multimission vehicles.

The multimission capability of the *Galaxy* class starship and its predecessors has, however, been shown to be an essential part of the vehicle mix. When operating beyond normal Starfleet patrol range, the capacity for autonomous execution of full-policy options is essential, though expensive. Accordingly, the *Enterprise* is equipped for nearly the entire spectrum of Starfleet missions.

This need for multimission vessels is made greater by Starfleet's continuing emphasis on deep-space exploration. Stellar survey operations beyond the Epsilon Quinonez sector alone are expected to utilize 22% of Starfleet's exploratory capacity over the next decade. And this estimate does not include follow-up planetary survey and cultural contact operations.

There are those who have argued for reductions in Starfleet exploratory operations; those who have argued to redeploy our fleet resources for domestic and civil missions. Yet the fruits of Starfleet's exploration and life-contact directives are a continuing source of vitality for the Federation itself. Domestic operations will continue to be a key part of our mission mix, but it is clear that we must continue to pursue Starfleet's primary objective: *To explore new worlds, to seek out new life, and new civilizations, and to boldly go where no one has gone before.*

UNITED FEDERATION OF PLANETS
STARFLEET COMMAND

AFTERWORD BY RICK BERMAN

People often say to me, "What a shame you can't suspend disbelief, sit back, and enjoy *Star Trek* like the rest of us." Fortunately, this couldn't be further from the truth. After twenty years in television, I can happily say that I am able to sit back, turn on the set, and join the crew of the starship *Enterprise* as it goes where no one (not even its producer) has gone before.

I don't think I am in any way unique in this respect. Most people involved in my business owe their commitment and their talents to the fact that they too can become happily lost in the illusion.

Although all drama relies on illusion, few projects I've been involved with rely on it as heavily as *Star Trek: The Next Generation*. And, unlike other television programs, every element of *Star Trek*'s illusion must be conceived from scratch. You don't go to Bullock's to buy an outfit for a Ventaxian. You don't go into the scenery docks to pull out the bridge of a Cardassian warship. There are no books to tell you how to form a prosthetic to create a Ferengi head or how to build a model for a Pakled cargo vessel. Every facet of each design must come from the imagination of the remarkably talented people who are responsible for creating this show week after week. Not surprisingly, it's just these kinds of unlimited possibilities that have enabled us to attract the caliber of people we have. But more on that later.

The greatest enemy of episodic television is time. On paper, it is virtually impossible to turn out feature quality work at a rate of twenty-six hours per year. But somehow we do it. An enormous degree of overlap is one of the secrets. At any given time, we'll be working on eleven episodes simultaneously. Three in various story and script stages, one being prepped to shoot, one on the stage, two in the editing bay, another being spotted for music and sound effects, two more being prepared for opticals, and still another on the sound mixing stage. Juggling this number of episodes at one time can be both terrifying and comical. We're constantly finding ourselves sitting in a production meeting or a cutting room wondering when Worf will do this or Troi will do that only to realize we're thinking of an episode we were dealing with earlier in the day. But this represents only one element of the constraints of time on *Star Trek*. The other has to do with what the audience has come to expect after twenty-five years.

Television has changed a good deal since the original *Star Trek* series. In the seventies and eighties the audience grew up. They grew accustomed to the extraordinary level of visual effects that they saw in films like *Star Wars* and *Indiana Jones* (and yes, even the *Star Trek* features). They came to expect this level of excellence. So, when it came to developing a new *Star Trek* series, we knew we had our work cut out for us. Foremost in that effort was to find the best possible people to bring it all to fruition; people with Roddenberry's vast imagination who understood the necessity of following the "rules."

Producing a television series always entails following rules. With some kinds of shows, the rules are more stringent than others. If you're producing *L.A. Law*, you have to be true to the laws of the State of California. If you're producing *St. Elsewhere*, you'd better know something about the practice of medicine, or at least have some knowledgeable advisors... preferably both. With *Star Trek*, we're in the unique and unenviable position of having two sets of rules to follow. First, we must be as diligent as possible in our depiction and description of science.

Although the scope of twenty-fourth-century physics can only be conjecture, we've got to base that conjecture on well-grounded twentieth-century information. Our second set of rules is a bit more unique. *Star Trek,* as a phenomenon, has existed for twenty-five years now. Seventy-nine episodes of the original series; five motion pictures, with another on its way; and *The Next Generation* with a hundred episodes and counting. During these twenty-five years, the rules and laws of *Star Trek* have been forged and scrutinized, perhaps more than those of any other television series in history. Whether elements like warp drive, dilithium crystals, transporter beams, phasers, or Romulan cloaking devices are feasible is not the question. They're all part of the *Star Trek* mythology and their nomenclature must be respected and adhered to.

No one is more important in the creative adherence to these two sets of rules than Mike Okuda and Rick Sternbach. Although we often rely on honest-to-God scientists who serve as our advisors, day in and day out our best sources of accurate "technobabble" are Mike and Rick. These two guys are so in tune with the style and texture of the series that they can flawlessly solve scientific "problems" before the writers and producers realize they've screwed up. When an alien spacecraft has to knock out a computer core without interfering with deflector shields, or a gaseous creature has to generate an energy field that transforms an isolinear chip into a transporter override, it's Rick and Mike who undoubtedly will come up with a logical and believable way to do it.... Needless to say, when it comes to monitoring (and correcting) story points that deviate from the "proper" *Star Trek* path, Sternbach and Okuda will waste little time.

As members of the art department, Mike and Rick's contribution to *Star Trek: The Next Generation* is incalculable. Every element of design, whether it be for a facial prosthetic, a costume, a prop, or an elaborate set, almost invariably has their hand in it. (They've helped design a few hands too, now that I think of it.) Shortly after joining this show, I learned that the term Jefferies Tube referred to an architectural section of a starship that was originally designed by a fellow named Jefferies back in the sixties. The term Okudagram has taken on an equally generic meaning at Paramount Pictures. Whether it's backlit, polar motion, or computer-generated, when you need an *Enterprise* graphic readout, you call for an Okudagram. Mike conceived of that "look" in 1987 and has kept it alive ever since. Come to think of it, I wouldn't be surprised if before too long anyone who needs an abstract idea turned into a "do-able" drawing will start using one of my favorite expressions for it... get it "Sternbached."

 –Rick Berman
 Executive Producer
 Star Trek: The Next Generation

INDEX AND KEY TO ACRONYMS

UNITS OF MEASURE

A.U. - astronomical unit, measure of length equal to the distance from the Sun to the Earth
Ångstrom - measure of length, one ten-billionth of a meter
arc seconds - measure of plane angle
C - celsius, measure of temperature
c - measure of velocity, the speed of light in a vacuum
cm - centimeter, measure of length, one hundredth of a meter
cm^3 - cubic centimeter, measure of volume
cochrane - measure of subspace field stress
delta-v - change in velocity, sometimes measured in meters per second^2
g - measure of acceleration equal to the Earth's gravitational field
g/cm^3 - grams per cubic centimeter, measure of density
gauss - measure of magnetic flux density
GFP - giga floating point operation - measure of computing speed, one billion floating point operations per second
GHz - gigahertz - measure of frequency, one billion cycles per second

GW - gigawatt, measure of power, one billion watts
hertz - measure of frequency, one cycle per second
Hz - hertz, measure of frequency, one cycle per second
K - Kelvin, measure of absolute temperature
kilohertz - measure of frequency, one thousand cycles per second
kilometer - measure of length, one thousand meters
kilopascal - measure of pressure, one thousand pascals
kiloquad - measure of data storage capacity
kiloquads/sec - measure of data transmission or access rate
km/sec^2 - kilometers per second squared, measure of acceleration
kW - kilowatt, measure of power, one thousand watts
light year - measure of length, the distance light travels in an Earth year, 9.5 trillion kilometers
m - meter, measure of length
m/sec - meters per second, measure of velocity

m/sec^2 - meters per second squared, measure of acceleration
m^2 - square meter, measure of area
Mach - measure of velocity in an atmosphere, the speed of sound
meter - measure of length
metric tonne - measure of mass, one thousand kilograms
MeV - million electron volts - measure of electric potential
millicochrane - measure of subspace field stress, one thousandth of a cochrane
millisecond - measure of time, one thousandth of a second
MJ - megajoule, measure of energy, one million joules
mm - millimeter, measure of length, one thousandth of a meter
mmHg - millimeters of mercury - measure of atmospheric pressure
MW - megawatt, measure of power, one million watts
nanocochrane - measure of subspace field stress, one billionth of a cochrane
Newton - measure of force
ns - nanosecond, measure of time, one-billionth of a second
warp factor - measure of warp velocity

ABOUT THE AUTHORS

Rick Sternbach currently works as senior illustrator on *Star Trek: The Next Generation*. Rick is responsible for the design of props, spaceships, and many other elements of the show. Twice honored with science fiction's prestigious Hugo Award for Best Artist, Rick also won an Emmy award as an assistant art director on the PBS series *Cosmos*. His other media credits include *The Last Starfighter* and *Star Trek: The Motion Picture*. Rick is one of science fiction's best-known artists and his work has been featured on the covers of such magazines as *Analog* and *The Magazine of Fantasy and Science Fiction*, as well as in the pages of *Aviation Week*.

Along with co-author Mike Okuda, Rick serves as a technical consultant to the writing staff of *Star Trek: The Next Generation*.

Michael Okuda is the scenic art supervisor for *Star Trek: The Next Generation*, and is responsible for that show's control panels, signage, alien written languages, computer readout animation, and other strange things. Michael's work on *Star Trek* was recognized with an Emmy nomination for Best Visual Effects. His other credits include *Star Trek IV: The Voyage Home, Star Trek V: The Final Frontier, Star Trek VI: The Undiscovered Country, The Flash, Flight of the Intruder,* and a bunch of commercials you probably haven't seen. Mike is from Hawai'i, but lives in Los Angeles, California, with his wife, Denise, and their dog, Molly.

Along with co-author Rick Sternbach, Michael serves as a technical consultant to the writing staff of *Star Trek: The Next Generation*.

Photo: Michael Paris